That Little Town Street

STACY ELIZABETH

Cover Art & Interior Doodles by Bailey DeBiase

@baileydebiase.ink | www.baileydebiase.com

Preface

Born and raised in Maine, I knew from the start this story belonged here. I'm more coastal than woodsy, so to the rocky shores we go. I hope you can see the blue hues of the ocean, hear the crashing waves against the rocks, and smell the sweet, salty air.

But more than anything, I hope that you dream of taking a walk down **That Little Town Street**.

Dedicated to those of you who thought you couldn't, but you did.

Contents

CHAPTER ONE

Eighteen Summers Later

VIV

My ass is asleep. I have to pee. And I'm hungry enough to suck Cheeto dust off a stranger's fingers. As if on cue, I feel a nose graze my temple and hot breath wooshes in my ear, followed by a low, desperate groan. This would probably turn me on under any other circumstances. However, at this point, it only confirms that Kevin feels the same way. And Kevin is my dog.

Take Route 1, they said. It will be fun, they said. Unfortunately... *they* is me. And they is an incompetent idiot. I stupidly added an extra frustrating hour and a half to a trip where I just wanted to reach my destination. I found myself asking Kevin, *Are we there yet?* Honestly, I figured I'd be up for the adventure of Route 1 in Maine the week before the Memorial Day holiday, but the weather is nicer than it should be this time of year, and others from away have the same idea. Spoiler alert: I was not up for it.

The only thing keeping me from completely losing my mind is the coastal-inspired playlist I curated for this trip. The smooth sounds of Noah Kahan's "Maine"... to the gentle acoustic guitar paired with the ethereal vocals of Hollow Coves "Coastline" wafts from the speakers.

Driving Route 1 along the coast of Maine is a lot like hunting for treasure. With every peninsula explored, a new set of potential adventures unfolds before you. But most travelers stop at the popular town of Bar Harbor on Mount Desert Island. They head to Acadia National Park to admire the vast views from the summit of Cadillac Mountain and pick up a bumper sticker to prove it, experience the ocean's natural power at Thunder Hole, or enjoy the cliff-enclosed stretch of coastline at Sand Beach. They peruse the downtown shops and restaurants in hordes, but few adventures take folks further than Schoodic Point and its expansive view of the Atlantic, unless Canada is their destination.

It's been nearly two decades since I last traveled this road. It was much more enjoyable when I wasn't the one driving. Back when Mom and I followed the same route, stopping at no fewer than five sprawling antique barns and flea markets to search for treasures to decorate the cabin. At that time, we didn't care how long it took to reach our destination because we had months ahead to enjoy it, and we cherished our adventures. I had hoped the drive would revive some of my best memories with my mother, but alongside those memories came a heavy wave of grief and an intense, empty feeling.

The road opens up once I pass the turn to Mount Desert Island. The line of slowly crawling traffic I'd been stuck behind all turns toward Ellsworth, heading for the road that leads them to the island. I've only been to Bar Harbor once, when I was twelve, and my mom thought it was a must-see stop for anyone from out of state. The streets overflowed with pedestrians rushing from shop to shop, darting into the road as if they owned the place. Finding a parking spot close to downtown was impossible. We drove around for a while before deciding that quiet Shearwater Cove was more our speed and getting the hell out.

"Smooth sailing from here," I say to Kevin. He nudges me again with his warm nose, so I reach into the back seat to give him a scratch under his chin. "We'll be there before you know it, pal." His tail happily thuds against the back seat, almost in beat to Taylor Swift's "Getaway Car" cranked on the radio—apropos of this particular trip. *Me too, dude, me too.*

Between Acadia National Park and the Canadian border, down east from Route 1, the small, one-traffic-light town of Shearwater Cove overlooks Narraguagus Bay. Mom kept a worn set of carefully notated directions in her glove compartment, detailing the precise mileage to the town road. That yellowed spiral notebook paper now rests on my lap as I approach the camouflaged turn. According to what Mom shared when she passed the cabin down to me, the town's residents don't actively seek to attract outsiders. This idea seems absurd since many of Maine's towns survive, and sometimes thrive, on tourist traffic.

The initial half mile of the road is a masterful disguise, crafted to deter any unwelcome visitors. Rutted gravel and wild, overgrown vegetation encroach from all sides, giving the impression of an abandoned path. A weathered Dead End sign looms ahead, convincing travelers they've surely taken a wrong turn. I'd wager Kevin's entire monthly food allowance that, if given the chance, the town would have eagerly installed a gate to secure its seclusion. The sign isn't misleading, though; the town of Shearwater Cove reveals itself just before the road's end, like a hidden gem embraced by nature.

Muddled memories from my childhood remind me that the few buildings that made up the town's main street were run-down and relatively nondescript. That's certainly not the case now. I wonder if I drove through a wormhole and somehow found myself in another fucking dimension. Each building I pass is painted in very bright colors. And not typical "businessy-type colors," no – we're talking bright yellow, hot pink, lavender – but it...*works*. The spring flowers poke through the ground in front of each business, and brilliant bouquets spill over the worn whiskey barrel planters along the main drag. It's by far the happiest little town street I've ever seen.

Shearwater Cove was never the wealthiest town, so their indifference to the tourists' deep pockets surprises me. I desperately want to understand their reasoning, but I also urgently require a bathroom, so that's an investigation for another time. My goal is to reach the cabin and stay there as long as my supplies last. I drive through town as quickly as the speed limit allows, hoping not to draw attention to my Massachusetts license plates.

Just off the main thoroughfare known as Cove Street, slightly beyond the main drag, there's a quiet, pothole-ridden dirt road marked by a stack of faded wooden signs nailed to a half-rotted hemlock tree indicating the families who own the properties along the road. Many of these signs have been touched up with new paint over the years, while the one I'm searching for is a weathered, barely legible sign that reads Walker's Rock.

While the weather is beautiful, the coastal air is still too cool to go topless, but with the Jeep's windows down, Kevin and I revel in the sensation of that salty breeze rushing through the car. My former apartment in Boston was near the coast, but the air never smelled as oceany as it does here, probably because it isn't mixed with the gas fumes from a million damn cars nearby. I won't miss that crowded city or its memories. My goal is to create new ones, only the good kind.

I crank the volume back up as I bounce down the rutted path to our cabin, where some spots are so tight that the tree branches brush against the side of the Jeep. Kevin, who enjoys hanging his head out the window, quickly retreats into the car's safety. Down Like Silver's pensive vocals to their song "Broken Coastline" feel so relevant to my new adventures. I sing at the top of my lungs, much to my co-pilot's dismay.

Most homes along the road are seasonal, and I expect I won't see many residents until the weather warms, so I'm unlikely to play the world's scariest game of chicken on this narrow road. I'm anxious as hell to get my anesthetized ass to our destination and out of this godforsaken vehicle. From the restless way Kevin paces the back seat, he's also eager to reach the cabin.

Mature pine trees darken most of the road as I pass the few other homes along the route. When the last house comes into view—a battered cabin overlooking the Bay—I'm fourteen again. My great-grandfather, Jackson Walker, constructed the rough-hewn log cabin from the trees cleared from this very property. He was, after all, a logger, and the cabin, so I've heard, was his pride and joy.

Over the years, as my grandfather, Noah, painstakingly cleared more land, several additions were crafted when he and my grandmother took over the property. On the bay side of the cozy cabin, he constructed an expansive back deck, nearly matching the cabin's entire footprint. This wooden platform offered breathtaking views of the shimmering waters. Before his untimely death in a car crash in the early '70s, he had earned a reputation as a local legend for his barbecues. He frequently hosted the town's most magnificent July 4th celebrations, which were marked by awe-inspiring fireworks displays that lit up the night sky with vibrant colors, their reflections dancing over the calm bay waters.

Walker's Rock was never intended to be an extravagant place. Unlike other "summer homes" in the area, the Rock's primary purpose was to provide its inhabitants with a comfortable spot to enjoy all year round. The breathtaking ocean views and stunning sunrises make up for the lack of luxury. Although the cabin showed some wear from the relentless coastal Maine storms, it remained structurally sound. From my vantage point, I see only a few repairs that require immediate attention.

Well, buddy, looks like we've got our work cut out for us," I mumble to Kevin, who has now taken up residence in the passenger seat for a better view. He looks at me side-eye like, *yeah, sure, let me find my fucking hammer.* If this dog could roll his eyes, he would do it often and direct all of those eye rolls at me.

My great-grandfather named the place Walker's Rock after the elephant-sized boulder just off the shore, not far from the end of the dock. The rock is barely visible at high tide, which can be dangerous for any boater unfamiliar with the area who gets too close. Enough of the boulder emerges as the tide recedes to tempt swimmers into reaching it. That is, if they can navigate the slick, natural steps carved into its side. Standing on the small flat top provides bragging rights for those who succeed, at least until the rising tide drives them away.

It's been eighteen years since I visited the cabin. Not that I didn't want to; I thought about this damn cabin every year since our last visit. That final summer, I was an awkward fourteen-year-old, sporting a face full of braces, giant glasses, and a terrible pixie cut that I thought made me look so glamorous and mature. In hindsight, though, I looked like a cross between Billy Ray Cyrus and Dorothy Hamill. And, of course, like any teenager at that time, I had a totally unhealthy obsession with Edward Cullen. I had no idea it would be my last summer at Walker's Rock, nor that the sheets Mom and I used to cover the furniture as we left that August would remain in place for many more summers. I had no idea that I would be a grown-ass adult the next time I laid eyes on this cabin.

The sparkling ocean beyond the cabin captures the attention of my furry co-pilot, and the thumping of his thick, black tail and low whine indicate that if I don't open his door, he is going to Incredible Hulk his way out of this Jeep. "Hold your horses, buddy," I say as I put his collar back on. "That water is gonna be cold, pal." His soulful brown eyes seem to say, *I. DON'T. CARE.*

I free Kevin from his vehicular prison. He finds a bush to relieve himself on, and as expected, he bolts down the dock and joyfully leaps into the chilly late May ocean with the enthusiasm of a champion belly-flopper. Not exactly the most graceful dock dog—but then again, he isn't quite two years old yet and is still in his awkward tween stage. He paddles around the

40-something-degree Narraguagus Bay like a recently freed hostage. My grandfather installed a floating dock ladder designed to make it easier for all the cabin dogs to get back up on the dock since the coast here is so rocky. I give him a few minutes before whistling him back to prevent hypothermia from setting in. He's incredibly handsome and equally clueless.

"Kev! We have all summer to swim. Get your furry ass over here!" He navigates the dock ladder like a champ, shakes off the water, and trots over to me with a customary Labrador smile bigger than I've seen in a long time.

As a kid, I hated that we had no sandy beach to play on. Traditional beaches were plentiful in southern Maine, but we only had rocky shores here. I think I wished for the beach because, for the longest time, I was a shitty swimmer, and I preferred frolicking in the surf. Jumping off the dock became much more enjoyable when I got older and truly learned how to swim. And the sound of the tide lapping at the rocks is far superior to that of sand.

I exhale deeply as I push through the cabin's front door, releasing almost two decades of musty air in a woosh. With the urge to pee reaching a dangerous Defcon level, I waddle pigeon-toed, thighs tightly squeezed together, to the single bathroom. Thank fuck, there's toilet paper. Everything is still right where we left it. The organized countertop is covered with neatly arranged bottles of now-expired sunscreen, toothbrushes, and the green aloe vera gel we used for bad sunburns. My heart clenches at the sight of the collection. I hike up my jeans and head back outside to unload the Jeep and check in with my best friend, Hadley.

VIV: I MADE IT! PAINFUL RIDE ON MY ASS.

HADLEY: YAY! UHHHH...YAY, YOU MADE IT, NOT THAT YOUR ASS HURTS.

VIV: YOU'RE GONNA LOVE THIS PLACE!

HAD: I CAN'T WAIT TO JOIN YOU ONCE SCHOOL LETS OUT. THESE KIDS ARE OUT OF CONTROL. I HOPE YOU'RE STOCKED UP ON ADULT BEVERAGES.

VIV: OH, I WILL BE BY THEN. I DON'T PLAN ON LEAVING THIS PLACE UNTIL MY SUPPLIES RUN OUT.

HAD: INTROVERT. PSSSH.

VIV: LOL

HAD: DON'T GO WILD ALL BY YOURSELF OUT THERE.

VIV: MIGHT BE TOO LATE.

Once I've informed Hadley of my safe arrival, I assess the cabin's condition while Kevin relaxes on the back deck, drying off in the afternoon sun. I'm thrilled to see that no rodents of any size seem to have taken up residence, showcasing the impeccable craftsmanship for which great-grandfather was known. No leaks have appeared since our last visit, and the outdoor furniture Mom and I stored inside is in perfect condition. The first order of business is to move that back out onto the deck to get it out of the way.

After we left the Rock at the end of that last summer we spent here, Mom got sick for the first time. Then life happened: I had school, summer jobs, college, a boyfriend, a real job, and a miserable excuse for a fiancé—all while caring for Mom each time her cancer returned. Each time, it was worse than before. Still, we discussed the possibility of coming to the cabin every June as the school year drew to a close. But every year, something inevitably occurred to keep us home in Boston, close to doctors and hospitals.

As I look around the cabin's living room, I can feel my mother's presence everywhere. It was the last place Mom was truly happy. She thrived in Shearwater Cove, spending time catching up with friends she had known her whole life, reading a stack of books nearly as tall as me over the summer, and then donating the entire pile to the town library. It was always hard for her to say goodbye when the summer ended. Having spent her first ten years living at Walker's Rock full-time, she felt more at home here than anywhere else.

Mom always had a talent for decorating. We never had much money while I was growing up, so she got creative. The worn leather furniture, which came from my grandparents' house, was moved to the cabin after my grandmother passed away. Mom refreshed the room with a once-vibrant braided wool rug from LL Bean in beachy colors—shades of green, blue, and beige—found at a yard sale. Various tables of different sizes and shapes that my grandmother had thrifted over the years were scattered throughout the room. Dusty seashells and brightly colored sea glass adorned every windowsill.

My grandmother's pride and joy was the only heating source for the cabin, located in the back corner of the main living area. After my grandfather passed away, she splurged on a new wood stove—a green 1975 Vermont Castings Defiant—to replace the aging pot-belly stove that was never very efficient. It's strange how one small wood stove can evoke some of the sweetest memories. Mom pushing the couch closer to the fire one Christmas we decided to spend here, covering it with pillows and fuzzy blankets. Each of us sitting at one end of the couch, reading books as the snow gently fell outside the window.

After opening all the windows in the cabin, Swiffering every surface in the living room, and sweeping the floors, I flop onto the couch to survey the space. I run a finger over the scratches on the coffee table made by Mom's adored golden retriever, Jack, who was always hungry and more than once tried to pull cheese and crackers onto the floor when left unattended. I glance at Kevin, who snores loudly, now sprawled out on the faded rug, and say, "You'd never be a bad dog like Jack, would you, handsome boy?" He lifts his head, chuffs, and collapses back down to the floor.

With the Jeep unloaded, the living room tidied, and the bedding freshly changed, I finally feel at ease, as if a great weight has been lifted from my shoulders. The cool sea breeze drifts gently through the open windows, carrying with it the salty scent of the ocean. It's as if the very air is filled with a sense of renewal, allowing me to breathe deeply and freely once more. The soothing sounds of the waves crashing against the rocky coast create a natural symphony that envelops me in calmness. As I listen, I can't help but imagine staying here indefinitely, wrapped in the peacefulness of this coastal haven. Compared to the frenzied pace of Boston, this place feels like a sanctuary for my mind and spirit—far better for my mental health.

CHAPTER TWO

Brews, Boats, and Bullshit

WILL

> TINY: MY OUTBOARD IS SMOKING, AND I HAVE A FISHING CHARTER SCHEDULED FOR SUNDAY. HELP!

> WILL: FUCK, TINY. I'LL SWING BY IN THE MORNING, BUT YOU KNOW IT'S PROBABLY A BLOCKED WATER INTAKE AGAIN.

Great. Another spinning plate to add to tomorrow's juggling act. Tiny needs to take an engine repair class—he'd save himself so much money on my services. With the brewery expanding six months ago, I may have to stop some of my current side jobs. Tiny's fishing charter boat problems are first on the chopping block. Dad and I have been the go-to team for anything needing a handyman for as long as I can remember. We've done landscaping, little league coaching, boat repairs, plumbing work, and small home renovations. As Dad gets older and his health declines, we primarily focus on boat storage and winterization; however, my passion is the brewery.

> TINY: BTW, I SAW A BLACKED-OUT JEEP WRANGLER DRIVE THROUGH TOWN TODAY WITH MASSHOLE PLATES. ANYONE YOU KNOW? KILLAH WHIP.

> WILL: NAH. PROB LOST.

> TINY: COOL.

Most days, I don't have to venture far from my road unless I need food, which is good because something always needs to be done at one of the many buildings on our property. Between the demands of the brewery and the house, Tiny will have to wait. Yet, despite his dependence on me, he's a steadfast sentinel for the town, his watchful eyes never missing a thing from his post in the little shack where he insists he operates his fishing charter. In truth, I suspect he spends his days scrolling through his phone, waiting for it to ring.

Coop's Cove Road was named by my grandfather, who purchased a 52-acre plot of land surrounding the road in the early 1940s, just before he met my grandmother, whom he married in 1948. The land is located just inland from Narraguagus Bay. While it doesn't directly border the water, the current main house, situated at the property's highest point, offers vast ocean views from a ridge. My dad inherited the land in 2002 after my granddad passed away at the ripe and crotchety old age of 84.

The mile-long driveway hosts several outbuildings. My grandfather built the original house where my dad grew up in the late 1940s. That old house sits at the entrance of the road, serves as the brewery's taproom, and remains as rustic as it was back then. Just behind the taproom is a brand-new metal building that houses the brewing equipment added on as an extension. Brewing beer began as a hobby, but people seemed to enjoy it, so I entered the competitive Maine beer scene on an incredibly small scale. My favorite part is the malting, mashing, boiling, and fermenting. I love experimenting with hops, malt, and yeast. Thus, my passion for good beer led to the establishment of ShearCove Brewery. Word of mouth has spread in the area, and we've seen more and more beer enthusiasts show up, much to the dismay of some of the town's old-timers.

SHAWN: YO, THERE'S SOMETHING WRONG WITH ONE OF THE TAPS.

Of course, there is. I can't leave him alone in the brewery for more than a few hours without him breaking something

WILL: DID YOU CHECK THE KEG? IS IT EMPTY?

SHAWN: YOU'RE AN ASSHOLE.

WILL: I'LL BE RIGHT DOWN.

I leave the paperwork needing my attention in my home office and head down to the brewery to tackle the problem. My taproom manager, Shawn, meets me at the door when I arrive. He's an imposing figure at 6 feet 7 inches, yet still the goofy jokester I've known since I was twelve, when his family moved to Shearwater Cove. Shawn is fantastic with customers and has a special way with our female clientele, but he's the least handy person I've ever met. Therefore, a malfunctioning beer tap isn't exactly his strong suit.

"Dude, what seems to be the issue? Why are you meeting me at the door?" I ask, pushing past him.

Shawn nervously pushes a hand through his hair, as he usually does when something goes wrong. "If I knew, you wouldn't be here," he grits through clenched teeth.

"What crawled up your ass?" I ask. Shawn's as easy-going as they come, so his current attitude is concerning.

"Sorry, man. A couple of women from out of town have settled at the bar inside and are relentlessly harassing me," he says, nodding toward the women in question. "And you know me, I love flirtin' more than most, but this is excessive. I hate when people stumble onto this town."

I shake my head with a chuckle. Shawn is a handsome guy, and I'm man enough to admit it. I understand why women can't resist flirting with him. With his sun-streaked light brown hair, long enough to give him a surfer dude vibe, and eyes the color of warm caramel... Gross, did I just actually describe my best friend that way? I gag a little. He's like a brother to me, and while he fancies himself a famous ladies' man, I know he has feelings for our friend Becky, even though he's too chickenshit to acknowledge or act on them.

"Oh, yeah, sorry," I reply. "Sometimes tourists get adventurous. I don't much like it either. Especially when they're drunk."

"Ah, yeah, about that. I saw a black Jeep cruise through town earlier," Shawn says.

"Tiny told me the same thing. Are you sure it's not your current fan club's transportation?" I joke and gesture to the bar.

"Nah, I saw them park. The Jeep went straight through town and never turned around. And I know it's not our regular seasonals on Monhonan because they never come until after the weather gets warmer."

"How did you see the Jeep if you've been busy fending off advances behind the bar?" I inquire, my brows narrowing.

"I needed some fresh air," Shawn says, refusing to look me in the eye.

I shake my head. "I thought you quit vaping. You know she's never going to give you a chance if you're still doing that shit."

"I know, man. I've been trying nicotine patches, but I just got stressed out and needed a hit," Shawn says guiltily.

"Well, knock it off. That shit will rot your lungs. I've lost one brother, and I don't need to lose you, too, to something this stupid." I see Shawn wince at the mention of my late brother Silas.

He nods and returns to his post behind the bar while I deal with the troublemaking women to give him a break. They're tipsy, which concerns me because they'll be driving out of here drunk. Shearwater Cove has plenty to offer, but lodging isn't one of them. If you don't live here, you can't sleep here.

"Ladies," I say, sidling up next to the drunker of the two and smiling at them big enough to show my dimples. "This isn't really the best place to get plastered. We have no accommodations available here in town, and you both seem well on your way to being unable to drive safely."

"Damn," the drunker of the pair garbles as she sways on her stool, not hiding the way she admires my body. "What do they feed the men in thith town? Ow, ow, owwwwww!"

"Suuuure, but I bet you have an extra room. Or a really big bed," the other replies.

"Ever been with two girlth at onthce?" The first slurs.

"Ok, aaaand time to go." My dimples vanish, and I fix my gaze directly on both of them to show I'm not in the mood for their nonsense today. Drunken disturbances at the brewery don't happen often, but when they do, it usually becomes the talk of the town for at least a week. With no local law enforcement, it's up to me to be the bad guy.

I settle their tab and gently guide them out the front door. They are not happy as they wobble to their car, vowing to ruin me on Yelp. The joke's on them because I don't give a shit.

"Ok, Shawn, let's see what you did to fuck up my tap lines."

"Fuck off. I did nothing. I replaced the keg earlier today, but it was working fine," he huffs.

"Well, it looks here like the coupler isn't fully locked onto the keg's valve," I say as I adjust it. "Should work fine now. I wish you were just a tiny bit more handy."

"Again, fuck off," Shawn lifts his middle finger. "You didn't hire me for my handyman chops." He waggles his eyebrows as I leave the brewery.

Heading back to my house, I pass buildings that represent the Cooper family's legacy. The old, unsophisticated pole barn my granddad built primarily stores our current boat projects and parts. To the right of the barn, we recently erected massive metal shelters where Dad and I winterize, shrink-wrap, and store boats at the end of the season.

I arrive at the house situated at the highest point of the land. The view still takes my breath away, even though I've lived here my whole life. My dad built the post-and-beam home we currently share after he and Mom got married. After Mom passed away during the COVID pandemic, I moved back in to keep an eye on the old man and his weak ticker. Melanie and I had just ended things, and I needed a change of scenery.

The unassuming cape-style front of our house is welcoming, with a covered front porch facing west. However, once you step inside, a breathtaking sight unfolds with a wall of east-facing windows framing a large fieldstone fireplace. The vast, open living area boasts a truly spectacular panoramic view of the ocean. The home, primarily a single-level structure, features only a loft area on the second floor, along with a cathedral ceiling that enhances the impressiveness of the main living space. Dad was a master carpenter in his day, and the love he poured into the house is evident everywhere.

Mom's domain was the chef's kitchen next to the main living room. She loved trying new recipes, but her true passion was baking. It's a miracle Silas and I weren't as wide as we were tall when we were children. The adjoining dining area was undoubtedly designed for entertaining—Mom and Dad enjoyed hosting extravagant dinner parties to showcase her latest dishes. Maybe someday, when I have someone to cook for, I'll spend more time mastering the art. Perhaps it will make me feel closer to my mom.

The smartest thing my dad ever did when building this house was to place the master suite at the opposite end from Silas's room and mine. When I moved back in a few years ago, I renovated my wing to create a second master suite, complete with a walk-in closet that makes me laugh because I only fill about a quarter of it with my flannel shirts, worn jeans, and my collection of boots in various stages of wear. I thought it would be appropriate to have that space between us for when I had women over. Sadly, I haven't been on a date since Mel and I broke up.

The open loft serves as my office and is one of my favorite spaces in the house. My antique cherry desk overlooks the first floor, offering the same east-facing view of the Bay. Behind the desk, a bookcase spans the entire wall, filled with collections of books dating back to my grandfather's time. Fortunately, this room is tucked away upstairs—it often looks like a tornado had recently passed through, and no one needs to see that mess.

Speaking of my dad, the house feels too quiet as I kick off my boots in the entryway. I need to keep an eye on the old guy because, even though the doctor advises him to take it easy and to spend only a couple of hours on projects, he often spends the entire day in his workshop.

"Dad!" I yell from the living room. "Are you here?"

"Jesus, kid, what the hell is on fire?" He skids to a stop in his stocking feet on the hardwood floor. "I was in the shittah."

"Oh, oops, sorry for the interruption." I need to calm the fuck down when it comes to Dad. "I didn't want to find you working on another project today. You should be relaxing."

"I thought I could just—"

"Nope." I cut him off. "You don't need to do anything right now. I'm heading upstairs to the office to do billing and payroll for the brewery. No boat calls today?"

"Ayuh. Just Tiny looking for ya," he replies. "Says something's wrong with the outboard."

"Oh yeah... he called my cell too. I'll swing by there in the morning."

"Tiny also said a Jeep from Mass went through town today. " Dad raises his eyebrows at me. "What do you think that's about?"

"God, Tiny's gossip skills work fast. I guess he comes by it honestly, considering who his parents are." I huff out a chuckle. "Dad, when did you last check on Walker's Rock?"

"Last month aftah that big storm. Not a scratch. That Jackson Walker was quite the craftsman. I think that log cabin would survive a bomb. Why?"

"Maybe I should check on it after seeing Tiny tomorrow morning. I'd be really surprised to see anyone there. It's been almost two decades."

"Probably the Callahans on Monhonan getting an early jump on the summah. They'd have Mass plates, too," my dad says as he heads to the living room to turn the Sox game on.

"Yeah, you're probably right. I'll check anyway. We had some high winds last week, so giving it a once-over wouldn't hurt," I say, and Dad nods in agreement before settling into his recliner for the game.

I head upstairs to the office and immediately feel overwhelmed. There are piles of paperwork waiting for me. I add Tiny to the schedule for tomorrow, knowing that Mike needs me at the marina at some point to help launch his dad's boat now that all the work has been completed. His dad, Jack, slipped on the ice and broke his wrist a couple of months ago. He's been an antagonistic asshole towards everyone this spring because he's been unable to work on his boat, which frustrates any fisherman.

Once the brewery and house bills are paid and the payroll is completed for my two employees, I head back down the road to distribute the paychecks and enjoy a beer. In addition to Shawn, who handles the majority of the taproom tasks, I hired Owen Peterson, a recent college graduate, to assist with the brewing process and support Shawn with any additional tasks. Together, we get shit done.

CHAPTER THREE

Who Brings a Gun to a Meet Cute?

VIV

I slept like the dead. I mean D.E.A.D. I didn't even wake up to pee, which neeeeever happens. I guess six and a half hours in the car will do that. Even Kevin never woke me up to go out. I mistakenly left a window in the living room open and woke up freezing, even with Kevin burrowed under my covers. May nights in Maine are not generally a "windows open" temperature. He's such a big baby. He can leap into a 40-something-degree ocean, but he cannot and will not be cold at night. I have to agree with him on that front.

I get out of bed, put on my socks and slippers, and shuffle out to the kitchen to make some coffee. Yesterday afternoon, after unpacking and cleaning, I was so exhausted from a day of travel that I passed out early. Today, my goal is to thoroughly examine the entire cabin to identify what needs fixing and improving. Since the weather is warming up this time of year, I can postpone projects intended to enhance the cabin's winterization. Then, I plan to relax for a couple of weeks before I begin my improvements. And when I say relax, I mean not moving from the couch until I've got bedsores. I have a pile of books and an endless number of shows to catch up on. I just want to wallow in my introverted nest of grief a bit longer before I join the living again.

Kevin jumps off the bed, stretches, yawns, then stretches again before positioning himself by the back French doors to be let out. When I don't immediately come to his aid, he groans, his thick tail brushing back and forth across the wide pine floor.

For fuck's sake.

"Cool your jets, pal," I say sarcastically. "I'm going to let you out unsupervised. Do not jump into that water. I will be watching, and I will not hesitate to murder you even if you are my perfect boy."

Kevin obeys. I would like to say this is an everyday occurrence, but when there's water nearby, I never know if he will heed the call of that little devil dog on his shoulder and go for it. I make him breakfast, freshen his water, start the coffee maker, and pop an English muffin in the toaster.

I'm generally not a seasoned planner, but I was smart enough to stock up on necessities before heading north. The last thing I wanted was to roll into town and immediately have to explain myself to anyone who might recognize the name on my credit card. Additionally, stealing my ex's MealPro delivery on my way out of Boston both entertained the shit out of me and will last me a few weeks. He's going to be so pissed when his food never arrives. One final *fuck you* to that miserable asshole.

As I wander around the cabin with my coffee, I reminisce about all the memories displayed on the walls: the photos of grandparents and great-grandparents I never met, my mom and me each summer until I was fourteen, and portraits of the many dogs that enjoyed the cabin and its deep blue sea. As a kid, I never appreciated the reminders of those who came before us. Now, I would give anything for a more recent photograph of Mom and me smiling broadly to add to the collection.

I let my fingers glide along the smooth, aged wood of the kitchen doorway, tracing the faint grooves carved by the pencil Mom used to mark my growth every summer. Each indentation tells a story of my journey from childhood. The last mark is thicker than the rest—a reminder that I stopped growing, and each year's measurement traced over the same five-foot line.

My great-grandparents married young. My namesake, Vivian, was just shy of her 18th birthday when she wed 20-year-old Jackson Walker in 1945. As a wedding gift, he purchased the land that would become Walker's Rock and spent the next three years constructing the log cabin they would call home. My grandmother, Patricia, was born here in 1947. My family lived in the cabin year-round until my mom was in elementary school, at which point my grandmother relocated to Portland for my mom's education. The cabin then became primarily a summer getaway, with a few Christmases added for good measure.

My great-grandfather was a skilled logger, incredibly handy, and also loved hunting. One cabin wall displays the dusty racks of a few unfortunate bucks and a mounted turkey fan. Some hunters have trophy rooms; he had a modest trophy wall instead. Beneath his prized dead animal parts sits a live-edge shelf adorned with faded pictures of him and some of his top kills. He might have had enough to create an impressive trophy room had he lived beyond his twenties. But like any woodsman, he worked in a perilous occupation and died in a logging accident when my grandmother was just a baby.

I'm lost in the stories of my predecessors when I hear Kevin's low growl, followed by the distinctive crunch of gravel in front of the cabin. I set down my coffee and peer out the front window to see a pickup pulling up in front of the cabin. Grabbing the antique gun from the wall next to the door for extra protection—even though it probably hasn't been loaded since Teddy Roosevelt was president—I slip its barrel between the front door and its frame. Who the fuck is this? I'm in no condition to receive visitors, nor do I want to.

"Who the fuck are you?" I yell at the figure climbing out of the F-250 while I hide behind the door.

He walks slowly toward the house with his hands raised in surrender, and I immediately realize how foolish I look. I'm not on the damn Oregon Trail in the 1800s; I'm in rural Maine, in a town of about 300 people who don't take kindly to strangers but are also not generally known for their violent tendencies. After almost two decades away from Shearwater Cove, I am most certainly a stranger.

"Who the fuck are you?" He repeats my words as he stands at the base of the front stairs.

Kevin's growling increases in volume, and now all 80 pounds of him push against the back of my legs, trying to get past me. I can't let him out. While he sounds menacing with that low, grumbly, big-dog growl, he will most certainly rush at this guy, push him to the ground, and then lick him to death.

"Um, well, seeing as I used *my* key to get into *my* house, I must be the owner," I respond snidely. Jesus Christ, you can't get anything past the people in this town.

"And *I'm* the one who looks after this house while the owner is away," he says.

"Funny. Because last I checked, the guy who looks after this place must be in his 70s by now. And," I peek above the gun to assess him, "you are clearly not in your 70s."

This is my property. Why am I explaining myself to this guy?

"Ok, ok, yeah. That's a good point," the not-70-year-old guy says. "My dad, Bill Cooper, takes care of the property, but I told him I had business at the marina today and I'd check on the place after numerous reports of a blacked-out Jeep with Mass plates driving through town." He nods his head to the side to indicate my Jeep.

Note to self: This town is full of nosy Nellies.

"Also, I know that .45-70 you've got pointed at me isn't loaded, and you just pulled it off the wall next to the door. I'll bet you a hundred dollars you can't even locate any ammo for it in that place."

What the...

I lower the antique weapon. "Anything else you'd like to tell me about *my* house?" My sarcasm drips as much as it can for the first thing in the morning.

"Well, the deer antlers on the wall are probably covered in dust, and—"

"Ok, I get it. You know the place. So now that we've established that, can you kindly go the fuck away?" Who does this guy think he is?

"You still haven't identified yourself. For all I know, you're a squatter I unfortunately need to evict, which I have zero time for today." He pulls off his hat and scratches his forehead with the same hand.

I catch a brief glimpse of his face and dark brown hair falling over his forehead, without the sweat-stained ball cap holding it back. He stands at the base of the porch stairs, close enough now that I can make out blue-gray eyes framed by dark brows, scanning the property and looking anywhere but directly at me. I was definitely not on his bingo card today. There's something so familiar about him. He stands with his arms crossed, shifting from one foot to the other, almost as if he's uncomfortable being such a big target in front of the house, even though he knows the gun trained on him isn't loaded.

"My family has owned this property since the 1940s, and I've decided to make it my permanent residence," I say, snapping his attention back to me.

I open the door a little wider and lower my weapon, and when he looks at me, I see a glimmer of recognition in his striking, unforgettable eyes.

When he quirks a lopsided smile, I know those dimples.

He speaks first, "Ani?"

Oh yes... I had been in my Ani phase, thinking Vivian was too much of an old lady's name to go by in high school.

CHAPTER FOUR

Not Just a Wrong Turn

WILL

The familiar red hair and sparkling jade-green eyes mark where the similarities end since I last saw her almost two decades ago. That summer, when she joined our friend group, the six of us spent nearly every waking hour together. This was no longer the girl I once knew. She was more beautiful than I remembered—and I had thought, even at fourteen, that she was stunning.

Her previously short hair now appears quite long, considering how much is piled atop her head, framed by long bangs that brush her eyes. Oh, and those eyes! They're a brilliant green so vivid that they seem almost unreal, no longer concealed by the thick glasses of her youth. When she recognizes me, those eyes sparkle like sunlight glimmering off an emerald. She is surely going to get me into some trouble.

"Billy?" She responds cautiously. "Is that really you?"

She flings the door open with a flourish, revealing her morning attire of baggy sweats and fuzzy animal paw slippers that look as if they could swallow her feet whole. Her long red hair is twisted in a chaotic, tangled knot. My breath catches in my throat at the sight, and time stands still for me to admire this unplanned morning chaos.

I'm just about to answer when I'm met by a streak of black fur hurling itself at my torso. I hit the ground with a loud ***OOOF*** when the 80-pound dog lands on my chest, pins me to the ground, and assaults me with hot breath and slurpy licks. All I can do is cover my face so he doesn't lick inside my mouth.

"KEVIN!" she yells, running down the porch stairs to grab the dog's collar and pull him off me. "What the fuck is wrong with you? Have you lost your fool mind? We do not jump on people, and we absolutely do not knock grown-ass adults to the ground. My god, Billy, I am so sorry for my menace of a Labrador."

Kevin looks prouder of himself than guilty for his actions, his tail wagging so forcefully that his entire body shakes from the movement. If I didn't know any better, I'd say he also wore a big, goofy smile.

"You named your dog Kevin?" I ask, pushing myself up off the gravel and brushing off the dust.

"What's wrong with Kevin? Doesn't he look like a Kevin? He's my angel boy when he's not being a fucking menace."

"Ok, well, if we're making new introductions, I actually go by Will now. It's a little surreal to see you back here, Ani. It's been a while."

"Well, here I am, and I go by Vivian, well, Viv, since I'm now an adult. It has been a while, Bil... Will." She turns and pulls Kevin back up to the house and slams the door behind him. "You want a cup of coffee? It's the least I can do for the rude welcome my idiot canine provided."

"I'd like that," I say, and she vanishes into the house, leaving me staring after her. This is not how I envisioned my morning unfolding. Mike and Tiny will have to wait a bit longer for my assistance.

Viv returns to the front porch with two steaming cups of coffee, and we sit on the front steps together.

"I wasn't sure anyone would ever come back to this place," I say. One thing that hasn't changed is her height, or lack thereof. I was tall for a 14-year-old—almost 6 feet 2 inches—and continued to grow a couple more inches in high school. She seems to be the same diminutive five feet she was when I met her. I'd be lying if I said her return to Shearwater Cove didn't make me happier than I'd been since Melanie and I were together, maybe even more so.

"It's nice to be back. I wasn't sure I'd ever return to this cabin, but here I am. I do need to ask you a big favor, though," she says, her tone turning serious.

"Anything you need, Viv. I'm sorry to come in so hot. We have a lot of neighborhood watchdogs around here, and you know how small towns get protective." I shake my head and blow out a chuckle.

"Yeah... I've lived in downtown Boston for ten years, and people generally mind their own business in the city. So, the small-town dynamic is not one I've been familiar with during my adult life."

"Right, makes sense. I forgot that not everyone grows up in a tight-knit community where everyone knows your business. I often wonder what that would be like," I say, staring longingly toward the ocean. "So what do you need?"

"Can you keep my presence here to yourself? I've had an incredibly tough year, and I need some time to myself to process things. There's nothing I prefer to share right now, but just know I won't remain a hermit forever. I am genuinely excited to be back."

"What about supplies?" I ask. "Are you all set with everything you need?"

"Yeah, I appreciate you asking. I arrived fully stocked, with enough supplies for at least a few weeks. I need to get my head in a better place before reconnecting with the folks in town."

"Viv, your family has been cherished in this town for as long as anyone can remember. People will welcome you back with open arms when the time comes. Until then, your secret is safe with me. Here's my number—reach out if you need anything before you're ready to face the town," I reassure her and hand her a business card. "I must move on to today's appointments. I'll make sure no one bothers you until you're ready."

I rise from the porch stairs and hand her my empty mug before walking back to my pickup. When I turn back, Viv holds her hand up in a sorrowful wave. I don't know what kind of terrible year she's had, but the expression on her face tells me she's dealing with some shit.

I'm officially an hour behind schedule when I pull into the marina. It's still early enough in the spring for more boats to be out of the water than in. Like Mike's dad, Jack, some diehards keep their boats in the water year-round. While lobster is his main catch, he's not opposed to fishing for whatever's in season. However, Jack slipped on the ice a few months ago, broke his wrist, and has been unable to do anything boat-related, turning him into an unreasonable bear. The doctor has finally cleared him to return to regular activity, so he's eager to get his 38' Calvin Beal—the *Betsy Ann*—back in the water.

"Hey, Mike!" I shout over the pressure washer he's using on his dad's boat, ensuring it's free of debris before they launch it. He waves back, barely looking up. This is the kind of friendship we have—words are often unnecessary. We've been best friends since elementary school, joined at the hip ever since. We played tee ball, then Little League, and both were starters on the varsity baseball team in high school. It's crazy to see him all settled now with a couple of adorable girls whom I love like my own.

I find his dad amidst a pile of pot wrap. "Hi, Jack, good day for you, finally. How's the wrist? Let me know if you need help getting your traps on the boat."

"Will, hey," Jack says, only half looking at me as he concentrates on swapping out the ropes on his red and blue striped buoys. "Ayuh, I'll definitely be happy to get out there. Between being in a cast the past two months and Mike thinking he can boss me around the marina store, I've had just about enough dry land for one wintah."

I shake my head and laugh. Jack Tucker is as old salt as they come. At 60, the lines in his tanned face are deep, highlighting light blue eyes that light up when he's out on the water.

Once we launch the *Betsy Ann*, I check to see if Mike needs anything else.

"Nah, I've got a pretty slow day, and I know Tiny is chomping at the bit for ya to come help him with his outboard. Is it just me, or does he need to take an engine repair class? He'd save so much money." Mike shakes his head.

"Don't get me started," I say. "Ok, I'll catch up with ya. It will be nice once it's warm enough for beers and burgers on the grill."

"See? Just as I told you, a blocked water intake. If you would just take an engine repair class, I wouldn't have to charge you for something this simple; you could fix it yourself," I lecture Tiny again. I feel like I do this a lot. He's a good guy. He runs a fantastic fishing charter that people rave about, but he's helpless with anything mechanical. Tiny claims to be more of a talker and less of a fixer, just like his dad, Earl, who owns Earl's Got Gas, Shearwater Cove's go-to for just about anything. Especially when it comes to town gossip.

"Where ya picking up your charter tomorrow?" I ask, sitting on the rail of his Sisu Eastern 22, which he named *Tiny Bubbles*, while he prepares for his group. Since we don't like to draw any unnecessary attention to downtown Shearwater Cove, he picks up his charters elsewhere. The 22-foot boat accommodates charters of typically two to four people, with no prior fishing experience necessary. He makes every trip memorable.

"In Steuben. It's three college friends having a reunion. I guess they all got high-stress jobs down in Portland and wanted a day out on the watah. Becky's gonna whip up some gourmet lobstah roll lunches for me to serve."

"Sounds good, Tiny. Be safe."

"Thanks for the help, Will. I'm going to look into the class, I promise. I guess I gotta grow up and take responsibility for my rig." Tiny sighs deeply at the thought of going back to school. "Oh, hey, did you ever find out anything about that black Jeep I saw yesterday?"

"Nah, I looked around and didn't see anything. Must've been a wrong turn that found their way back to the main road. You know, we always get folks that have no idea where they are." I chuckle, hoping Tiny doesn't dig deeper.

I'm exhausted, and it's only lunchtime. Now that Tiny mentioned a lobster roll, I decided to head to Cove Lobster for some takeout.

"Will!" Becky yells when my order is ready.

"Thanks, Becky," I say, taking the tray with the lobster roll, homemade kettle chips, and my iced tea to an empty picnic table. My stomach growls, reminding me that I haven't eaten since early this morning, and Becky makes an award-winning lobster roll. She steams the lobster in its juices, giving them a briny flavor that showcases its freshness. The chilled lobster consists of a mixture of tail and claw meat split into bite-sized pieces, overflowing a buttered and toasted New England-style hot dog bun. Becky always gives customers the option of melted Kate's butter, mayonnaise, or both. Definitely both. Becky's German Shepherd/Lab mix, Shirley, saunters over to my table, hoping to find some snacks on the ground. It's hard to resist Shirley with her cockeyed ears, so I sneak her a couple of bites of my lunch; she wags her fluffy tail in thanks and continues to the next diner.

Chef Becky left Shearwater Cove, the only one in my friend group who went to college. She graduated from Johnson & Wales in Rhode Island with a degree in Culinary Arts, hoping to secure a position at a fine dining establishment in Boston or Portland. However, like most of us from the Cove, the lure of the town proved too strong. Mary Pelletier, Earl's wife and owner of the Cove Cafe, brought Becky back home by offering her carte blanche on the menu for the new seafood takeout lunch spot at the edge of the waterfront park. She couldn't resist.

Becky still pines for my other best friend, Shawn. Since we were kids, she's had heart eyes for him, but for the longest time, he was too oblivious to notice. They dated during our senior year of high school, but he still failed to appreciate a good thing when he had it, which led to their breakup, and she moved south for college. To this day, they're both still single, and I often catch one of them staring at the other. I can honestly say that if I were in their situation, I'd jump at the chance to be with someone I'd yearned for so long.

CHAPTER FIVE

Binge–Reading and Bed Sores

VIV

HADLEY: VIVIAN PATRICIA JAMES, GET YO HEAD OUT OF YO ASS AND ANSWER MY TEXT! WALLOWING TOO LONG AT OUR AGE IS BAD FOR COLLAGEN. MAYBE. I DON'T EXACTLY KNOW.

VIV: SORRY, HAD. I'M STILL LYING LOW AND BINGE-READING APOCALYPTIC THRILLERS. ALSO, LET'S NOT TALK ABOUT OUR AGE, PLEASE.

HAD: UH, DUDE, THAT DOES NOT SOUND LIKE A GOOD WAY TO IMPROVE YOUR MENTAL HEALTH.

VIV: COULD BE WORSE. WHEN ARE YOU COMING?

HAD: ARE YOU SAYING MY COMING TO VISIT IS WORSE?

VIV: HA! NO WAY!

HAD: SCHOOL'S OUT NEXT WED, SO I'LL BE UP ON THU. THINK YOU CAN TAKE A FUCKING SHOWER BY THEN?

VIV: BITE ME.

HAD: LOVE YOU TOO, SWEETS.

VIV: SHOWERS ARE OVERRATED. I SMELL FINE.

HAD: DOUBT IT. OH, I HAVE NEWS. NOT VERY GOOD NEWS.

VIV: GOD. DO I WANNA KNOW?

HAD: WHEN I GOT HOME YESTERDAY, ERIC WAS ON MY STEPS.

VIV: THE FUCK?

HAD: I DIDN'T KNOW HE KNEW MY ADDRESS.

VIV: NEVER TOLD HIM. FUCKER MUST'VE PRESSED SOMEONE.

HAD: IT FREAKED ME OUT. HE'S PISSED.

VIV: HE HAS NO RIGHT. HE KINDLY CAN GO FUCK HIM-SELF.

HAD: HE HASN'T TRIED TO TEXT YOU?

VIV: DUNNO. BLOCKED HIS SELFISH ASS.

HAD: SMARTY PANTS.

VIV: I HAVE MY MOMENTS.

HAD: HE MUST BE EXTRA PISSED IF HE TOOK THE TIME TO DRIVE TO ME IN PLYMOUTH.

VIV: I HEARD HE'S FUCKING SOMEONE ON THE CAPE.

HAD: AH, THAT MAKES SENSE.

VIV: I HOPE HE GETS SYPHILIS AND HIS DICK FALLS OFF.

HAD: THAT'S THE SPIRIT.

VIV: CAN'T WAIT FOR YOUR ARRIVAL.

HAD: HAVE YOU BEEN INTO TOWN YET?

VIV: FUCK NO.

HAD: YOU HAVEN'T SEEN ANYONE BUT KEVIN?

VIV: WHAT'S WRONG WITH KEVIN?

HAD: HA, THAT LITTLE ASSHOLE MISS ME?

VIV: I DID HAVE A VISITOR...

HAD: COME AGAIN.

VIV: MY MOM HIRED A LOCAL GUY TO MONITOR THE HOUSE. SOMEONE SAW MY MASS PLATES, SO HE SENT HIS SON TO CHECK THEM.

HAD: I SENSE A SILENT AND...

VIV: I KNEW HIM FROM THAT LAST SUMMER WE WERE HERE. HE REMEMBERED ME.

HAD: DID YOU REMEMBER HIM?

VIV: UH-HUH.

HAD: WHAT AREN'T YOU TELLING ME?

Viv: Nuthin.

Had: Don't believe you. I'll have better luck getting you to talk in person.

Viv: Fine.

Had: Fine. See ya next week, muffin!

Viv: xoxo

CHAPTER SIX

Goodbye Funk, Hello World

VIV

Wallowing ends now. I must be developing those bed sores I wished for from the amount of time I've spent on the couch over the past three weeks. I'm glad I cleaned the cabin and unpacked before going into hermit mode, or I'd be in trouble. My supply of purloined frozen meals is running dangerously low, and I am really tired of powdered coffee creamer. It's a bad sign when you smell so bad your dog won't even sleep with you anymore.

"I'm showered, shaved, and ready to snap out of my funk," I say to Kevin, who acknowledges me with a microscopic lift of his head from his spot in the afternoon sunshine coming through the windows.

Grocery shopping is a special kind of torture, but I predict that grocery shopping in a small town where I'm a mildly familiar outsider resembles a circle of hell even Dante isn't aware of. But I am a strong, independent woman who can handle this. Who am I kidding? I grab a ball cap and sunglasses just in case I chicken out. Also, if I don't have food and booze in this house by the time Hadley arrives, she's going to dice me into tiny pieces and feed me to the fishes.

The jingle of the keys rouses Kevin from his slumber, and he's already got his nose pressed against the front door. Fucking dog won't let me take a shit without him lying at my feet, so I figured getting out of the house without him would be a lot like escaping Alcatraz. I've never seen a mammal go from snoring to turbo like Kev.

Despite my dread about finally going into town, I'm curious about who's still around and why the hell all the buildings are painted in a palette of colors that seem to have come from a unicorn's ass. I hope others from the old crew are still local—it would be nice to catch up with Evvie and Becky. They're probably married with kids and jobs, leaving no time to entertain the lonely single lady from away, whom they might not even remember.

The town's main street is Cove Avenue, and the bright yellow building that houses Earl's Got Gas greets you as you enter town. As a kid, the name Earl's Got Gas would always send me into fits of giggles whenever I saw it. Mom tried to remain composed about it, but she often ended up giggling right along with me.

Earl's facelift is immediately apparent, with a new sign that advertises "Other Stuff" in addition to gas. Earl Pelletier opened the gas station in the 1970s as a one-stop shop for all fuel sources, auto repairs, and cigarettes. In the 1990s, he added fishing gear, camping supplies, and essential outdoor clothing. Twenty years later, he expanded with a small grocery store for locals who preferred not to drive to the market in Milbridge.

With my list in hand and, because I am, in fact, a chicken, my disguise securely in place, I push through Earl's front door, having left Kevin in the car. It feels like a flashback to my childhood as Earl sits behind the counter, holding court with a handful of his cronies, most likely retelling tall tales that have become taller with time. Even after all these years, I recognize him immediately. It's hard to forget the deep, creasing dimples in his cheeks and his navy-blue eyes that crinkle when he smiles. Only the color of his hair has changed over the years, having faded to a sandy white.

I wander the aisles with the small cart, adding necessities. By necessities, I mean snack foods resembling a nine-year-old boy's dining habits and an alcohol collection commonly found in a fraternity house. If there's one thing Hadley and I enjoy, it's a feast of Twinkies and PBR. I also pick up a four-pack of local craft beer, margarita fixings, some fancy cheeses, meats, and crackers for when we feel lavish. I replenish my coffee supply, select an actual liquid coffee creamer, grab some eggs and bacon, and head to checkout. I figure now that I've put my reclusive life behind me, there's no need to hoard supplies.

I set my provisions on the counter as Earl rings me up. Aside from a polite greeting, he's unusually quiet for the town's biggest tea spiller. I hand him my credit card, catching his sidelong glances as if he thinks he should know me. He looks at my card, looks at me, and then back at the card again. "Vivian James," he reads out loud.

"Yes, sir," I reply.

"Patty's granddaughter," he says with a smile, a statement more than a question. The guy has a memory; I'll give him that.

"Yes, sir," I answer with a smile. I'm no stranger to the rumors that Earl had a major crush on my grandmother after my grandfather passed away, and before he married his wife. He openly wept at the rear of the church during her funeral.

"Ohhhhhhh, man. Well lookit you, all growed up. I haven't seen you in, what? Twenty years? Gosh, you look just like your grandma."

"That's a lovely compliment. Mom and I were last here in 2006," I smile.

"Oh, I remember Maggie James. How is she doing these days? Did she come with you?" Earl asks, dropping names as if we were here last year.

"Mom passed away about nine months ago. Breast cancer."

"Like her momma, eh?"

I blow out a breath and nod. "She put up a bit more of a fight, but it just kept coming back with more of a vengeance each time."

"Oh, I'm sorry about that, darlin'. I hope you're sticking around for a while. It'll be nice to have a fresh face 'round these parts," Earl says. "Your momma and your grandma sure were great gals."

"Planning on staying at least through the summer. Maybe longer if I can get the cabin in shape for permanent residence."

"Ayuh, we got a couple of handymen I'm sure would give ya a good price on the job. You remember Will Coopah? He's got a few businesses here in town, and he's good with his tools."

My ridiculously immature brain only registers the part about being "good with his tools." I chuckle to myself and attempt to keep a straight face.

"Oh yes! Good to know. Thanks, Earl. I appreciate the recommendation. I'm still compiling my list of projects." I grab my groceries and head for the door. "It's so good to see you again, Earl."

"You too, darlin'. Don't be a strangah!" He calls out with a wave as I push through the doors.

I return to the car, only to find Kevin chatting with the locals. His big, black head sticks out of the window as two older ladies admire his handsomeness and stroke his velvety ears.

"Well, doggo," I tease, "seems like you've already found yourself a fan club."

"Oh, he's a handsome boy," fan #1 declares.

"And he's such a gentleman!" says fan #2, aggressively scratching under his chin.

"He thanks you for your lovely compliments." I chuckle, opening the trunk. "He's here all summer and loves attention!" I hear them both giggling as they walk away.

It's such a beautiful day, and with my perishables safely stored in my cooler, I decide it's ice cream weather. Since Kevin has been an exceptionally good boy, he deserves a pup cup for his patience and politeness. A few doors down from Earl's is the bright turquoise building that houses Tucker's Tasty Treats. Some of my fondest childhood memories in Shearwater Cove involve Mrs. Tucker sneaking me extra scoops of my favorite ice cream, much to Mom's dismay.

I clearly remember walking into the shop early that summer and seeing a line of really loud kids my age sitting at the counter: Billy and his best friends Shawn and Mike; Evvie, who always had googly cartoon eyes for Mike; and Becky, who had the same googly cartoon eyes for Shawn. Nervous about being just a summer visitor, I quickly ordered my ice cream and left the shop, trying not to make eye contact.

It was Evvie who chased after me, the most outgoing member of the small group.

"Hello, hey, wait a second," Evvie called, breathless after running after me.

I stopped as I tried to eat my ice cream before the thing embarrassingly melted down my arm. "Yeah?"

Evvie continued. "You don't look familiar. Are you just here for the summer? We don't get a lot of summer folks around here."

"Yeah, I'm here for the summer with my mom," I said. "My name's Ani."

"You should come hang out with us," Evvie says, her eyes pleading. "We could use another girl to even out our group."

"Um, ok, I guess, if you don't think anyone will mind."

Evvie waves me off with an eye roll as if she is the boss of the small group of teenagers, thus making all the decisions.

"I'm Evvie, by the way! Come back in, and I'll introduce you to the gang. We all live here year-round, and honestly, I need some new stories," she adds with an eye roll. "Those stinky boys only ever talk about video games!"

For the rest of the summer, it was a gang of six. Evvie, Becky, and I were inseparable, often breaking away from the boys to discuss makeup and clothes, which Jonas brother was the cutest (Nick, obvi), and the latest season of *One Tree Hill*. But much to the boys' dismay, the main topic of conversation revolved around the recently released *Twilight* novel (Team Edward forever), and we couldn't stop obsessing about the upcoming release of *New Moon* at the end of the summer. Will, Mike, and Shawn were just as sick of hearing about sparkly vampires as we girls were of hearing about *Grand Theft Auto*.

It was the best summer vacation I could remember in Maine. Mom was so happy that I found some kids to hang out with, and she enjoyed listening to the teenage conversations when the group came to Walker's Rock to hang out. Mom often talked about making Shearwater Cove our permanent residence, so I'm sure that seeing me make friends so quickly boosted her confidence in that plan. Plus, Mom loved being able to tease me relentlessly about the blush that crept into my cheeks when Will talked to me. My whole life, I've dealt with that embarrassing blush—the curse of the redhead.

As I pulled myself out of my trip down memory lane, I entered the ice cream shop, greeted by the jingling of the bells on the door. The same bells rang out, but the interior had been updated in bright pink and teal to complement the teal exterior. Mrs. T didn't seem to be working, but a young woman in her early twenties sat on a stool, scrolling through her phone behind the tubs of various ice cream flavors.

"Welcome to Tasty Treats. What can I tempt you with today?" The girl asks. God, this town loves its alliteration.

"I would love a hot fudge sundae with all the fixings, but no nuts. If you offer pup cups, my friend here would love one, too. "

"Of course. And who's your friend? He's quite a looker."

I smile. "This is my angel boy, Kevin. He loves swimming, car rides, and ice cream.

"Well, he's come to the right place!" The girl chuckles. "I'm sorry, I don't recognize you, and I try to greet all our customers by name. Mrs. T says that's the best way to get the good tips!"

"Oh, sorry! I'm Vivian James. I used to come here as a kid, and my family owns the place out at the point—Walker's Rock."

"I'm Tristin. I moved to Shearwater Cove two years ago and manage this place for Mrs. Tucker. It's very nice to meet you, Vivian. I'll get your ice creams right away!"

"Thanks, Tristin. Is Mrs. T around, or is she pretty hands-off now that she has a capable shop manager? I'd love to say hi."

"She's in every morning for a few hours to ensure we're good on supplies. I think she's next door having her hair done right now. Her daughter-in-law, Evvie, owns the salon," Tristin said.

"AHA! Evvie married Mike. I knew them as a teenager, but I haven't been back here since I was fourteen, so I never saw that relationship bloom!"

Tristin laughed. "Oh yeah, they've been married for ten years now, I think. Evvie opened Shear & Shave about six years ago. Mike owns Shearwater Cove Marina. Such an entrepreneurial family. And they have two of the most adorable little girls."

"Wow, seems like I have much catching up to do with the old gang – that's if they even remember me! Come on, Kevvie, let's eat our ice cream outside." Kevin will do anything for ice cream, so he follows me out obediently. "Thanks, Tristin! It was nice meeting you. I'm sure we'll see each other again."

"You too, Vivian! I hope you come back soon!"

Once we finish our ice cream, I secure Kevin's leash to the lamp post and peek my head into Shear & Shave. Mrs. Tucker sits under the hairdryer, flipping through a magazine, while who I assume is Evvie spins in the salon chair, scrolling on her phone. When more goddamn bells jingle, both women look up, seemingly confused by this person who appears familiar yet like a stranger at the same time.

Evvie says, "Welcome to Shear & Shave. What can I do for ya?"

"I'm not sure if you remember me, but I used to summer here about 20 years ago," I say sheepishly.

Mrs. Tucker speaks loudly from under the dryer. "Gosh, she looks very familiar, doesn't she, Evvie?"

"She certainly does, Betsy," Evvie replies as she walks over to turn off the dryer.

"It's those pretty green eyes. How can anyone forget those eyes? And that beautiful red hair," Mrs. T says.

"Ani?" Evvie asks.

"Yeah," I say. "It's actually Vivian, well Viv, really; I haven't gone by Ani since I was a stupid teenager. Gosh, I can't believe you remembered my name."

"Cursed with a memory like an elephant, I'm afraid," Evvie says with a chuckle as she stands and walks slowly over to me, never taking her eyes off my face. She gently pulls me into a hug that feels as if no time has passed and tells me there are no hard feelings about all the years between visits.

I hug her back, holding on for a moment longer when she tries to pull away. "I'm so glad you remember me," I whisper into her shoulder.

"Wow," Evvie begins, pulling away. "Vivian, we had no idea what happened to you. You were gone when I returned home from my grandparents' house, and I never saw you again. Becky and I wondered about you for a couple of years and tried to find you on MySpace and Facebook."

"I know, and I'm sorry. Mom forbade me from signing up for social media until I was sixteen." I apologize. "Not long after we left that summer, Mom got sick, and she battled for years and just never felt well enough to come back here. She passed away last September. I'm just really happy to be here now, in a place that meant so much to her." I quickly wipe at a tear I didn't realize had leaked from my eye.

Evvie hugs me again. "Well, you're here now, and we're not letting you go this time! So I hope you're staying for a while."

"I mean, but you have Mike now. Why do you need me?" I chuckle.

"Oh, HA! It took me a while. Trying to peel him away from those stupid video games they played. I guess it took me getting boobs to make that happen."

"Evelyn Ann, don't say that kind of thing in front of your mother-in-law!" Mrs. T interjects. Evvie and I burst into a fit of giggles.

Mrs. Tucker steers the conversation back to Mom. "I'm sorry about your ma, Viv. She was a wonderful friend during our childhood, and I remember all those summers she spent here as an adult. I wish we had known."

"Mom declined a service since it was only the two of us left. However, her one request was for her ashes to be spread at the Rock. I thought I'd gather some of her old friends this summer to do it."

"That must've been you in the black Jeep everyone was all flustered about a couple of weeks ago," Mrs. T says.

"It sure was, Mrs. T," I confirm. "I needed a few weeks to pull myself together. The last year has been a rough one."

"Obviously. And I think you're old enough to call me Betsy now, Viv."

"Thanks, Betsy. Hopefully, you can help me track down her old crew."

Betsy nods and replies, "Of course, dear."

Evvie says, "Viv, you must come to our house this weekend for a BBQ. Mike would love to see you."

"Does Mike even remember me?"

"He remembers the girl who had heart eyes for Will Cooper."

"Oh god," I throw my hands over my face. "Kinda hoping no one remembered that!"

"I don't forget much, as we've already determined," Evvie says, raising her left eyebrow slightly.

"Oh man, it's so great to see you both. I should head out so my dog doesn't think I've abandoned him tied to the light post in a strange place."

"A DOG? Go get him this instant," Betsy squeals.

Upon my return with Kevin, both women immediately fall to their knees to give him plenty of ear scritches and nose kisses.

"And what's your name, you handsome fella?" Evvie coos.

"This is Kevin. He just celebrated his first birthday in April. He likes swimming, car rides, tackling unsuspecting adults, and ice cream," I proudly reel off.

"Did Kevin get a pup cup next door?" Betsy asks.

"Gleefully. And messily."

"Give me your number, Viv," Evvie says, standing back up. "I'll get in touch with the details for our gathering. We'd love for you to join us."

"That would be amazing. I was so afraid I'd have been forgotten," I laugh. It feels good to laugh. There hasn't been much laughter this past year, and I think I'm now ready to start shedding all this drama and sadness.

CHAPTER SEVEN

The One That Got Away... and Came Back

WILL

A June Saturday with bright sunshine and bluebird skies makes for a perfect day for the first barbecue of the season at Mike and Evvie's. After a long, cold winter and an unusually wet spring, the arrival of warmer weather thrills us all. The Tuckers love to entertain, which I appreciate because, while I have the space for big parties, I could possibly be the worst host imaginable. Evvie excels at throwing parties, regardless of their size.

Last year, they installed an in-ground pool, and I know their wild girls will be in that sub-70-degree water as long as their parents allow them. They began asking about the pool around Memorial Day, but Mike refused to open it until mid-June because they would completely ignore the cold.

I'm not sure how he can resist those two little angels. I'd give them everything they ever asked for if I were in his shoes. Olivia is seven, with dark hair, while Amelia is almost five with white-blonde curls—they both have their dad's striking blue eyes. And boy, do they love getting into mischief! Olivia has recently discovered pranks, and no one is safe around her. Like any little sister, Amelia longs to be just like her big sissy but hasn't quite mastered the art of the practical joke. I'm definitely getting Liv a Whoopee cushion for her birthday in September. Her parents might kill me, but it will be worth it.

I swing by my brewery for beer since that's always my contribution to any barbecue. I grab a couple of different styles that I know everyone will enjoy. Some of my friends aren't exactly adventurous in their beer choices, and that's okay. I also pick up some bags of ice to fill the cooler in the back of my pickup and get all the beer on ice.

As usual, I'm the first to arrive. I always am. Sometimes, I think they intentionally give me an earlier time because they know I'll either help set up for a gathering or keep the girls entertained so they're not underfoot. I enjoy option two the most. When I push through the gate leading to Mike and Evvie's backyard, I'm met with squeals of delight as Mike tosses each of the girls into the pool. I have to laugh because they're each wearing tiny wetsuits to ward off potential hypothermia.

Mike catches sight of me just as he hurls Olivia into the pool for one final splash. I crack open two ice-cold beers, the crisp sound cutting through the warm air, and hand one to my best friend. Together, we settle into a pair of comfortable chairs on the patio to keep an eye on the children as they play in the pool. Evvie waves to me from the back deck where she's thoughtfully arranging the table with colorful plates and silverware.

"Will! What kinda beer did you bring me?" Evvie asks.

"Is that a trick question, Ev? I have some Ranch Waters in the cooler right here," I say as I toss her an unopened can.

Evvie catches it like a major league first baseman, laughing. "Oh, you just knew I'd be testing you to see if you remembered my favorite drink from last summer. I think Becky will be just as thrilled."

As lifelong friends often do, we settle into an easy conversation about nothing in particular while we wait for the rest of our group to arrive. I know Becky is coming, and Shawn will be on his way after he gets Owen settled to manage the brewery while we're gone. Mike's older brother, Cameron, should be here with his son, Lucas. I hear Betsy and Jack in the house, arguing about where to put the potato salad they brought. Betsy says it should go in the refrigerator, while Jack thinks putting a mayonnaise-based salad outside is perfectly fine. Jack should stick to what he knows, which is definitely not barbecue side dishes.

The grandparents' arrival elicits another round of squeals as the tiny humans bribe their grandpa to continue the tossing. Betsy ruffles my hair from behind before taking a seat on the patio with us.

"Will, honey, is your dad joining us today?" Betsy asks. She has known my dad since they were kids and was one of my mom's closest friends.

"Not today. He overdid it yesterday working in his shop, so I'm sure he's lying on the couch watching the Sox game. He needs to knock it off."

"It has to be hard for him," Betsy says, "he's always been such a busy, active guy."

"Which is fine if he would just do less and take things more slowly. He can still do everything he loves, just in smaller quantities," I sigh. "I lost Silas and Mom both before they were supposed to go, and I don't want to lose Dad too."

"I get it, Will, but try to cut him a little slack. Seems like he's trying." Betsy squeezes my arm before returning to the house to help Evvie.

I'm deep in thought about my dad when I hear more voices coming from the yard. Becky arrives with a batch of her renowned homemade sea salt kettle chips. While I handle the beer and ice for any barbecue, Becky takes the role of the chip lady. Everyone in town craves the salty crunch of her chips. Cam, Mike's brother, brings a crock of baked beans, and his son, Luke, who immediately joins his younger cousins in the pool.

Cameron returned to Shearwater Cove when Luke was just a baby. The boy's mother quickly decided she wasn't cut out to be a mom, and after she left, Cam believed that being closer to his family would be best for both of them. He opened a small bakery food truck named The Coffee Car in the brewery's parking lot, which serves gourmet coffee and a limited selection of baked goods. The truck is open only until noon, allowing him time to work at the marina helping Mike. Lucas will be a junior in high school when classes start back up in the fall. He's the star of the track team, maintains good grades, and works part-time for Becky at Cove Lobster.

Mike has the grill fired up when Shawn finally arrives with even more beer. Although the extra beer is unnecessary, Mike appreciates adding it to his collection.

"Owen's all set for the afternoon?" I ask Shawn. "I know it's not his first time manning the ship solo, but sometimes he gets nervous if no one is there to answer one of his 300 questions."

"He's good," Shawn says, staring over my shoulder. I don't have to turn around to know who he's looking at.

"Jesus, you're painful. Just go talk to her." I walk away, leaving him standing there, gawking at Becky.

Burgers are finished, and all the sides are on the table when Evvie's doorbell rings. I look around, confused because we're all here, and none of us would ring a damn doorbell. Evvie rushes to the front door and returns to the back deck with someone following behind her... is it? No. But I think I see red hair. The air rushes out of my lungs because the last time I saw Vivian, she did not look... this... good.

Evvie guides Viv to an empty seat, encouraging her to fill a plate while she makes introductions.

"Shawn, Becky, Mike... do you remember Ani from the summer before we went to high school?" Evvie asks.

Mike's lips quirk in a wicked smile. "Ani? Holy shit. What brings you back to the Cove?"

"Well, my full name is actually Vivian. It's a stupid story, but I thought it was too much of an old lady's name, so I was trying out nicknames that summer. So you can call me Viv," she says shyly.

"Oh my GOD, Viv!" Becky shouts. "Evvie and I wondered for months what happened. We figured you had to go home, but then you never came back the following summer."

"She popped into the salon a couple of days ago, and I thought Betsy was going to fall out of her chair!" Evvie laughs, nodding at Betsy.

"Wait. Are you the girl who had the hots for Will that summer?" Shawn chimes in, struggling to catch up with the conversation.

"What the fuck is wrong with you, man?" I scold.

"Language!" Evvie reminds me, glancing down at the kids eating on the patio with raised eyebrows.

"Sorry," I whisper.

"God, don't scare her away, you buffoon," Becky chides.

"What?" Shawn asks innocently. "Tell Mike's face that."

"Jesus Christ, Shawn," Mike shakes his head as he continues the introductions. "Viv, this is my older brother Cam, who was unquestionably too cool to hang out with us kids back in the day. And that handsome young dude sitting with my girls is his son Luke."

"Nice to meet you, Cam," Viv says. "And I can't tell you how happy I am to be back here and to see you all again. Jeez, it's blowing my mind to see you as adults now. When I decided to come back here, I wondered if anyone would still be around."

"Becky is the only one who escaped for college," Evvie says. "But she couldn't stay away. Couldn't stand being away from us!"

'You wish," Becky says. "If it weren't for the opportunity Mary gave me to run my own place, I'd probably be living a completely different kind of life in Boston right now."

I see Shawn wince at those words. He needs an industrial-sized crowbar to dislodge his head from his ass. He'd probably be a lot less cranky if he just told her how he feels. I think it's jamming up his chakras or something.

I can't stop staring at Viv. She looks so comfortable being back with us. She's dressed casually in her baggy jeans rolled at the ankles and a green hoodie that makes her jade eyes almost glow. The hair that had been piled on her head when I saw her weeks ago now falls in long waves down her back, with her bangs brushing against her eyes. The smattering of freckles across her nose remains, and she wears almost no makeup, except on her lashes. I thought she was pretty when I was fourteen, with glasses and braces. Fuck me, I'm in deep trouble now.

After finishing dinner, Betsy and Jack pack the girls up and take them back to their place for a sleepover. Cam and Luke take off since Cam gets up early to open his food truck. And then there was the original group of six. Something that hasn't happened in almost two decades. The conversation around me flows like no time has passed, but I just observe. When I saw Viv a few weeks ago, she said she had a shit year, but she seems good now—like all she needed was a couple of weeks to decompress.

I might be the only one here who sort of understands what that terrible year was like, as my dad checked in on Maggie occasionally. He was aware of her struggles with breast cancer and Viv's determination to take charge of everything while trying to be a teenager with school and then transition to an adult with work, all while managing her own life. In the last conversation Dad had with Viv's mom, she confided that she would be going into hospice and didn't have much time left. That was late last summer. But I'll let Viv tell her own story when she's ready.

I see Viv going into the kitchen, and I follow. She's at the sink filling a glass with water, so I lean casually against the kitchen island, waiting for her to turn around.

"FOR FUCK'S SAKE, WILL!" she gasps, almost dropping her entire glass. "What kind of creepy stalker are you?" She puts a hand to her chest, her eyes wide, and I realize I may have wanted to be less ninja in my approach.

"Ooops," I say sheepishly. "I just wanted to catch you alone to see how you were doing since we last saw each other."

"Ah, yes. I'm doing much better. Thank you for asking. I went into town yesterday and everything. Sweet Earl remembered my mom and grandmother. And as you know, I ran into Evvie and Betsy."

"Look at you go," I joke. "But in all seriousness, I'm happy you're feeling better. I should've said something before, but I'm sorry about your mom, Viv. My dad kept in touch with her occasionally, checking in on you both and keeping up with the cabin. He told me she went into hospice last summer."

"I wondered if you knew. Mom never told me that she kept in touch with your dad, only that he was looking after the cabin for us. It was a rough final six months for her."

I nod in agreement, and together we make our way back to the deck. The sun has dipped below the horizon, casting deep purple and gold hues across the sky. An early summer chill lingers in the air, brushing against our skin, while the soft rustle of leaves provides a soothing backdrop to the evening.

"I hate to do this," Viv starts, "but I've got a hungry lil pupper at home who is probably pacing by the front door, considering how he might stave off starvation should I not return. So I must be getting back home to feed the beast."

"Next time, the beast is also invited," Mike says. "Look at this lovely fenced-in yard."

"As long as you don't mind him belly-flopping in your pool," Viv replies. "He can't be trusted around any body of water."

"I know a couple of little girls who would love to have a furry swimming friend," Evvie jokes. "Surely bring that handsome pup anytime!"

"Thanks again for the invite. You have no idea how much this means to me," Viv responds. "Oh, my friend Hadley arrives next week from Massachusetts. She's a teacher and plans to spend a few weeks here—maybe the whole summer. I'd love for you all to meet her."

"That will be lovely," Evvie says with a smile. "We'll see you soon!"

The rest of the crew says their goodbyes. I can't help but feel hopeful as I watch her drive away. Maybe this summer, she won't vanish into thin air.

CHAPTER EIGHT

No Richards Allowed

VIV

I spend a few moments in my Jeep before leaving Mike and Evvie's. My heart races, and I can't determine whether it's because Will startled me in the kitchen or because he looked so damn good doing it. The boy I knew back in the day was tall and so skinny he was almost transparent. His typical shaggy hair fell into his eyes, so I never got to luxuriate much in those captivating gray-blue eyes. He wore thick, black-framed glasses and hadn't gotten the memo about deodorant use. But I didn't care. My heart fluttered every time I saw him that long-ago summer.

That boy is long gone. In his place stands a man with the same shaggy dark brown hair, but it doesn't hide his eyes this time—eyes the color of an overcast day. He's taller, if possible; the glasses are missing, and he exudes an intoxicating mix of hops and pine—I almost passed out from the deliciousness of that scent when he surprised me in the kitchen earlier. He was without his ball cap and dressed in what I assume is his standard uniform: worn jeans, a pair of well-loved rustic brown Blundstones, and a t-shirt under a flannel shirt. And then there's the neatly trimmed beard and full lips... and...

"Snap out of it, Vivian," I berate myself for the impure thoughts of this man I haven't seen for almost twenty years. For all I know, he could be the town manwhore. Yes, please. GAH, stop. But just the few conversations we've had since my return, and the fact that his dad kept up with Mom's health over the years, tell me he's a genuinely good guy. Helpful, empathetic, dependable, handsome... I'd like to see what's under that T-shirt... "For fuck's sake, stop," I mumble to myself.

My primary reason for coming to Shearwater Cove is to escape the shit-show of a life I left behind in Boston, not to mention the grief I've been dealing with since Mom passed away. I need as much distance as possible between me and my ex, Eric the Ass Face. Those charming qualities that Will possesses? Eric is the exact opposite. He only lends a hand when it serves his interests. I'm frustrated that it took me three years to see through his douchebaggery.

Our relationship was likely doomed from the start. We met at the onset of the COVID pandemic while walking along the Charles River in Boston. He was walking in the opposite direction, and his pace slowed as I approached him. I resisted the urge to look at him. For starters, I was very serious about social distancing and, well, serial killers. Then he boldly turned and followed me. Motherfucker.

"Excuse me," he said as he closed the gap between them. "Don't freak out... I'm not a crazy stalker."

"Said every crazy stalker, ever," I replied, keeping a good six feet between us. I was nothing if not cautious.

"This may sound forward or like a bit of a line, but you are beautiful. Ok, even that sounded forward to me. Too much time by myself these days, I guess."

Uh, ok. Very forward. Am I here for it?

"I get that. Living alone in times like these can be painful. But on the bright side, it gives you extra time to work on your pickup lines." I mock.

"Well," the stranger stalker said, "maybe I'll see ya around again?"

"If you're lucky," I joked.

He smiled, headed back the way he came, and then turned for one last sheepish wave.

I chuckled as we parted ways. He was a pretty good-looking guy, not really my type, but honestly, I hadn't dated in so long that I wasn't exactly sure if I still had a type. He needed a haircut, but who didn't at this point in the pandemic? Something about the way he bashfully glanced at the ground while telling me I was beautiful made me reluctant to shut him down completely.

We indeed met again. And again. And again. Since it had become such a regular occurrence, Eric and I decided to turn it into an evening ritual. I increasingly found myself looking forward to my walks with Eric. After a few weeks, we began planning more adventurous activities—picnics in the Boston Public Garden, kayaking on the Charles River, and plenty of walking. He was easy to be around, with no pressure to do anything indoors.

Six months later, I made the most significant mistake of my life and decided to move in with him, forming an official pod. This was more for convenience than anything else, so we wouldn't feel lonely while socially distancing ourselves from the rest of the world. Mom warned me it was too soon, but I didn't necessarily have suitors knocking down my door. She always said she wanted me to be happy above all else. And I really did enjoy spending time with him.

Hadley arrives tomorrow, and thankfully, my entertainment items will be here today. She's known to lose her temper without a television or music source. I'm expecting a delivery from Amazon, but I honestly have no fucking idea how they would ever find this town.

VIV: HEY, WILL, IT'S VIV. DOES AMAZON DELIVER TO SC?

I bite my thumbnail while waiting for the three dots to appear.

> WILL: HEY, VIV! YEAH, BUT THE DRIVERS ARE INSTRUCTED AT THEIR WAREHOUSE TO DELIVER ALL PACKAGES TO THE STEUBEN GENERAL STORE. PROBABLY SHOULD MEET YOUR FRIEND THERE TOO. SHE'LL NEVER FIND OUR ROAD.

> VIV: OK, COOL. GOOD CALL WITH MEETING HADLEY AT THE STORE. TY!

A small emoji reaction appears on my last text. Wait, did he really just add a winky face emoji? I put my phone down on the scarred coffee table with a slight case of the "WHY THE HELL DID HE SEND ME A WINKY FACE EMOJI? WHAT DOES IT EVEN MEAN?" I don't have the stomach for mixed messages, Will Cooper.

> VIV: GONNA MEET YOU TOMORROW AT THE STEUBEN GENERAL STORE ON ROUTE 1. I HAVE TO PICK SOME STUFF UP THERE ANYWAY.

> HAD: CAN'T WAIT TO SEE YOU TOMORROW! I MISS MY BEST BITCH.

> VIV: I CAN'T WAAAAIT!

I check my list. The guest room sheets have been laundered, and the bed is made. The cupboards are stocked with junk food and booze. All deck furniture has been cleaned and arranged to provide the best possible ocean views. A new umbrella was purchased for the table, as the last one had fallen prey to rodents in the shed. The coolers have been taken out and hosed down. The cabin has been swept, vacuumed, dusted, scrubbed, bleached, buffed, sprayed, and fluffed. Kevin has been bathed, much to his chagrin.

"Stop moping," I yell to him after hearing a rather obnoxious sigh from where he's lying near the door. "You, my friend, are untrustworthy on a good day, but that distrust multiplies exponentially after a bath. You must think I was born yesterday."

I glance over at him, and he's doing that thing dogs do where they lie on their bellies with their heads resting on their paws. Then, they look up at you with just their puppy eyes without actually lifting their heads. This canine will not be the boss of me.

"I have such a surprise for you, Kevin. You will forget all about this animal cruelty by tomorrow." I bend to give him ear scritches, and he falls onto his side with a pleased groan. Hadley tops his list of favorite people, even higher than me, and I feed that ungrateful little shit.

I'm exhausted and decide to crawl into bed early. I take Kevin out one last time on his leash to do his business because, you know, trust issues. Then, we both snuggle in for the night. I'll need all the rest I can get because the next two months will be non-stop with my best friend.

Hadley is expected mid-afternoon, giving me time to finish some last-minute chores. I take a shower, walk Kevin, and then take another shower after he took off after a squirrel while on his leash and dragged me through a mud puddle. How he escaped without a splatter, I'll never know... He's absolutely working my last nerve today. I don't know if he even deserves his surprise.

I prepare a Kong filled with treats to keep Kevin occupied. He's going to be pissed that he's not coming along for the ride, so this will help ease his frustration a bit. I grab my keys, sunglasses, and bag, drop the Kong, and rush out of the house before he even realizes I'm gone. I leave a little early so I have time to track down my packages.

I arrive at the General Store and find the guy who manages all the Shearwater Cove deliveries. Once the packages are loaded into the Jeep, I spot Hadley's bright red Toyota Tacoma barreling down Route 1. She nearly overshoots the store's parking lot in her haste. She skids to a stop and steps out of the truck, and I charge at her like a deranged toddler, leaping into her arms. I say "toddler" because that's exactly what all five feet of me look like next to her six-foot frame. She's dressed as usual in baggy overalls rolled at the ankle, beat-up Birkenstocks, and a tank top, showcasing her intricately tattooed arms—the most beautiful colorful garden of wildflowers, including some bumbles, hummingbirds, butterflies, and other garden-y friends. Her bleached blonde hair is twisted into a thick braid that falls down her back.

"Haddy!" I exclaim, my legs wrapped around her waist as she cradles my bum like she's holding a baby. "I've missed you so much!" I give her loud, juicy kisses on each cheek.

"Oh, my best little friend! It's so good to be here, but fuck me; my ass is dead asleep!"

"Asses generally don't make it this far without going numb, but we're almost home. It's going to be the best summer with just us girls. No dick allowed." Do I really mean that? Because if there's one thing single Hadley and single Vivian love to do, it's flirt with the cute guys. So maybe just a smidge of dick this summer.

"Ok, let's get moving. I'm jonesing to snuggle with my furry lover." Hadley jumps back in her truck and motions to me to get going, spinning her finger.

I lead Hadley to Walker's Rock, and she exits her truck with a million questions tumbling from her lips. "Why are the buildings painted like that? Why is the road practically hidden? Who was that silver fox I saw walking in town? How many people live in this town? How do they survive without the tourists?"

"Take a breath, girl. We have all summer to investigate the deep, dark mysteries of Shearwater Cove!" I grab packages and turn towards the cabin. "Ok, I need you to stay right there and brace yourself for Hurricane Kevin."

Hadley positions herself in a high squat and claps her hands, indicating she's ready for the incoming storm. I slip into the house, but he doesn't meet me at the door. Uh oh, he still seems to be cross with me. I check the bedroom, and he's curled into a sad little pile, facing away from the door. "Kevvy, come see who's here! You have a visitor." He looks back at me over his shoulder, sits up, stretches, and slowly gets out of bed. "I mean, don't rush on my account. I'm sorry for leaving you behind, buddy."

I open the front door, and when he looks up to see Hadley, his ears perk up, and he peeks back at me. "Go. Go see Haddy!" He races out the door, leaps from about eight feet away, and lands in her arms, just like I did. She hugs him tightly as he furiously licks every inch of her face.

"How's my handsome, precious, perfect angel boy?" Hadley coos at him. She sets him down, and he immediately drops to the ground and rolls over for belly rubs. She falls to her knees and strokes every inch of his fur, and when he glances over at me with wide eyes, his tongue lolls out the side of his mouth. The dude is in heaven.

"Don't spoil him!" I bark.

"He's already spoiled," Had barks back.

"Is not."

"Is he sleeping under the covers?" She asks.

"Maybe..." I mutter.

"What was that?"

"Yes, ok, is that what you want to hear? We're sleeping together."

We both burst into uncontrollable laughter. It's so great to have my best friend here. Things are unquestionably looking up.

CHAPTER NINE

Flooded Kitchens and Bad Decisions

WILL

My phone starts chiming very early. I try to bury my head under the pillow, but it won't stop. I finally have a rare Saturday morning with nothing on my schedule, but the universe has other ideas. Who the fuck needs me this early? The brewery isn't even open. Tiny sure as shit isn't awake at this hour. It could be Dad texting me from the opposite end of the house. An old-manish groan slips out as I begrudgingly slide out of the comfort of my bed and shuffle over to my phone. It's not Dad.

> VIV: WILL!! ARE YOU AWAKE?

> VIV: I'M SORRY TO TEXT SO EARLY.

> VIV: I NEED YOUR HELP!

> VIV: SOMETHING'S WRONG WITH MY PIPES.

> VIV: OOH, I MEAN, NOT *MY* PIPES. THAT'S WEIRD. THE HOUSE'S PIPES.

> VIV: THE KITCHEN IS FLOODED.

> VIV: I'M SO HUNGOVER. I JUST WANTED A GLASS OF WATER.

> VIV: I'M SO SORRY. YOU'RE THE ONLY HANDYMAN I KNOW.

> VIV: I'VE USED EVERY BEACH TOWEL IN THIS CABIN.

> VIV: FUUUUUUUUUCK. MY HEAD HURTS.

Oh my god, this is not what I expected. Viv's friend Hadley arrived two days ago, so I'm sure there's been some celebrating. But what the hell else are they doing over there? I know how old the cabin's pipes are, so it's no surprise there's been an... event.

WILL: I'M HERE. GET TO THE WATER SHUT-OFF VALVE UNDER THE SINK TO STOP THE FLOW. BE THERE SOON.

VIV: YOU ARE A LIFESAVER.

Fuck my life. Sometimes, I wish I were more like Shawn—clueless about the DIY world. I grab yesterday's jeans from the pile on the floor and toss on an old T-shirt. This is most certainly going to be a dirty job.

After grabbing my bag of plumbing supplies, I swing by The Coffee Car because, if there's no water, I imagine two very hungover women would do several illegal acts for a coffee right now. When I arrive at Walker's Rock, there's no sign of life. My knock on the door elicits some low woofs, and I hear Viv yell that the door is open.

The situation here is dire. The kitchen floor is covered with what must be every beach towel this cabin has ever used since the beginning of time. Kevin won't even get out of his chair to greet me. On the worn leather couch sit two women who seem to be in a world of pain and refuse to make actual eye contact with me. The coffee table is cluttered with dirty dishes, junk food wrappers, shot glasses, and an empty bottle of tequila. Oh dear.

"Well," I start, "looks like you two had yourselves a night."

They lift a synchronized middle finger toward me.

"Why are you talking so loudly?" Viv asks.

I laugh and set the two cups of coffee on an empty spot on the coffee table. They grunt a *thanks* and voraciously descend on the cardboard cups of liquid life.

"And you must be Hadley," I say to the blonde woman, who is currently holding her head in her hands. She mumbles a hello.

Alright, a lively crew this morning. I return outside to my truck to fetch additional towels and my shop vac to tackle the mess.

"Viv, I need you to get me a laundry basket or something to put all these wet towels in before I take them outside."

She extracts herself from under the blanket on the couch and shuffles into the bedroom. She's wearing a faded tie-dyed sweatshirt that hangs off her slender frame and sleep shorts. Really short sleep shorts. I tell myself not to stare at her bare legs. I ignore my own warning. Her legs aren't long. How could they be when she's only five feet tall? But damn, they certainly look long enough to wrap around my waist. No. Stop thinking about her legs, deviant.

Viv picks up all the wet towels and clears everything from under the sink. I use the wet vac to soak up the remaining moisture on the floor. She returns to her spot on the couch while I start working on the damaged pipes. I realize I've forgotten my belt when I lower myself to the floor, and at the same time, I notice that the two women on the couch have a bird's eye view of me. I swear, if either of them mentions plumber's crack, I will... probably just be glad someone is looking at my ass.

While working on the problem, I hear Viv and Hadley whispering on the couch. Check that. They think they're whispering. I can hear them loud and clear.

"Is that THE Will?" Hadley asks.

"Shhhhh," Viv scolds. "Ya, that's him."

Hadley lets out a low whistle. "Damn, girl. He's hot."

"Shhhhh, Jesus, Had, not so loud."

"His ass is fine."

Viv sighs. "I know."

"Whatcha gonna do about it?" Hadley demands.

"Nothing. It's not why I came here."

"Why did you come here if not to start over?" She fiddles with the frayed edge of the blanket.

"Good point. But does starting over have to include a guy?" Viv says, and I try my hardest not to turn around to see what her face is saying.

"I'm not saying you have to drag him into your bedroom right this second." Hadley chuckles.

I crack my head on the edge of the cabinet. "Ow, fuck!" I cry out.

"Are you ok?" Viv asks, concerned.

"I'm fine," I respond. Jesus fuck, do not think about Viv dragging you to her bedroom. Do not think of anything bedroom-related. Not soft beds. Great, now that's all I'm thinking about.

"Ok," I clear my throat, rising from the floor. "I've fixed the leak for now, but I really think you should have someone come in and professionally replace these pipes, Viv. They seem to be original to the house."

"How long will the repair last?" Viv asks.

"You should be fine for a few months. But get on a plumber's schedule for the fall."

"Is there even a local plumber?" she asks.

"There's a guy in Steuben who comes highly recommended. I can give you his number," I say.

"Thanks. A lot. I mean it. I'm so sorry for dragging you out of bed on a Saturday. I'll add plumbing to my list of repairs this place needs."

I need to get the hell out of here before the word "bed" is repeated, and I pop a boner right in front of these two.

A few hours later, I'm perched on a stool at the rustic wooden bar in my brewery, surrounded by conversations and clinking glasses. The rich aroma of hops hangs in the air, mingling with the faint scent of polished wood. I can't stop thinking about this morning's events, and I tell Shawn what happened. The whole experience left me craving a beer and a cold shower.

"Wait, you heard them talking about you?" Shawn's eyes go wide.

"Um, yeah," I say. "It was awkward, to say the least, although it was cute how they thought they were being so quiet."

"So you met the friend?" Shawn's eyebrows waggle.

"Down, boy," I laugh. "She's not your type. At all."

"Wait, I have a type?" Shawn asks.

"You have a very specific type," I say, shaking my head. "Haven't you learned that in the last twenty-five fucking years?"

"Maybe another type will get me over that type," he says, tapping his index finger on his chin.

"No type is going to get you over Becky. Once you realize that and grow a set of man-sized balls, maybe the two of you can be happy! I'm so tired of watching you two circle each other like wrestlers. Just make the move already."

Shawn gives me both middle fingers and changes the subject. "So what are you going to do about Viv? She clearly has the hots for your fine ass."

I shake my head and stare into the pint glass. "I don't know, man. I'm getting the feeling whatever drama she's running from did a real number on her."

"Maybe the cure for her drama is your fine ass." Shawn cracks himself up.

"Enough about my ass," I jab. "You're obsessed with it."

"Not the only one," he mumbles.

Settled at the bar with my laptop, I'm immersed in planning the logistics for brewing a new Czech Pilsner. I'm focused on gathering everything I need before starting the brew—Saaz hops, Czech lager yeast, and confirming I have enough Pilsner malt. Shawn's shadow darkens the bar top in front of me.

"Looks like you might have some company." He nods towards the entry-way.

I glance over my shoulder just in time to see Vivian and Hadley strolling towards me. They both look only slightly better than they did this morning. Viv still wears her baggy sweatshirt but has swapped out the sleep shorts for cutoffs and worn-out sneakers. Hadley is dressed in a full sweatsuit and flip-flops. Is that velour?

"Well, look what the cat dragged in. Or maybe more fitting, dragged out of the litter box," I joke, turning around on my stool. Vivian flips me off. Such a minute gesture. Such big feelings in my pants.

"Hair of the dog, boys. Give us alcohol now," Viv says as she taps her knuckle twice on the bar top beside me.

Shawn looks at me with raised eyebrows over the small one's demands.

I scowl at him and turn to the two sets of bloodshot eyes staring at me as if they might flay the skin from my body if they don't get alcohol immediately.

"Shawn, get these lushes a beer, will ya? And pour them each a shot from that bottle of Espolon Blanco I keep in the back room. That should cure what ails them," I say.

Hadley starts to dry-heave and heads straight for the front door. Viv, turning a cadaver shade of gray, rushes to the restroom.

Shawn and I look at each other and immediately bust out laughing. "They said hair of the dog, and there was a very empty bottle of tequila on the coffee table this morning," I chuckle.

"You're a monstah," Shawn drawls.

"But a monstah with a great ass," I joke.

"Ayuh," he says.

"Viv woke me up as the ass-crack of dawn this morning with her leaky faucet, so I just wanted to get back at her a little."

Hadley returns to the bar first, using the back of her hand to wipe her mouth. Great... there's vomit somewhere in my parking lot. I hope she was courteous enough to puke in the bushes. Vivian joins her moments later from the bathroom. Surprisingly, the color has returned to their faces.

"Malicious. Fucking. Stunt. William. Cooper," Viv reprimands, poking me in the chest to punctuate each word.

"Hey," I say, rubbing the spot on my chest her pointy little finger just jabbed. You mentioned the dog's hair, and the dog I spotted on the coffee table this morning was named Don Julio."

"That was just mean," she whines. "But I must say, I feel a million times better after blowing chunks."

"Yeah, like I could actually put food in my mouth now. Oh, and apologies for the azalea bush," Hadley smirks.

CHAPTER TEN

Pancakes, Park Dances, and Poor Choices

VIV

Hadley and I leave the brewery, driven by a strong need for food. We walk down the street to the Cove Cafe, which is quiet after the lunch rush. We're greeted by a striking older woman with warm hazel eyes and a stylish haircut, colored a few shades darker than the lavender paint on the cafe's exterior.

"Welcome to the Cafe," purple hair greets. "My name is Mary, and I know everyone in this town, but you two don't look familiar."

I find humor in the need for every town inhabitant to point out that we are strangers here. I might as well rip the band-aid off right away.

"Hi, Mary, I'm Vivian James. You might remember my mother, Ma—"

"Maggie James," Mary interrupts.

"That's right," I agree.

"My gosh, I haven't heard Maggie's name in years. How is your ma? What's kept you away all these years?" Mary asks.

I feel tears prick the back of my eyes. "Ah, Mom passed away in September after a long battle with breast cancer," I say quietly.

"Like her mom before her," Mary says softly.

"And my great-grandmother, too," I continue.

"I'm sorry to hear about Maggie. She was always so sweet to everyone in town. And I knew your grandmother too, you know," Mary says.

"I figured you must have, since I heard Earl had a crush on her after my grandfather died."

"Ayuh, that he did," she laughs. "Patty adored Earl but would not give him the time of day romantically. Lucky for me, he didn't drag it on for too long, or I might not have married him."

"I never knew my grandmother, but from the pictures scattered around the cabin, she was quite a beautiful woman," I say wistfully.

"Your mom looked just like her, and you do too. Hard to forget a family of gorgeous redheads," Mary chuckles.

"Well, that's very kind of you, Mary. And I'm being rude not introducing my friend, Hadley Baker. She's visiting for the summer."

"Very nice to meet you, Hadley! Why don't I get you girls to a table with some menus," Mary says, gently touching my arm.

She leads us to a spacious two-top against a half-brick wall and places our menus on the table. The upper half of the wall is painted a soft beigey-sage color and features a collage of old framed black and white photos depicting the town over the years. Rough-hewn exposed beams and copper tin tiles decorate the high ceiling, while a black concrete-topped bar stretches along the left side of the restaurant.

The restaurant's interior exudes a sophisticated elegance that contrasts sharply with its brightly colored exterior. Inside, a grand wooden chandelier with Edison-style light bulbs stretches over the entire length of the bar, casting it in a warm glow. Each table is lit by quirky lamps crafted from antique copper pots, adding a unique charm and character to the room. Although Mom and I didn't frequent this place often, I can confidently say it was never this classy.

"Can I get you girls something to drink?" Mary asks as she walks over to our table.

"I'll just have an ice water," I say. Hadley nods in agreement. Both of us feeling the desperate need to hydrate. "And coffee for me."

"Can I also have a coffee and a Diet Coke?" Hadley asks.

"Oh yeah, Diet Coke for me too," I say.

"Did you girls have a rough night or somethin'?" Mary asks.

"You could say that," we reply in unison with a laugh.

Mary comes back with our assorted beverages, while Hadley and I order a stack of blueberry pancakes accompanied by a large side of crispy bacon. If anything can absorb the sourness in our stomachs, it's got to be pancakes.

"Mary?" I call out as she's walking away. "I know I was just a kid the last time I was in Shearwater Cove, but the buildings. When were they painted? That little town street is just a joy to look at."

"Oh, the town received an anonymous grant about fifteen years ago. It was substantial enough for the renovation of all the businesses and the construction of the waterfront park. We never named the park because it felt strange to name it anything other than after its benefactor, yet we never discovered who was responsible."

"It's been driving us crazy wondering about the story behind the paint colors. And also how the town can close itself off from the tourist business."

"One of the stipulations for how the grant was spent was to make the town colorful. It was so drab and rundown twenty years ago. If tourists can find us, good for them. As I mentioned, the grant was sizable." Mary excused herself to place our order in the kitchen.

"Had, I think we should maybe take a detox day today and do something other than drinking ourselves into a stupor," I suggest, guzzling half the water Mary just set down.

"Boring but acceptable," Hadley says with an eye roll.

"Don't you roll your eyeballs at me, Hadley Jane Baker."

"Don't you roll your eyeballs at meeee," she mocks like a five-year-old.

"Twat."

"Shrew."

"I've missed you, Haddy. Life's just so much more interesting with you in it." I reach across the table with a smile and squeeze her forearm.

Hadley and I met as freshmen at Boston University when we were assigned as roommates. I lived close enough to home that I could have commuted, but my mom insisted I stay in the dorms to experience college life fully, as she had missed it. It also meant I was just an easy drive away if she needed help getting to her doctor's appointments.

We were as different as a giraffe and a meatball. I was raised by a single mother without any other family to rely on. Hadley's parents were old hippies who raised her and her three younger brothers in Northern Vermont. They form a close-knit family that loves each other dearly, but there's always some feud brewing between two of the three brothers that leads to major drama. Hadley is never involved in the feuding, mainly because, as she claims, she's too smart for that shit. But in reality, it's because early on, Hadley perfected a wrestling move called the leg trap camel clutch, which all of her brothers had previously fallen victim to. Now, they're just deathly afraid of her.

After we finish what were possibly the best fucking blueberry pancakes in the galaxy, grab to-go cups for our coffees, and thank Mary profusely, we decide to take a walk through town. Hadley suggests a detour through the park along the waterfront. The wide wooden walkway snakes along the curves of the coastline, bordered by flower gardens on one side and Naraguagus Bay on the other. There are vintage black iron lamp posts and a row of brightly colored Adirondack chairs facing the water. Three docks jut out into the bay where a few daring teenagers are doing cannonballs into the frigid Atlantic.

As we head back toward the main street, we notice a spacious lawn with a gazebo at one end, seemingly designed for weddings, and a small pavilion for performances. Hadley breaks into a sprint toward the stage. What the fuck is she doing?

The park is not exactly busy, so Hadley takes it upon herself to provide the entertainment for the few unsuspecting walkers. As I approach the stage, I can see that she is performing her best, definitely not suitable for children, pole dance with the stage roof support beam. I see a mother quickly shield her kid's eyes as he starts pointing at Hadley, picking up her pace to get away from the stage. Oh dear.

I shake my head and try not to collapse into a fit of laughter; instead, I take the responsible approach and hop onto the stage to pull her off. The thing about trying to force Hadley to do anything she doesn't want? She has about a hundred pounds on me and is as stubborn as a mule.

"I swear to god, Had, if you get me kicked out of this town, I will spoil every single show you watch for eternity," I threaten as I tug her toward the edge of the stage.

"You wouldn't!" she shrieks, finally jumping down from the stage. She threads her arm through mine, which, due to our height difference, positions her torso at about a 70-degree angle as we walk back to the brewery where my Jeep is parked.

"Hey, Had? What do you think about us throwing a July 4th celebration at the cabin? My grandfather used to be famous for them, and it might be fun to try to recreate his epic parties. It's still a couple of weeks away, so we have plenty of time to plan it."

"I think that's a great idea. I guess it's a good thing I loaded a tote full of fireworks in the back of my truck before I came up." Her eyes light up.

"Your brother Henry, I assume?" I ask.

"Guy has a literal armory of pretty exploding things."

"Why doesn't that surprise me?"

"Because he's missing parts of three fingers on his left hand?" she asks.

"Right," I say, "I forgot about that."

"Also, Hayden and Holden are too fucking concerned with their looks and what missing fingers would do to their status with the girls to get near explosives."

"Are they out of college yet?" I ask about the twins as we walk.

"Seniors. Fraternity bros. And I believe they've got some degrading wager going on that I don't even want to think about. They'll both be lucky to make it out of UNH with a degree, let alone find a real job," Hadley says. "My poor parents. Those three have taken years off my mother's life."

We return to the Jeep to head home. I know Kevin will be pouting again over our abandonment—spoiled angel baby—so Hadley plays fetch with him off the end of the dock to tire him out. I clean up the house after the first few days of Hadley's visit, which has descended into complete chaos.

We both agree to an early night with our books, maybe some gummies, and many hours of uninterrupted sleep, and we retreat to our respective bedrooms. I hop into bed and take out my phone.

> **VIV:** WE WANT TO DO 4TH STUFF OUT HERE. FIREWORKS. FOOD. THOUGHTS?

> **WILL:** DUNNO. MIKE USUALLY BUYS A SHITLOAD OF FIREWORKS, AND WE SHOOT THEM OFF AT THE TOWN DOCKS IN THE PARK.

> **VIV:** EVERYONE CAN STILL SEE THEM FROM THE ROCK, RIGHT? I WANNA RECREATE THE OLD DAYS.

> **WILL:** LEMME CHECK. LET YOU KNOW LATER.

I mean to add a thumbs up reaction to Will's text and add a winky kissy face instead. That is definitely not what I meant to do. Fuck. What is wrong with me? Please ignore it. Please ignore it.

> **WILL:** WHAT ARE YOU TWO UP TO?

Ok, sounds like he's ignoring it.

> **VIV:** EARLY NIGHT. YOU.

> **WILL:** SAME. SOMEONE WOKE ME UP EARLY TODAY.

VIV: OOOPS.

WILL: OK, G'NIGHT.

VIV: YOU TOO.

His winky kissy face reaction in return proves that he did not, in fact, ignore it. And then to follow it up with a rolling-on-the-floor laughing emoji? That's just cruel.

Mother. Fucker. I should not be allowed to use emojis. Ever.

"Hadley? Are you asleep?" I call out.

She says nothing, but I hear her heavy footsteps as she rushes into my room and leaps onto the end of my bed. The impact disturbs Kevin from his slumber, and he begrudgingly jumps off with a huff and heads for the couch.

"I am not asleep. I am not tired. Why? You wanna start drinking?" She quirks a devilish grin.

"For fuck's sake, Had, no. I will not be drinking tonight. But maybe I should after the absolute fucking ignoramus I am."

"God, what did you do?" she asks, concern lining the space between her eyebrows.

"Wellllll...."

"WHAT?"

"I just texted Will," I confess.

"Ok. About?" she asks.

"4th of July. Having it here." I say.

"What's wrong with that? Seems relatively tame," she comments.

"I sent him the winky kissy emoji." I cringe just thinking about it.

"Maybe he didn't notice?" she asks hopefully.

"I thought maybe he could be adult enough just to ignore it."

"He didn't ignore it, did he?" She flops back on the bed, covering her face with her hands.

"He did not." I sigh.

"Winky kissy face emoji?" she asks, her voice muffled by her hands still covering her face.

"Uh-huh. Followed by a laughing emoji. I want to die."

"I'll go outside and start digging your grave," Hadley jokes, sitting back up. "Give me your phone."

"No. Why? No!" I clutch my phone to my chest.

"You cannot be trusted to not be a complete fucking weirdo when it comes to Will." Hadley grabs for my phone, and as I turn away from her, she ends up grabbing my boob.

"Ow!" I whine.

"Stop, that didn't hurt," she chides.

"Did too. You're mean," I grouse, holding on to my abused boob.

"I'm going to bed. Do not, under any circumstances, text that man again tonight. I will swap out all your chocolatey snacks with raisins," she threatens.

"You wouldn't! Fine. I'll put it on the dresser. It needs to be charged anyway," I pout like a petulant toddler. "I wish I had asked him what he was wearing."

"Oh my god. Just stop. You're clearly overtired. Go to bed."

"Nighty night, Hadley Jane. I looove you."

"G'night, Vivian. I love you, too, but sometimes you make it so hard."

CHAPTER ELEVEN

Pitching Tents and Playing it Cool

WILL

Vivian is the biggest mystery in my life at the moment. In one breath, she's lamenting about her shit year, and I overhear her saying she's not ready to move on with another guy. In the next, she's sending me a fucking winky kissy emoji? My head is spinning. I need advice, and Evvie is the only person qualified to provide it. I also need to discuss Viv's July 4th request with Mike. I'll swing by the house first and the marina second.

When I pull up to the house, I'm relieved to see Evvie's SUV, not Mike's truck. Evvie appears at the front door. "Hey, stranger, what are you doing here?"

"I need help," I reply.

"Mike's not here if you're looking for him. He's down at the Marina."

"Actually, I came to see you," I say sheepishly.

"Oh boy. This sounds like girl problems. Come sit on the front porch with me while I wait for the girls to get dropped off."

We both sit on the top step, my head hanging slightly. Evvie is turned toward me, waiting for me to begin. I throw my hands up in surrender.

"She sent me a winky kissy face emoji." I start.

"She whhhhhhat?" Evvie sits straighter at full attention.

"I didn't know what to do, so I tried to ignore it. And I know she was stone-cold sober. I just started asking her random questions, trying to get it out of my brain. Then I did something I regret more than that mohawk back in high school. I sent one back."

"YOU SENT HER A WINKY KISSY FACE?" Evvie yells. "You are a cruel, cruel man, Will. I'm sure she did it by accident, and she was just hoping you'd ignore it, but you couldn't help yourself."

"But it gets worse," I mumble.

"What did you do?" She puts her hand on my arm like she's going to pinch me, and the answer I give her will determine how much.

"I sent a laughing emoji right after." Evvie grabs a piece of my arm skin. "OUCH! Stop pinching me, you bridge troll!"

"Will," Evvie begins, "You've been part of my family since the third grade. You've been one of my best friends in the world. You've put up with my relationship with Mike throughout high school. You stood up for us at our wedding. You're the godfather to my girls. I trust you with every part of my life. But you CANNOT be fucking trusted to text with a woman. You're too out of practice. It's been years since you've been in a relationship."

"Ev, I fucked up with Viv the first time around, and I don't want that to happen again. And the way things ended with Melanie... "

"I know, pal. That breakup was hard on all of us. But that was four years ago. FOUR YEARS, Will. You're not getting any younger," Evvie smirks at me.

"Fuck off," I mouth. My phone chimes with an incoming text.

> VIV: HEY, MAYBE THE SIX OF US COULD GET TOGETHER AT THE ROCK TOMORROW NIGHT TO TALK 4TH PLANS. IT'S SUPPOSED TO BE UNSEASONABLY HOT.

Which means the clothing will be small. Fuck me.

"Ev, this is Viv texting. I was going to swing by to see Mike next, because Viv mentioned throwing a 4th party at her cabin and shooting off fireworks from there. That was why she texted me before the emoji debacle."

"I think that sounds great. I'm sure Mike will, too. And the girls will love jumping off that dock of hers."

"Are you guys free tomorrow night to go out there and start planning?"

"The girls are staying with Betsy and Jack, so yeah, that would be fun. I've been dying to meet her friend, too!"

"Oh, Hadley. She's something." I laugh and turn back to the text.

> WILL: YUP. 6 PM WORK?

> VIV: PERFECT. CAN YOU BRING US SOME BEER FROM THE BREWERY?

> WILL: OF COURSE, ANY SPECIFIC STYLE?

> VIV: JUST MAKE SURE IT'S WET.

I choke on absolutely nothing and start coughing uncontrollably. Evvie starts pounding on my back to help. I hold up my hand to indicate I'm ok.

"What's wrong?" Evvie asks.

"Oh, just Viv talking about things being wet," I say like a horny teenager.

"Jesus. You men never change."

> WILL: IT WILL BE THE WETTEST.

> VIV: BRING YOUR BATHING SUITS IF YOU DARE TO BRAVE THE WATER.

> WILL: CHALLENGE ACCEPTED.

"Ok, now that I've sent her yet another suggestive text, I'll be on my way to the marina," I say, standing up from my seat.

"Are you going to tell me what the fuck up was with Viv?"

"Nope," I say, popping the P.

"Coward."

"Absolutely," I agree. "Can you start making a list of people we should invite to Viv's 4th party?"

"Sure thing. Tell Mike I've already approved our outing tomorrow night and that I'm going to volunteer him for burger duty."

"Viv says to bring suits if we dare. That Masshole is trying to provoke us." I salute Evvie and hop in my truck to head for the marina.

I catch up with Mike to share the plan; afterward, I message Shawn and Becky to check their availability.

The following day is scorching hot. Maine's springs and summers are fucking weird. One minute, you're in jeans and a flannel; the next, you want to peel your skin off to escape the heat. Today is a peel-the-skin kind of day. I've sweated through three T-shirts, and I can't wait to put on shorts after I leave the stifling barn. Dad needed help with a minor engine repair, and the air conditioning in the shop was just a little too ancient to keep up with the oppressive heat.

Once we're done, and I convince Dad to rest in the air-conditioned house for the evening, I put on swim trunks and a dry T-shirt before heading out to Walker's Rock a little early. When I arrive at the front of the house, no dog rushes to knock me down, but I understand why when I hear the thundering music from the back deck.

As I walk around the side of the house to the back deck, I'm greeted by a sight that will not soon leave my brain. Or my pants. Two of the shaded chaise loungers are occupied by sleeping women clad in very tiny bikinis. They could either be sleeping or passed out, as more empty bottles are scattered on the deck than we recycle in a week at the brewery. The dog is stretched out in the shade of a nearby tree, and the music blares from a Bluetooth speaker on the table. I don't recognize the band, but it can only be described as angry, fuck the patriarchy music. How the hell are they sleeping through this noise?

I turn down the volume, and all three sleepers bolt upright. I notice that while Viv's bikini is tiny, it covers everything modestly—Hadley's—not so much. And she gives no fucks about that. Kevin slowly walks over, panting heavily, looking for a quick head scratch, and I kindly oblige.

"WILL! You're early!" Viv says as she leans back on her elbows.

While Hadley's bathing suit barely covers her nipples, it's Viv I can't stop looking at. I hope she doesn't find it creepy. Her petite frame is thin yet curvy. Her breasts are small but appear so perfectly shaped that I'd almost question their authenticity. Her arms and legs are toned without being overly muscled. And her hair... God, that hair... if only I could run my fingers through it. It's styled into two Princess Leia-like buns on either side of her head. If I don't stop looking at her, my swim trunks won't be able to hide anything.

"Sorry, Viv. I'm sweatier than a priest at a strip club and was hoping to jump in the water before everyone else gets here. Wait, are you guys drunk?" I ask, gesturing to the empty bottles carpeting the back deck.

"Oh, haha," Viv chuckles. "Not yet. Those are an indication of our time together since Hadley's arrival. We thought it would be funny to just let them pile up, but planned to clean them up before you arrived."

Viv puts on an oversized Red Sox T-shirt and begins loading the empty bottles into a trash bag while tidying up the back deck. I walk down to the water for a dip. I drop my T-shirt at the end of the dock and brace myself for the shock this dive will deliver to my system. By this time of year, the water hasn't reached 60 degrees yet. But it's so fucking hot, I hold my breath and plunge in.

"Motherfucker!" I yell as I surface. I guess I no longer need to worry about a boner. I've never been one for ice plunges for good reason. Holy shit. I quickly scramble back onto the dock and lie flat in the sunshine to try and warm up a bit so my legs work again.

With my trunks nearly dry, I slip my T-shirt back on and head to the deck. The music, less angry this time, has been turned up to a more acceptable level. The rest of the group arrives, and I greet everyone and then grab the cooler of beer from my truck.

"I'm so happy you're all here again with me—just like when we were kids," Viv says to the group, holding up her can of beer in a toast. "Cheers to my Shearwater Cove peeps. And our special guest, my best friend, Hadley Baker. Hadley, you know Will, that's Mike, Evvie, Shawn, and Becky." She points to each one and says their name.

"CHEERS!" Everyone replies in unison. "And welcome, Hadley," Evvie adds.

"I've asked you all here," Viv begins, "because I'd like to host July 4th here. Hadley has a truck full of fireworks, and we thought it would be fun to set those off on the point." She gestures to the small piece of the property that juts into the water.

"Mike and I think it's a great idea!" Evvie exclaims.

"Ha, so you don't have to host it at your house," Shawn mocks.

"Shut up," Evvie retorts.

"I'm all for it," Becky says.

"I've started a guest list," Evvie says. "It's the seven of us: my kids, Cameron and Luke, Betsy and Jack, Bill, Tiny, Mary, and Earl. We should invite Tristin since the ice cream shop will be closed. What about Dr. Jane and her twins, Owen and Nora?"

"That's great. Perfect. All of those people and anyone else you can think of. All are welcome," Viv says. "I also have plenty of room around this yard if anyone wants to pitch a tent and stay over."

"I bet Will would like to pitch his tent," Shawn mumbles.

"Shawn, do you have something to share with the class?" Mike asks.

"Nope, just thinking that sounds fun, pitching a tent and all." Shawn struggles to keep in an adolescent giggle.

"Then it's settled. Food, drinks, tents, explosives! Sounds like the perfect celebration to me," Hadley says.

Mike fires up the grill for his famous smash burgers while Viv and I grab the accouterments from inside the cabin. The group falls into easy conversation about who will be responsible for what on the 4th. After sunset, the air finally cools down enough to start the fire pit, and we all gather around the circle.

"Man, I never saw stars like this in Boston," Viv observes, her head tilted back.

"The beauty of being in the middle of fucking nowhere," Shawn says.

"I knew there had to be a good reason to live here," Hadley jokes.

"It's hard to explain all the good reasons to someone who has always lived in a big city," Evvie says wistfully. "I love that my girls can ride their bikes in the park while I sit and read my book. And that anyone they encounter knows them by name and would protect them at any cost. We can leave our homes and cars unlocked. And if I forget my wallet at the store, Earl will tell me to get him the next time I come in. Stay here long enough, and you'll feel the pull of the Shearwater Cove family and never want to leave."

"That sounds lovely, Ev," Viv says. "I've only been here for a month, but Boston feels further away than ever."

My head snaps up at that comment. Since Viv arrived, I've been waiting for her to say she's leaving or that she's decided to sell the cabin. But the way she's talking right now, all that worry could be behind me. I find myself looking forward to a July 4th celebration more than I have since childhood.

CHAPTER TWELVE

You Could Wear a Burlap Sack

VIV

The weather has been stellar. Hadley and I have spent all our time sitting on the back deck, enjoying each other's company, the spectacular view, and numerous alcoholic beverages. Kevin celebrates his freedom from city life by repeatedly jumping off the dock and then lying in the sun to dry off. It's definitely shaping up to be a summer for the books.

Having Hadley here with me has been so healing for my soul. I can't imagine sitting alone on the back deck that Mom and I enjoyed for so many summers. Mom would read her books while I spent hours making friendship bracelets, painting rocks, or working on some other craft project. We would throw the ball for our golden retriever, Jack, until he collapsed from exhaustion on the deck beside us. We would join Jack in jumping off the dock when the weather was hot enough to drive us from our chairs. And we would float. Float for hours on those hot days, dreaming about what it would be like never to leave Shearwater Cove.

Hadley closes her book with a snap, pulling me out of my trip down memory lane, and turns to face me. Uh oh. This cannot be good. She has something on her mind that I'm sure I don't want to discuss.

"Vivian."

"Hadley."

"Let's cut the shit. Tell me what the fuck happened with Will when you were kids. The way you two have been tiptoeing around each other like a couple of ballet dancers, something had to have happened." Hadley turns herself in her deck chair and takes off her sunglasses. Ok, she means business.

"It's just one of those embarrassing teenage dramas I don't like to remember." I sigh.

"It's me, Viv. ME. We tell each other everything. It can't be any more embarrassing than that time in college when you—" I press my palm over Hadley's mouth to keep that story from being released into the atmosphere.

"Okay, okay! You're right, I don't often keep stuff from you," I comply.

"Oh, goodie!" Hadley claps and bounces in her seat.

"I can't believe how much happiness you're getting from my embarrassment." I shake my head.

"I need stories, Viv. They're my life's blood."

"Okay, do you see that rock out there at the point? You can only spot it at low tide; when it's visible, it beckons to you. So, that last summer I was here when I was fourteen, that's when I met the group. Evvie approached me first and pulled me into their fold. It was the best summer I'd ever experienced in Shearwater Cove. We spent a lot of time here because of that rock. We challenged each other to swim to it and tried to scale the slippery ridges on its sides to reach the top. Swimming to it was easy. Scaling it, not so much. No one could ever do it." I reach over to grab my iced tea for a sip.

"Challenge fucking accepted." Hadley declares. I laugh at her confidence but know that she'll succeed.

"If we were together, it was always the six of us. Granted, we would often break into groups—girls and boys. The boys were so tired of listening to us swoon over Edward Cullen, and we girls wanted nothing to do with their dumb-ass video games. But we were always in the same general area."

"Anyone who thinks Jacob Black is superior to Edward Cullen is an absolute fuckwit," Hadley interjects.

"Oh, I know. Fortunately, the three of us were one hundred percent Team Edward. Of the three boys, Will was the quietest. I learned later in the summer from Evvie that his older brother Silas had been killed the previous summer during his first tour of duty in Iraq, and he was still struggling fiercely with that loss. But I still crushed on him hard. His quiet demeanor, his shaggy brown hair, and the way he would glance at you from under that hair falling into his eyes. And whenever I caught a glimpse of his eye color—bluish-gray framed by these incredible long, dark lashes—it sent strange tingles through my stomach, among other places, that I wasn't yet familiar with."

"Oooooh, that boy made you horny!" Hadley squealed.

"I was fourteen. I had no idea what those tingles meant. I knew I would do anything to spend time alone with him. That wasn't how our group operated—definitely an all-for-one and one-for-all attitude. It confused me because I could see how Evvie and Mike looked at each other, and I wondered if they wanted to be alone. Or the hearts in Becky's eyes every time Shawn looked her way. I believe we were all feeling feelings new to us, unsure of what to do with them."

"At fourteen? You really did lead a sheltered life, my Viv." Hadley laughed.

"I was a late bloomer, to say the least. I barely had boobs at fourteen!" I blurt out.

"I had boobs at ten," Hadley replies. "I envy your late blooming."

"Towards the end of August, I started to feel antsy. I wasn't ready for this summer to end. I made Mom promise we would stay until the last possible moment before we had to return home for the first day of school. Then I found out that most of the group had end-of-summer plans—Evvie was going to stay with her grandparents in New Hampshire; Mike and Shawn were attending a sleep-away football camp at the University of Maine in Orono; and Becky's parents had enrolled her in a junior cooking class at Southern Maine Community College near her grandmother's house."

"Ohhhhh, I see where this is going. Please tell me you threw yourself at Will!" Hadley exclaims with an eyebrow waggle.

"I wasn't sure I would see Will again without the buffer of the other four. But, like every other summer day, he showed up at Walker's Rock in his swim trunks with his beach towel. Without the constant chatter of the others, he was slightly more talkative. We hadn't spent much time talking to each other for most of the summer, so the conversation was light and general. We discussed our upcoming freshman years of high school and the sports we were planning to play: I was a runner as a kid, so I would try out for all the track teams, while Will played basketball and baseball."

"And like every other summer day, our goal was staring back at us during low tide—Walker's Rock. I raised my eyebrows at Will, and we both sprinted toward the dock. The swim to the rock was fierce. I mean, if one of us was going to reach it, we wanted to be the first. To claim the crown of the rock. So there was a lot of splashing, dunking, and kicking to distract our competitors. I was small but scrappy and made it to the rock first that day, and surprised even myself as I scurried to its flat top with little effort. I stood there, arms raised in the air, wishing the whole crew was there to witness it."

"My girl, I knew you could do it!" Hadley cheered on. "What was different that day that made scaling the slippery sides easier?"

"Wouldn't you like to know?" I tease. "Will reached the rock soon after my triumph and also successfully made it to the flat top. We looked at each other, feeling the same way—why wasn't anyone else there to see it? No one would believe us."

"Fucking get to the good stuff, Viv." she urged.

"We decided to hang out on the rock until the tide chased us away. The flat top wasn't huge, so when we sat down, our hips were so close they touched. Our bare arms brushed together. My skin buzzed. He didn't pull away from the contact; he peered at me from beneath the wet hair that hung in his face. I was certain he was going to kiss me. I wanted him to kiss me. I needed him to kiss me. It was a new feeling for me: that fluttering, the heat, the longing. When I turned my face toward him, he reached his hand to the side of my face. Oh god, I thought it was actually happening." I was lost in the memory when Hadley interrupted.

"DID HE FUCKING KISS YOU OR WHAT? God, girl, this slow-burn suspense is killing me."

"Well, he leaned in. I leaned in. I closed my eyes and slightly parted my lips. This was going to be my first kiss, and I didn't want it to seem like my first kiss. But nothing happened—no warm lips, nothing. I opened my eyes to find that Will had plucked a large, slimy piece of seaweed from the side of my face. Then he stood up, dove in, and swam back to the dock. He left me there, stunned, embarrassed, and horrified. It was the most pathetic feeling I'd ever experienced up to that point in my life."

"Dude."

"I know."

"Still not more horrifying than my first blow-job."

"Definitely not, but at fourteen, it was really my first true embarrassment," I sighed.

"So what happened? Did you see him again before you left for home?"

"Nope," I say, with a pop of the P. "I made up some story for Mom about everyone leaving for family obligations, and we might as well go home so I have more time to prepare for my freshman year."

"She bought it?" Hadley asks.

"If she didn't, she never let on. She agreed, and we packed and left a few days later. I never saw anyone else, never exchanged contact information, nothing. I thought about them all for a few months, but then Mom got sick, and I had other, more important issues to focus on. At the time, I figured it was for the best."

"Holy shit. I wonder how things would've been had he kissed you that day?" she wonders.

"Probably for the best," I repeated. "Mom was never well enough after that summer to make the trip. So I just would've resented her for keeping me from him."

"True," Hadley agrees. "But look at him now. LOOK AT HIM."

"I know. It's killing me not to reach out and touch his lips and feel the scratch of his beard against my palm. His hair no longer hides those eyes. He was so skinny when we were kids, and now seeing him all... you know, buff and manly, it's stirring feelings in me that I thought I'd never experience again after Eric's complete devastation of my self-confidence."

"God, I hate that gangrenous ball-sack of a human," Hadley sneers.

"Nice use of the word 'gangrenous,' Had," I compliment.

"Thanks. It was on my Word-of-the-Day calendar, my last day of school." She laughs and continues, "Really, Viv. I could unalive that guy for what he did to your faith in yourself. For someone to be so unconcerned about your well-being because all he could think about was how it would negatively affect him? God, it turns me into a burning ball of rage. You deserve so much better."

"I know, Had, I love you for your secondhand rage, and your undying support and nursing skills, of course. I'm just glad I finally saw through his gaslighting and did what was necessary for me. I wasn't risking my health for him." I lean over and hug Hadley. We generally don't have a mushy friendship, but she's been there for me at the lowest points of my life, and I wouldn't trade her for all the money in the world. She's my ride-or-die, no matter the situation.

"I got you, Viv. But I will say, I think Will is the Bizarro-Eric and might be exactly what you need."

"I think you may be right. But do you think he feels the same way?" I bite my lower lip, waiting for her response.

"I've seen how he stares at you when you're not looking. I've watched him lick his lips. I've noticed him adjust himself in his pants. I've seen him flush at the sight of you in a bathing suit. My god, it sounds like I'm describing a pervert!" Hadley cackles. "And whenever you send him an inappropriate emoji or say things like, 'make sure the beer is wet,' he probably creams his drawers. I think July 4th will be the perfect night to make your move! We'll need to find the ideal outfit to bring him to his knees."

"Uhhhh, Hadley! You know I hate perfect outfits. What's wrong with cutoffs and a tank top? I just want to be comfortable," I whine.

Hadley grumbles, "Fine. Whatever. Although you could probably wear a burlap sack, and he'd get hard."

"Oh, god. How about I promise not to throw my hair into a messy bun?"

"Deal," she agrees.

CHAPTER THIRTEEN

God Bless America and Ice Machines

WILL

July 4th always feels like the official kickoff to summer, even though the calendar officially marks it a couple of weeks earlier. In Down East Maine, shit just happens later. Slow, like life here. We've always celebrated the holiday grandly in Shearwater Cove. All the town businesses shut down, ensuring no one gets left out. Doesn't that mean I should be relaxing at home, sipping coffee in the morning sunshine on my back deck overlooking the Bay? Yeah, I thought so too.

Shawn called from the brewery to say that the ice machine has stopped, well, making ice. This was a significant concern since I was responsible for bringing ice to this afternoon's party. Fuck. Even if I fixed the machine, it would never produce the necessary amount of ice for this event.

> WILL: HEY EARL... YOU AROUND?

EARL: JUST EATING BREAKFAST.

> WILL: HOW MUCH ICE DO YOU HAVE AT THE STORE?

EARL: PLENTY. GOT DELIVERY YESTERDAY.

> WILL: CAN WE MEET AT NOON SO I CAN LOAD UP? ICE MACHINE AT THE BREWERY SHIT THE BED.

EARL: SEE YOU THERE.

> WILL: TY

EARL: WHO'S TY?

> WILL: NO ONE.

EARL: WHY'D YA MENTION HIM?

> WILL: TY = THANK YOU

EARL: KIDS THESE DAYS. GEEZ.

> WILL: GOODBYE, EARL.

I call the brewery to inform Shawn that I've found an ice alternative, but I ask him to make sure all the beer we're bringing for the party is in the coolers, since it will be a while before we can put it all on ice.

I'm almost tempted to turn off my phone so that no one else can reach me. However, if Viv needs me, I'll come running, so the phone stays on.

"Dad!" I yell. "Are you in the house?"

"Stop yelling. I'm right here," he says as his head pops up from where he was lying on the couch.

"Oh shit, sorry, didn't see ya," I say, over my armful of sleeping bags. "Are you planning on sleeping in my tent with me tonight at Walker's Rock? For the 4th party? Just want to know if I need two sleeping bags."

"I dunno, son. I'm feeling a little under the weather today. I may skip this year's party."

"Dad, what's wrong? You never miss the fireworks," I ask, my gut clenches slightly.

"Ah, I think I overdid it yesterday in the barn with this awful heat. I'm just exhausted. And I'll be able to see the fireworks from here," he replies.

"Are you sure that's all it is?"

"Ayuh. Just need a day of relaxin' without anyone yapping my ear off," he says with a smile.

"Ok, Dad. But you need to promise me that you'll call me if you start to feel worse," I demand, feeling relieved that it only seems to be exhaustion and not something more serious.

"Of course. Don't worry about me tonight. Have fun with your friends. Give everyone my regards," Dad says as he lies back on the couch and turns on the TV.

"You'll be missed, for sure." I throw one sleeping bag back in the closet. If Dad's not coming, I'm not bothering with the tent. I'll just sleep in my truck if I need to—it's more comfortable than the ground.

I finish loading my truck with three bulky coolers, five weathered camp chairs, my well-worn cornhole boards, and a stash of leftover fireworks from last year. I secure everything in place, and I'm on my way to meet Earl when my phone chimes with an alert, breaking the quiet morning air.

> VIV: HADLEY DROPPED OUR ONLY BLOCK OF CHEDDAR IN THE DIRT. CAN EARL BRING ONE FROM THE STORE?

> WILL: ON MY WAY THERE NOW FOR ICE. AND NOW CHEESE, TOO.

> VIV: SINCE WHEN DO YOU BUY ICE?

> WILL: SINCE MY ICE MACHINE IS BROKEN

> VIV: HOW'D THAT HAPPEN?

> WILL: NO IDEA. SHAWN PROBABLY LOOKED AT IT WRONG.

VIV: YEAH, THAT'LL DO IT. LOL

WILL: HA!

VIV: SEE YA

I arrive at Earl's parking lot just as he does, and we meet at the front door while he unlocks the store.

"I appreciate this, Earl. I would be in big trouble if I failed to bring the most important item for a summer party!"

"For sure. Vivian would kick your ass," Earl jokes.

"Oh, yeah. Viv needs a big block of cheddar. Hers met an untimely death in the dirt." I huff out a chuckle.

"Cheese abuse is no laughing matter, William," he says sternly.

"Tell that to the cheese abusers later today," I reply. The phone in my pocket chimes again.

VIV: CAN YOU ALSO PICK UP MUSTARD, PICKLES, TRISCUITS, PAPER TOWELS, CITRONELLA CANDLES, AND BUG SPRAY?

WILL: JESUS CHRIST, VIV. DID YOU EVEN MAKE A SHOPPING LIST?

VIV: I DON'T WANT TO TALK ABOUT IT.

> **WILL: THIS STUFF MUST'VE BEEN ON HADLEY'S HALF OF THE LIST.**

> **VIV: BINGO.**

> **WILL: YES, I'LL GRAB THE STUFF.**

"So it looks like I need to do some extra shopping for the party, if you don't mind," I say to Earl, grabbing a basket.

"I'm feeling less and less confident about Vivian's ability to throw a party right about now," Earl shakes his head.

"I won't tell her you said that."

"Please don't. That friend of hers scares me just a little." Earl follows me around the store as I collect the needed items.

"She scares the hell out of us all, Earl."

The suffocating heat has finally given way to refreshing sunshine and cool breezes. The clear blue sky stretches infinitely, and the crisp air makes it the perfect day for a party.

I dump all the ice into the coolers in my truck and add the perishables until I reach the Rock. After collecting the beer from the brewery, I'm on my way to help Viv and Hadley set up the party. Upon arriving at the cabin, I unload the coolers and place the groceries Viv requested into the fridge.

"Viv, why is the only meat in the fridge a package of hot dogs? There will be a revolt if everyone has to Hunger Games it over a couple of franks," I ask.

"Do ye have such little faith in me, William? The dogs are for the kiddos. I've asked Jack to bring a few dozen lobsters and steamers to do a bake." Viv shakes her head like she can't believe I've actually questioned her party-planning skills.

"Ok, then. Impressive. Expensive."

"Meh," she waves her hand at me as if to say don't worry about it.

Kevin patrols the kitchen while Viv and Hadley prepare food. He focuses on the bags of chips, the trays of veggies, and the dips, all crowded on the countertop. He watches hungrily, hoping for a mistake. With every second that goes by, he tries harder in his game of patience, concentrating as if employing doggy Jedi mind tricks, attempting to will the food into submission.

"Will, can you please take Kevin outside with you? If I trip over him one more time, I'm going to murder his furry ass." Viv nudges Kevin in the butt, he grunts and begrudgingly follows me outside, clearly not happy about being denied snacks.

"Come on, Kev," I encourage, "we've got serious stuff to do out here for the explosives that are most likely going to scare the ever-loving shit out of you tonight. Our apologies in advance for that."

Kevin is the type of dog who looks at you while you're talking to him as if he knows exactly what you're saying, and if he could form words, he'd have a goddamn conversation with you. I'm sure his day will significantly improve once the kids arrive and give him all the attention he deserves. I genuinely hope the fireworks don't traumatize him.

Viv has assigned me the task of organizing the launch pad area for the fireworks. With the leftover rockets I had from last year, the tote of supplies Hadley brought, and the collection Mike has been storing all year, our fireworks display will be unforgettable. Fortunately, we anticipate an offshore breeze tonight, creating the perfect conditions for the fireworks.

After finishing my outdoor tasks, I grab a tennis ball and head to the dock, with Kevin following close behind. I'd like to wear him out so he won't pester the guests.

"Thanks for playing with him," I startle, not hearing Viv sneak up behind me.

"Jesus fuck, Viv," I turn quickly. "Do we need to put a fucking bell on you? You're like a ninja."

"Not my fault you're hard of hearing," she teases.

"What?" I say, holding my hand to my ear like an old geezer.

"Get that puppy good and tired. I don't need him knocking down the small children," she says, affectionately knocking her shoulder into my arm. "And thank you for bringing all the stuff. I'm glad I didn't have to bury Hadley's body today."

"No problem. Kev and I needed some guy time. He's a good boy," I compliment.

"So are you, Will Cooper," she says with a smile, turns on her heel, and heads back to the house, and I stare at her ass way longer than is socially acceptable. Pull your shit together, man—approach with caution. Do not, I repeat, do not scare her away.

The guests have arrived, and chairs clutter the deck and lawn. Jack has the lobsters and clams nestled in their bed of seaweed, ready for cooking. I bring beers to Jack, Mike, and Cameron, who are tending to the seafood in the pit oven. Betsy and Evvie watch the children jumping off the end of the dock with Kevin, each kid again wearing a wetsuit. There's a lot of laughter, squealing, and splashing.

I watch Vivian comfortably mingle with the guests, her demeanor warm and inviting as she carries a tray of cheese and crackers, offers drinks, and ensures everyone is happy. She stops to chat with Dr. Jane, our local veterinarian, engaging in a spirited conversation—no doubt, about her beloved black lab. Dr. Jane and Vivian share a hug. I recall hearing that Jane and Viv's mother shared a close childhood friendship, a connection that seems to show in their interaction.

I can't help but smile as her sparkling green eyes meet mine. She flashes a grin that says agreeing to throw this party was exactly what she needed. Dressed in her usual well-worn cutoffs and a casual tank top, she radiates effortless style. Her hair, typically piled on top of her head, now hangs loose in shaggy, tousled waves that cascade over her shoulders, adding a carefree air to her appearance.

Viv walks toward our group tending the lobster bake with cheese and crackers, and we all grab a handful. As she walks away, I feel her finger drag along the tops of my shoulders. What the...? When I turn around, she's smiling at me over her shoulder. Ok, then. This is getting interesting.

The sun is setting. The food has been served and devoured—the only evidence is the piles of discarded lobster and clam shells. Tents have been set up before it gets too dark. Mike and Evvie built the cutest little pillow pile for the girls. Citronella candles burn across the yard to ward off the mosquitoes.

Some of us are beginning to feel the effects of the many beers we've consumed. And by "some of us," I mean me. I'm in that sweet spot of drinking—the moment between buzzed and completely shitfaced. From the looks of it, Viv might be feeling the same way.

Mike waves me over to where he's preparing the fireworks display. He has already given his girls sparklers, which they gleefully wave around as they weave through the guests who have staked out their spots on the lawn. I hope he's taking the lead on this task because I probably shouldn't be near explosives at this point in the night. Cam and Hadley are there to assist, or at least Cam will be helping. Hadley stands beside him with her hand on his arm, looking up at him with what can only be described as pure lust. What is happening right now?

With the fireworks under control, I search for Vivian. We haven't talked much tonight, with her hostess duties keeping her occupied. I find her cleaning up inside and gently tug on her arm to come outside with me. I arrange us on the deck couch with throw blankets to ward off the chilly night air.

"Hi," I whisper.

"Hi," she whispers back.

"You've been busy. I haven't seen much of you," I say.

"The night is still young," she says mischievously.

Well, that comment just punched me square in the gut. Change the subject, Will, before this blanket becomes a tent.

"Ah, so what's going on with Hadley and Cam?" I ask, narrowing my eyes.

Viv laughs. "She's seen him a few times walking around town, and each time, she demands to know who the 'silver fox' is. Well, she finally met the silver fox and has sunk her teeth into him. I think our friend Cam is in a little bit of trouble."

"Oh dear," is all I can come up with.

"I hope Cam knows what he's in for. I also hope he's not sharing a tent with Lucas because that might get awkward."

"Betsy and Jack are taking the girls and Luke back to their house after the fireworks," I confirm.

"I'm not sure if that's good or bad," Viv chuckles, scooches closer to me, and rests her head on my shoulder. This might be my favorite night of my life.

"Quick question, I meant to ask earlier. Is Kevin ok with fireworks?" I ask, desperate to think of something other than her warmth pressing against me.

"That big dope? He's totally ok. I did put him in the house, though. Those kids exhausted the poor guy. He could barely hold his head up long enough to eat his dinner."

We fall silent as the fireworks show begins. Mike, an explosives master, treats us to a twenty-minute display of colorful bursts in the night sky. A spherical burst of colored stars, a cascading explosion resembling a weeping willow, a fast-burning blast with streaking trails, and a single bright comet that leaves a glittering stream. And then everything happens all at once. The yard erupts in oohs and aahs, and once it ends, there is applause.

At some point during the fireworks, Viv's arms slid comfortably around my waist, and I instinctively draped mine across her shoulders, feeling the warmth pressed against my side. I wished this moment would last a little longer, but around us, guests who were not camping out were starting to pack up. Reluctantly, Viv rises from the couch, her touch lingering for a brief moment before she moves to say her goodbyes, leaving a void where her warmth had been.

After we bid farewell, the remaining group consists of just eight of us: our original crew, along with Hadley and Cam. We arrange ourselves around the fire pit and keep tossing back the drinks. I feel an urge to pull Viv onto my lap right now, but when I look at her, she's gripping her phone so tightly that I can see her knuckles turning white in the firelight, and the color has drained from her beautiful face. Her eyes are wide with fear as she slowly stands from her chair, scanning the darkened property.

"Viv? What is it? You're scaring me," Hadley says, going to Viv's side.

CHAPTER FOURTEEN

Tequila, Temptations, and Threats

VIV

"Viv, you ok?" Will asks.

I barely hear the questions. I can't speak. The text message on my phone sends chills down my spine, and my blood runs cold. It's from an unknown number with a Boston area code, and the message...

UNKNOWN: I KNOW WHERE YOU ARE. I'LL BE COMING
FOR THE DOG YOU STOLE FROM ME, BITCH.

I can't breathe. My chest constricts, and I feel Hadley's arms around me as I struggle to catch my breath. She slowly pries the phone from my hand.

"Hadley, what the fuck is going on?" Will asks.

Hadley looks at my phone, and her face is as pale as I'm sure mine is right now.

"I will kill that motherfucker!" Hadley yells.

"Whoa! Violence!" Shawn exclaims. "I'm in. Who are we killing?"

"Who?" Will, Evvie, and Becky all shout at the same time.

"It's my ex, Eric. He must've borrowed someone's phone to text me because I blocked him," Viv says in a hushed tone. "He says he knows where I am."

"Is there any way he could?" Will asks.

"I never told him about this cabin, so I don't know how he'd ever know." I shake my head. "He can't find me. He wants Kevin back." I sob into my hands.

Hadley squeezes me tighter, and I feel Will's hand on my thigh.

"We're not going to let that happen," Hadley assures me.

"He hates Kevin. He never liked that the dog picked me every time. He yelled at him all the time," I say. "He's a different dog here. More relaxed.

Not being ordered to lie on his bed and not to bother anyone. Which is so hard for a puppy."

"Kevin is not going anywhere," Will asserts. "Over my dead fucking body."

"I appreciate that, really, I do. But you don't know Eric. If he knows where I am, he won't show up at my front door and demand I give him the dog. He's going to be sneaky about it. I'll never know what's happening until Kevin is gone. Or worse."

"Kevin will get a 24/7 security detail if needed," Mike offers, leaning forward in his seat with his elbows on his knees.

I huff a chuckle. "That sounds like a great idea, Mike."

"After the way he treated you, he can't just let you have this one thing, can he?" Hadley asks angrily. "You basically left everything behind but your clothes and your dog."

"He just wants to hurt me and knows this is the best way." I rub my face with my hands and release a frustrated groan.

"Why does he think he can steal Kevin?" Evvie asks.

I blow out a breath. "Eric and I were engaged for a few months. He proposed just after my mom went into hospice care. I don't know if he did it to get my mind off my mom's situation or if he did it to put the attention back on him. He didn't like not being the center of my world."

"Asshole," Hadley mutters.

"On the day he proposed, he arrived home from work with a picnic basket, which was unusual because he didn't enjoy eating outside, much less on the ground. As I wrapped my arms around his neck to kiss him hello, the tiniest, blackest little puppy pushed his head out of the picnic basket and barked the softest little bark. I remember scooping that puppy out of his basket and squeezing him so tightly that he just fell limp in my arms. When I lifted him from my chest to admire his handsome face, I noticed the ring hanging from his collar."

Becky let's out an "Ooooooh!"

"Definitely not," I say.

"Don't tell me it was an emerald cut?" Evvie scoffs.

"Oh yes, it was," I say. "Not exactly the ring I would've picked, but at the time, I figured it was the thought that counted."

I smile as I continue, remembering Kevin as a puppy. His fur was so black it almost had a blue tint; his nose was the color of charcoal, and his bubblegum pink tongue desperately tried to lick any part of me he could reach. His dark brown, soulful eyes were filled with love. His little puppy eyebrows gave him a perpetually worried look that he has yet to outgrow.

"When Eric and I had talked about getting a dog, I imagined we'd go to the local shelter together and find the perfect homeless pup. But when I set Kevin down on the ground, and he stumbled over his giant paws, I was done. In love."

"Eric asked me what I thought. It's a fucking puppy, you moron, is what I wanted to say. But I told him it was the best baby any girl could ever hope for—the one big thing we had in common was our lack of interest in having children." I start laughing. "Sorry, it's funny because I thought he was talking about the puppy, but he was really talking about the stupid ring. He never actually asked if I wanted to marry him—he just assumed the ring spoke for itself. We never once discussed getting married, so I was confused by this sudden proposal. I shrugged and said sure, then snuggled with the puppy."

"Oh my god!" Evvie squealed. "He was probably livid that you paid all your attention to Kevin!"

"Yup. I sat on the ground next to him, and he immediately fell over so I could rub his belly. You've all experienced that. He's such a sucker for a belly rub. I said I wanted to name him Kevin. Eric, of course, rolled his eyes and muttered that it was a stupid name for a dog, but I didn't care. I had always wanted my dog to have a regular old human name. And he was undeniably *MY* dog. He was my shadow. Eric often accused me of loving the dog more than I loved him. Spoiler alert: I did. He would yell at Kevin for no reason other than to assert his authority. The more Eric yelled, the more Kevin avoided him, and I showered him with even more love."

"Eric did very little to help with the dog. He expected me to handle all the feeding, walking, bathroom breaks, and vet visits. Fortunately, Kevin adored car rides, so I never had to leave him home alone with Eric when I went out. Everyone loved that big softy. He loved everyone—never met another animal or person he didn't instantly get along with—except for the person who constantly yelled at him."

I reach for my warming beer and take a couple of swigs.

"So, let him come. Let him try to take Kevin. I doubt he'll succeed. That dog hates his guts. And I refuse to let that asshole ruin my summer." Now that I've put the story out there, not one person sitting around this fire will let anything happen to my baby.

"That's the spirit," Hadley cheered. "I'm also looking for an opportunity to kick that asshole square in the nuts."

I watch the guys around the fire pit flinch at the thought, and I laugh. Hadley has such a violent way with her words, and I know that if anyone here will fight for Kevin, she'll battle the hardest. Her hatred for the way Eric treated me in the months leading up to my mother's death burns bright and hot.

We all agree there will be no mercy if Eric finds his way into Shearwater Cove and the group relaxes again. Hadley sneaks into the house, grabs a bottle of tequila, limes, and shot glasses, and turns up the music on her way back to the firepit. Uh oh. This is not going to end well. I could use a night that doesn't end well to banish Eric's threats from my memory.

"Let's play a drinking game!" Hadley begs.

"Had, you know we don't play drinking games with tequila," I respond sternly.

"You're no fun, V." She looks around the circle with a devilish grin. Everyone avoids her eyes.

"We're not twenty-one anymore, Had," Becky says. "I would be in an alcohol-induced coma after a tequila-based drinking game."

"Same," Shawn agrees with a nod, and stares at Becky just a beat too long. I'm not the only one who notices.

We spend another hour drinking, sharing stories, drinking more, and telling more stories until people retreat to their tents. Mike and Evvie go first, claiming they must pick up the girls earlier than they'd like tomorrow.

Hadley dances suggestively to "Pony" by Ginuwine, which I'm sure she specifically added to the playlist so she could Magic Mike the pants off Cameron. And he seems... agreeable. I suddenly feel like they should be left alone.

I see Shawn going to his tent and Becky to hers. It makes me a little sad that they're both so stubborn. I stand up to head inside, but I sway so severely that Will is forced to hold me upright.

"Ok, Tipsy Tinkerbell, let's get you into bed." Will puts his arm around my shoulders and pulls me in.

"I'm not tired," I slur and try to pull away to do my own indecent dance performance.

"Nope." Will grabs at me again before I spin myself off the deck.

"You're no fun," I pout.

"You're cute when you're drunk," Will leans in to whisper.

I giggle and shiver at the feeling of his breath hitting the shell of my ear.

"So are you," I say, pressing my finger into the side of his cheek.

He gently lifts my finger off his face, and without a moment's hesitation, I thrust it into his mouth. His lips close around it, and the sensation is electric. When he reaches up to remove my finger, he does so with excruciating slowness, dragging it past his lips while maintaining a tantalizing connection with his warm tongue. I lose feeling in my face. Hooooooo-ly shit. That was hot.

"Vivian," Will says, his voice low and raspy, "Don't start something you're not prepared to finish."

"Willllll, take me to my bed." I drag out his name, tugging his arm towards my bedroom. I think I'm being sexy, but in reality, I'm just being an obnoxious twat. I can't help but get super flirty after multiple tequila shots.

"Jesus fuck," he mumbles quietly. "Ok, I'll help you get *into* bed."

"And you'll get in too," I demand.

"Ah, no. Not this time, Viv," he replies, suddenly sober as a judge.

"Yes," I say, crossing my arms like an insolent toddler.

"Just lie on the bed, dammit," he orders.

"Oooh, I like controlling Will," I tease and crawl across the bed toward him on all fours. "What else do you want me to do?"

"Fuck, Vivian. Just let me help you," he pleads.

"Ok, ok, I'll lie down. But you have to lie down with me until I fall asleep," I negotiate.

"Oh, no, I don't think that's a good idea," he pushes back.

"Then I'm going back outside to drink more," I snap back.

Will grabs my arm before I can get past him and tosses me back on the bed. My breath whooshes out of me, and I start laughing.

"Ok, boss. I'll go to bed. Get these shorts off me," I demand.

"How about I leave the room while you do that yourself?"

"Chicken. I have underwear on," I pout. "Just help me."

"Fuck me," he mutters. I lie perfectly still and watch his face while he removes my shorts. His eyebrows shoot up to his hairline when he sees the tiny red thong I'm wearing. I hear him let out a low groan.

"I didn't say what kind of undies they were." I wink and giggle, pulling the covers over me to put him out of his misery. "Ok, you lie on that side of the bed. Just until I fall asleep, then you can retreat to your tent. I mean, unless you want to make your own tent under my covers."

"You will be the death of me, Vivian James."

"But it will be a good death, right?" I ask sleepily.

I wake up to the early morning sun beaming through my window. The brightness seeps through my eyelids, making it feel like someone is stabbing my retinas with tiny knives. *Owwww... what have I done?* I feel Kevin's weighty frame on the bed behind me. But when I open my eyes for real, Kevin is standing by the bed, his big head resting on the edge near my pillow. Having my attention, he softly whines and wags his tail. The poor guy needs to go out. If Kevin is currently looking at me, who the hell... I shoot straight up in bed, and my head immediately feels like it might crack open. Will's fully clothed form sleeps beside me. The fact that he is fully clothed is the most critical observation. What did I do last night to warrant this?

Padding to the back door, I open it to let Kevin out for his morning constitution when I recall last night's threatening text. I step out onto the deck to keep an eye on him and notice Becky sneaking back to her tent. I don't have to look in Hadley's room to know she didn't sleep there last night. Well, at least someone got lucky last night. I feed Kevin and grab water and ibuprofen before returning to the bedroom.

Will sits on the edge of the bed, facing the window, rubbing his temples. I scoot across the bed on my knees, and he turns to look at me.

"Water? Ibuprofen?" I ask.

"Yes to both," he says.

"I'm guessing that your presence in my bed this morning means I was being a flirty asshole last night?" I ask, raising my eyebrows in worry.

"Definitely flirty," he says, throwing the pills in his mouth and washing them down with several gulps of water.

"Considering I woke up in just my underwear, I'm going to assume there was a very obnoxious point where I demanded you remove my shorts?" I ask. "Normally, I'd just pass out fully clothed."

"It was mildly awkward," he says. "But you didn't jump my bones or anything."

"Ok, phew," I say, relieved. "Tequila makes me very drunk and very flirty."

"No shit," Will mumbles. "Yeah, you also put your finger in my mouth at one point. I wasn't one hundred percent sure if that was supposed to be flirting."

"Oh, boy." I shake my head. "Well, you have officially met Tequila Trashed Viv, then."

"I like my nickname better—Tipsy Tinkerbell," he chuckles, returning to his spot against my pillows.

I would kiss him if every tooth in my mouth weren't currently wearing a sweater. He looks so good, with his hair tousled from sleep and the pillow creases in his cheek. He's still wearing his shorts and T-shirt, but his feet are bare. We've spent a lot of time together this summer, and I still have yet to see him shirtless. I barely caught a glimpse when he jumped into the water the other day—definitely not close enough to really admire.

My inner evil genius thinks that maybe I can persuade him to go for a swim with me today. I know a guy who has a hard time resisting a challenge.

CHAPTER FIFTEEN

Between a Rock and a Hard Place

WILL

Viv prepares coffee for us and discovers a box of chocolate donuts that someone must have brought with them, while I cook a batch of greasy bacon. It's not exactly the breakfast of champions I envisioned this morning.

"Wait, you want to swim out to the rock today? Hungover?" I ask once Viv drops the challenge on me.

"I figured you'd be dying to redeem yourself after I beat you to the top the last time," she throws down the gauntlet. "And surprisingly, I'm not that hungover now—and I have bacon!" She holds up a crispy piece I just took out of the pan.

"That is surprising considering your actions last night."

"Hey, you're the one who suggestively sucked my finger as you pulled it out of your mouth," Viv looks at me with a glint in her eye.

"Oh, so you remember that, huh?" I mumble. She just grins.

"Okay," she begins. "Once we're both in our swimsuits, I'll count down from three on the deck steps, and then we'll race to the rock. Look out there—the tide is perfect for this!"

I scoff. "No way those short legs will even come close to beating me to the water."

"I was a sprinter on my high school track team, mister." She starts doing quad stretches and lunges.

"And my legs are twice as long as yours. No contest."

"Care to place a wager on this race?" she asks.

"Abso-friggin-lutely," I agree. "If I win, you go on an actual real date with me. We're talking about a nice dinner out. The works."

"Can you please clarify 'the works'? I don't want to get stuck in some basement bondage room after our meal."

"Party pooper," I say. "I would say 'the works' just leaves our night open to continuing after dinner if we find we want to spend more time together."

"Hmmm," she ponders, her finger tapping that bottom lip I long to nibble. "Okay, Will Cooper, you're on. And mainly because I kicked your ass once, I can do it again."

I stretch out my arms before me and shake them like an Olympic swimmer preparing for the starting blocks. "You're going down, James."

"Wait! What if I win?" she asks.

"I'm so confident I'm going to win that I'll offer you my handyman services for a whole weekend, free of charge."

"I could definitely use some help around here," she chuckles.

Viv shoos me out of the house while she changes. I run to the truck to change into swim trunks, and we meet on the back deck. Just as Viv is ready to start the challenge, we see Hadley stumble out of Cam's tent, holding what appears to be most of the clothes she wore last night. We both wolf-whistle through our fingers, and she flips us off.

"Ready, Cooper?" she checks. I nod. "Hadley! Count us down from three while you're doing your walk of shame!"

"Go fuck yourselves," Hadley yells. "THREE!... TWO!... ONE!... GO!"

Viv and I bolt toward the dock. Fortunately, Kevin is still in the house, or he would've excitedly knocked at least one of us down. She's surprisingly quick for a toddler-sized adult, deliberately running like an absolute menace, zig-zagging to prevent me from passing her. But once we reach the dock, she stumbles slightly, and it's all over. I get around her, hit the perfect spot at the end of the dock, and dive in.

Surfacing nearly halfway to the rock, I glance back to see where Viv is, only to be pulled under by my foot. Scrappy, I'll give her that—and, damn, she's a fast swimmer. Escaping her grasp isn't easy, but I finally break free, and with a few more strong strokes, I reach the rock first. As I begin to scale the slippery natural steps, she grabs the back of my swim trunks, nearly pulling them down while also halting my progress. I want this fucking date, so I push her off me with my foot, and she loses her grip. I pull myself onto the flat top and lie on my back to catch my breath.

I sit up in time to see a defeated Viv pull her small, dripping wet frame onto the rock to join me. The water droplets covering her lightly bronzed skin make it appear like she's sparkling in the sunshine. We're both breathing heavily as we squeeze into the small space on the rock. And exactly like when we were fourteen, our hips touch, our bare arms press up against each other, but this time, I don't plan on being a complete imbecile.

"I won," I mumble.

"I know," she agrees.

"You have to go on a date with me," I say.

"I know."

"And 'the works' too," I remind her.

"I know."

She's quiet for a minute before slowly rising to her knees and facing me. She lowers her eyes to my lips, and I lick them self-consciously. She lifts a hand to my cheek and brushes my cheekbone with her thumb. I suck in a breath at the contact. As she moves her face closer to mine, I'm buzzing with anticipation. Is she going to kiss me? She leans in, runs her tongue along the crease of my lips, followed by the softest kiss. And that buzzing shifts to my pants. I'm frozen. She then whispers in my ear with a soft breath, "That's how it's done, you seaweed-plucking idiot."

She didn't forget about the seaweed. Then she's gone. By the time I jump into the water to extinguish the fire in my pants, she's already climbing onto the dock.

I noticed that the tents had all been packed, and everyone had left while we were at the rock. When I arrive back at the cabin, Viv is wrapped in a towel, waiting for me on a deck chair.

"So in all the excitement of the race and your victory, I forgot to take a minute to admire..." she gestures to my torso, "... this. Those don't look like gym muscles, Will."

My eyebrows shoot up, and I let out a shaky breath—I wasn't expecting her to say that. She stands from the chair and slowly walks around me. I freeze in place. She runs her index finger across the tattoo that spans the width of my shoulders. Her touch heats my skin. Is she about to objectify my body? Probably yes. Was I okay with that? Also, yes.

"What is this bird?" she asks without removing the finger from my skin.

"It's a Shearwater," I say, my voice low.

"Of course. I should've known. How very on-target of you."

She continues exploring me, pausing at the tattoo on my bicep. Her brow furrows in curiosity.

"Narraguagus Light," I say.

"Significance?" she asks.

"It's the lighthouse I can see from my house. But also, there's an old family story that my great-great-grandfather was its keeper at some point in the 1800s. And I like lighthouses," I say with a shrug.

She lets out a contented sound, continues to my chest, and places a warm hand on the tattoo over my heart.

"I like this one most," she says softly, tracing the outline of the compass rose.

"It was my first," I say through clenched teeth, and my heart starts to race. God, her touch is killing me. I start thinking about gross things to keep my dick from making himself a player in the conversation. Feet, cat puke, gangrene, amputations. Ok, down, boy.

"Significance?" she asks again, clueless to my inner monologue.

"I had just graduated from high school with no college plans. I was having a hard time finding my way. Not sure what I wanted to do with my life. The compass represented guidance and direction, and let's be honest, I could use all the help I could get at that point. I credit it for helping me navigate those challenges," I reply, running a nervous hand through my still-damp hair. "I know it sounds like such a cliche, but it worked. I enrolled in an engine repair class and found my niche."

"Oh," she sighs, "Then it's definitely my favorite tattoo."

"How do you know? You haven't seen them all." I quirk my eyebrow at her.

"Will Cooper! Are you hiding a tramp stamp somewhere?" she laughs, pushing me with that soft hand still covering my tattoo.

"I guess you'll just have to find out for yourself." I smile big enough for my dimples to make an appearance as I stumble back from her shove. Oh, this was going to be fun.

"Tease. So, are you going to tell me where the muscles come from? I didn't see a fancy gym anywhere in town. And you were a damn beanpole the last time I saw you." She's not the least bit shy about checking me out from stem to stern.

I flop onto the cushioned deck couch and stretch out my legs. Viv follows suit, folding into the spot beside me with her legs tucked under her.

"It's called filling out, Viv. It happens to men when they become grown-ass adults. Plus, I spend my days lugging kegs and other heavy shit. I guess they just happened," I say, my smile quirking up on one side.

"Ok, well, keep up the good work," she encourages, patting me on the shoulder. "Can I ask another question?"

"Shoot."

"That scar on your shin. That looks like quite a story," she replies with a look of concern on her face.

"Oh yeah, that one. Not my finest moment," I answer, looking down at my feet. "It happened about ten years ago. My dad and I were working on this sweet 28-foot Bertram with twin Mercury 300s. One of the outboards had just shit the bed, and the guy wanted to see if we could repair it since they cost about $25,000 to replace."

"Jesus Christ on a cracker. That's expensive," Viv exclaimed.

"Right? Dad and I were up for the challenge. We'd never encountered an outboard we couldn't fix. We were hoisting the motor off the back of the boat—it weighed about 600 pounds, so it was difficult to manage. We needed to use two chains because it was so large, and one of the chains must've had a defect because, as we moved it toward the engine stand, that chain broke loose. The engine swung at me hard enough to snap my tibia and fibula. Man, did it hurt like a motherfucker. And it messed up my leg to the point of needing surgery with plates and pins. So yeah, I was left with this gnarly scar. Does it make me look badass?" I ask, trying to lighten the mood.

"Totally. But ouch. Did you fix it?" she asks.

"Fix what?"

"The big engine, you dummy!"

"Of course we did. I was on crutches, so Dad had to do most of the work, but we saved the guy ten grand. And it was a good payday for us."

Viv hops off her chair, leaving her towel behind. "You hungry?" she asks.

"I could eat," I answer.

"I didn't realize it was lunchtime already. Stay here. I'll be right back." She disappears into the cabin with me longingly focused on her ass, still clad only in her bathing suit.

I hope she covers that up while she's in there. No, I don't. Yes, I do. Fuck. I lean forward with my head in my hands. I remain in that position when she returns with a whole tray of leftover snacks and sandwich fixings from yesterday's party, with no cover-up in sight.

"I've got enough leftovers to feed us for weeks," she laughs. "So, eat up, pal."

We sit quietly, constructing absurdly tall sandwiches and attempting to fit them into our mouths politely. We spectacularly fail and laugh at the mess we've left behind on the deck. As if on cue, Kevin wakes from his nap and rushes over to clean up whatever has fallen onto the deck. From the enthusiasm with which he devours the leftover food, you'd think the poor dog was never fed.

As much as I don't want to leave this cozy situation right now, I need to get home to check on Dad and ensure he's not doing something stupid. And I need a shower like nobody's business.

"I hate to do this because we seem to be having a great time catching up, but I really need to head home and check on Dad," I say, following Viv into the cabin with the leftovers.

"Ok," she says, a mild flare of disappointment ghosting her eyes.

"When are you available for our date?" I ask.

"Anytime," she waves her hand at the surfaces cluttered with empty beer cans and bottles. "Obviously, I don't have anything essential going on around here."

I laugh and run my hand through my hair. "How about tomorrow night?"

"It's a date," she agrees.

She walks me to my truck, and as I hop into the driver's seat, she places a hand on my forearm through the open window and looks me straight in the eyes. "I'm really looking forward to discovering what 'the works' includes."

Jesus Christ. This shower might be longer than usual—and ice cold.

CHAPTER SIXTEEN

Hot Date, Cold Dessert

VIV

I hate to see Will go, but there is information I need to get from my best friend, and I have so much to tell her. I rush back into the house and kick open her bedroom door.

"Hadley Jane! Get your hungover-whore-ass out of bed immediately! It is two o'clock in the damn afternoon," I yell in my most obnoxious voice.

She groans and pulls the covers over her head. Fuck that. I pick up an extra pillow off her bed and start beating her with it.

More groans. "Stop hitting me, you trash goblin!"

"GET. OUT. OF. BED." I punctuate each word with another pillow whack. She wants angry, I'll give her angry. I'm enjoying this way too much until Hadley finds my arms and drags me into her firm grasp.

"Just shut up and lie here with me for a minute. I had a long night," she says, looking at me with a side-eye glance.

"Which is exactly why I'm in here, goddammit! Tell me everything."

"I don't know what you're talking about. We just talked all night," she says innocently.

"BULL. SHIT. I swear to the gods, Hadley, if you got laid after only a couple of weeks here, I will replace your shampoo with Nair," I threaten.

"Good thing I look good bald, then," she smirks.

"Hadley!" I say, shooting straight up on the bed.

"Vivian," She responds, also sitting up. "I have taken a lover."

"He's so quiet around us when we're all together. I didn't know he had it in him."

"Oh, Vivian... there's so much you don't know," she says, flopping back onto her pillow.

"Spill it. I mean, he is a beautiful man. But he also seems too responsible for a one-night stand in a tent with someone he literally *just* met."

"Have you never heard of lust at first sight, my innocent little friend?"

"I mean, so you really did just Magic Mike the pants off him," I say, shaking my head.

"Precisely." She nods her head in agreement with herself.

"Sooooo...?" I look at her, raising my eyebrows as high as they go.

"My god, you're impatient. Let's just say that sinking my hands into those luscious silver locks while his face was buried between my thighs is not a feeling I'll forget soon."

Now, it's my turn to flop back onto the pillow. "Holy shit," I muttered.

"And the delicious sensation of his beard on the inside of my thighs. And the way his blue eyes crinkled at the corners when he looked at me as he got me off."

"Not fair," I pout.

"And that was before I crawled onto him to straddle his lap. Naked."

"Ok, enough. I get the whole lubricious idea. Was he good?"

"Yup," she said with a pop of the p. "And I plan on doing it again tomorrow night at his place, you know, just to confirm."

"Good, I won't have to listen to it. Ohhhhh, about tomorrow night," I start.

Hadley looks at me quizzically, twirling her finger, signaling me to continue.

"Will and I are going on a real date," I say, wringing my hands together.

"It's about fucking time!"

"I know. I lost a bet."

"It took a lost bet to get you to go out with that fine specimen of a man?"

"I would've gone either way. It was just more fun this way," I chuckle.

"I love your evil side, Viv." Hadley shakes her head. "Where are you going? WAIT, where did Will sleep last night?"

"He said it would be a surprise, so I'm keeping a very open mind." I waggle my eyebrows. "And he slept next to my passed-out ass. He was a good sport about it. Although I made him take my shorts off, and I was wearing that tiny red thong, so you can imagine his face."

"I love it! And I'll be at Cam's, so you'll have the place to yourself."

"Where will young Lucas be while you two are howling like feral cats?"

"How dare you think I sound like that in the throes of passion!" She puts a hand to her chest with an exasperated expression. "He's going camping with some buddies."

"I'm nervous, Had," I confess.

"Viv, no. Don't be. Will is not Eric. Will is so far from Eric that they're not even on the same planet." She puts her arm around my shoulders and pulls me tight.

"But I haven't been with anyone since, you know—"

"That should be the least of your problems right now," she cuts me off. "Stop thinking that you're less."

"I know. I can't help it sometimes. Fucking Eric."

"Fucking Eric is right," she repeats. "If I ever lay eyes on that asshole again, I'm going to show him my famous wrestling moves and hopefully snap one of his legs."

"Love you, Had. Always got my back."

"Look, V. Like I've said before, I've seen how Will looks at you. And I also saw how Eric looked at you. It's as different as night and day."

"Tell me more," I say, resting my chin on my hands and fluttering my eyelids.

"Will looks at you as if you're the sun. When you rise each day, you brighten his world. You provide him with energy. Eric looked at you as though you were there to serve him. There was never light in his eyes, only disdain and contempt."

"Uh, wow, I never noticed that look in either of them."

"Then you're not paying attention."

We both fall into silence. How could I have been so foolish as to stay with Eric as long as I did? And I'm sure Hadley is reliving her sexy times with the silver fox. I hope this nervous feeling in my belly subsides by tomorrow because I don't want to mess this up.

Hadley and I spend the rest of the day snuggling on the couch, reading. We've decided to have a smutty book club this summer, and our chosen tome is a dark erotic romance featuring a masked, muscled man that leaves us both stomping our feet and giggling over the super spicy parts. I could use the inspiration. Becky and Evvie also joined the book club, but I believe they're both horrified by this book choice. I told them they could select the next one.

I turn in early. After the last few days, my body needs a recharge, and I don't want to look like a haggard sea witch for my date.

I let myself linger in bed until mid-morning. With nothing pressing to do, I welcome the time to rest my mind. In retaliation for yesterday, Hadley kicks my door open and proceeds to body-slam me in the middle of my bed. *OOOF!*

"Please refrain from breaking me in half before my big date," I struggle to say, with her body covering me.

"Mwaaaahahaha," she evilly laughs. She removes herself from me and sits back on her knees. Bouncing on the bed, she asks, "What will you wear? Please let me help pick out something to knock his socks off!"

"Hadley, I'm gonna need more than his socks to get knocked off," I say with a smug grin.

"Yee-haw!" Hadley howls, taking off an imaginary cowboy hat and waving it around. "My girl's gonna get lucky tonight."

"Ok, let's not get ahead of ourselves," I try to rail her in. "Not sure I'm ready for the full scope of your idea of luck." I roll my eyes. "Did you let Kevin out and feed him?"

"Of course, I took care of Kevin. And don't be a prude. You could use some good dick. Might cure the darkness that still hangs over your head from that shriveled ball-sack of a man."

"Not being a prude, just careful."

"Careful, schmareful."

"Seriously?"

"Rip the band-aid off!"

"Hadley."

"Vivian."

"Let's just pick something out that will make his eyeballs *boing* out of his head like a cartoon character."

"Deal," I agree, and she starts flinging things out of my closet onto the bed. "I'm going to shower. Choose something nice for me, will ya? I can't handle these kinds of decisions."

I glance up to see Hadley rubbing her hands together with the expression of an evil scientist. I might be in trouble. More importantly, Will could be in even greater danger.

After exfoliating and conditioning, shaving all the places, and moisturizing, I'm all shined up and ready for anything. Well, maybe not *anything*. But some things. Certain things. Oh, god, what am I doing?

I head back into the bedroom to see what outfit Hadley has put together from the pile of random clothes we tossed on the bed. I'm not exactly known for my stylish clothes or fashion sense. Given that the weather isn't stifling hot today, she's done a pretty great job.

She dug out a pair of simple dark wash skinny jeans I forgot I even owned and paired them with a jade silky tunic-style tank top, the fabric sheer from just below my boobs. The nude open-toed platform wedges will give me a little extra height, so it doesn't look like Will is dining with a child.

"Hadley!" I yell out.

"What? Where's the fire?" she asks, running into my room half-dressed.

"Nice work with the outfit," I compliment. Trying not to think of Will peeling those skinny jeans down my legs. Hot damn. Jesus, you don't need to be horny now, you idiot.

"Right? I think you should make him work for it on the first date." She arches an eyebrow, considering the same about the skinny jeans.

I'm not exactly sure what my expectations are for tonight—we're just getting to know each other again. However, I don't want to be caught off guard wearing boring undergarments. Will seemed to enjoy that tiny red thong I wore the other night, so I chose the same one in black along with its matching lacy strapless bra. I slipped on an oversized T-shirt and headed back to the bathroom to do my hair and makeup.

Now fully dressed, Hadley appears in the bathroom mirror as she walks behind me.

"Full eyes, Viv. Give him the works—the liner, the mascara, and a subtle cat eye. You know what I mean," she insists. "The only other thing you need is a soft lip shade. You already have some nice color from your time outside. And sexy hair... big, full waves. Don't straighten that shit."

"Aye, aye, captain," I respond and get to work. The finished product is spectacular, if I do say so myself. I rarely do full makeup anymore. Eric ruined it one night when he told me I was wearing too much eye makeup.

I hear my phone ping in the other room.

WILL: PICK YOU UP AT 6?

VIV: WORKS FOR ME. OR CAN I MEET YOU IN TOWN?

WILL: UH, ABSOLUTELY NOT. WHAT KINDA DATE DO YOU THINK THIS IS?

VIV: JUST TRYING TO SAVE YA SOME TIME.

WILL: PFFFFFFT.

VIV: LOOKING FORWARD TO TONIGHT.

WILL: ME TOO.

VIV: SEE YA SOON

I'm dressed by 5:30 and start pacing the cabin. Hadley sits on the couch, watching me with a look of slight concern on her face.

"Dude, you keep pacing like that, you're gonna have to shower again."

"I'm just trying to work off the nervous energy."

"Sit down. You don't want your hair to get frizzy from too much activity. At least before you actually, you know, participate in an *actual* activity." She laughs.

"Hmm, good point," I agree.

"Ok, I'm heading out to Cam's. Promise me you'll sit perfectly still while you wait for Will to arrive."

"Promise."

"Good. Have a good night, honey. See ya tomorrow!" Hadley heads out the front door, and I hear her yell, "Don't do anything I wouldn't doooo!"

"Well, that leaves my night pretty open," I yell back as the door is closing.

Will pulls up to the cabin just before six. He hops out of the truck and meets me halfway to the house.

"Um, why do you have Kevin on a leash with a bag full of various dog treats with you? I'm fairly certain the restaurant doesn't allow dogs." Will inquires, his distractingly muscular arms crossed over his chest.

"Shawn is on Kevin's guard duty tonight, so I made sure to bring his favorite treat."

"Shawn's?"

"Kevin's!" I shove him playfully.

"Is there a girl dog in that bag?" Will asks, chuckling.

"No, dummy. It's a M-A-R-R-O-W-B-O-N-E." I whisper. Now he's just being a smartass.

"Ah," he says, opening the passenger-side door for me. The truck sits high, so I'm grateful for the step and handle that help me get in gracefully. He opens the back door for Kevin, who leaps in like a champ. "I'm glad you're not taking any chances by leaving the furry dude alone. The one drawback of not having close neighbors is that they can't keep an eye on your stuff while you're out."

"Where are we going?" I ask impatiently.

"Surprise."

"Are we leaving Shearwater Cove because I can think of only one dinner place?" I say, looking out the window.

"But you don't know all its secrets."

"Oooh, I'm intrigued," I purr. I think I see his knuckles whiten slightly on the steering wheel.

After getting Kevin settled with Shawn, we arrive at the Cove Cafe, where Mary greets us at the hostess station with a wide grin. There are two things I didn't notice the last time I was here: first, each ceiling beam is wrapped with tiny twinkle lights, giving the whole place a fantastical appearance, and second, there's a walled-off area towards the back that I assume is for special occasions. Mary leads us to that back area, and now I'm wondering: is this a special occasion?

"Will, why are we going to the back?" I whisper.

"Because I don't need my nosy neighbors in our business. I'm just trying to make this date memorable, Viv." He leans down and whispers back, the words tickling my ear and sending shivers down my spine. Oh, god.

Mary leads us to the restaurant's private area, known as *The Snug*. A solitary antique wooden table, trimmed with copper, is set for two, topped with a cluster of flickering candles and a small vase of freshly picked wild-flowers. The high-backed cushioned chairs create a cozy atmosphere that eases my earlier nerves. An ornate fireplace, likely original to the building, is also adorned with candles since the weather is too warm for an actual fire.

We engage in an easy conversation at our table. The noise from the rest of the restaurant fades into a distant murmur behind the wall, and I feel as if it's just the two of us. We order cocktails—a margarita for me and a dirty gin martini for Will—figures he likes it dirty. Pull it together, Viv.

Mary surprises us with a new appetizer that the kitchen has been working on. The app isn't fancy by any means, but the lobster tater tot with spicy remoulade has us both begging for more. For dinner, we share an arugula and beet salad along with a bowl of buttered lobster pasta with cherry tomatoes. When Mary offers us dessert, I notice Will's blue-gray eyes crinkle slightly as he tells her we have other plans. *Gulp.*

After gathering a sleepy Kevin from Shawn's, Will quickly stops at Earl's. He refuses to show me the contents of the bag he brings back to the truck. I pout. He laughs. God, I hope it's ice cream. The nerves that disappeared during dinner now return with a vengeance, knowing we'll be alone. Back at the cabin, we unload the dessert fixings: ice cream, hot fudge, whipped cream, and cherries—*double gulp.*

"In all the excitement of dinner, I forgot to mention how handsome you look tonight, Will," I say, awkwardly waving my hand at him. His hair is its usual tousled mess that works for any occasion. He's wearing a more dressed-up version of his standard outfit: dark jeans and a lightweight cotton plaid button-down in blues and greens. He kicks off his unscuffed brown Blundstones and shrugs off the plaid shirt, revealing a simple white T-shirt underneath. Oh boy.

"Thanks, Viv. You look pretty great yourself," he flirts, and I feel the fierce blush crawl up my neck. "That tank top is making your eyes so bright, and I'm trying very hard not to stare... actually at all of it." He blows out a breath.

"Well, thank you, kind sir," I say with a curtsy, trying to keep things light. It's suddenly getting very stuffy in this cabin. I open a few windows, trying to cool it off. I wipe my sweaty palms down the front of my jeans.

"Shall we make our desserts?" I ask.

"Absolutely," Will says nervously.

Ok, at least I'm not the only one freaking out right now.

CHAPTER SEVENTEEN

Sticky Fingers and Sweaty Jeans

WILL

Viv gathers all the necessary tools for our ice cream sundaes: bowls, spoons, a scoop, and some M&Ms for extra toppings. The ice cream is my favorite local flavor, Moose Tracks. It's vanilla ice cream with swirls of chocolate fudge and chunks of mini peanut butter cups. It's the best for a hot fudge sundae, and I would fight anyone who disagrees.

"Moose Tracks," Viv squeals. "That's my favorite."

"Phew," I sigh. "Glad my choice wasn't an epic fail."

She smiles at me and continues with the task at hand. Starting with the ice cream base, we both chose two scoops, followed by the hot fudge she heated on the stove, and topped it with whipped cream from the can because that's the best kind. We both add cherries, M&Ms, and more hot fudge. Obnoxious but delicious.

Sitting on the couch, we quietly eat our masterpieces until the only sound in the cabin is the tink-tink of spoons scraping the bottoms of our bowls.

Viv grabs her phone and connects it to the Bluetooth speakers, selecting a soft, sultry playlist. She takes our dishes to the sink and returns to the couch with a devilish look in her eye, holding the whipped cream canister.

"What do you plan on doing with that, Vivian?" I ask.

"I plan on squirting directly into my mouth," she winks at me. I think my brain just short-circuited.

I watch her carefully because the look in her eyes is pure mischief. She strolls nonchalantly around the cabin with that canister, occasionally squirting a bit into her mouth and singing softly to the music coming from the speakers. Her voice is gentle and lovely. Kevin is groaning in his sleep, momentarily distracting me—and it's all the time she needs.

Before I know it, Viv is back on the couch, but this time, she's straddling my lap and covering as much of my face as possible with whipped cream. I struggle to get a hold of her arms to make her stop, but her cackling laugh makes me laugh too hard, and I can't see a goddamn thing. I finally wipe enough of the whipped cream off my face to see her. That mischievous look in her eyes has shifted to something else. Something a little naughty.

She tosses the canister onto the floor. I can't help but stare at the sugar lingering at the corners of her mouth.

The playlist shifts to a seductive number. The voice is familiar, but it's not a song I've heard. Maggie Rogers, maybe? Yup... Oh, boy.

She's looking at me like she wants to lick me clean, which I would be totally fine with. Her legs squeeze my lap, and she shifts just enough to awaken my desires. Her sticky hands softly stroke the hair on the back of my head.

"Vivian, what are you going to do now?" I murmur, looking up at her bright green eyes. Outlined in the black eye makeup, they look fucking sinful.

"I'm just wondering how long you'll sit here covered in whipped cream."

"Kind of hard to move right now." For several reasons.

She shifts her hips again, and I can't take it anymore. I thrust my hands into her luscious hair and pull her to my whipped cream-covered lips. She startles for a minute and then settles into the embrace. I try to pull away, but she holds me in place, licking the friggin' cream off my face. A new one for me, but I'm fucking here for it. The music fades into the background as the situation becomes more heated.

I'm sure the hip shifting is being done on purpose to see how much of a rise she can get out of me. I grab her around her hips and flip her onto her back with a small, surprised squeak. I tilt my head to the side to get the right angle and return for more sugary, sweet kisses. This time, she parts her lips, inviting me in. Or tongues meet in a frenzy, licking into each other's mouths.

I pull away momentarily to take off my T-shirt, mostly so I can wipe the rest of this whipped cream off my face, but also because I'm boiling with her under me. I hear her groan as her hands find my bare torso. Someone is dying to get out from behind a zipper right now, but he will have to wait his turn.

Viv pulls me back down to her… "Take off my pants," she whispers into my ear. Fucking what?

"Ah, are you sure?" I ask, thinking maybe this is too fast even for me.

"I'm boiling my ass off, Will, and these pants are melting my skin. Just take them off me, dammit."

Oh. Well, that's mildly deflating on so many levels.

She continues, "I'm looking at a leather-pantsed-Ross episode of Friends level of discomfort right now. These jeans are pasted to my sweaty legs. Please. Fucking. Help. Me."

I sit back on my heels and can't help but laugh at the desperation on her face right now.

"William Cooper, Jr., I will fuck your shit up."

Ok, scary threats. I unbuckle the belt and slowly unbutton and unzip, trying hard not to look directly at her underwear, especially after what happened the last time she ordered me to remove her pants. I get hold of the waistband of her jeans and start peeling them down her sweaty legs. She wasn't kidding. They're nearly at one with her skin. I get them to her ankles and think I'm finally home free when I accidentally look up and see the thin, tiny black triangle that covers only what's essential. Fuck. Fuck. Fuck. No. Gross thoughts, Will. Nope, I can't think of anything gross.

"Viv? Again?" I say, looking away and gesturing to her undergarments.

"Oh, oops, sorry. I'll go put some shorts on." She so did that on purpose.

"Well, you don't have to... Do you need help with the top also?" I ask, waggling my eyebrows.

She rolls her eyes obnoxiously and walks into the bedroom, and I am met with the most delicious view of her bare ass that might be the thing I see every time I close my eyes for the rest of my life. While she's changing, I head to the bathroom to clean up my sticky face, splashing it with ice-cold water for good measure.

As I turn to leave, she's leaning against the doorframe, wearing tiny sleep shorts and a cropped T-shirt. I can't help myself. I grab her by the arm and spin her toward the sink vanity, lifting her small frame onto the edge of the sink and sending bottles of beauty products scattering to the floor. *Ooops.* I wedge between her legs and tilt her head to face mine, and plunge back into her mouth, sucking her tongue into mine. I'm not sure if the moans I hear are mine or hers. She's got to feel how hot I am for her right now. I move my hands from the sides of her head to the bare strip of skin the cropped shirt reveals. She grabs me by the belt loops and pulls me tighter into her. Yup, sure she can feel it now. Her arms snake around my back, pawing at my flesh while we pant against each other's mouths.

She wraps her legs around my waist, and I pick her up, cradling her ass.

"Which way?" I ask gruffly.

"Bedroom."

"Really?"

"Just fucking do it," she demands.

I toss her onto the bed and crawl toward her as she retreats to the pillows. I find her mouth again and decide it's the only place I want to be right now. Her sigh against my lips sends a thrill down my spine. I slowly move my hand on her hip up her side, slipping under her shirt. She freezes.

"Viv?"

"Can we not... do that?" she asks.

"Of course, anything. You call the shots. Tell me to stop when you need me to," I say in a husky whisper. "Are you ok?"

"Just, yeah, I'm ok. It's just... I guess it's hard to explain. I'm sorry. I didn't mean to be a tease."

"Stop it. You're not a tease. And you don't have to tell me anything, Viv. When you're ready, I'll be here."

"Thanks. I think maybe I just want to sleep now," she exhales, her expression sad when she lifts her head to face me.

"Ok, I'll grab my shirt and—" She cuts me off.

"No, I want you to stay with me, okay?" There's a pleading look in her eyes that I can't refuse.

"Um, yeah. I'll stay." I really hope to uncover this mystery of Viv's soon. I hate the frightened look that crossed her face when I slid my hand under her shirt. The last thing I want to do is scare her, especially considering the recent threats from her ex.

"I need to let Kevin out before I snuggle in. I'll just be a minute," she says, moving to get out of bed.

"No, you stay. I'll let him out. Is that all?"

"Can you lock up? Hadley's staying at Cam's."

"Uhhh, *what*? Really? Wow, that happened fast. Like lightning-fast. I didn't know the old dude had it in him." I shake my head as I rouse Kevin from his slumber for his evening constitution.

"You guys treat him like he's geriatric. Isn't he only in his late thirties? Not much older than us," she asks before I leave the bedroom.

"Yeah, but because he was such a dink to us when we were kids, we treat him like he's way older. Childish, I know, but it's fun." I reply. "But good for them. He deserves some fun in his life. He's always had too many responsibilities."

"Please put Kevin's leash on him. I don't want him wandering into the trees where you can't keep an eye on him." She asks, jumping off the bed and heading to the bathroom.

"Yes, ma'am. Be right back."

After locking up, I head back to the bedroom to find that Viv has washed her face clean of any trace of makeup. If possible, her eyes appear greener, and her freckles are more noticeable. She looks so fucking sexy, and with her hair piled on top of her head, god, I don't know how I'll ever keep my hands to myself.

"Do you mind if I take my pants off?" I ask sheepishly. "Jeans aren't very comfortable for sleeping."

"Of course, don't be silly. I think we've determined you won't sneak-bone me in the middle of the night," she chuckles.

"I mean, that's *my* plan, but I can't speak for him," I say, pointing at my crotch.

"Oh, Will Cooper. Still fourteen inside that head, aren't ya?"

"Don't you know it, babe. But I can tell you what's not still fourteen," I raise my eyebrows a couple of times and flash a set of deep dimples. She smiles, and we settle in for the night on our respective sides of the bed. I'm not sure I could take more contact tonight.

"Goodnight, Will. I really enjoyed our date tonight... and 'the works' too." She says, turning on her side to face me.

"G'night, Vivian," I reply.

CHAPTER EIGHTEEN

Boners, Boundaries, and Dirty Books

VIV

I wake up lying on my side, hugging the edge of the bed, refusing to open my eyeballs yet. I'm confused. Usually, Kevin doesn't take up that much space on his side of the bed. Ugh... this stupid dog. It feels like he's got a paw stuck right into my ass and one draped over me. What kind of pretzel position is this idiot in? For fuck's sake, dog.

"Kevin, dammit, get your paw out of my—" I stop talking.

I stop talking because I remember it's not Kevin on the other side of the bed behind me. Opening one eye, I'm met with a muscular arm draped over my middle. So, the paw sticking into my backside... is not... a paw... Oh god.

I scoot forward, hoping to slip out of bed without waking Will, but his strong arm tightens around me when I attempt to escape, dragging me back against his body. This isn't your average, run-of-the-mill morning wood... no, my friends, this is morning redwood. I don't know what to do. I was never a big snuggler, so I've never experienced this in my past relationships. Should I just wait for it to deflate on its own? Should I shake him awake and pretend not to notice? I would need to be paralyzed not to notice. Should I make a break for it and jump out of bed like I have a bathroom emergency? Shit. Shit. Shit.

I lie as still as a corpse, with probably the breath of one, too. I haw-haw into my hand, and yup, god, I almost shrivel from the stench. Well, it appears I'm trapped with a rather sizable boner sticking nearly into my ass. Don't think about it. Don't think about it. Great, it's all I can think about. Aaaaaand now I need to pee. Will's arm loosens as his breathing deepens, indicating he's once again asleep, and I quietly make my escape. Phew. That. Was. Close. Close to what? I'm not entirely sure.

I throw on a sweatshirt and let Kevin outside. The sun casts the Bay in an exquisite orange glow, so I curl into a deck chair to enjoy the scenery while Kevin searches for the perfect blades of grass to defile. Once he's finished, I feed and water him and brew the coffee. I carry the two mugs back into my room to find Will sitting up, leaning against the pillows piled at the headboard, utterly oblivious to my morning skirmish with a particular body part of his. He's flipping through a book—motherfucker.

"Good morning," I sing, handing him the steaming mug. "Um, where'd ya find that book?"

"It was here on the nightstand. What the hell are you reading?"

"It's for my Book Club. Hadley picked it," I blame. Lies. I picked it. I fucking picked the book about a thirst-trappy masked muscular stalker man.

"I'm not really enjoying it much," I lie again. I'm enjoying it too much.

"I might not even finish it." More lies. This is actually my second time reading it.

"Somehow, I don't believe you because these pages look, errr, well-loved," he says, tossing the book back on the stand.

"Used bookstore," I say. God, why can't I stop lying about this stupid book?

"You little liar," Will says with a smirk. "Viv likes to read all the smut."

"Do not."

"Vixen."

"Shut up."

He glances at me with an impish smile as he sips his coffee. I crawl back under the covers next to him and grab my phone to silently scroll through Instagram while he's busy relishing his supposed discovery of my deep, dark secrets. Instead, I'm met with thirty-seven unread texts. What the fuck?

GROUP TEXT with EVVIE, BECKY, HADLEY, VIV:

Ev: I HEARD FROM BETSY, WHO HEARD FROM EARL, WHO HEARD FROM MARY, THAT WILL TOOK VIV OUT TO DINNER LAST NIGHT!

BECK: YEEHAWWW

Ev: JESUS, VIV. WAKE UP AND TELL US ALL THE DEETS, DAMMIT.

BECK: WE NEED THIS. I'M SO BORED.

Ev: NOT WHAT I HEARD.

BECK: WHAT DO YOU MEAN?

Ev: MIKE SAID THAT TINY SAID HE HEARD FROM OWEN THAT SHAWN HAS BEEN SNEAKING OUT OF THE BREWERY FOR LUNCH A LOT.

BECK: GOD, THE RUMOR MILL CHURNS SO HARD AROUND HERE.

VIV: DID SOMEONE SAY HARD?

HAD: DAMN! ENJOY HAVING THE HOUSE TO YOURSELF?

BECK: WAIT, WHERE WERE YOU, HAD?

Ev: HADLEY WAS AT CAMERON'S.

HAD: UHHHHHGGGG

Viv: BUSTED!

BECK: WAIT, WHAT'S HARD, VIV?

Viv: SOMEONE'S MORNING WOOD...

HAD: RIDE 'EM, COWGIRL!

Ev: MY INNOCENT EARS!

Viv: AS IF!

BECK: WHAT'S MORNING WOOD?

Viv: GIRLS' NIGHT. CABIN TOMORROW? BOOK CLUB.

Ev: I'M IN.

BECK: SAME.

HAD: I LIVE THERE.

Viv: I'LL MAKE MARGARITAS.

Ev: OLE.

When I can't stop giggling, Will attempts to grab my phone. I lock the screen before he can reach it and toss it onto the nightstand. I slide down into a more horizontal position and turn onto my side. Will mimics my position, and we lie facing one another.

"Do you want to talk about it?" he asks.

"About what? That book I'm reading? Absolutely not."

"About what happened last night?"

"Not at the moment," I sigh. "I'm not quite ready. I'm sorry."

"You have nothing to apologize for, but I think I could keep up. You're...okay? Right?" he asks, worry lining the space between his brows.

"Physically, yes," I reply, "But I'm still working on my mental well-being."

"Viv..." he whispers.

"I promise you, Will, it's nothing you did. Just something I need to come to terms with." I lean over, give him a quick peck on the lips, and curl into his chest. He wraps his free arm around my shoulders, resting his chin on my head. The faint scent of pine and hops relaxes me like some manly aromatherapy. He whispers softly, "I'll be whatever you need me to be." And my heart aches and melts at the same time.

I wake from my mid-morning nap to find the bed beside me empty. I assume Will must have left for the brewery and didn't want to disturb me, but I hear his soft voice in the living room. I pad over to the doorway to see who he's talking to, only to discover him curled up with Kevin. Will is sipping a second cup of coffee, his feet stretched out on the couch. Kevin is wedged between Will's legs and the back cushions. My 80-pound puppy can squeeze into the smallest spaces. They're both so fucking adorable.

"Are you comfortable, Kevin?" Will murmurs. Kevin lifts his head to look at him and sighs contentedly as he curls back into himself. "I'll take that as a yes, then." He takes a few more sips of coffee and whispers, "I hope your momma is okay, buddy. She seems a little sad about something. I wish she would open up to me. But maybe she opens up to you instead, and that's okay too."

Oh my god. A gasp slips from my lips, and I slap a hand over my mouth, hoping he didn't hear me eavesdropping on this heartfelt, one-sided conversation he's having with my dog. My heart clenches—I want so badly to tell him everything. I'll share it all the next time he asks me on a date. However, after last night's debacle, I'll be lucky if I get a second chance.

"Hey," I say, emerging from my spying spot. "I thought you'd have taken off already."

"Nah, Shawn and Owen are at the brewery, and I don't have anything boat-related on my schedule. So, I thought I'd keep Kev company while his mom catches up on her sleep. I texted my dad, and he's fine, so I'm all yours today if you're not busy. Maybe we could visit the park in town and take Kev for a wa—." I cover his mouth with my hands.

"Don't you know you're not supposed to say that word in front of him? He'll turn into the Tasmanian Devil so fast that it will make you spin, too.

The trick is to sneak it up on him, nonchalantly. And whatever you do, do not make eye contact."

Will freezes in place and gradually diverts his gaze from the dog, afraid of what might occur if they make eye contact.

"I mean, it's not like looking directly at the opened Ark of the Covenant or anything, Will. Your face will not melt off," I laugh. "Why don't you head home, and I'll get ready and meet you at the brewery in an hour. Does that work?"

"Indeed," he says, carefully sliding off the couch so as not to disturb the sleeping baby. He also gives me a sweet kiss on the forehead as he passes by to gather his things. Well, shit. The sweet man certainly deserves to know the whole story, and I think it's time I suck it up and spill my guts.

"Come on, Kevvy, let's run some errands," I say, jingling his collar and hoping the word *errands* will distract him from the actual plan. He ambles sleepily to the door, and we head to the Jeep. When I start removing the top, his ears perk up, and his tail wags so fiercely that his entire hind end sways. Nobody enjoys the freedom of a topless Jeep ride quite like Kevin. He hops in eagerly, ready for the wind in his ears.

We pull into the brewery parking lot, and with Will nowhere in sight, we head inside. I'm unsure if dogs are allowed in the taproom, but we'll find out. Upon our entrance, Shawn's face lights up at Kevin's presence, and he and Owen rush over to greet him. Not me, mind you. Not even a nod or a hello. It's butt scritches for the Lab. The excitement draws Will from the back, and he comes over to greet me. At least someone is happy to see me.

Kevin snuffles in Shawn's pockets as if he's digging for treasure, and he rewards the dog's begging with a few treats.

"Wait... did you just produce dog treats from your pocket?" I ask, confused. "What's up with that? You don't even have a dog."

"I just like to be prepared when I see one out and about. Plus, if you looked in the mirror, you'd see the expression on a woman's face when you give her dog treats. I mean, Will better watch out because the mix of lust and adoration on your face right now should scare the shit out of him." Shawn turns back to Kevin, who now seems superglued to his leg.

"Oh, Shawn, you really need to get better at reading facial expressions!" I joke.

Shawn sticks his tongue out at me, gives the dog another treat, and focuses on scratching the spot just above Kevin's tail. He tippy-taps his feet in a little happy dance at the butt scritches.

"Well, there's no getting rid of him now. You will forever be the Treat Man, and that fucking dog never forgets a guy with a pocket full of goodies," I shake my head. "Come on, buddy—time to let Treat Man get back to work."

The brewery is relatively empty, so before I clip Kevin's leash back on, I want to show Will what happens when I say the magic word that transforms him into a whirling dervish.

"Kevvy, W-A-L-K?"

He tilts his head to the right.

"Wanna go for a…"

He tilts his head to the left.

"WALK!"

Kevin spins full-on in circles. Like dizzy on a merry-go-round, puke-your-guts-out spinning. I look over at Will and cackle at the look of sheer terror I'm sure is a result of his near mistake with that word earlier. My little buddy loves a nice walk. I clip the leash, and the three of us push through the front door, heading towards the park. I hadn't been back since the day Hadley and I explored, when she tried to get me kicked out of town with her lewd behavior.

I lucked out in the furry friend department. Although still quite puppyish, he walks exceptionally well on a leash and knows to heel when necessary. He only becomes very excited when he sees other dogs his size. Small dogs scare him, and he gives them a wide berth.

"Gosh, the park is so lovely," I comment as we walk towards the boardwalk bordering Narraguagus Bay.

"It is. Building took a while, but the whole town was so happy to have green space like this for activities."

"Mary told Hadley and me that it was built with funds donated by an anonymous benefactor. So, no one knows who it was? Really?" I prod.

"Not that I know of. I never really thought much about it," he shrugs.

"I find it funny that it's just called the waterfront park," I chuckle.

"Everyone in town agreed that if we couldn't dedicate the park to its donor, we just wouldn't name it at all."

"That's what Mary said," I reply.

We walk in silence, with only the squawks of the seagulls perched on the nearby docks and the competitive shouts and laughter of the kids playing soccer disturbing our peace.

"You hungry?" Will asks.

"One thing you'll learn about me quickly, Will, is that I will eat all the time if food is offered."

Will laughs and pulls me toward the path leading out of the park near Becky's take-out place. Oh. Ohhhhhh. Lobster rolls. Now I'm starving.

CHAPTER NINETEEN

You Had Me at Lobster Roll

WILL

Viv and I walk up to the window of the small forest-green building that houses Cove Lobster Co. Becky's dog, Shirley, lifts her head from her spot beneath the green and white awning shading the take-out window. Her tail wags when she sees Kevin, but she doesn't move.

"Will! Viv!" Becky waves when she sees us. "Shirley, go see Kevin! Go ahead."

Shirley's ears perk up, which always makes me laugh. She's got the big ears of her German Shepherd ancestors, but they flop over like the Lab part of her. And they move independently of each other. She and Kevin spend the next several minutes sniffing butts, then Shirley takes off with Kev hot on her heels.

"They'll be okay, right?" Viv asks nervously.

"God, yes," Becky says. "Shirley won't go far and will keep an eye on him. She's very bossy."

"Like her momma," I mutter.

"What was that, William?" Becky narrows her eyes at me.

"So, we'd love a couple of jumbo lobster rolls," I change the subject. "Viv, butter, mayo, or both?"

"I've never been offered *both* before! Decisions, decisions," she says, tapping her chin. "What do you get?"

"Always both," I say.

"Both, then."

"You won't regret it." I support. "Let's grab a table."

Becky serves us our iced teas along with an extra-large basket of her famous chips. We find a picnic table nestled among the trees, away from the others—a perfect spot to keep the dogs from bothering anyone.

"I can't believe it's taken me this long to get a lobster roll from Becky," Viv remarks. "Is it weird that I'm ridiculously excited?"

"Not at all," I say. "She makes the best I've ever had, and there's no shortage of them around here. Someday, I'll take you to Lunch on the Wharf in Corea; it's a cool little spot with a lobster roll that's almost as good."

"Sounds fun!"

"Will! Viv! Your rolls are ready!" Becky yells from the take-out window.

"I'll grab them," I say.

"Extra napkins!" Viv yells after me.

"She must think I'm a moron," I mutter under my breath, chuckling.

"Not my first lobster roll, Viv!" I yell back. I hear her mutter something I'm sure is a threat of bodily harm.

I return with two of the most enormous lobster rolls I've ever seen Becky serve. I think she's trying to impress Viv—and I'm all for it! I see Viv's eyes widen like saucers when I set the tray on the table.

"Jaysus!" she exclaims.

"Right?"

"This ain't your mama's lobster roll," she jokes.

"They're not usually this big. I think she's showing off," I respond.

"Show off all you want, Becks. I'm not even sure how I'll get my mouth around this thing."

I choke on my iced tea.

"Are you okay? Do you need the Heimlich?" She jumps off her bench and runs over to me.

"No," I say between coughing fits. "Tea. Wrong pipe."

"Pull it together, man!"

The size of the rolls presents a challenge for both of us—not that we're complaining; we're definitely not. No one ever complains about too much lobster. More meat ends up on the tray in front of us than in our mouths. We fight over the fallen lobster and share a few bites with Kevin and Shirley, who each have a river of drool sliding down their chests. We devour all but a few chip crumbs, say our goodbyes to Becky and Shirley, and head back toward the brewery.

"Can we walk back near the road? I feel like I can't get enough of this town. The colorful buildings make me so happy."

"Of course," I reply. "I forget that not everyone has a town like ours. I'll be the first to admit that when the buildings were first painted, I wasn't a fan. But each business has really embraced it, and with the flowers complementing them, it just makes spring and summer such a picturesque time in Shearwater Cove."

"I know! When I first walked into Evvie's salon, I was absolutely tickled that the interior accents matched the hot pink of the exterior."

"Evvie really leaned in, and so did Betsy. I don't think you've been to Cam's coffee truck yet, but I love that he painted it bright lime green. It's hard to miss when you're driving through town."

"Ok, that's amazing! Maybe some day, I'll get my ass into town before he closes." Viv exclaims.

"On the next rainy day, I'll take you to see the library. Remember that anonymous donor? They allocated fifty percent of the donation to renovate the library. There probably won't be many erotic romances for you, though." I glance at Viv just in time to dodge her attempted shove.

"Oh, you're *hi-LAR-ious*. But yes, I would love to see the new library. My mom used to take me there at the start of each summer to choose my stack of books. She said it was one of my grandmother's favorite places."

"It's a date, then. And speaking of dates, when can we see each other again?" I bend a little to look her in the eye.

"Oh, really? I figured I fucked things up after the last one."

"Viv, no. Jesus. Just because you didn't want to do the things on the first date doesn't mean I'm giving up on you. What kind of monster do you think I am?" I shake my head, grab the hand not holding Kevin's leash, and spin her to face me. "I want to get to know you better—all of you. And if that includes some challenging things, I won't run away. I promise."

"Ok," she exhales like she's been holding her breath, waiting to see if I still want to see her. "I have book club tomorrow, so maybe this weekend?"

"Oh, to be a fly on the wall when you women talk about that dirty book."

Viv pushes me, and I almost stumble into the bushes.

"Friday?"

"How about you come to the cabin, and I'll feed you and tell you all my deep, dark secrets." Worry lines the space between her brows.

"Sounds perfect," I say, reaching over to tuck the hair that has escaped her braid behind her ear.

We arrive back at the brewery, and I persuade her to come in for a beer. The afternoon drifts on with easy conversation—Shawn can't help but share a few dad jokes, even though he is, in fact, not a dad. Kevin lounges beneath our stools, clearly exhausted from today's walk. I can't recall enjoying a day so much.

"What do you think of that pilsner?" I ask Viv.

"It's nice. Crisp but smooth. Dangerous because I think I could drink several. What's it called?" She subtly winks at me. I see it. I think. Did she really just wink at me? Or maybe she has something in her eye.

"Definitely dangerous. It's called Narraguagus Light Pils," I murmur. "I'm working on a Czech Pilsner next. I think you'll like that one too. Smoother and softer with a slightly fuller body."

"Hmmm. Yeah... that sounds so good." She sighs, rolling her eyes.

Jesus. Is this beer talk making her moan? That definitely sounded moan-y. Nothing could turn me on more than a woman who appreciates good beer. I look up at Shawn, whose eyebrows are raised almost to his hairline. He looks at me over Viv's head like, dude, are you hearing this? I give him a look that tells him to shut the fuck up.

"Viv, how do you feel about Farmhouse Ales?" Shawn asks.

Viv's head snaps around to me, and her eyes narrow.

"William Frederick Cooper, Jr., are you holding out on me?"

"Okay, first of all, my middle name is *not* Frederick, and secondly, you've been in this brewery like twice, and the first time, you were vomiting in the bathroom. So, we haven't exactly gotten to tour the various tap offerings. Take it you like a farmhouse?"

"Only my favorite beer style, Will. Do you brew it with any fruits?" She asks excitedly.

"Shawn, do we brew our farmhouses with fruit?" I joke.

"Well, Vivian, as a matter of fact, we do," Shawn continues.

"I'm going to fucking punch one or both of you in seconds if you don't just give me a sample of all of them." She's kneeling on her stool as if she's about ready to leap on Shawn like a spider monkey.

Shawn holds his hands up in surrender. "Okay, okay, settle down, tiny human. I'll get you your beer sampler."

Shawn places a flight of four farmhouse ales in front of Viv. We only have six taps in the brewery, and one is always reserved for the pilsner, one for the lager, and then we experiment with the other four. Right now, lucky for Viv, they're all fruited farmhouses.

I wave Shawn away so I can show off the beer creations.

"All of our Farmhouse Ales are aged in stainless tanks. Eventually, I'll do some barrel-aged stuff, but at the moment, tanks are all I've got. Number one is our Pigeon Hill Cherry. Number two is the Schoodic Point Apricot. Number three is the Wyman Wild Blueberry. And number four doesn't have a name yet. It's a recently aged Peach."

"Oh god, I love peach beers so fucking much!" Viv squeals.

"Maybe we'll call it Walker's Rock Peach?" I half grin as I look over at her. Her eyes widen and then go soft.

"Really?" she whispers.

"Yeah," I whisper back.

"I like that idea!" she declares. "Will you bring a growler of it to my place for our date?"

"Absolutely," I agree.

My phone rings, and I consider not even looking at it, but it could be Dad. When I look at the screen, sure enough, it's the old man.

"Dad, everything okay?" I ask.

"Ayuh," he responds. "Just wondering if you're close to home. I've got myself into a pickle with a project at the barn and need an extra set of hands."

"Are you trapped under anything or injured?" Viv looks at me like I have two heads for my question.

"No, son. Just need some help," I hear Dad chuff out a laugh at the question.

"Okay. Good. I'm down at the brewery, so I'll be home shortly." I hang up the phone and turn to face Viv.

"You go help your dad," she says, understandably. "I should head back home anyway. I'm sure Kevin would appreciate a soft bed and some snacks after his extremely rough day."

"Alright," I say. "I'll see you Friday night then. Does six work?"

"Sounds great." Viv hops off the stool, grabs the front of my T-shirt, and pulls me in for a quick kiss. I hear a sound coming from Shawn, and I know that if I look over at him, he'll have both hands pressed to his mouth, desperate to keep his comments on the inside. He's not usually very good at that.

CHAPTER TWENTY

Margaritas and Mask Kinks

VIV

The patio table on my back deck is strewn with the remnants of our Mexican fiesta: chips, guacamole, salsa, queso, taquitos, tacos, and, most importantly, margaritas. The Boozy Book Club gathering is now on pitcher number four of these sour and salty libations, and fueled by tequila, our debate on the current book selection grows progressively louder and more belligerent.

The meeting began with Evvie feeling completely appalled by the book choice, and I blamed Hadley for her obsession with smut. She always tried to get me to read the kinky stuff when we were younger, but I was too much of a prude. However, after what happened with Eric, I needed to escape into books that required little to no complex thought. I wanted to experience actual feelings again—and nothing sends unadulterated tingles down your spine (and to other places) like a steamy story.

"I just don't understand the point of the mask," Evvie complains.

"Jesus, Ev. It's a kink," Hadley argued.

"But why?" Evvie asks, clearly confused.

"Says the girl who's been with the same guy since sophomore year in high school," Becky chuckles.

"Bite me, Becks. Mike and I can be... adventurous."

"Your idea of adventurous is fucking on the couch when the kids are away." Becky shoots back.

"Says the girl who hasn't had sex in what...two years?" Ev taunts.

"Okay, okay," I pipe up. "The purpose of the Boozy Book Club is, first and foremost, the booze. Stop being mean to each other. Hadley, please explain to our friends the purpose of a kink."

"Me?" Hadley shoots me a dirty yet demure look—if that's even possible.

"As if you keep any secrets." I chuckle.

"True. True," Hadley laughs. "A kink is just a little somethin' extra to get your motor running. You know, like a fantasy or being dominated...

Honestly, you might not know what does it for you until you give it a try. For example, I like to be choked a little."

As if on cue, Becky chokes on her margarita.

Evvie's big blue eyes pop out of her head.

"And Vivian's—" Hadley starts before I cut her off.

"Hadley—"

"—is a little more vanilla. She likes to be called a *good girl*—but it has to be whispered softly in her ear."

"If one of you spills that little secret to Will, I promise to end you."

Becky mimes zipping her lips. Evvie throws her hands up like she wants no part of that conversation.

"I mean, a kink doesn't have to go to the extent they do in this book. There doesn't need to be knife play, creepy masks, or stalking. Just something that gives you a rush of adrenaline that makes the sexy times more exciting," Hadley continues.

"How did you discover the *good girl* thing?" Becky asks. "And why wouldn't you want Will to know if you like it so much?"

"College incident. And it's not the same if he's been *told* to say it."

"And?" Evvie says, looking between Hadley and me.

Hadley shakes her head. "Not my story to tell."

"Aw, come on, Viv!" Becky pleads. "Give me something. I need a little excitement."

"Wait," I respond, "Didn't I see you sneaking out of Shawn's tent the morning after the 4th party?"

Evvie's head snaps around to Becky. "Erm, what?"

"Nothing happened," Becky says, looking down at her lap. "I did sneak into his tent, yes. I had plans. But Shawn was so sauced that he passed out before I could make a move. I lay down next to him for a while, waiting to see if he would wake, but then I fell asleep. When I woke up, it was morning, and I left before he woke up."

"So nothing," Evvie laments. "Dammit, Shawn. Stop being such a fucking chickenshit."

"Right?" Becky sighs. "I'm done. I'm gonna join a dating app or something. My vibrator is exhausted."

"A girl's gotta do what she needs to do for herself," Hadley says. "Men shouldn't be in charge of a woman's pleasure. Especially men who are too stupid to know a good thing when it's standing right in front of them."

"Here, here," I say, lifting my margarita.

"Way to get the spotlight away from your 'college incident,' Viv," Becky chides.

I look at Hadley, and she just leans back in her chair, crossing her arms over her chest. I could smack the smirk right off her gorgeous face.

"Why do I seem to be the one always spilling my guts about shit?" I ask.

"Because, let's face it, babe, you've got a lot of guts to spill," she huffs out a laugh.

"I will torture anyone who repeats even a word of this story. Got it?" I ask, staring down at each friend until they nod in agreement. I take several gulps, finish off my margarita, and refill my glass before beginning. They all lean forward in their chairs, waiting for me to start.

"I was a freshman in college. I met him at some stupid off-campus party Hadley dragged me to."

"Sounds like you're blaming me for your actions," Hadley mutters. I silence her with a look.

"This guy was hot—like Henry Cavill with tattoos. His muscles, the hair, the chin dimple, and that whole package made it extremely difficult to look away. At one point, he caught me staring at him from across the room and crooked his finger, beckoning me to come over. He stood alone in a dim corner, looking all mysterious and delicious. Hadley and I had pre-gamed pretty hard before arriving, so I felt good—buzzy, light, and sexy. The music. The crowds. It was something entirely new for an introverted high school nerd."

Evvie and Becky lean in even more, resting their chins on their hands.

"He gripped my hips and started dancing with me, backing me into the corner, pulling me in flush to his body. I went with it, enjoying the buzz vibrating through my body. He had his knee between my thighs, sort of like they did in Dirty Dancing. I was wearing a skirt, so there wasn't much between us."

I pause to take a few more gulps of my drink.

"So we were dancing, and there's a little grinding going on, we're both clearly enjoying the bit of friction, but that's the only contact we had. No kissing or groping or anything. He bent down to my ear, his voice was low and seductive, and said, *Be a good girl and lift your skirt a little more for me.* Aaaaaand I fucking orgasmed right there. There was no hiding it, the way my body froze and then shuddered. He pulled away and looked at me with wide eyes, and I bolted. He had barely touched me. I was so fucking embarrassed I avoided him at all costs. I assume he must've been a senior because I never saw him after that year. I never even knew his name."

"Dude," Becky says.

"I know. But that's not even the worst part."

"How does it get worse than *that*?" Evvie asks, visibly concerned.

"No guy has given her an orgasm since," Hadley tells them.

"Bingo," I agree.

"Wait! Are you telling us no guy has given you an orgasm since your freshman year in college?" Becky asks.

"Oh, Becky, you think *your* vibrator is tired?" I sigh. "It's one of the reasons I broke it off with Eric. I was tired of the constant chafing associated with his half-hearted efforts to get me off. He was such a douche; if I tried to direct him, he'd just push my hand away like a petulant child claiming to know what he was doing. He couldn't have found my clitoris if Google Maps gave him turn-by-turn directions."

"Jesus. I can't believe there are more reasons than that to dump him," Evvie shakes her head.

"Yeah, he was just the whole package of steaming dog shit," Hadley comments.

"Amen," I agree.

"I truly hope Will is a considerate lover," Evvie declares, squeezing my arm.

"Ew!" Becky squeals.

"What?" Evvie asks.

"You've been hanging around with your mother-in-law too much. Totes something Betsy would say," Becky scrunches up her face.

"Ew!" Evvie repeats. "God, I need more girls' nights."

"I think we all do, babes," Hadley agrees. "Ok, so really? What did you all think of the book? Entertaining, right?"

"I had to Google some things in incognito mode," Evvie confesses.

"Same," Becky agrees. "Although I thought the main character was hilarious with the way he treated her cat like their child."

Hadley shakes her head in disbelief.

"Also, why do we need to read a book for an excuse to get together?" Evvie asks. "Can't we just have a boozy girls' night? Trying to read smut with little kids asking me two hundred questions an hour is a pain in the ass."

"Yes! I hate feeling like I have homework," Becky adds.

"Guess it's just you and me reading all the spice," Hadley says to me.

"I volunteer as tribute." I joke, with a Katniss salute.

"Oh, something else..." I continue, and all three snap their heads toward me. "Will and I have date number two tomorrow night."

All three women begin talking at once, bombarding me with questions: Where are you going? What time is it? What are you doing? And what are you wearing? When I mention that I'm cooking dinner for Will, Hadley emphatically shakes her head in disapproval.

"Viv, you know I love you, but if you're interested in Will sticking around long enough to take his shirt off again, please, for the love of god, get some takeout."

Evvie and Becky nearly fall off their chairs laughing. I might need to make a new plan for our date now. Admittedly, my cooking skills are not particularly impressive.

"Okay, smartass," I bite back at Hadley, "What do you suggest?"

"Oh, you definitely don't want my suggestions," she says with an evil smile.

"Right. What on earth was I thinking? How about you, Becky? Any ideas?"

"Girl, if I were in your position right now with Shawn, food would be the last thing on my mind. I think his poor dick would fall off from overuse."

I blow out a breath and bury my face in my hands.

"It's okay, Viv," Hadley says, rubbing my back in gentle circles. "Get some takeout from the Cafe and enjoy yourself. He's not expecting anything you're not ready for."

Chapter Twenty-One

What We Leave Behind

WILL

> WILL: HEY, DO YOU WANT TO COME TO MY HOUSE FOR OUR DATE? I JUST PUT MY DAD ON A BUS TO BOSTON TO SEE HIS BROTHER FOR THE WEEKEND.

> VIV: THAT SOUNDS GREAT. CAN I BRING KEVIN?

WILL: I'LL BE SAD IF YOU DON'T.

VIV: EXCELLENT.

WILL: DOES THIS MESS UP YOUR COOKING PLANS?

VIV: NAH, I WAS PLANNING ON TAKEOUT FROM THE CAFE. MARY'S MEALS ARE MUCH MORE EDIBLE THAN MINE. ARE YOU OK WITH THAT?

WILL: THAT'S PERFECT. I'LL GO PICK SOMETHING UP.

VIV: GREAT. WHAT ELSE SHOULD I BRING?

WILL: HMMMM...

WILL: TOOTHBRUSH?

VIV: HMMMM...

WILL: STOP.

VIV: THINKING.

WILL: VIVIAN.

VIV: YOU WANT ME TO SLEEP OVER?

WILL: YES.

VIV: WHAT IF YOU FIND ME COMPLETELY REVOLTING AFTER OUR TALK?

WILL: IMPOSSIBLE

VIV: WE SHALL SEE...

Mary outdid herself with the meal she prepared for us. It's a seafood bake that simply needs to be put in the oven, and she assured me that if I followed her directions exactly, the dish would turn out perfectly.

I hear Viv's Jeep rumble to a stop in front of the house, and I trot outside to help her with her things. I'm sure Kevin's overnight bag is probably bigger than hers. She lets the dog out of the car, and he rushes over with a polite greeting, quite different from our first meeting. I'm glad he has added me to his list of non-tackleables. When I look over at Viv, her mouth hangs open in surprise.

"You okay, Viv?" I ask.

"Will," she whispers, "Your house is breathtaking."

"I wish I could take credit for it. My dad built it in the late eighties. He's incredibly proud of it."

"As he should be. What's your Dad doing in Boston?" Viv asks.

"His younger brother, my Uncle Charlie, lives just outside of the city and asked my dad to come down for the weekend for a Sox game," I reply.

"Oh, fun! I love any chance to visit Fenway," she exclaims.

"You're a baseball fan?"

"Duh, how do you grow up in the Boston area without living and dying by how the Sox are doing?"

"I guess that makes sense. Come on, let's go inside, and I'll give you the tour," I say, touching her arm and picking up her very light overnight bag. She grabs Kevin's giant bag of belongings and follows me inside.

As we walk to the house, Viv continues to ooh and ahh over the exterior—the welcoming front porch with the handmade Adirondack chairs Dad constructed a few years ago, and the sprawling flower gardens scattered around the property, with fieldstone pathways connecting each one. Dad's strengths are carpentry, mine are keeping the plants alive. I find gardening almost as soothing as crafting beer recipes.

"I'll give you a full tour of the gardens another time. Dinner's in the oven and will be ready soon." I say to distract her from all the pretty flowers.

"Okay, but what's with that area over there?" She asks, pointing to an overgrown field. "Seems weird that you have all these pretty flowers, and then...*that.*"

"*That* is my daisy field. They just haven't bloomed yet."

Her eyes go wide. "You have a whole field of daisies? My absolute most favorite flowers? Will! I can't wait to see it!"

"It's quite a sight when it's in full bloom," I say, rubbing the back of my neck. "Come on, dinner now, flowers another time."

She follows me reluctantly into the house, and we kick off our shoes in the small foyer. She unclips Kevin's leash and threatens him with bodily harm if he misbehaves. She enters the main living area and gasps loudly.

"Will! Oh my god, this room is a dream. That fieldstone fireplace! And oh, I love the cathedral ceiling with the beams. Look at that view!" She slowly turns in the center of the large room, taking it all in. "That kitchen! Holy shit! It's designed for a professional chef. Why do you have it?" She looks at me with a half grin as she traces the gray veins on the marble-topped island.

"HA-HA, funny, Viv. Actually, my mom was quite the cook. She loved hosting dinner parties, but her true passion was baking. Food was her love language. Dad built this kitchen just for her."

"That's so sweet. I wish I had met her. She sounds like a pretty amazing woman," she compliments.

"She was. I miss her." I feel Viv's hand on my arm as she rubs my bicep.

"I know exactly how you feel."

"You certainly do," I agree, squeezing her hand in response.

"Okay, the meeting of the sad saps is officially over. Where should I put my things?" she asks.

"Since I don't have a guest room, I guess you'll have to stay with me." My smile spreads wide, showing off my dimples. Look, I know the effect they have on women, and I'm not afraid to use them, especially for Viv. I notice her eyes darken, and a pink flush rises on her cheeks. Mission accomplished.

"My dad and I are at opposite ends of the house. He's down that hallway in the original master suite he shared with my mom," I say, pointing to the left of the kitchen. "The loft above the kitchen is where my office is, but it's a complete disaster, so you are *not* going up there."

"You're no fun," she chuckles.

"At your size, you could vanish amidst the piles of paperwork up there and not be found for months. And my room is this way," I say, leading her towards the right side of the house.

The oven timer rings to signal that dinner is ready, so we drop off Viv's bags and head back to the kitchen. Kevin follows us from room to room, unsure of where to settle. She runs back to the bedroom to grab his travel dog bed and plops it on the carpet in front of the fireplace. The dog chuffs as if to say thank you and turns a few times before relaxing.

Viv climbs onto a stool at the island while I take the dinner out of the oven. The golden-brown seafood bake sizzles, and we both groan at the mouthwatering aromas wafting from the dish.

"This smells divine! What is it?"

"It's Mary's famous seafood bake. She prepared it for me with detailed instructions so I didn't fuck it up in the oven. It's lobster, scallops, and shrimp in a lobster bisque-style sauce, topped with Parmesan bread-crumbs. And also, because Mary cares about our nutrition and, apparently, our eyesight, she gave us some roasted carrots."

"God, it all sounds so orgasmic! I can't wait to put it in my mouth."

"And I can't wait for you to put it in your mouth," I say with a wink.

I serve the casserole and carrots into the bowls and grab the growler of Walker's Rock Peach I brought home from the brewery. We eat at the table without much talking. But we groan. We drink. We groan. We eat some more. We groan louder. We complain about being too full. We make a mental note to thank Mary profusely.

"Damn, that was the best meal I've eaten since I've been here," Viv praises.

"Totally agree. Why don't you take your beer to the couch, and I'll get the leftovers into the fridge."

As I link my phone to the Bluetooth system, a soothing playlist flows through the house.

"Ooooh, who's this? I've never heard this song before." Viv asks over the back of the couch.

"It's The Maine. Can't even remember how I came across them on Spotify, but it's good, right? This song is called "thoughts i have while lying in bed.""

"Nice. I'll have to check out more of their stuff."

When I join Viv on the couch, she nervously chews on her bottom lip. I can tell she's anxious about sharing her story. I pull her closer, wrapping my arm around her shoulders.

"Would it help if I told you about my past with my ex?" I ask, trying to comfort her. I feel her nod against my shoulder.

"I met Melanie six years ago on one of Tiny's fishing charters. His old boat accommodated more people, so every so often, if I had time, I'd help him out. The charter consisted of a group of coworkers from Bangor on a team-building fishing trip. I could tell from the start that Melanie was not up for a day at sea. We had barely made it fifty yards from the dock when she started to look green."

Viv pushes herself off me to sit facing me, listening to the story.

"While Tiny handled the people who were fishing, I tried to help Mel manage her seasickness. Tiny keeps a stockpile of remedies, and we tried them all: ginger, peppermint, acupressure wristbands, Dramamine, deep breathing, focusing on the horizon—nothing worked. She felt so miserable and embarrassed. But I stayed with her, telling her silly stories to try to distract her from her discomfort. By the time we made it back to shore, she felt well enough to scold her coworkers for choosing such a terrible team-building exercise. Then they piled into their cars and drove off. I didn't even get a thank you."

"A couple of months later, she showed up in Steuben asking where she could find the guy Tiny with the fishing charter. They gave her directions to Shearwater Cove, and I ended up running into her at Earl's. I was so confused. She told me she felt terrible for not thanking me after the char-ter—that if it hadn't been for me, she might have thrown herself overboard to end her suffering. She mentioned that she had quit her job and was in need of a fresh start. She said she couldn't stop thinking about me during the past few months. I mean, she was beautiful, and I had thought of her often as well. She didn't seem prepared for life in a small town like this one, but neither of us paid any attention to that warning."

"We clicked immediately and spent all our free time together. She found an apartment nearby and secured a remote job. After nearly a year of dating, we decided to move in together. Everything was great for a while—until the pandemic. Then everything fell apart between us when the world shut down. She resented living in a small town. She resented having to socially isolate. She resented me, making that clear every day. She blamed me for keeping her in what she called 'a miserable, boring excuse for a town,' which hurt. I told her that if she didn't like it, she could leave. She thought

I would follow her, but I didn't. And that was that—it ended as quickly as it started." I shrug, unsure of what else to say.

"Well, she sounds high maintenance," Viv says, after a long silence. "And possibly prone to making impulsive decisions."

"You have no idea," I laugh, though there's an edge to it. "We were only together for two years, but it felt like a lifetime. At the time, I didn't recognize the impact she had on my mental well-being, especially after the world shut down. It was only after she left that I could finally breathe again, but part of me wondered if I should miss her more."

"I appreciate you sharing your story, Will. Have you heard from her over the years?" she asks.

"Nope, she made it clear on her way out that there would be an ice age in hell before she ever set foot in this town again. I have no idea where she is or what she's doing, and I intend to keep it that way."

"So, what you're saying is that you don't have a hidden desire for her to come back into your life?"

"Definitely not. My current desire is sitting right next to me," I say, my voice unexpectedly huskier than usual. I'm about to glance up to see if Viv understands my meaning, but before I can raise my head, she's crawling into my lap.

"We'll finish our conversation in a minute," she commands. "Right now, I want you to kiss me."

How can I say no to that? I pull her closer, and our lips collide. The spark that's been smoldering in my chest all evening now bursts into a full-on blaze. Her position straddling my lap only intensifies those flames, and I'm sure she can feel it. I hope she can feel it. I want this woman. Badly. But I'll wait for her to make the first move. I'll wait for her to be ready for all of me.

CHAPTER TWENTY-TWO

Fun Bags and Red Flags

VIV

I reluctantly pull away from Will's warm lips because if one of us doesn't stop this freight train, we're going to end up naked before I get the chance to reveal my secrets. I continue to straddle his lap as I search his eyes for any signs of doubt.

"Viv, I'm not going to change my mind," he says. "I really want to support you in any way possible. And I don't want you to be scared that I'm going to flee. I've never been a runner."

I exhale a long breath, which I hadn't realized I was holding, and Will raises one finger as if signaling for me to hold on a minute.

"One more thing," he starts. "If you continue to sit on my lap like this, I'm not sure I'll hear anything you say over the rush of blood through my veins."

I laugh and slide off him, sitting cross-legged while facing him. He turns slightly toward me, one knee resting on the cushion in front of me. His arm snakes across the back of the couch, and I weave my fingers through his, using him as a lifeline.

"So, you know my mom died of breast cancer. What you might not know is that both my grandmother and great-grandmother also died from the disease. Both were relatively young."

Worry creases Will's forehead. "Viv, are you—"

I cut him off. "I'm not sick. But for the last ten years, I've been so worried I would get it too. I've had so many mammograms that my breast size was a DD-flat. Each time, it came back clear. I did genetic testing, and the results were clear. But the fact remained that I came from three generations of women who succumbed to the disease. No doctor could tell me what my future held—and I sought second, third, and fourth opinions. Finally, one of my mom's new doctors suggested that I just schedule a double mastectomy and call it good. No one had ever given me that option."

"I immediately set the plan in motion. My mom was incredibly supportive and thrilled to know I wouldn't endure the same agonizing suffering. I met with the surgeons and the reconstruction team, and my spirits soared—like a weight had been lifted off me. I was making the best decision to secure a

long and healthy life, along with peace of mind. I felt that almost immediately."

Will squeezes my hand and reaches his other hand to wipe the tears I didn't
realize were rolling down my cheeks.

"The only thing left to do was make sure Eric would be able to help
out, knowing that it would be two weeks of a pretty awful recovery. The
conversation did not go well."

"I was setting the table for dinner one night and said, *So, I have a date
for my surgery.* And he responds, *Surgery? What surgery?*" I shake my
head, reliving the most ridiculous conversation that has ever happened.
"I told him, *the double mastectomy I told you about, to make sure I don't
get breast cancer?* Oh, he thought I was joking. He believed that because
I had cleared genetic testing and all my mammograms, I wasn't pursuing
anything further. All I wanted was to give myself a chance to live past my
50s. I also wanted to get rid of the double Ds that just weighed me down."

I glance up at Will to see his eyes as wide as saucers. "Put your eyes back
in your head, Cooper. They killed my back. I couldn't wait to get rid of
them."

"Eric's brain functioned like nothing I had ever seen before. He accused
me of *getting rid of the thing he loved most about me.* Yeah. You heard that
right. All he cared about were the fun bags—not one ounce of his dark
soul cared about my health. He couldn't stop citing the clear tests I'd had
over the years as a reason for me to reconsider. And then things got a little
nasty."

Will's hands ball into fists, and I know that if he ever came face-to-face with Eric, he'd break his nose. "What an asshole," he mutters.

"I say to Eric: *So you're willing to risk my life just so you can fondle a set of giant knockers?* He walked out of the room without answering. When he returned, he told me he wouldn't be able to take time off from work to play nursemaid, even though I hadn't even given him the dates yet. You wouldn't believe how angry I was. We spent the next several hours battling."

"Did he hurt you, Viv?" he asks.

"Physically, no, but every point I made about all the things I did for him during the years we were together—listening to him complain about everything, supporting him through the pandemic when he was at his lowest. He responded with pure selfishness every time. It was always me, me, me. He whined about me spending too much time with my mother. I was slowly losing her to the ravages of a terrible disease, and all he could think about was how it affected him."

"I hate this guy," Will says.

"The final straw was when I said I thought we were a team that supported each other. Do you know what he said to me? He said, *my team has big tits, Vivian.*"

Will's mouth hangs open.

"I know, he's a diseased ball-sack. But something occurred to me as I slammed the bedroom door on him. He never did anything for only me—never bought me flowers or told me I looked pretty or gave me an orgasm."

My timing is impeccable. That last comment comes just as Will takes a big swig of beer, which immediately geysers all over the floor.

"Jesus Christ, Viv," Will laughs, beer dripping from his chin. Would it be weird if I leaned over and licked that off his chin? Maybe another time.

"So, I said, sayonara, sucker, and moved in with my mom. I didn't want to place the burden of being a nurse on her in her weakened state, so I decided to postpone the surgery until after she was gone. At that point, we knew she had only a few months left, and I wanted to spend as much time as possible with her. It truly was the best decision of my life."

Will is quiet. He just stares at me, as if he wants to say something, but he needs to find the exact right combination of words. He whispers, "Are you okay now?"

"I think so," I say, wiping away more tears. "It's taken me a while to overcome the crippling grief I felt after my mom passed away. But also, to let go of the intense anger I feel towards myself for wasting so much time on such a pig."

"So, did you just take off and never see that guy again?" Will asks, slightly confused. He knows exactly what he's doing when he changes the song to Taylor Swift's "The Smallest Man Who Ever Lived." It's just what we need to lift the mood again.

"He tried to call me. When he came home from work and found Kevin and me gone, he left me about 137 messages, so I blocked him. I left him a note with the ring on the table, asking him to please kindly shove the ring up his ass." I shrug and finish off my now-warm beer.

Will pushes a hand through his hair. "God, Viv, I'm so sorry you dealt with all that stuff by yourself."

"Oh, no. I stayed with Hadley after my surgery. She took time off and was there for me every step of the way. Some of those steps were not very pretty. She emptied my drains like a champ, took me to follow-up appointments, and made me delicious soups. Most importantly, she did everything for Kevin. I couldn't walk him for months. She's my true love."

"She's a good friend," Will says, suddenly looking nervous. "Can I ask you something?"

"Of course, shoot."

"Did your ex really never give you an orgasm?"

I blow out a breath. "Nope. His only concern regarding an orgasm revolved around himself. So, I did the bare minimum since that was his approach. And became a very good faker. Honestly, Will, I'm not sure anyone could get me off at this point in my life. I'm destined to be pleasured only by my trusty vibrator, Rip."

"You named your vibrator?"

"Why wouldn't I? I need to scream someone's name, and Rip is a good, manly cowboy, so..."

"Rip? From Yellowstone?"

"Do you know another Rip?" I ask.

"I can't believe I'm having this conversation with you."

"You asked."

"I'd like to give it a try," Will says, his voice low and huskier.

"Huh? Try what? Rip? Damn, Will, didn't know you had it in you."

"Fuck, Viv. No. An orgasm. I bet I could get you there."

"Oh, really? Those are some very confident words, Mr. Cooper."

"Come here," he demands.

"Wait. So you're completely okay with looking at some hideous boob scars? And you're not mad about my much smaller rack?"

"You could be completely flat, and I'd still want you like crazy."

"Oh fuck... kiss me, Will Cooper."

"Is that all you want me to do?"

"Let's start there."

He pulls me back to my spot on his lap. He stands, and my legs try to wrap around him. It's difficult when you're vertically challenged. He kisses every inch of my neck as he walks us to the bedroom. I look back to make sure Kevin isn't trying to follow us because that would be... awkward.

Will effortlessly tosses me onto his expansive California king bed, my body landing with a soft bounce on the plush mattress, almost propelling me off the other side. We both dissolve into a fit of giggles, our laughter echoing around the room like a pair of mischievous teenagers terrified of being discovered.

"Hold on a sec," he says, running back to the living room. He comes back with his phone, and I peek over his shoulder to see him searching for a song. I love that he feels the need to pair music with the occasion.

There must be speakers in every corner of this bedroom because I'm immediately enveloped by the opening notes of Matt Nathanson's "Run". I look at Will, and my eyebrows shoot straight up to the middle of my forehead. This is, without a doubt, the sexiest song on the planet. He's going all out in his quest to make me come, and I have zero problems with that. My heart starts racing, and I'm having a hard time taking a deep breath.

Oh god.

Will stands and pulls me to my feet. I watch him slowly unbutton his shirt and shrug it off, leaving him in a white tee, jeans, and bare feet. Gahd. And then no white tee. Gulp. I watch him reach for the hem of my sweatshirt and slowly pull it off over my head.

He licks his lips as he gazes lazily at me in a cropped tank top and cut-off jean shorts. He runs a finger down the front of my body, between my breasts, to the edge of my tank. I might melt into a puddle faster than Frosty in the greenhouse.

A sharp gasp escapes my lips as he swiftly removes my top, leaving me bare from the waist up. A pleased hmmmm escapes him when he discovers I'm not wearing a bra. My fingers hungrily reach for the zipper of his jeans, but he swats my hand away. "Not yet," he whispers in a low, husky tone just below my ear before softly kissing me there. His hand slides to my lower back, slowly guiding me onto the bed. He hovers above me, one elbow supporting his weight, surrounding me in a haze of lust and expectation.

"So beautiful," he murmurs. As he gazes, I trace the lines of the compass rose on his chest, feeling him shiver beneath my touch.

Will unfastens my shorts and leisurely slides them off. He groans when he realizes I'm not wearing any underwear tonight. He pauses to look, then begins to touch. His hands explore every part of my exposed skin. Being laid bare before him is liberating in a way I never anticipated. I have no desire to cover myself. Perhaps it's the way his eyes turn the color of a stormy sky, or the way his breath feels as it puffs onto my skin... whatever the reason, I feel a deep tingling sensation at the base of my spine. Could it be?

CHAPTER TWENTY-THREE

Hit Me With Your Best Shot

WILL

All I can do is look. And touch. And admire. All she's been through, she's opening herself up to me—trusting me. I don't see scars; I see bravery. I don't see broken; I see badass.

"Will," she sighs.. She reaches up to pull me down to her mouth. I cage her head between my elbows, trying not to crush her beneath me, at least, not yet. But I can feel her arching up into me.

Not exactly sure how much longer I'll be able to stay trapped in these jeans, but I want this to be about her. After our talk, I can't think of anything I'd rather do than worship this woman. I kiss her mouth. I kiss her neck. I kiss a line to her breasts when I feel her tense under me.

"Viv. Let me," is all I say.

She nods. I kiss her scars, trailing down to her hip bone. A swirl of my tongue elicits a faint gasp. I lick a path to her inner thigh, and when I feel her hands in my hair, I glance up at her, questioning.

"Give it your best shot," she breathes.

Is she challenging me? I have never been one to run away from a challenge.

Her inner thighs become my current obsession as I shower them with intense kisses and licks, savoring the silky skin that smells of fresh air and lavender soap. Her body reacts with subtle squirm beneath my touch. Without hesitation, I delve to her center, and the air around us fills with her explosive, breathy gasps, followed by the hypnotic repetition of my name. Each syllable makes me harder as I continue my relentless worship, kissing, sucking, and licking with an insatiable hunger, driving her to writhe and twist on the bed in pleasure. In this moment, I realize I could spend forever here, lost in this paradise between her thighs.

Her fingers tighten in my hair, the grip becoming increasingly firm, signaling that I must be on the right track. Her breaths come in rapid, shallow bursts, so close to the edge of hyperventilation. Seizing the moment, I thrust deeper with my tongue. Her body responds with a sudden jolt, a tremor running through her as waves of sensation ripple outward. I don't move, allowing her to experience every sweet wave of her orgasm on my face.

When she pulls me back up her body to crush her mouth on mine, I can't help but smile smugly against her lips.

"Will," she whispers, "That was— I'm not sure I have words. Amazing. Surprising?"

"Surprising?" I ask, confused.

The look she gives me says it all.

"You mean, he never..." I say.

"Nope."

"Did you ever ask...?"

"Yup. He scrunched up his face and made a gagging noise."

"Mature."

"I know," she says, shaking her head. "Will..."

"Hmmm."

"You have too many clothes on." She waggles her eyebrows at me.

"Be my guest."

Her eyes flicker with a sudden, intense darkness as she reaches forward to unbutton my jeans. The soft rasp of the zipper resonates through the now quiet bedroom. She scatters kisses across my chest, tracing the thin lines of my compass rose tattoo with her tongue, igniting even more fire within me than I can handle. She kneels at the foot of the bed, her movements deliberate and teasing as she peels my jeans off and adds them to the growing pile of discarded clothing. Clad only in my boxer briefs, my desire for her stands boldly at attention.

Viv greedily pulls my boxers off, finally freeing my hard-on from its cotton prison. The look on her face can only be described as pure lust. And then she sees it. The mystery tattoo I alluded to.

"Will Cooper!" She sits back on her knees and points at my upper thigh. "Is that a mermaid tattooed on your upper thigh?"

She falls back onto the bed in a fit of giggles. Well, this is going swimmingly.

"I lost a bet."

"Who made you do that to yourself?"

"Shawn."

"Oh, well, that makes perfect sense," she chuckles.

"It's a long story."

"And not one we have time for tonight." Her smile disappears, and her green eyes turn feral. Oh boy, she's not planning on wasting any time. She disappears behind a curtain of hair as she leans over my lap, and I feel her lick the entire length of my dick, and I almost lose it right there.... It's been... *a while*. I gather her hair in my fist so I don't miss another minute. I must find a distraction to keep me from blowing my load like a twelve-year-old who just discovered the joys of jerking off into a sock. Right, socks. Dirty socks. Stinky socks.

When her mouth slides over my tip, all thoughts leave my head. I'm pretty sure my brain followed closely behind. Holy shit. She takes me in one deliciously agonizing inch at a time, and I'm not sure what happens next because I think I black out. Her tongue swirls, and when I hit the back of her throat, I'm done. Ruined. And scene.

She looks up at me and wipes the corners of her mouth with her thumb and forefinger. Her lips twist into a dark, amusing smirk. "Well, that didn't take long," she says. "I must be spectacular at that." A quick raise of her left eyebrow is the only clue to her teasing.

"I was in the same boat," I say, shrugging.

"Wait, your ex didn't—"

"Nope. She generally didn't go much out of her missionary-position comfort zone."

"Well, she missed out."

She pulls the covers over us and nestles into the crook of my arm, draping her arm across my body. I hug her close, thinking that nothing could beat this date. We lie there in silence for a while, sated, quenched, and happy—until we hear the faint sound of Kevin whining outside the bedroom door. Viv moves to get up, and I stop her.

"You stay here; I'll get him. I'll be right back." I lean over and kiss her quickly. The beauty of living where I do? I could let the dog out stark naked, and no one would care. And it's precisely what I do. I got a funny look from Kevin, but maybe it was just him saying, 'Yeah, buddy, way to go!'

"Did you take the dog out naked?" Viv asks as I jump back into bed.

"Why wouldn't I?"

"Because... I don't know... people?"

"People don't venture this far up the road if they know what's best for them. I have a standing agreement with everyone that you cannot pass the storage building without confirming with me."

"Well, that sounds friendly."

"Some folks don't mind a pop-in. My dad and I are not those folks." I say with a shrug.

"Are you nudists?" she asks, laughing.

"Maybe?" I joke.

"So what do you want to do now?" She asks.

"Good question. Dessert?"

"I thought that's what this was." She purrs, waving her hand between the two of us.

"Okay, second dessert, then."

"Yes."

"Without the whipped cream attack."

"I can't make any promises." She says, jumping out of bed and grabbing my discarded white t-shirt from the clothing pile.

Fuck me, she looks good in my shirt. I pull on my boxers and follow her to the kitchen.

We build hot fudge sundaes that are equally as obnoxious as the ones we ate on our first date. We give Kevin a little bowl of whipped cream for being such a good boy while Mommy got her orgasm. We cuddle up as close as two people can on the couch and still manage utensils without clanging elbows. I honestly can't remember a time when I've felt so at peace, so at ease with a situation. Viv is so easy to be around, just like when we were kids, and she integrated seamlessly into our group, as if she were meant to be a part of us.

"Are you as exhausted as I am right now?" I ask, taking our bowls to the sink.

"Oh my god, I'm so glad you said it first. I didn't want to seem like a loser for wanting to go to bed."

"I can't think of anything I'd rather do more than snuggle under the covers with you in my arms. It has nothing to do with me not being used to all this... *physical*... activity."

"Wow!" she exclaims. "From the looks of those muscles, I thought you'd be in better shape."

She squeals as I throw her over my shoulder and head to the bedroom.

CHAPTER TWENTY-FOUR

What Safe Feels Like

VIV

I wake up in my new favorite place—nestled against Will's warm, muscled body. Yes, I love it even more than waking up with Kevin's furry frame smushed against me. I might even love it more than ice cream. His deep breathing tells me he's still asleep, so I use my time wisely. I prop myself up on one elbow and gaze at his beautiful face. I don't often have the chance to study him like this without him knowing.

His silky, dark brown hair is longer on the top than on the neatly cropped sides, creating a perpetually tousled and effortlessly charming look. The urge to run my fingers through those soft locks takes every ounce of my willpower to resist. One of his dark eyebrows sits slightly higher than the other, adding a hint of mischief to his resting expression. With his eyes closed, the long, luxurious lashes resting against his cheeks create a shadow that seems almost sinful. Why do men always have such enviable lashes? His bottom lip, slightly fuller than the top, is irresistibly pouty and just begs to be nibbled on—perhaps that's the perfect way to wake him. His usually neatly trimmed beard has grown thicker than usual; the extra length adds a rugged charm. I'd like to think it's because he took my compliment to heart when I admired the extra length a couple of weeks ago.

Lost in the memories of last night, I feel his gaze on me as he slowly opens an eye, watching me while I study him. The early morning light barely filters through the curtains, and it's clear neither of us is quite ready to start the day. With a gentle shift, he rolls onto his side and draws me close, pressing me against the warmth of his firm, naked body. The sensation of his hard, morning form against mine is irresistible, and I press even closer with a slight wiggle. His hand, strong but tender, finds its way to my hip, gently halting my eager movement.

"Don't start anything you don't plan on finishing, Vivian." He whispers in the most delicious, husky morning voice that makes me desperate to, in fact, start something. I move against him again.

"Vivian." He warns. Pressing my luck is fun.

"Will." It comes out breathy.

Before I can even move again, he's got me pinned underneath him. Wow, he's quick for a big guy who just woke up. His lips find mine, neither of us caring about morning breath. And now I'm turned on. I mean, I've never been one for morning sex, but mainly because Eric the dickhead refused to do anything involving bodily fluids before teeth were brushed and bodies were washed.

The grind of Will's hips snaps me back to the moment, and oh, hey there, big fella. His deep growl when I wrap my legs around him sends a surge of desire through me. And yes, sir, I am all in for morning sex. If this is what he wants to remember as our first time, abso-fucking-lutely. He leans over to the nightstand and starts rummaging. What the...?

"Will," I interrupt.

"Hmmm."

"What ya looking for?" I say, rubbing my hands over his very well-sculpted pecs.

"Condom."

"Don't bother."

"Oh, so you don't—"

I cut him off. "Oh, I do. I'm on the pill."

"Ah, that's... good. So good." He's above me now, eyes the color of storm clouds focus on me. "Are you sure?"

"Will, I swear to god, if you're not inside me in the next three minutes, I'm literally going to die." I think our date last night awakened something deep inside me.

It's definitely less than three minutes. It's probably even less than a minute. He slides into me so agonizingly slow that I start thrusting my hips against him. He just smiles at me.

"You're very impatient, babe." Babe. I'm dead.

Just as he's entirely inside me, and I wonder if it's possible to lose consciousness from too much pleasure, he kisses up my neck and sucks my earlobe into his mouth, sending shivers everywhere. When his hips start to move again, I'm lost in my head at the exquisiteness of the whole situation. I almost don't hear him when he whispers during one particularly mind-blowing thrust. "That's a good girl. Take all of me."

And I'm done. Finished. Demolished. Obliterated. Eradicated. Annihilated. Liquidated. I come harder than I have in my whole sexually pathetic life. Okay, I am definitely now one for morning sex. I'm going to fly a banner over the cabin about how much I love morning sex. A few thrusts later, Will follows my destruction.

"Holy fuck." He breathes out.

"You can say that again."

"That wasn't a figment of my imagination, was it?"

"The sex, or the mind-blowing orgasm?" I ask.

"Both. I guess."

"Totally real. And totally amazing." I say, unable to persuade my limbs to start working again.

"Totally." He agrees, rolling onto his side with a roguish smile ghosting his lips. "Do we have to get up?"

"I need a shower in the worst way," I say, slipping out from under him to get cleaned up.

I'm rinsing the shampoo out of my hair when he steps into the stall, looking quite sinful. He backs me against the wall of the shower, and I notice that he's definitely ready for round two. It lasts so long that our skin becomes pruned like a raisin by the time we finally emerge from beneath the cooling spray.

Will and I spend the next two days relaxing on his back deck, reading, talking, eating, talking some more, drinking, and eating some more. We spend the evenings curled into each other in Will's bed, alternating between binge-watching *Ozark*, which he's never seen, and fucking like sex-starved teenagers.

Kevin feels the exact opposite about being here. He lopes around the house, annoyed at being pulled away from his swimming spot. Hadley texts often, mainly to make sure we're hydrating and to find out when I'm coming home. I've been gone for just the weekend, and she's acting

WHAT SAFE FEELS LIKE   225

as if I've abandoned her for weeks. If anyone is doing the abandoning, it's her—she's been spending nearly every night in Cameron's bed.

Ping.

> HADLEY: OK, SLUT. WE NEED A GIRLS-ONLY NIGHT. I'VE FORGOTTEN WHAT YOU LOOK LIKE.

> VIV: WHO YOU CALLING SLUT, HUSSY?

> HAD: WE HAVE MUCH TO DISCUSS.

> VIV: INDEED.

> HAD: ARE YOU COMING HOME SOON?

> VIV: WILL'S GOING TO PICK HIS DAD UP AT THE BUS STATION AND GRAB DINNER FOR US. I'LL BE HOME IN THE MORNING.

> HAD: LATER, HO.

Kevin and I explore Will's flower gardens while he's off picking up his father, and he tries to pee on almost all the pretty flowers. I jerk his leash, letting him know to find somewhere else, and he looks at me as if I just kicked him.

"Oh my god, Kevin. We're going home tomorrow, and you can swim as much as you want. Such a sour puss this weekend. Also, I'm telling Will you're trying to murder his flowers with your urine."

He lets out a soft grunt and continues to sniff each blade of grass in search of the perfect one to defile.

Will and his dad arrive home with pizzas and beer. Kevin nearly pulls me right over, trying to tackle the stranger he hasn't met yet. Before we settle around the table, Bill bends down to scratch the dog's neck, gives me a big, warm hug, and whispers his condolences before he pulls away.

"Thank you, Mr. Cooper," I say, releasing him.

"I think you can call me Bill, kid."

"Well, thank you, Bill. Mom never told me that you two kept in touch. I appreciate you checking in on her over the years."

"Of course. Maggie was a good friend," he says sadly. "And she helped me get through some grief of my own when Will's ma passed."

We spend the rest of the evening enjoying pizza and listening to Bill elaborate on his time in Boston and the Red Sox game. He mentioned that their seats were on the Green Monster, much to his delight, and they even saw Big Papi signing autographs in the stands.

Bill checks out, saying he's worn out from his wild weekend. We take Kevin for an evening walk and head to Will's room for more binge-watching. I drag Kevin's bed into the room with us so maybe he'll stop being so mopey. What I didn't expect was for him to jump on the bed and squeeze his large body between us.

"I guess Kevin makes the rules tonight, and I think this means hands off my mom tonight, pal." I joke. I can see that Will is mildly annoyed that he is not able to pull me into his big spoon.

"That's cool, Kev. Don't think I'll forget this subtle cock-blocking act. Probably for the best. I'm not sure I can trust you not to wake up my dad with your moans of pleasure." His grin widens, showcasing his deep, dazzling dimples that appear when he's being a smart-ass. I'm ready to crawl over my dog to ride Will like a mechanical bull when he looks at me that way. Instead, we prop ourselves up on the pillows to see what shady business dealings Marty Byrde is involved in now.

CHAPTER TWENTY-FIVE

Boil, Cool, Kiss

WILL

The last few weeks with Viv have been the happiest I can remember. We spend nearly every morning on one of our decks, drinking coffee and doing Wordle together, and every night, if Hadley hasn't abducted her for some no-boys-allowed evening, we're entwined on the couch. We generally save our raucous sexcapades for when we're alone at her house. For one, I don't need my dad to hear any part of that, and two, with Hadley spending more and more time at Cam's, the cabin is all ours. It's also better for Kevin's mental health, as he tends to become irritable when he's unable to swim at his leisure.

We've spent a lot of time exploring the trails that my dad and I have cleared over the years around our 52-acre property with the pup, taking picnic lunches to scenic spots whenever I wasn't busy with work. We enjoy day trips in Viv's topless Jeep to nearby tourist destinations like Schoodic Point and Prospect Point Lighthouse, which we view from across the harbor since it's an active U.S. Navy installation. And we finally made it to Lunch on the Wharf for lobster rolls. We both agree that while their roll is nearly perfect, Becky's still holds our top spot.

We celebrated Amelia's fourth birthday with a small pool party at Mike and Evvie's at the end of July. Kevin enjoys a good party, especially one with a pool and ten little girls fawning over him. Despite his young age, he's remarkably good with kids. They grab at his tail and ears, tightly hug his neck, and drape their tiny bodies over him. He does more than simply tolerate it; he loves all the attention.

Hadley and Cam joined us for many dinners. Viv is trying to spend as much time as possible with her best friend before school starts, when she has to head back south. While we're thrilled for their happiness, I worry about how Hadley's departure will affect Cam. He's never been lucky in love, and the way he looks at her suggests he's fallen for her hard. Historically, his son Luke has been tough on Cam's love interests, but not on Hadley, which I'm sure contributes to his growing feelings.

But mostly, we talk—we talk so much, trying to fill the gaps of the last eighteen years. She shares the struggles of her mom's illness while balancing school and caregiving. She reflects on the times when her mom was in re-mission, during which they made elaborate travel plans that never came to fruition. She also expresses how nervous she felt throughout her twenties at the thought of developing breast cancer. We discuss how much she missed her summers in Shearwater Cove and how she wished her mom could have enjoyed one more summer here before she passed away.

I shared with her the loss of my older brother, Silas, and the impact the events of September 11th had on him as he was entering his teenage years. He joined the Marine Corps' Junior Reserve Officers' Training Corps in high school and left for basic training a week after graduating. My parents begged him not to enlist, knowing how deadly the war in Iraq had been, but nothing could change his mind. Shortly after completing boot camp, he was deployed to Fallujah and tragically lost his life to an IED. Everything happened so quickly, and my parents and I were left in a state of shock for a long time. I tell her that meeting her that summer was a bright moment in an otherwise dark period of my life.

She enlisted my help to assess what work needed to be done on the cabin. We created a prioritized list, and I shared the names of reputable contractors for each task. She joked that Earl still recommends him as a handyman, and I mentally noted that I should ask him to stop. I assisted her in ordering wood for the colder months and built a rack to store it, keeping it sheltered under the front porch roof.

I installed a couple of security cameras around the property, even though we haven't heard anything else from that asshole ex of hers. Hopefully, he was just trying to scare her. Mission accomplished if that's the case. With extra deadbolts installed and cameras she can monitor from her phone, she feels comfortable leaving Kevin home alone again.

It's been an incredible few weeks, and I look forward to what our future holds if she does, in fact, commit to staying in Shearwater Cove.

Viv's out with the girls tonight, so I'm heading to the brewery after hours to get started on the new Czech Pilsner I've been planning all summer. I finally think I have the perfect recipe, and once I arrive at the empty building, I begin heating the water to mash the grains. Once it reaches the right temperature, I add the grains to soak for an hour. I love a deserted brewery—no one to ask me questions or give me shit.

I connect my phone to the Bluetooth speaker and crank up The 1975. The upbeat notes of their popular yet volatile song, "Love It If We Made It," fill the small taproom. I turn on my laptop and open a planning document for my next beer. I recently found some oak barrels that were used to age tequila through a contact in Portland, so I'm planning my first barrel-aged Gose, which I think Viv is going to freak out over.

After the grains have soaked, I begin boiling the wort, setting timers for when I need to add the Saaz hops. The first addition is after thirty minutes for the bittering, so I head to the storeroom to check the canning inventory and find I'm nearly out of four-pack can carriers. The timer alerts me for the next step, and I add the initial batch of hops to the mix and set the timer again.

My phone chimes.

VIV: OPEN THE DOOR.

Hmmm, bossy tonight. She must be feeling tipsy. I head out to the tap-room and stand near the door.

> WILL: BUSY.

Banging on the front door.

> VIV: ANGRY.

Teasing Tipsy Tinkerbell is one of my favorite pastimes. She gets riled up so fucking easily.

> VIV: WILL.

More door banging.

> WILL: HOLD, PLEASE.

My timer goes off, and I add the next batch of hops to the mixture; this one is for flavor. The scent of hops has become one of my favorites.

> VIV: IF YOU DON'T LET ME IN THIS INSTANT, I'M GOING TO PEE MY PANTS. AND THEN I'M GOING TO DISMEMBER YOU.

> WILL: SOUNDS LIKE YOUR POOR PLANNING IS NOT MY EMERGENCY.

> VIV: OH MY GODDDD.

Door kicking.

> WILL: BABBLING BROOKS.

> VIV: ASSHOLE.

I may have gone too far. She's starting to sound pissed, so I unlock the door, and she sprints past me as quickly as she can with her thighs pressed together. I can't help but laugh at the way her feet flail out to the sides as she runs.

"I thought you were with the girls?" I ask as she walks past me after a trip to the ladies' room, slapping my ass in mock anger. It only revs my engine.

"I was. I figured I'd walk over here to get a ride home with you," she says, climbing onto a stool at the bar. "I didn't know you were a fan of The 1975. God, I love this song."

Of course, she does. "Sex."

"I like this song too," I say, raising my eyebrows and grinning at her. She smacks me in the chest, and I feign injury. "So much violence tonight."

"Oh, stop. You love it when I'm rough," she jokes, pulling me in for a quick kiss. Down, boy. We still have work to do.

"I hope you weren't in a hurry to get home. I've got another hour or so here before this new beer is ready to ferment for the next few weeks." I'm anxious to complete my tasks now so I can get her back to the cabin.

"Oooh, can I watch?" she asks, bouncing a little on the stool.

"Of course, come on out back with me. Bring your stool." I hold the door open, and she drags her bar stool to where my wort is boiling. "I thought you'd be out with the girls until much later."

"Evvie got a call from Mike. Amelia wasn't feeling well, and she wanted Mommy. So we just called it a night. And now I'm glad because I get to see this," she says, pointing to the bubbling liquid.

"Pretty cool, right?"

"So cool. And kinda sexy," she murmurs the last part, but I hear her, and it makes my heart race just a little. If she keeps this up, I'm going to have to scrap this batch.

The timer goes off.

"What's that for?" She asks.

"The last batch of hops needs to be added. For aroma." I reply.

"Then what?"

"Then it needs to boil for a bit longer," I say.

"Then what?"

"The wort, which is this boiling stuff, needs to be cooled quickly."

"How do you accomplish that?" She asks, now fully invested in the process.

"I have an immersion cooler that does the trick. My last step tonight is to add the yeast and store it away for fermenting."

"Then what?" She asks, smirking because she knows asking too many questions drives me insane.

"Then I take you home and fuck your brains out," I growl, trapping her head between my hands and kissing her hard to punctuate my last statement. I feel her go soft in my hands, leaning into my mouth and nearly falling off her stool again. She grabs hold of my belt buckle to pull me closer and twines her arms around my neck, deepening the kiss. I'm sure she can feel how serious I am about what I plan to do to her after we finish here. She pulls away, wide-eyed, and I see the pink flush creep into her cheeks in the bright lights of the brewery.

"Well, Mr. Cooper, I do believe your not-so-little friend fancies a little playtime," she teases, lightly running her palm over the front of my jeans—good lord in heaven. I've never dated a woman who made me feel like I could come in my pants with just the briefest touch. But then again, none of those past women were Vivian.

The teasing persists as I finally get the wort ready to ferment. By the time we leave the brewery, *I'm* ready to ferment. We barely make it home without ending up naked in the truck. I pull her from the passenger door, tossing her over my shoulder to a cacophony of squeals. Kevin meets us at the door, needing to go outside. So I latch his leash on with my free hand and carry a shrieking Viv back outside. While Kevin does his business, she beats at my back with her tiny fists, begging to be let down.

Back in the house, Kevin returns to his spot on the couch with a satisfied sigh. Good boy, no cock-blocking plans tonight. I take Viv to the bedroom and dump her on the bed. I strip down to my boxers, enjoying the ravenous look on her face when she sucks her lower lip into her mouth. Her devilish eyes darken to more of a pine green color as I crawl after her on my hands and knees, gripping behind her thighs and pulling her underneath me.

CHAPTER TWENTY-SIX

What Happens in Portland...

VIV

While I sit on his bed, Will packs for an overnight trip to Portland that he's been very secretive about. I closely observe the items he loads into his bag, trying to gather a clue about what the actual fuck he's doing down there. He claims he's going away on business, and when I asked if he wanted some company, he declined. I was surprised he turned me down. Lately, he's been eager to spend all our time together, so of course, my stupid self-confidence seems to have gone on vacation, and now I think something is off. Does he suddenly need some alone time? Does he have a side piece down south? I hate secrets, and it's killing me that he won't spill them.

Will chatters on, asking me what I have planned for the rest of the day. He promises to be home by dinner tomorrow and inquires if I need anything in Portland. *Yes, jerkface, I need to come with you!* echoes in my head, so I'm super glad he's not a mind reader because the inner voice that just yelled that sounded like a spoiled brat.

I flop back onto the pile of pillows and stick out my bottom lip at him in an exaggerated pout. "We haven't spent many nights apart lately. I'm just going to miss having a warm, hard body curled around me."

He climbs over me on the bed and sucks my pouty lip into his mouth. I grip his t-shirt and keep him there while I try my best to convince him to cancel his trip.

"Vivian," he mumbles against my mouth. "I have to go if I'm going to get to all my meetings."

"Okay, okay, I'm going. See you tomorrow," I say with a quick peck on his cheek.

I text Hadley before leaving Will's to see if she can keep my poor, lonely ass company this afternoon. Plus, our time together is getting shorter as the start of school approaches. I hate to see her go. She's really connected with the folks here, and I know she's dreading the day she has to leave Cam behind.

> VIV: HADDY, WHERE ARE YOU?

HADLEY: ON MY KNEES.

VIV: JESUS CHRIST, HADLEY.

HAD: YOU ASKED.

VIV: I REALLY WISH I HADN'T.

HAD: I'M DONE. HE'S DONE. WHAT'S UP?

VIV: WILL'S GOING AWAY FOR THE NIGHT.

HAD: YOU DON'T WANT TO BE ALONE.

VIV: NOPE.

HAD: BE THERE SOON.

VIV: YOU'RE THE BEST.

HAD: THAT'S WHAT CAM SAYS.

VIV: STOP.

Like our early summer days, we sit on the back deck overlooking Narraguagus Bay with our books and our drinks. She regales me with the various sexual positions she has tried in the past week, and some sound familiar. For example, I may have read them in a recent book club book. Poor Lucas—I hope his bedroom is soundproofed or in another zip code. I wish my entire brain were soundproof right now.

"So, what's going on with you and Will these days?" she asks.

"You know what's going on. Same as you, minus the kinky bondage room I'm positive Cameron has in his basement. Things are good. I'm happy, Haddy."

"I know, Viv. I haven't seen you smile this much, well, ever. He's really good for your soul."

"And my vagina." I laugh.

"That's my girl," Hadley chuckles. "But honestly, it's like ever since we met, there's been a dark cloud hanging over you—first with your mom's illness, and then with assface. It's just nice to see my best friend blissed out over a guy."

"Back atcha, babe," I say, squeezing her hand. "Had, what are you going to do when it's time to head back to Plymouth? Have you and Cam talked about that at all?"

"Every time I try to bring it up, he changes the subject. I don't think he wants to think about it, even though I'm due to go home in a couple of weeks. It's going to be hard to leave. I think my feelings for him are kinda big," she sighs.

"Ever thought about staying?"

"Only every damn day."

"What's stopping ya?"

"I guess just my commitment to teaching those budding artists." She says with a slight air of sarcasm.

"I'd love for you to stay. We seem to have a good thing going here. We're both happier than we've ever been. We've found good, kind men, Hadley. That's not something to take lightly." I say.

"You know, Viv, I think I was worried you wouldn't want me to stay, so hearing you say that makes me so happy."

"Hadley! How could you ever think that?"

"You have Will now. He's your go-to now, your confidante."

"You shut your whore mouth right now. You know there's shit I cannot talk to Will about, that only you can help me with." I move over to Hadley's lounge chair and hug her tightly. "I honestly think you staying in Shearwater Cove would make my life perfect."

Hadley blows out a breath. "Okay, then. Let's see how Cam feels about the idea."

"My guess is he'll be thrilled."

Evvie arrives after lunch with the girlies, and they quickly put on their life jackets to join Kevin in a game of who can create the biggest splash off the end of the dock. The 80-pound lab certainly wins that contest—he has perfected a doggie-belly-flop to an Olympic level. Evvie, Had, and I sit along the edge, dangling our feet in the water while the girls squeal in delight at Kevin's antics. They imitate his frantic doggie paddle as they race him back to the dock.

"Ev, kinda seems like the girls would love a dog of their own," I say, nudging her shoulder.

"Mike keeps threatening to surprise them with a puppy, but damn, we've got enough on our plates right now with running two businesses and chasing two kids. I mean, he's off to Portland tonight, and I'm already feeling overwhelmed without him here to help."

"Wait," I start. "Did Mike go to Portland with Will?"

"Yeah, Will didn't tell you?"

"Will was treating this trip to Portland with a CIA-level of secrecy. I got next to no details." I huff.

"Oh my god," Evvie laughs. "That is such a Will move. He must be down there organizing something for you!"

"Me?"

"Uh oh, Viv. I wonder what it could be?" Hadley splashes her feet in the water with excitement.

"Oh, please." I scoff. "I doubt it has anything to do with me. Honestly, now that I know Mike is with him, I feel so much better."

"Did you think he was meeting a woman?" Hadley asks.

"Maybe?" I reply sheepishly.

"As if, Viv. I've known Will almost my whole life, and he's never cheated on a girlfriend, and I've never seen him this happy." Evvie adds.

"That makes me feel better," I exhale.

"You gotta remember the piece of shit she was with last, Ev." Hadley snarls.

"Speaking of that piece of shit, have we heard anything from him since his July 4th threat?" Evvie asks.

"Oddly, no. But Will installed security cameras around my property just in case. We're still not letting Kevin out off-leash in the dark, either."

"Good, that makes me feel better about you being out here alone," Evvie says. "Hey, I thought Becky was joining us this afternoon?"

"She texted that she'd be a little late—something to do with staffing at the restaurant. Any movement with her and Shawn?" I ask.

"Cold honey runs downhill faster than Shawn moves in a romance," Evvie jokes, and we all laugh.

"Poor guy. What's jamming him up?" Hadley asks.

"I think you know that they dated briefly in high school. By the time Shawn got up the nerve to ask her out, senior year had just started. Becky starts applying to colleges, and Shawn gets pissed because he doesn't understand why she wants to go away when they just got together. And then Becky gets pissed because she feels like he's trying to control her and squash her dreams. So Shawn pulls away, trying to backpedal on some of the stuff he said. Then she breaks up with him because she says there's no way long-distance would work for them. It was an absolute mess. Really fucked with our group dynamic for almost our entire senior year." Evvie recounts.

"My god, if that doesn't sound like both of them," I laugh.

"Right? They would be so good together now, and I know Becky wants to try again, but he's such an idiot." Ev says.

"What can we do?" Hadley asks. "I mean, I've been here for less than two months, and I didn't have a problem."

"Amen to that!" Evvie and I say in unison.

"I mean, maybe it's going to take old school manipulating—telling Shawn Becky likes him and telling Becky Shawn likes her. Like we're a bunch of children." I shake my head at the fact that this is even necessary.

"Shawn is a huge flirt, but when Becky's in the vicinity, he turns into a mute," Hadley observes.

Kevin lifts his head from where he's drying off in the sunshine on the dock at the sound of a car. I give the girls a look, signaling the end of our current conversation topic. We need to develop this plan before putting it into motion. Evvie's kids scurry out of the water when Becky arrives, giving her soggy hugs before jumping back in. Becky strips down to her bathing suit and leaps in, chasing after them and grabbing at their little legs as they scream and giggle.

"Oh my god, I needed this dunk," Becky exclaims, floating on her back in front of us. "The restaurant was so nuts we almost ran out of lobster."

"Sounds like a good day," I say.

"I'm gross and sweaty, and I need a drink. Someone promised me a margarita." Becky says, pulling herself onto the dock.

"Amelia! Olivia! Time to get out of the water!" Evvie yells. She's met with considerable protest, but the girls exit the water nonetheless.

As Hadley and I prepare a fresh pitcher of margaritas, Evvie helps both girls into dry clothes and settles them on my couch with Kevin to watch *Frozen*

2. After spending so much time in the water, they're likely to be asleep within minutes. The four of us sit at the large round deck table under the umbrella. The westerly winds from the Bay today create a perfectly glorious day for lounging. As summer begins to wind down, part of me looks forward to being in Shearwater Cove for the fall colors.

"I have a question," I say, sipping my margarita. "The summer flowers around town look so great with the brightly colored businesses. But what happens in the fall when the color scheme changes?"

"Oh, Viv, be careful whom you ask about this topic. There are some strong feelings around here," Evvie says. "It's not easy to pair fall-colored mums and pumpkins with a bright pink building. We all tend to prefer white, pink, and yellow mums, steering clear of deep reds and oranges. There's a guy not far from here who grows white pumpkins, and we buy them all. It's definitely a complete pain in the ass. And don't even get me started on Christmas!"

We spend the afternoon chatting about everything: my plans for the cabin renovation and Hadley's plans with Cameron. Both Becky and Evvie are excited to hear she's considering relocating to the Cove. Evvie can't wait for school to start so she can take a break from the girls. During the summer, she works by appointment only, allowing her to spend time with her daughters, so she's looking forward to being in her salon more.

Olivia wanders out to the deck. "Mommy, the movie is over. Can we go home?" I check my watch, and it's almost dinner time. Oops, we completely lost track of time, as we often do.

"Of course, baby. Is your sister asleep?" Evvie asks. Olivia nods. "I guess that's my cue to get these two home." She scoops up Olivia and carries her into the house.

We follow her inside to help gather and carry everything while she takes the sleeping Amelia to her SUV. As we assist Evvie, Hadley's phone rings, which is strange because who even talks on the phone anymore? When she hangs up, the expression on her face indicates that she's needed somewhere else.

"Everything okay?" I ask across the driveway.

"Viv, Cam just received a huge order for the bakery for tomorrow, and he asked me to come back to help him. I really hate leaving you here alone."

"Had, I'll be alright. I've got my bodyguard here to protect me if needed," I say, nodding toward Kevin. Although at the moment, he's trying to bite his own tail, so I really hope his services aren't needed.

"You'll call me if you need anything?"

"I will," I assure her.

"I think I'm going to head home too," Becky adds. "I'm exhausted. Hadley, are you okay to drive?"

"If you don't mind dropping me off, that would be great," Hadley says.

"Yup, I'll meet you at my car." Becky hugs me and heads out.

After Kevin and I have dinner, I take him outside for his post-dinner bathroom ritual. As we walk around the house, I'm sure I see something rustling in the trees. It's so dark out here that it's hard to tell if the sound is made by an animal or a person. However, the fur on Kevin's back stands up, and I hear a low growl that I know signals danger. After he finishes his business, we quickly retreat to the house. I rush around, making sure that all the windows are shut and locked and that the deadbolts are secured on the doors. Sensing my fear, Kevin doesn't leave my side. I take out my phone.

> VIV: WILL? I THINK SOMEONE IS OUTSIDE.

He responds instantly.

> WILL: DID YOU LOCK EVERYTHING?

> VIV: YUP. I WAS OUT WITH KEVIN. HE STARTED GROWL-ING AT THE TREES. MAYBE A CRITTER?

> WILL: COULD BE, BUT JUST STAY INSIDE AND MAKE SURE THE CAMERAS ARE ACTIVE. I'LL CALL SHAWN TO COME OVER.

> VIV: CAMERAS ARE ON.

I had barely hit send when I get an alert from one of the cameras. I open up the feed and can just make out the outline of a figure against the darkness.

VIV: WILL! THERE'S SOMEONE OUT THERE. I JUST SAW THEM ON THE CAMERA. SHOULD I CALL THE COPS?

WILL: FUCK. HOLD ON FOR TWO SECONDS. MAKE SURE YOUR CURTAINS ARE CLOSED.

VIV: YEAH, THEY'RE ALL CLOSED.

WILL: I JUST TEXTED SHAWN. HE'S GONNA COME AND STAY UNTIL I GET HOME. HE'LL BEAT THE COPS, SO DON'T BOTHER. PLUS, HE'S PRETTY MENACING IN THE DARK.

VIV: K. KEVIN IS STICKING TO ME LIKE GLUE, SO I FIGURED IT WAS SOMETHING.

WILL: GOOD BOY. I'LL BE HOME BY LUNCH TOMORROW.

VIV: JUST HAVE SHAWN TEXT ME WHEN HE GETS HERE.

WILL: WILL DO. HANG IN THERE. GRAB THAT OLD .45-70 IF YOU NEED TO SCARE SOMEONE.

VIV: YES, BECAUSE IT WAS SO SUCCESSFUL IN SCARING THE SHIT OUT OF YOU.

WILL: I WAS PETRIFIED.

VIV: WHEN WILL SHAWN BE HERE?

WILL: HE SAID FIVE MINUTES. I'LL STAY ON THE PHONE WITH YOU UNTIL THEN.

VIV: THANK YOU. I'M A LITTLE FREAKED OUT RIGHT NOW.

CHAPTER TWENTY-SEVEN

Footprints and Fuckery

WILL

Waiting for Shawn to arrive at Viv's to reassure me that everything is okay is a special kind of torture. It's hard for anyone from away to pass through Shearwater Cove without being noticed and endlessly discussed, so if someone is out at Walker's Rock, they must have come by rowboat for Viv not to have heard them. If I find out it's one of the hoodlums Luke hangs out with playing some prank, I might blow a gasket.

"I had a thought. Does Luke still hang around with those kids that Cam thinks are troublemakers?" I ask, my fist tightening around the beer bottle in front of me.

"Sometimes. I think Cam's thrilled that Luke is working for Becky this summer and not hanging out at the park docks with them—idle hands and all. I've caught them a few times skulking around the marina, not realizing I have cameras everywhere. Earl told me he's caught them shoplifting at his place. They don't even live in Shearwater Cove."

"Jesus. Do you think they could've ended up at the cabin?"

"I don't think so, but it's worth looking into. The father of one of the kids keeps his boat at the marina, so I've talked to him a couple of times about it. He just waves me off, like *boys will be boys*, which pisses me off so much. I've concluded they're just rich kids with very little supervision or responsibilities, and not much is going to change."

"Why does this shit happen when I'm away?" I ask Mike as we sit at Flatbread Pizza's bar. If we both hadn't already had several beers, I would suggest we head home right now.

"Murphy's Law, my friend," Mike says, holding up his beer in a mock toast.

"Murphy sucks. Shawn better be on his way over there or I'm going to lose my shit," I curse.

"Despite some of his quirks, Shawn is a loyal friend who'll drop everything to help out. You know that," Mike says.

"I know, I just—" I'm cut off by the ping from my phone, relieved to see it's from Shawn.

SHAWN: I'M HERE.

I show Mike the text and then quickly text Viv to let her know Shawn has arrived, so she won't be freaked out by him tripping the cameras. Mike nods as if to say, *I told you so, dummy.*

WILL: AND?

SHAWN: I'M WALKING THE PERIMETER. SOME FOOT-PRINTS, BUT NOT SURE IF THEY'RE NEW.

WILL: CAN YOU CHECK THE DOCK?

SHAWN: YOU THINK SOMEONE CAME BY BOAT?

WILL: IT'S THE ONLY EXPLANATION IF NO ONE SAW THEM IN TOWN.

SHAWN: MUDDY FOOTPRINTS ON THE DOCK, BUT NO BOAT.

WILL: SO SOMEONE COULD'VE BEEN THERE.

SHAWN: YEAH.

WILL: FUCK. CAN YOU STAY WITH HER?

SHAWN: OF COURSE.

WILL: I TOLD VIV YOU'RE THERE.

SHAWN: I GOT IT, WILL. STOP WORRYING.

WILL: CAN'T HELP IT. FEEL HELPLESS BEING 3 HOURS AWAY.

SHAWN: SEE YOU TOMORROW.

"Do you mind leaving early tomorrow?" I ask Mike. "I'm feeling very helpless right now, and I don't like it one bit."

"Of course," he replies. "Do you think it could be Viv's ex trying to scare her?"

"I almost hope so. Between you and me, I'd really love to punch that guy."

"Oh, I get it. And I'm sure Evvie will be ecstatic to have me home earlier than expected. She texted me earlier with a picture of the girls." He holds up his phone, showing a photo of both girls, zonked out, in their car seats. "She took them to Viv's to swim, and they spent a couple of hours jumping off the dock with Kevin."

"Damn, those two are cute," I say. "I'm glad they all got together today. Viv wasn't happy about being *abandoned*, as she put it."

If my heart rate and anxiety don't decrease, I'll never be able to sleep tonight. I'm glad that Mike and I were able to get everything we needed today so that we can hit the road early tomorrow. Also, being in the 'big city' really makes me appreciate the quiet life in my small town. My contact for the tequila barrels really came through for me with three of them. I'm excited to get back to the brewery and craft a recipe for this new barrel-aged beer.

I also purchased something extra that I've wanted for a while, so it's a good excuse for my trip since the new beer will be a surprise for Viv. I've been eyeing a used Grady-White for some time and found a great deal on a Fisherman 180 in Falmouth, which I also purchased. Mike came with me to take a second look, and aside from some cosmetic fixes, the hull and outboard seem solid. It's just a simple 18-foot center console for Viv and me to explore the islands in the area and maybe do a bit of fishing. We'll have it in the water before Labor Day for sure.

Mike and I make it home from Portland in record time. I drop him off, leave the boat and trailer at my house, check on Dad, and immediately rush to Viv's. She must have heard the crunch of gravel because she's out the front door and launching herself at me like a tiny missile as soon as I step out of the truck. The comfort and relief I feel when she wraps her legs around my waist and hugs me is as if a weight has been lifted off my shoulders. I look up to see Shawn, who salutes me as he walks to his car, and I mouth a *thank you* over Viv's shoulder.

I carry her into the house, desperately trying not to trip over Kevin, who also looks very happy to see me. I'm exhausted, and I just want to strip off my clothes and take a long nap, cuddled up to Viv.

"I barely slept last night, even with Shawn on the couch," she whispers.

"Me neither," I whisper back. "Let's take a nap."

"Is that code for something, Cooper?" she asks with a laugh.

"This time? It's code for I'm exhausted."

"Me too. Let's nap," she agrees.

When I open my eyes again, it's mid-afternoon, and I'm starving. Viv is still sound asleep, and I manage to untangle myself without waking her. I find nacho fixings and prepare a big batch of cheesy chips. She's just waking up when I return to the bedroom with snacks and iced tea for us. She narrows her eyes at me.

"Nachos in bed, Will? I just put fresh sheets on the bed. Do you want to be sleeping in crumbs tonight?" She asks, concerned.

"If I'm sleeping with you, I can weather a few crumbs. Or maybe you could not eat the chips like Cookie Monster eats cookies," I chuckle.

She playfully smacks me on the chest, but there's no further protest about eating nachos in bed. We really should inspect the area around the cabin while it's still daylight, so we both throw on some clothes. Kevin is happy to get out of the house after being cooped up. I see the footprints Shawn mentioned—and I know they're not mine, Shawn's, or Mike's because none of us have feet that small, and they look fresh. We make our way down to the dock, and Viv gasps when I share my theory.

"So, someone came by boat?" She asks.

"Looks like it. Shawn told me last night there were some muddy prints down here. I didn't want to freak you out too much. I can put a camera with good night vision down here, too, if you want."

"Yeah, I think that's a good idea. Fuck me, why can't I just enjoy my life without someone trying to fuck with me?" She asks, clearly frustrated.

"Do you think it could be your ex?" I ask.

"As far as I know, he wasn't exactly a boat guy, so I'm not sure. Or maybe he hired someone to scope out the place. That's more his speed. If he could hire someone to do his dirty work, he'd be all for it."

"Alright, let's go with that. If this hired help found what he needed, then he's probably long gone," I comment. "But just to be on the safe side, can you text me a picture of him that I can share with Mike and Shawn?"

"Yeah, I'll dig one up," she says, chewing on her bottom lip. "I may have deleted them all after I left, so I'll see what I can find on social media."

"Would you feel more comfortable if we stayed up at my house for a few days?" I ask.

"I would. I just don't think I can relax here until we figure this shit out."

"Sounds like a plan. Why don't you go in and pack a bag, and I'll look around some more to see if I can find any clues."

"Okay, Columbo," she quips.

Of course, Dad is thrilled to have the company, especially Kevin, to whom he has developed an unhealthy attachment. He often complains that they don't visit enough. He immediately takes Kevin's bag and bed from Viv and informs us that he will be in charge of the dog during their stay. Viv raises her hands in surrender after handing over the items. She looks over at me as if to say, *Should I be worried?*

I tug Viv closer and whisper, "Let him have this. I think he's been feeling useless since the doctor clipped his wings, and he has more free time than he knows what to do with."

"I'm sure Kevin will love being the center of attention, especially since he's away from his personal swimming hole. But I'm feeling a bit hurt by how easily he just left me behind."

"Awww, is your baby growing up? He doesn't need his mommy anymore," I tease. "At least if he's sleeping at the other end of the house, I don't have to worry about him cockblocking me again."

"Now, who's being unreasonable?" Viv teases back.

I grab her around the waist and pull her close, kissing her. She parts her lips, inviting me in deeper, but then pulls away unexpectedly.

"What's wrong?" I ask, as I feel the concern marking my brows.

"Nothing, I just don't want to do this... here," she says, gesturing around the living room.

"Sorry," I say, pulling her back to me and groping her ass. "I just can't help myself around you." She giggles a little too loudly, which brings my Dad back to the living room.

"Is everything okay? I thought I heard a scream." He asks, Kevin's right on his heels. I hide my hands behind my back like I'm a teenager again, getting caught trying to get to second base.

"Fine, Dad. Viv's just a little too ticklish." I roll my eyes.

"Sounded like someone was torturing a chicken out here," Dad says with a smile, and Viv rolls her eyes at the remark.

"Viv and I are planning to meet friends out tonight. Are you okay with Kevin considering we're back here because someone was lurking around the cabin?"

"Dumb question, son. I have weapons, and I know how to use them. Go have fun. We'll be fine." Dad assures me as he and Kevin head to the couch to watch television.

"Two peas in a pod," Viv says, smiling at the lounging duo.

"Why are we going to the brewery?" she asks.

"We're meeting Mike and Shawn to discuss the recent events at the cabin."

"And to ply me with beer so maybe you can take advantage of my drunken state later?" She asks, one eyebrow raised.

"Really, Viv, is the drunken state essential?" I tease.

"Nah, but I really want some beer. Lots of that yummy Walker's Rock Peach, please."

"Okay, okay, let's go, sweets."

CHAPTER TWENTY-EIGHT

Bang, Bang on the Door, Baby

VIV

Will and his friends huddle to discuss my creepy stalker while I enjoy my delicious peach beer and make plans to bring the rest of our crew to the brewery tonight, since I need some fun. After last night's events, I need to be surrounded by my friends, plenty more beer, and loud music. The guys are so engrossed in their conversation that they don't notice me flitting around the taproom, my nose buried in my phone.

GROUP TEXT with EVVIE, BECKY, HADLEY, VIV:

VIV: LADIES! COME TO THE BREWERY!

EV: ISN'T IT PAST CLOSING TIME?

BECK: YOU WANT ME TO PUT ON HARD PANTS?

HAD: BUSY.

VIV: UNACCEPTABLE.

EV: I HAVE CHILDREN.

VIV: GET A BABYSITTER.

BECK: I'M ALREADY IN MY PJS.

HAD: BUSY.

VIV: SUCK IT UP BUTTERCUPS. GET YOUR ASSES OVER HERE.

EV: GOD, LET ME SEE IF BETSY'S FREE.

VIV: HADLEY JANE, PUT YOUR CLOTHES ON AND BRING THAT FOX WITH YA.

BECK: NOPE. I'M TAPPING OUT.

VIV: SHAWN'S HERE, LOOKING FINE.

BECK: GODDAMN ALL OF YOU.

The banging on the front door captures the guys' attention. They all look up, concern creasing their brows, undoubtedly wondering who on earth is trying to get into the brewery after hours. Before any of them can get up to check, I sprint to the front door.

"Vivian!" Will yells, stomping toward me. "Do not—"

I grab the knob and unlock the door.

"—open that door." But before he can reach me, I fling it open and let the group inside.

"It's just our friends, silly," I say to his perplexed face. "We're gonna have a little party!"

"A what?" Will asks.

"Come on, Cooper. Don't be a killjoy," I whine. "I had a bad night, and I need fun." I wrap my hands around the back of his neck and toy with his hair. I know this move usually turns him to liquid, and I'm not above using it to get my way.

"Fine. Fine. Okay." He says, pulling my hands into his and kissing each palm. "I know this is tough on you. Have your beers with our friends."

"Yay!" I stand on my tiptoes, giving him a kiss that lingers a beat too long.

"Where are the kids?" Mike asks Evvie.

"Viv was pretty adamant about us all being together, so I figured I'd just leave them alone since they were asleep."

"Are you insa—"

"Your mother came over. Jesus, you're so gullible." Evvie laughs and grabs a beer from me.

I connect my phone to the Bluetooth and blast Pink's "Raise Your Glass," and the guys all collectively groan. Hadley grabs my hand and twirls me until I can barely stand. Becky chugs the beer in her hand and joins our dancing. We sing at the top of our lungs.

The song changes to Flo Rida's "Low," and Evvie excitedly flips her hair and body rolls down the front of her husband, leaving his mouth agape. Hadley makes some extra crude dance moves in the vicinity of Cam's crotch that might be better suited for a stripper pole, followed by some surprisingly impressive twerking.

"Oh shit," I hear Mike murmur to Shawn as I twirl past them. "This is not going to end well."

"Dude, maybe you'll get extra lucky and fuck somewhere other than your bed tonight," Shawn teases loudly.

"Ohhhh!" I yell, holding up my beer in a mock toast.

"Fuck off. All of you." Mike shakes his head and leans against the bar, arms crossed, and his crystal blue eyes never leave his wife's suggestive dance moves.

"Hey, Shawn, tell me the story of Will's mermaid tattoo!"

Shawn's eyes go wide. "No. That's a story for Will to tell.

"Come on!" I whine.

He makes the lip-zipping motion and says nothing else.

I love it when we're all together, having fun. No worries about someone trying to break into my cabin. No worries about a boyfriend judging my poor decisions. Now, if we can get to the bottom of this rando lowlife creeping around my cabin, I can get on with my new and improved quiet life in Shearwater Cove. I'm lost in my thoughts, watching my friends enjoy themselves, dancing around like fools, when someone commandeers the Bluetooth and changes the whole vibe in the room. When I look at Will, the way his mouth hitches up on one side tells me he's responsible.

The elegant, haunting notes of Lord Huron's "The Night We Met" drift through the taproom, enveloping the room. Will strides confidently across the scarred wooden floor, his eyes locking onto mine as he draws me into his arms. I glance around, taking in the scene of our friends paired off, swaying softly to the music's rhythm. Even Shawn and Becky are together, though there's a slight gap between them, reminiscent of couples at a middle school dance. My breath catches as Will's fingers weave into my hair at the nape of my neck, his other hand pressing me closer against him, resting at the small of my back. Our difference in height is a bit awkward for slow dancing, but it hardly matters as the warmth of his presence surrounds me. With my face buried in his chest, I inhale the sweet, familiar scent of pine and hops and lose myself to our movement. Will bends to my ear, brushing the shell with soft lips.

"Want to get out of here?" he whispers. His tongue flicks along the outer edge of my ear, and a jolt of desire shoots up my spine.

"One hundred percent," I purr.

"Shawn, lock up when you guys are done here?" Will asks.

"Oh, wait a goddamn second!" Evvie scolds. "You drag us down here to party, and now you're bailing on us?"

"Have you seen my sexy boyfriend?" I ask, nodding my head toward him. "Unless you want to witness something you'll never be able to unsee, you'll be happy we're leaving."

Hadley pushes Cam to the front door hurriedly. "Yeah, we're out, too."

"I have a fucking babysitter, people!" Evvie whines.

"Babe, let's go down to the Cafe for a nightcap," Mike suggests, which seems to please Evvie.

"Later, losers," Evvie yells as they bolt out the door.

"Alrighty then. Guess it's back into my PJs for me," Becky says.

"I can drive you home if you want," Shawn offers quietly.

"That would be great. And, um, the safe thing to do," Becky replies.

Will looks like he's about to make a snide comment, so I elbow him in the ribs and give him my shut-the-fuck-up look. It's like seeing animals in the wild—don't make any sudden moves, or they both might flee in opposite directions.

"Well, that's weird," I say.

"What's weird?"

"Weren't we about to leave everyone behind? Now we're alone," I say with a sly smile.

"Well, look at that, we *are* all alone." Will slowly backs me up until the bar stops our progress.

He lifts me effortlessly, placing me on the bar so our mouths are level. Gently, he nudges my knees apart and steps into the space between my legs. I wrap my arms around his neck and lock my legs around his waist, holding him close to me.

"I think this might be my favorite place to be," he murmurs.

"In the brewery?" I ask.

"Between your thighs with you wrapped around me. I mean, I prefer this position minus the clothing, but right now, I'll take what I can get." He presses his lips firmly against mine, and our tongues twine, each exploring stroke slow and deliberate. I groan into his mouth and feel him undeniably harden against me.

"Let's go home," I whisper into his mouth.

"And try to be quiet with my dad there? Hell, no. You cannot be trusted, and also, I've fantasized about fucking you on this bar for months now."

Fuuuuuuuuck. I glance over his shoulder to make sure the window blinds are closed up tight.

Our clothes quickly fall to the ground in a pile, and he draws me toward the edge of the sleek, polished bar top. As our bodies press against each other, I can feel the heat and electricity between us, and seeing this man shirtless doesn't help the situation. I can't help but admire the sculpted ridges of his body that always seem to invite my fingers to explore. His muscles flex under my touch, warm and unyielding as I trace my favorite tattoo on his chest. His firm, well-toned arms hint at years of hard work rather than a gym obsession.

His gaze sweeps over my body with an intensity that sends a shiver down my spine, and a low, appreciative moan escapes his lips. His index finger gently glides across the raised, pink lines of scars that bisect the front of my breasts, tracing each mark with a tender touch.

"I could look at your naked body all day," he rasps.

"Even my ugly scarred boobs?" I ask, my voice barely audible.

"Especially your badass scars and battle-tested boobs. There's nothing ugly or less about any part of you, Viv."

His teeth graze my neck, igniting anticipation and eagerness within me. Holding me tightly, he gradually enters me, and together, we release a shared gasp. He stills momentarily, giving me time to adjust to the overwhelming sensation, then moves in slow, rhythmic pulses as I cling to him.

"Oh my god." It comes out of him in a breath. "Don't move. Stay very still. Or this is going to be very quick."

I can't help but roll my hips with a devious grin, and a low, husky growl rumbles from his throat. His eyes lock on mine, a faint sheen of sweat visible on his brow.

"Vivian..."

"Will... oh god, that feels so good. More."

"More, what?" I feel his smile against my cheek.

"You. More of you," I say, and he starts a more delicious movement, bringing us to the brink.

"Oh, Viv…" he groans and softly says, "I love you."

Excuse me?

"What did you just say?" I ask, releasing my grip on him. We're still connected, but all movement has come to a complete stop. I study his face to see if I can detect any bullshit, but his beautiful face reveals only honesty, his gray-blue eyes sincere.

"I'm sorry," he responds, nervously raking a hand through his hair. "Too soon?"

"Say it again," I demand, needing to hear it again.

"I love you."

"Again."

"I love you."

"Show me."

His movements become increasingly frantic, a desperate urgency powering each thrust. Waves of pleasure rush through my body, culminating in one mind-blowing orgasm that leaves me breathless. He follows swiftly with his own equally explosive release, which is evident by the look of sheer euphoria on his face and his shuddering body.

"I love you too, Will," I say into his shoulder as we heave with exhaustion.

He grasps my face between his big, calloused palms and kisses me sweetly. "I'm really happy because when I said it, you looked mildly terrified."

"I heard the words, and for a moment, I wondered if they were merely figments of my imagination. It felt as though my mind was playing some cruel prank. The idea of falling in love again seemed almost impossible. I had convinced myself that I didn't want to fall in love again." My lip quivers as the words spill out.

"Vivian, I've loved you since I was fourteen. I thought about you nonstop after that summer. I begged my father to find out if you were ever coming back, but he simply raised his hand and told me it wasn't a good time. I thought I'd never see you again, let alone get a second chance at not fucking up my shot."

A tear falls down my cheek, and he wipes it away with his thumb. "I never want to be apart from you again, Will. I want to stay in this quiet little town and make a life with you."

"Geez, I might have to kick my dad out of the house." He laughs, and I slap him on the chest.

"Bill Cooper will stay precisely where he is. I've got a perfectly fine place where we can be alone when needed. Let's get cleaned up and go back home. We've had ourselves a night."

"That we have," he agrees, helping me down from the bar top. We clean up, dress in silence, and head back up the hill to Will's house. Of course, Kevin can't even be bothered to acknowledge our arrival, likely having been spoiled all evening by Will's dad.

After a quick shower, we climb into bed, and Will curls around me as we fall asleep. I'm almost positive I still have a smile on my face as I doze off.

CHAPTER TWENTY-NINE

She Found Her Way Home

WILL

Viv and I have settled into a perfect routine. She spends her days at the cabin, creating lists and hiring contractors to prepare for the work needed before the cold weather arrives. I spend my days shuffling between duties at the brewery and assisting my dad with a couple of outboard engine repairs. We stay at her place every night, but see my dad frequently for dinner. He gets grumpy if he doesn't get to see Kevin often since they've become best buds, and Kevin loves being spoiled.

I completed the minor fixes on the used Grady-White I bought in Portland, but Viv still thinks that was my only reason for the trip. Our first voyage on the 18-foot vessel takes us out to Pond Island to see the Narraguagus Lighthouse—Viv had been badgering me to see the inspiration for the tattoo on my bicep. Now a private island, we couldn't explore the light-house in person, but it was fun to float just offshore while I recounted its significance.

Built in 1834, the lighthouse stands at the entrance to Narraguagus Bay. It was designed to help with navigation through the bay to the port of Milbridge, which was a vital deep-water shipbuilding hub at the time. Although it's not the most visually appealing lighthouse, its history has always fascinated me because I am a descendant of one of the former keepers from the 1850s. The light, which was deactivated in 1934, is now privately owned.

I introduced Viv to the thrill of fishing for striped bass. She had never held a fishing pole before and was excited by the feeling of the fish hitting the lure and struggling to reel in the decent-sized catch. During one afternoon trip, we caught a keeper and grilled it for dinner. Viv's eyes widened with delight at her first taste of the firm, flaky white fish. It has quickly become my favorite fish to eat and one of the few meals, other than burgers and hot dogs, that I've mastered on the grill.

Every Friday night, we enjoy drinks and dinner at the cabin with anyone who is able to join us. Hadley and Cam come every week. Mike and Evvie arrive when Betsy is available to watch the girls. Shawn and Becky often show up separately but leave together, thinking they're being sneaky, but we're on to them. This week, Friday night's gathering will be a celebration. Hadley has finally decided to leave her teaching job in Massachusetts and stay in Shearwater Cove. We all breathed a sigh of relief—both Viv and Cam are especially thrilled about her decision. Watching Viv immersed in this new life, a serene smile always on her face, fills me with a deep sense of joy and satisfaction. She's here with me and plans to stay.

"Hey, Will?" Viv snaps me out of my reflection.

"Yeah, babe. What is it?"

"So, the anniversary of my mom's death is coming up on September 13th." She starts.

"Oh, I didn't realize it was coming up so soon," I say.

"I know. It kind of snuck up on me. We've been so busy this summer. The reason I bring it up is she had some precise instructions in her will for the one-year mark."

"Okay…"

"She forbade me from having a service after she passed away. I was the only family she had left, and she had no real close friends who stuck by her through all her health struggles. All she wanted was for me to find my way back to Shearwater Cove and spread her ashes at Walker's Rock. She wished to be laid to rest in the place she loved the most."

"That makes sense," I say. "Do you think she would've wanted her local friends here to be there?"

"Definitely. I actually talked to Betsy about it a couple of months ago, and she agreed to help me gather everyone. I'd like to plan it for the 13th at sunrise. I know it will be early, but that was absolutely her favorite time of the day to sit out on our back deck."

"I don't think that will be a problem," I reply. "Viv? Question... I've never heard you talk about your dad. Is it weird for me to ask what happened to him?"

"Not weird. I just don't know that much about him. From what Mom said, she got pregnant on their second date, and she didn't find out she was pregnant until after he'd left to go back to UCLA for his senior year. Once she told him, he seemed happy and promised to come back east right after he graduated. But soon after I was born in April 1992, Mom found out he'd been caught in some crossfire during the LA Riots and didn't make it. She didn't really have time to be sad, having to now care for a newborn, and so it was just us."

"Jeez, Viv, I'm sorry to hear that," I say, leaning over to squeeze her hand.

"It's fine. Honestly. She knew him for such a short time, there wasn't much she could tell me about him."

"Okay. So do you plan to spread her ashes off the point?"

"I think that's the best place. Hopefully, the winds will cooperate and not blow my mother back into my face. Although it would be just like her to get the last laugh."

I frown at that thought and make a note to help her decide on the best direction to scatter the ashes beforehand. Fortunately, the sunrise winds are relatively calm.

"I actually have a whole list of things I need to do on that day, but only the spreading of ashes needs to include others." Viv pulls at her bottom lip.

I'm curious. "Like what?"

"No idea. I was given a large envelope after her death with her instructions. She actually made me a checklist, which made me laugh because she knows how much I love to check off boxes when I've completed a task. There are a few sealed smaller envelopes inside that I'll have to open after we spread her ashes."

"You won't have to do any of it alone, Viv. I'll be there every step of the way." I reach for her, pulling her into my lap for a hug. She leans into my chest, resting her head against my shoulder.

"I'm so glad I'm not doing this on my own. And Mom would be so happy that I've found my way back here and back to this group of amazing friends. And to you."

"We are pretty amazing, aren't we?" I smile into her hair.

"I wouldn't want to be anywhere else." She looks up at my smiling face. "I love you, Will Cooper. Until we decompose into worm food."

"I love you, too, Vivian James," I say, squeezing her closer and smiling at her attempt at using of a lyric from one of our favorite songs.

She hugs me around my middle with a contented sigh.

"I hate to ruin this moment, but I need to run to the brewery for a few hours to do some repairs."

"Did Shawn break shit again?" She asks, laughing.

"Not this time. Unless he's not telling me something."

I leave Viv curled up in a deck chair with Kevin and a book, then I head to the brewery just before closing time. When I arrive, Mike is sitting at the bar, talking to Shawn. My two best friends wave me over, both wearing concerned expressions. I hate that look—it's never good for me since whatever is causing that look is most certainly going to be my problem to solve. Throughout our friendship, I've always been the fix-it guy.

"What's going on?" I ask.

They look at each other, and Mike motions for Shawn to tell me.

"So..." he starts. "There was a weird dude here this afternoon for a few hours."

"What do you mean, weird? How was he weird?"

"I didn't like his look. He had these creepy, unnaturally blue eyes, and he almost looked like someone stretched skin over a robot."

"Uh, what?" I ask, confused.

Mike interrupts. "His looks don't matter. What matters is that he was asking about the town and real estate for sale. He inquired about the various businesses and their owners, and he seemed particularly interested in this place. Also, he said he was boating along the coast and asked about the house on the point."

"Walker's Rock," I breathe.

"Yeah. Do you think it could be Viv's ex?" Shawn asks.

"I hope not," I say, dragging my fingers through my hair, tugging it nervously. My stomach ties itself in knots at the thought that this asshole is lurking around town.

"Sounded like he's staying somewhere near Gouldsboro. Mentioned he'd be back to see if he could meet with a realtor and tour some properties for sale," Shawn replies.

"Over my dead fucking body," I hiss.

"No way, dude," Mike agrees. "We need to follow this fuckwad the next time he shows his face. So, Viv never showed you a photo of him?"

I pull out my phone and hold it up to my friends. "Is this him? Viv dug this photo up for me just in case he found his way here."

"That is exactly the same guy. Can't forget those eyes." Shawn says with an exaggerated shiver.

"Fucking great," I say, shaking my head. "I think I'd like to keep her clear of this place, though, so she doesn't come face-to-face with that asshole."

"Good idea." Mike agrees and runs his hands down his face in frustration.

"We'll just need to be diligent, and we need to bring Kevin with us everywhere. I can't leave him behind at the cabin after this revelation."

"We'll take care of this guy. He had soft hands," Shawn comments. "Didn't seem like a terribly scary guy."

All three of us stand over six feet tall and present a rather intimidating front, especially Shawn. As goofy and kind-hearted as he is, he's been known to jump right into the middle of a brewery fight and literally toss anyone out. I'm definitely not afraid of Mr. Soft Hands, but I cannot, under any circumstances, allow him near Viv.

"Why don't you see if Viv will send Kevin up to stay with your dad?" Mike suggests.

"That's not a bad idea, but again, she'll think it's a weird request." I purse my lips in thought. "You know, I could have Dad ask her himself to keep me out of it. She won't be able to say no to the old guy if he says he's lonely."

"Good idea." Shawn cracks his knuckles. "I'm so ready for this dipshit's face to meet my fist."

"Calm down, Chuck Norris," I joke.

"What? I haven't given anyone a good beating recently."

"We also need to keep this from Evvie and Becky, too," I say, looking at each of my friends with serious eyes. "Those two can keep a secret about as well as Amelia!"

"Awww, don't throw shade on my little angel!" Mike emphasizes.

"That kid tells on herself," Shawn says, and Mike and I laugh and nod in agreement.

I quickly finish the repairs needed around the brewery, pick up a pizza at the café, and race back to the cabin. The sun is setting, and Viv and Kevin are exactly where I left them, although a blanket has been added since the back deck is now shrouded in shade. This late in the summer, the air cools quickly along the coast once the sun sets. When I open the door to the deck, they both turn to look at me but don't get up from their chairs. Viv offers me a sweet, loving smile that punches me in the heart.

"Is that pepperoni?" She asks.

"Pepperoni and Greek olive tonight, babe."

"Oh, fancy. Come over here and kiss me, handsome."

"Good book?" I ask as I bend over to kiss her soft lips.

"Yeah. I've hardly moved, and that's just because Kevin refused to get the blanket for us."

"Psssh. Ungrateful. Do you want to eat out here?"

"Nah, let's go eat inside. Maybe a movie? The latest Quiet Place is streaming," she says.

"Oh yes, I love it when you claw at my chest and climb into my lap when a movie scares you."

"I promise to be extra scared then," she murmurs, biting her lip. That simple action ignites something almost primal in me, a jolt of need I feel deep in my bones—and other places.

CHAPTER THIRTY

Small Life, Big Love

VIV

The abundance of good news I've received over the past few weeks has me floating on a cloud. Will Cooper loves me. Hadley is staying put. There are no recent signs of my creepy yard stalker. Renovations on the cabin are progressing well. Did I mention that Will Cooper loves me? I know; sometimes I can't believe it either. The good definitely outweighs the sadness I know will come with laying my mother to rest soon. But at least I'll be surrounded by people who care about me and cared for her.

Will left early to help his dad with something boat-related, and then he was needed at the brewery. The familiar sound of tires crunching on gravel indicates that Hadley has arrived. She has been spending most of her time at Cam's, but today, I need her help. I have to start planning this gathering for my mom, so I've invited Evvie and Betsy as well.

"Hey, Had," I say when she walks through the front door.

"Hey, Sweets." She reaches for a piece of scone off the tray I have prepared for our meeting, and I slap her hand away. She pulls it back with an insulted look.

"No. Wait for the other guests to arrive."

"Can I at least have some coffee?" she asks, bottom lip pouting.

"Have at it."

"I'm exhausted," she sighs, settling into the wooden chair at my table. "I don't know that you have a mug big enough for the amount of coffee I need."

"Are you complaining?" I ask, giving her a playful smile.

"Hell, no. That man has some impressive stamina for his age. I thought at some point he'd wave the white flag, but damn, I can't tire him out. And believe me, I've tried."

"My GOD, he's not that old!"

"Maybe it's the silver hair." Hadley shrugs. "Or maybe the silver hair is the root of his sexual superpowers."

"Jesus."

Thankfully, Evvie and Betsy arrive before this conversation becomes any more ridiculous or indecent. The four of us crowd around my kitchen table with oversized mugs of coffee and a plate full of Cam's famously delicious blueberry scones, as we plan a special send-off for my mother. Part of me dreads this memorial service because it feels like my final goodbye—like I'm leaving her behind. But it was her wish, and I must honor her last request.

"The most critical part of this service will be ensuring it happens at sunrise. I cannot mess that up. Do you have any suggestions on how to coerce a group of people to be somewhere at 6 a.m. on a Friday?"

"Food." Betsy and Evvie say in unison.

"I suggest contacting Cameron and Mary the day before. I'm sure Cam would be more than happy to make a fresh batch of pastries the prior evening. And ask Mary to prepare two or three of her famous scrambled eggs and bacon casseroles. It feeds a ton of people, and it's so delicious. I'm happy to make a giant fruit salad," Betsy says, of course, having all the answers.

"I can pick up the plates, utensils, cups, and napkins," Evvie says. "And we'll need a couple of big urns of coffee, which I can arrange."

"My gosh, you two are absolute lifesavers. Will and his dad are getting me a bunch of folding chairs for additional seating," I add. "Should I send out an invitation or something?"

"I have some errands to do at Earl's after I leave here, so I'll let him know to spread the word. There's no one in town capable of gathering a crowd like Earl Pelletier," Betsy says with a chuckle.

"Maybe you should be the one to sweet-talk Cam into making us some fresh goodies," I say to Hadley. "Something tells me there's not much that man won't do for you."

"On it. I'm also on the hunt for those paper lanterns to release into the sky in Maggie's memory—I've been hoping to find environmentally friendly lanterns, but isn't regular paper generally pretty biodegradable?" Hadley asks.

"Oh, I love the lantern idea. The sky won't be full daylight yet, so it's going to look so cool to see all those globes float away. Such a perfect send-off for a bright light like your mom." Betsy quickly dabs a napkin at the corners of her eyes.

"I guess the only thing left to do is write the eulogy," I scrunch my face up. "I've always hated public speaking, but then adding on the emotional aspect, I really hope I don't fuck it up."

Evvie squeezes my hand. "You've got this, Viv. I would suggest asking the group if anyone else wants to say anything after you're finished."

"Great idea," I agree. I feel good about our plan. And I know I can count on Earl to get the word out to everyone who meant something to Mom.

"So, Hadley," Betsy says. "I hear you've decided to move to Shearwater Cove permanently. I can't tell you how happy Jack and I are. Cam moved back here when Lucas was just a baby, and there have been girlfriends here and there for him, but none that make his eyes light up like you do. And your relationship with Luke—well, there's a lot of Hadley this and Hadley that when we spend time with him. Thank you for making my boys happy."

"Hadley, I demand you marry Cam this instant so Betsy can be your mother-in-law!" I yell excitedly.

Hadley completely ignores my comment and changes the subject. "My parents and brothers are going to visit for Thanksgiving. I'm looking forward to them meeting everyone. I only hope the Baker Boys don't embarrass the shit out of me. My brothers can be... *a lot.*"

"Didn't one of them blow off some fingers?" Evvie asks. "I thought I heard Mike and Cam talking about it after the Fourth party."

"Oh yes. That would be Henry. He's an Explosive Technician with a construction company in Vermont, near where I grew up. The guy lives for blowing shit up."

"Hadley's stories about her brothers never cease to entertain me." I giggle. "When we met our freshman year of college, the twins were just little kids. They're the youngest, and now they're in college, majoring in girls and frat parties."

"This should be quite an interesting visit—especially when we get your brothers together with Michael and Cameron." Betsy rubs her brow the way only the mother of boys can. "Well, girls, I must carry on with my daily errands. I know Tristin is waiting for me to pick up some supplies for the shop. And I'll be sure to give Earl his instructions."

"Bye, Bets," Evvie says, standing up to kiss her cheek. "I'm right behind you. I've got to collect the girls for a playdate, and Mike needs to get to the Marina."

Hadley and I walk them out to their respective vehicles and bid them farewell. With all their help, I feel as if most of the weight has been lifted from my shoulders. This town has a good heart and genuinely takes care of its people. Evvie and Betsy have hardly disappeared from sight when I see Will's truck approach, and strangely, he's not alone. I wasn't expecting him until later, so I hope everything is okay. As they park, I realize that he's with his dad.

"Hey, Coopers," I greet—a quick kiss for Will and a tight hug for Bill.

"Sorry to barge in on you guys. I hope we didn't interrupt." Will apologizes. "Dad actually has something he wanted to ask you, Viv."

"Oh, really? What is it?" I'm super curious now. Bill Cooper is usually not so mysterious.

"Well," Bill says, removing his ball cap and scratching his head. "You two have been spending a lot of time out here, and I really miss Kevin. I'm wondering if maybe I could take him for a few days or so?"

My heart clenches, this man... these men. "Of course, you can. I'm sure Kevin would love it. He especially loves it when he's the center of attention, but as long as there are not too many human food treats this time." I scold even though I know that won't happen. Bill loves to sneak Kevin all the good table scraps.

"Yes, ma'am," he says, nodding.

"Where is he?" Will asks. "I'm feeling mildly offended he hasn't raced out front to greet us."

"He's probably sleeping in the sun or hunting critters. He currently has a pretty intense feud going on with a family of chipmunks." I motion for the guys to follow me out back to find the chosen one.

"Those chippies will do a number on the property. It might be good for him to scare them away," Bill says.

I nod and scan the area for the big black dog. I see him at the rocks near the water's edge, clearly interested in what is likely a dead fish. Jesus.

"Kevin James, you better not be getting ready to roll in something stinky," I yell across the yard. He instantly looks up with an incredibly guilty expression on his perfect face, and upon noticing we have company, he trots over for greetings.

"Let me go in and pack up his stuff, and you'll be good to go. Just please remember to put his leash on when taking him out in the dark."

"Of course," Bill says. "Come on, big guy. Let's go do our best lazy bachelor impressions. I'll take good care of him, Viv."

"I know you will."

"I'm going to run these two back up to the house, finish a few things at the brewery, and I'll be back for dinner," Will says, leaning in for a quick kiss before returning to his truck.

It's barely noon, and Hadley is making a pitcher of margaritas. She does a little shimmy in response to the height of my concerned eyebrows. I am not day-drinking. I am not day-drinking. She forces a deliciously salt-rimmed glass into my hand, and I guess I'm day-drinking. I'd be lying if I didn't admit this morning was hard, putting those plans for Mom into motion.

"I'm not saying we have to get drunk," Hadley says, lifting her glass. "I'm just saying, why not? I need to drive back to Cam's later, so just a couple."

I grab the chips and salsa, and we make our way to the back deck. We might as well enjoy these days while we can—before we know it, these warm summer days will be distant memories. I love summer so much, but I also cherish the coziness of winter. Dressing in layers and snuggling under blankets on the couch feels delightful. I don't feel guilty about staying inside all day just to read a good book. I love sweaters and jeans, thick socks, and cozy boots. Flannel sheets, fires in the wood stove, and soft snow falling outside the window bring me comfort.

"Viv, can I ask you a question?" Hadley asks, running her finger through the condensation on the outside of her glass.

I scowl at her, wondering what's so serious. "What is it? You're kind of freaking me out a little."

"What are you going to do for work here in Shearwater Cove? You must be running low on savings; I haven't seen you work since before your surgery."

I huff out a chuckle. "I was wondering when you were going to ask that question."

"I'm just worried about you. You've never been good with idle hands."

"You know that my grandmother died pretty young and that my grandfather passed away when my mom was a baby?"

"I remember."

"My grandmother got a pretty sizeable settlement after my grandfather was killed in a car crash. My mom told me that she had found a financial guy who had made some astute investments that were passed down to Mom after she died. And just before Mom passed away, she basically gave me all that money and the cabin. I'm sorry I didn't tell you. It was hard for me to wrap my head around it. It's not a ton, but if I keep the investments active, and the stock market doesn't crash, it's plenty for me to live comfortably on for however many years I have left." I look at Hadley, whose mouth is hanging wide open.

"Are you saying you're rich?" she asks.

"I'm comfortable," I correct. "I'm not going to be buying a private plane or a second home or a sports team."

"Oh, but imagine owning a sports team, with all those tight asses to gawk at?" Hadley swoons, batting her eyelashes at me.

"Not enough for that. Sorry, babe."

"Jesus Christ, Viv... look at all the seagulls out there," she exclaims, pointing towards the spot where Kevin was earlier.

"Oh, yeah, I should probably take care of whatever's there. Kevin had investigated it pretty closely earlier, before he left with Junior and Senior. It's probably a dead fish."

I grab a shovel from the small shed, and Hadley and I assess the situation. Waving our arms wildly, we successfully scare off the squawking flock of seagulls. When we finally see what attracted all the attention, it is, in fact, dead fish. It looks like a bait bag full of fish chunks, and I have no idea where it came from.

CHAPTER THIRTY-ONE

Butter Her Up

WILL

The sheer happiness on my dad's face when he spends time with Kevin makes me consider getting him a dog. But what if it's not just the dog's company but Kevin specifically that brings him joy? He chatters with the lab while they sit on the couch watching the Red Sox. Dad explains who the players are, and Kev looks at him as if he's trying to decide who his favorite is.

I leave the best buddies to bask in bachelorhood and set out for Viv's. I'll miss having the big oaf loafing around the cabin, but I'm glad he's somewhere safe until we figure out this shit with Viv's ex. I've grown pretty attached to that dog, and I would hate to have to whoop some soft-handed loser city boy's ass if anything happens to him.

My phone pings with a message from Shawn.

SHAWN: VIV'S WEIRD DUDE IS BACK.

WILL: ON MY WAY.

SHAWN: COME IN THE BACK. HE SEEMS KINDA JUMPY TODAY.

WILL: PROBABLY GUILTY OF SOMETHING.

SHAWN: I'M GOING FULL-ON INQUISITIVE BARTENDER RIGHT NOW.

WILL: GOOD, KEEP HIM TALKING. HAS HE SAID ANY-THING ABOUT A REALTOR?

SHAWN: YEAH, ASKED ME FOR A RECOMMENDATION. I RECOMMENDED YOU.

WILL: AH, PERFECT.

SHAWN: I TOLD HIM YOU RENT OFFICE SPACE FROM US, AND I CAME OUT BACK TO TEXT YOU.

WILL: BE THERE IN A MINUTE.

I sneak in through the back door and throw on a button-down shirt that I had hanging in my office to create a more professional vibe. When I enter the brewery taproom, I spot the guy immediately, recognizing the creepy blue eyes from the photo. Shawn described him perfectly—he really does look like a robot with skin. I didn't think that was possible. I decide to introduce myself with a fake name just in case, and I'm really curious to see if he has the balls to use his real name.

"Excuse me, are you looking for a realtor?" I ask.

"I am. And you are?" he asks, looking down his nose at me.

"Bill Harris, Shearwater Realty. Nice to meet you." I reach out my hand to shake his, and he doesn't reciprocate. Okay, major douchebag alert.

"Name's Mitch. I'm in the market for a vacation home, and I happened to be boating nearby and saw a few properties that sparked my interest. It's quite a puzzle to find out how to get into town, but I think that makes it that much more charming." He sips his beer, never looking directly at me.

"It's rare that we have a property for sale around here. Folks like it in Shearwater Cove, and they tend to stick around. Was there a particular property you saw?" I ask.

"Well, I did notice one on the point. Looked like a nice one, very private, with a dock. Just what I'm looking for." Motherfucker.

"I'm quite positive that particular property isn't for sale. I happen to know the family, and they've owned it for generations." I respond.

"Come on, pal. Isn't everything for sale for a price?" His use of the word *pal* makes my skin crawl, and I see Shawn wince sympathetically.

"Sometimes. And sometimes not. You should probably pick another property." I clench my fists at my side.

"I can offer the owners double what the place is worth," he says, grabbing the top of my bicep like we're buddies.

I remove his hand from my arm. "Do you always bully people into kowtowing to your requests?" I ask, my voice even.

"Excuse me?" His head snaps toward me. "I don't know what kind of business owner hires someone so rude to potential customers with unlimited funds to spend, but I would like to speak to your manager.

"I'm the owner of this business," I say, crossing my arms.

"Well, then, I'm sure there's another realtor in this podunk town, and I'd love to give my commission to your competitor."

"I'm sorry, did you not notice that this small town has fewer than a dozen businesses? Do you really think a town that tries its best to remain unnoticed would have two realtors? There are no homes for sale here." Damn, I don't want to run him off before I get the chance to scare him shitless. "Look, let me speak to the owner of the house on the point and see what they think. Do you have a number where I can reach you?"

"I'll be back here in a couple of days. We'll connect then." He tosses a twenty-dollar bill on the bar for a seven-dollar beer and leaves.

I rush to the front window and see him getting into an expensive red SUV. He won't be hard to follow. I tail him all the way to Elsa's Inn down in Prospect Harbor. I feel a little better knowing where he's staying, but damn, this guy is a fucking asshole. I'll need to get Viv on board, but once

I tell her what he's doing, I think she'll love nothing more than to fuck with this shit stain.

WILL: I'M ON MY WAY. TAKEOUT?

VIV: LOBSTER ROLLS. BIG ONES.

WILL: I'VE GOT SOMETHING BIG FOR YOU.

VIV: WILLIAM. I'M HANGRY.

WILL: OKAY, BE THERE SOON.

VIV: 10-4 RUBBER DUCK

WILL: WAIT, YOU KNOW CONVOY?

VIV: MY MOTHER LOVED THAT MOVIE!

WILL: GOD, I LOVE YOU.

VIV: BACK ATCHA, COOPER.

Viv moans in pleasure with every bite of her lobster roll. I honestly don't know how I'm going to make it through this meal without dragging her onto the kitchen table and fucking her senseless. She has melted butter dripping down her chin, and her eyes are closed. I can't stop staring, my lobster untouched. I finally stuff the thing into my face so fast that I barely taste it. She finishes hers, and I barely let her wipe her hands on the napkin before I toss her over my shoulder.

"Will! I'm covered in butter!" she squeals.

"Exactly. And I can't fucking wait to lick it off you."

"Oh. I could go melt some more if you're interested," she purrs.

"No need," I say as I hold up the extra container that came with our lobster rolls. "And I don't even have to wait for it to cool off."

"Sneaky boy. Also, we are not getting butter all over the bed."

"Well, shit, that's no fun."

I do a quick about-face, carry her back to the kitchen table, and sweep the takeout containers onto the floor. I lower her to sit on the edge of the table, her bare breasts greeting me as I slowly strip off her t-shirt. The butter from her chin has dripped all the way to her cleavage, so I lean down and lick from her chest to her mouth, plunging my tongue into her waiting mouth.

"Vivian," I breathe against her lips. "You can't moan like that during dinner."

"Hmmmm," she teases. "Why not?"

"Because eating with a raging hard-on is not fun."

"I could help you with that problem." She hooks her finger in the front of my jeans and pulls me forward.

"I'm not done eating yet," I murmur into her neck, my voice a low growl filled with hunger. I tip the container of melted butter against the curve where her neck meets her shoulder, letting it trickle down her body. I gently guide her to lie flat on the table, her skin warm beneath my touch. The rich saltiness of the butter mingles with the sweetness of her skin, igniting a craving within me. She writhes beneath the caress of my tongue as I slowly lap up every drop of butter from her breasts down to where it has pooled just above her hip bone.

I'm sure if I try to fuck her on this table, it will end very badly, so I pick her up and carry her to the bathroom. Once the shower has warmed, I strip off her remaining clothing, followed by my own. She backs up under the steamy spray, leaning her head back into it. I can't help but take advantage of her exposed throat and graze my teeth along the slender column of skin, prompting more soft groans to escape her lips. If I thought I couldn't get harder, I was wrong after that whimper.

"Will..." She exhales my name as if it's the very breath that gives her life. Methodically, I help her clean the slick, greasy mess I made of her. Focusing with deliberate care on the soft curves of her breasts, I glide kisses through the frothy lather. My soapy hand glides with purpose to the apex of her thighs. When I trace a single finger around her clit, she releases a sharp, breathless gasp. The soft sounds ignite an intensity in me, prompting me to lift her effortlessly, her incredible ass resting perfectly in my hands. Instinctively, she wraps her smooth legs around my waist, aligning us perfectly.

"Bed," she demands. We turn off the running water and overlook the towels, and I leave a trail of wet footprints leading to her bedroom. She's nearly climbing my damp chest, sucking at my neck, biting my earlobe. I want to sprint to the bedroom, but I think slipping and falling would really kill the mood.

She lies back in the middle of the pile of sheets and blankets on her unmade bed, stretching her arms overhead and arching her back. The heap of bedding situates her hips at a higher position, giving me an angle we have yet to experiment with. I hover over her on all fours, and she's rubbing her wetness on the leg I have wedged between her thighs. *Oh, fuck me.*

Our kisses become increasingly more desperate and urgent with each passing second as we deny ourselves the sweet release of pleasure. I explore her mouth with my tongue, drawing out small whimpers from her—whimpers that send electric pulses down my spine, pooling low in my stomach.

"Vivian," I husk against the shell of her ear. "What do you need, baby?"

She reaches for my uncomfortably hard dick, slowly stroking. "I think you know what I need. Nice and slow." This woman has no idea what effect she has on me. I would give her the world if she asked for it. But what she needs right now is going to be agonizingly slow for both of us.

Pressing the head of my cock to her slick entrance, I make one shallow thrust, waiting for her to adjust. She grabs onto my hips like handles and attempts to pull me in deeper.

"You said slowly," I murmur in her ear, holding my ground.

"I lied."

"You know what happens to bad girls?" I ask, eyes full of mischief.

"Spankings?"

"Vivian."

"Do it."

"You think you can take it all?"

"I always love a challenge," she groans.

She barely completes her sentence before I'm fully inside, striking the spot that only this angle can reach. Her gasp echoes through the room, urging me to draw out that sound once more. I withdraw almost entirely with a torturous slowness, then thrust back into her. Her gasp is even louder this time, followed by her breathless plea, "Will, oh god. Oh my god! Please don't stop."

"That's a good girl," I say, urging her on with those words.

"Mmmm, that feels so good," she bucks her hips to meet mine.

I wrap my arms around her lower back, pulling her closer. I keep thrusting until I feel her body tremble. I follow through with my orgasm until stars blur my sight, and I finally collapse in exhaustion.

CHAPTER THIRTY-TWO

A Fishy Situation

VIV

Waking up sprawled across Will's chest may just be my new favorite thing. The sound of his deep, sleepy breaths, with my ear pressed against him, creates a calming effect I never thought possible. He's like my own personal brand of Xanax. With his muscular arm wrapped around me, it feels as though nothing bad can happen.

Trailing a finger down the ridges of his abs, I follow the path of fine hair that leads to— oh, hello. He slowly awakens to my tongue running across the crease of his lips, with my hand wrapped around his morning hard-on. An easy smile spreads across his face as he fists my hair to pull me into a deeper kiss.

"Good morning, beautiful," he murmurs sleepily. "How'd you sleep?

"Perfectly as usual," I purr. "I always do when I'm with you."

"Hmmm," he moans. "I love waking up with your skin against mine."

"What do you want to do today?" I ask.

"Well, I'd like to start by finding out if you plan to do anything with that hand or if you're just going to hold onto my dick all morning?" He laughs into my hair.

"Actually..." I slide my leg across his lap and sit up, straddling him. "I thought maybe I'd just try this..." I sink down onto him so slowly, I swear I see his eyes roll back into his head.

Once we've extracted ourselves from the tangled mess of sheets, the rest of the morning is spent relaxing with our coffees on the back deck. Will is on one cushioned chair flipping through a boating magazine, while I'm on the other, using his lap as a footrest as I scroll through Instagram. The sun shines, the air feels dry and breezy, and I know that as long as I stay in this cabin, I will never tire of looking out at the ocean. I will always want this view, regardless of the season. The feel of Will squeezing my ankle draws my attention as I look up from my phone.

"Want to go get some brunch?" He asks.

"Hmm, yes," I groan. "Piles of bacon and eggs, please."

"I could really go for a big ol' plate of Mary's cooking. It seems like some-one's been keeping me up late. I need to recharge my energy." He moves my feet from his lap to the deck. "Let's go get dressed."

Note to self: When you're in a hurry to get somewhere to eat because you're so hungry you might die, do not, and I cannot stress this enough, get dressed in the same room as your extremely handsome, exceptionally built, incredibly sexy boyfriend. Once he's naked, it's hard to let him put clothes on. By the time we finally made it to the Cove Cafe for brunch, we were close to starvation. Thankfully, Mary immediately showed us to a table and fed us plates piled high with bacon, eggs, hashbrowns, toast, and fruit. And we both ate every crumb of food on our plates.

Will isn't needed at the brewery until later in the day, so we walk around town and pop into the Salon to say hi to Evvie. She's busy with a haircut while her two little girls sit at a small table in the waiting area, coloring pictures for their mom to hang up. Their little eyes light up when they see Will, and both leap into his arms.

"Hey, if you want them out of your hair for a little bit, we can take them to get an ice cream," I whisper to Evvie so the girls don't hear me.

"Oh my god, that would be amazing. I have another appointment right after I'm done with this cut." Evvie squeezes my hand in thanks.

"Who wants ice cream?" I ask, walking back to where Will is critiquing the art projects.

"ME ME ME ME MEEEEE!" They wave their little arms and jump around excitedly at the invitation.

Will and I walk hand in hand with the girls, listening to them enthusiastically discuss which flavor of ice cream they want, whether they want jimmies, and if they'll add whipped cream—we smile at each other over their heads. The familiar bells on the door clanging as we push through it, we stand behind the short line of families enjoying the last days of summer.

"Welcome to Tucker's Tast—" Tristin begins her greeting. "Oh, hi, you guys! So nice to see you!"

"Hey, Tristin," I say. "We're keeping an eye on the squirts for a few hours and needed a treat."

"Who's first?" Tristin asks.

"ME!" Olivia's hand shoots up like a rocket. "I would like cotton candy in a dish with jimmies and whipped cream."

"Please." Will reminds her.

"Please!" She adds loudly.

"And for you, Amelia?"

"I would like cotton candy with dimmies and ripcream."

"It's jimmies," her sister corrects.

"That's what I said, dimmies." Amelia scowls.

"I've got it," Tristin responds. "What about the adults?"

"Hot fudge sundaes?" Will looks at me hopefully.

"With extra whipped cream," I say, nodding my head.

"Great! Coming right up."

While Tristin works on our ice creams, Will and the girls go out front to find a table for the four of us. Once she has loaded up a tray with our order, I grab a stack of napkins and head to the table. The girls happily chatter about Barbie dolls, American Girl dolls, and, of course, their favorites, Anna and Elsa. Will leans forward, riveted by the conversation, and I can't help but smile at him. I can tell he is mining for birthday ideas for Olivia, which is coming up early next month.

"Where's Kebin?" Amelia asks.

"He's hanging out with my dad," Will answers.

"I miss him," Olivia adds.

"Me too," I say, now really needing to swing by on the way home to give him some scritches under his chin.

Will's phone rings, and I hear only his side of the conversation. "Dad, what's up? Wait, wait, slow down." He pauses, his brows drawing together in concern. "He threw up? When? We'll be there in a minute."

I bolt to my feet, now realizing that they're discussing Kevin. My stomach begins to roil with nausea. My angel puppy isn't feeling well, and I'm sure he needs his momma.

"Sorry to cut our ice cream date short, but Vivi and I need to make sure Kevin is okay."

Both girls nod, pick up their ice creams, and follow Will back inside the Salon. "Sorry, Ev, we gotta bolt. Something's up with the dog." Evvie nods and waves.

"What did your dad say? How many times did he vomit? Is he eating? What's he doing now?" I pepper Will with questions.

"He said he only threw up once, but that was all he said. Let's not jump to conclusions."

"I jumped to all the conclusions before we even reached the truck," I say, gnawing on my bottom lip nervously.

Will skids to a stop in front of his house. His dad meets us on the front porch, clearly worried about the situation.

"Tell us what happened, Bill," I say, looping my arm through his.

"He ate his breakfast fine this morning. He went out and did his usual business. I even kept him on his leash so he wouldn't get into the flower gardens, so I knew he didn't get into anything. At about noon, I fed him lunch, and he had no interest in it. I thought it was weird because, well, it's Kevin. But then he threw up and did a lot of dry heaving. Now, he's lying on the floor in front of the back door and hasn't moved. I will say I thought it was odd that his vomit smelled a lot like fish. I didn't think you fed him fishy-smelling food."

"I don't. So that's weir—" My eyes widen, and I feel the color drain from my face.

"Viv, what is it?" Will asks, grabbing my shoulders.

"I didn't think it was a big deal," I say.

"What?"

"Yesterday, when you came to pick up Kevin, he was into something at the edge of the yard. I didn't think anything of it at the time, but after you left, Hadley and I went to check it out. It was a bait bag full of fish chunks. Honestly, I just thought maybe a seagull had swiped it from the deck of a fishing boat and dropped it accidentally on my lawn. But I also thought it was weird the fish was cut up in uniform chunks."

"Yeah, that's odd. Bait isn't generally cut up into neat little chunks," Will says. "What did you do with it?"

"I tossed it in the garbage."

A retching sound coming from the kitchen interrupts our conversation. I turn around to see Kevin throwing up again. But that's not what worries me most. He doesn't make an effort to stand or lift his head; he merely vomits where his head lies on the floor.

"Will, his breathing looks labored," I say, now worried this is more than a little upset stomach.

"I'll call Dr. Jane and let her know we're coming into her office."

The three of us have to carry the eighty-pound lab to Will's truck because he's unable to walk on his own. I sit in the back seat with his big, blocky head on my lap, stroking his ears. "You're going to be ok, angel boy. You have to be ok. I won't let anything happen to you." I whisper to him.

On our way to the veterinarian's, I text Hadley to let her know what's going on.

> Viv: Kevin's sick. On way to vet now.

> HADLEY: I'LL MEET YOU THERE.

> VIV: HE HAS TO BE OKAY.

> HAD: I KNOW. HE'S YOUNG AND STUBBORN. HE'LL BE FINE.

We arrive at Shear Cove Animal Hospital in record time. Dr. Jane meets us at the door and directs us to an empty exam room, where we set Kevin on the table.

"I think he got into a bait bag full of fish that was on my lawn yesterday," I say quickly. "He's thrown up a few times and wouldn't eat his lunch."

Dr. Jane's eyebrows draw together, clearly concerned that a lab didn't eat his lunch.

"Let me do a quick exam first," she says, methodically checking Kevin's vitals, doing a general physical assessment, and looking at his gums. I'm no veterinarian, but his gums looked paler than usual. "He's presenting with symptoms of poisoning. Possibly a rodenticide. Rat poison. We'll administer activated charcoal to soak up any remaining poison. Then, depending on the severity, we can give him Vitamin K1, which is the treatment for common rat poison."

"Should we get the fish to be tested?" I ask.

"We really don't have a test that will give us any immediate results, so we'll treat him as if we know for sure he's been poisoned."

I hear Hadley tear into the front door of the Animal Hospital, demanding to be shown to Kevin's room. She quiets as she enters the exam room, and

I feel her arm circle my waist. She's come for support, nothing more. And to make sure her favorite canine is okay.

"Is he going to be alright?" At this point, I've chewed my lip to the point I now taste blood, and I'm slightly wobbly on my feet.

Dr. Jane steadies me with her hand on my arm. "I'd like to keep him overnight here under our supervision. I'll give him fluids to combat the dehydration from his vomiting episodes."

"Absolutely. I need to stay, too," I say.

"I'll stay too," Will says, pulling me close to him to keep me steady.

"Of course. We'll need to put him in a kennel, but I can pull a couple of chairs back there for you. The next twelve hours will be critical. He's not coughing up blood, so that tells me it's most likely a mild case of poisoning."

"I'll go grab you both a couple of sandwiches and drinks from Earl's," Hadley offers.

"We're good, Hadley," Will says.

"You'll thank me later," Hadley says and rushes out the door.

"I can't fucking believe this shit. I'm going to get to the bottom of this. That bait bag didn't just land there by chance." Will drags a palm over his face, scratching at his beard.

"Let's worry about that tomorrow once we know our baby is going to be alright."

Once Dr. Jane has Kevin set up in his kennel and we're set up in our chairs, she excuses herself to see another patient. I feel fortunate that Jane has an emergency-first policy at her clinic and that Bill noticed Kevin was off and called us to come home. I know he loves that damn dog almost as much as I do and certainly doesn't want anything bad to happen to his best buddy.

Author's Note: It's just a mild poisoning. Kevin will be fine.

CHAPTER THIRTY-THREE

Dirty Deeds Done Dirt Cheap

WILL

Spending the night at the veterinary office and attempting to sleep in a chair is not advisable. I wake up, lifting my head with a neck pop that sounds like a firecracker. It must be early, given the soft light pouring through the window. I notice that the chair next to me is empty, but I quickly spot Viv. She's curled up on a blanket on the floor, facing Kevin's small kennel. Her hand is pushed through the gap between the bars, holding his paw. Gentle snores come from both of them.

The news must be relatively good, considering there were no emergencies to wake us up overnight. From my vantage point, Kevin looks comfortable. The sight of Viv holding her beloved pup's paw squeezes my heart. I take a quick photo so we can reminisce later about how fucking cute this picture is once Kevin is out of danger.

When I return to the room after locating the restroom, Viv sits with her back against the empty kennel nearby. She looks up at me, worry creasing her brow; her green eyes are rimmed in red from crying. I slide down to the floor beside her and silently pull her into my lap, my arms wrapped tightly around her as she buries her face in the crook of my neck. We sit like that for so long that I wonder if she has fallen back asleep.

I notice some movement in the neighboring kennel. When I look over, Kevin's black nose presses against the door. I gently shake Viv and point towards him. She jumps to her feet, startling both me and the dog.

"Kevin," she breathes, as if she's been holding her breath the entire time he's been sleeping. The sound of his wagging tail brushing against the floor of the kennel is the sweetest I've heard. "I need to text Jane. She said to let her know when he wakes up."

I wrap my arm around her shoulders. "He's going to be ok, Viv," I say softly into her hair. I feel her nod in agreement as she hugs my middle.

Dr. Jane arrives promptly, and after another examination, she's pleased with his progress. She decides that one more bag of fluids is necessary before we can take him home. While administering the fluids, she reviews the post-visit instructions: small, bland meals, keep him hydrated, and rest. Most importantly, if anything seems off, we should bring him back immediately.

Viv and I thank her, and she can't help but pull Dr. Jane into a tight hug for saving her sweet baby. After the last dose of fluids, Kevin is ready to go—ready to walk out of this place on his own. I'll be pretty happy never to see that puppy so helpless ever again. I have a pretty good idea of who's behind this, and once I get the proof, there's going to be hell to pay.

During the drive home, Kevin's head hanging out the window proves he's feeling much better. Viv calls Hadley to tell her everything is going to be okay and to thank her for rushing to the vet's office to be with us.

When we get back to the cabin, we give the puppers a small portion of food that he gobbles up. Viv breathes a sigh of relief that his appetite has returned.

"I have to head to the brewery in a few hours, but I need a nap," I say. Viv nods in response and pulls the dog into the bedroom with us. We lie on the bed, facing each other, with Kevin stretched out between us.

I wake to my alarm telling me it's time to get to work. "Babe," I whisper. When her eyes open, I tell her I'll be back later and kiss her softly. She nods, stretches, pulls Kevin closer to her, and falls back to sleep.

As I leave the house, I shoot off a text to Mike and Shawn.

> WILL: MEET ME AT THE BREWERY IN 20.

> SHAWN: IT'S MY DAY OFF, MAN.

> MIKE: EVERYTHING OK?

> WILL: NO. SOMEONE POISONED KEVIN.

SHAWN: WHAT THE FUCK?

MIKE: COMING.

SHAWN: SAME.

The brewery is closed today, so I slip in through the back door and turn on a single light at the bar. Mike and Shawn follow closely behind, both clearly eager to uncover who tried to hurt Kevin. I share the events of the past few days with them, and I notice Mike tense up.

"What is it?" I ask.

"There have been complaints about minor thefts from boats at the marina. Nothing big, mostly stupid stuff like beer from coolers, but one fisherman reported that several of his empty bait bags had been stolen. I thought nothing of it and figured maybe the wind had blown them off the boat, but he said they were securely stowed away."

"Don't you have cameras around the boat slips?" Shawn asks.

"I do, but they only show the dock area in front of the boats, so if someone walked down the dock to get on a boat. If someone pulled up to the back by boat, I can't see that. Anything that happens on the boat is the owner's responsibility." Mike says. "It's not the greatest system, but I just don't have the budget for more cameras."

I chew my lip, lost in thought. There must be more to this, and I'm convinced that once we get to the heart of the issue, it will have Viv's ex's name all over it. The sound of my phone pinging snaps me out of my head.

UNKNOWN: WILL, IT'S TRISTIN. OWEN GAVE ME YOUR NUMBER. I NEED TO TALK TO YOU OR VIV.

WILL: COME TO THE BREWERY.

I hold up my phone so they can read the message. Mike's brows shoot up so high they almost disappear into his hair.

"What the fuck is that about?" Mike questions.

"No idea, but it must be serious if she had to ask Owen for my number," I respond.

There's a knock at the front door, and Shawn rushes over to let Tristin in. She's visibly rattled.

"Hey, come on in," Shawn says.

"Thanks," she says. "I know you're closed today, but I could really use a beer right now."

"Of course," I say, pouring a farmhouse from the tap. "What's going on, Tristin?"

"I just closed up the ice cream shop, but right before closing, these three guys came in—maybe high schoolers, I dunno, but they're not from here. None of them looked familiar. I know I'm relatively new to this town, but I had never seen them before." She takes several gulps from her beer. "They were being obnoxious—trying to get me to give them ice cream for free. They joked that if they spit in the tub, I'd have to give it to them. It was just fucking weird."

"Sounds like those hoodlums that Luke was hanging out with before Cam put his foot down," Mike comments.

"They were definitely hoodlummy," Tristin continues. "While the one guy was trying to {air quotes} sweet-talk me, the other two were discussing how to spend the money they just earned for pulling off a prank for someone. They were vague, but I heard them say Walker's Rock and something about poisoning someone."

I am fuming. It feels like my head is about to pop entirely off my body. When I find those little fuckers, they'll be sorry they ever stepped foot in Shearwater Cove.

"So Kevin spent the night at Dr. Jane's last night due to poisoning," Mike says. I'm still too mad to speak.

Tristin gasps. "Oh no, is that sweet boy okay?"

"He'll be fine." I'm finally able to speak. "I think only because whoever did the poisoning was too stupid to put enough in there to be deadly."

"Or maybe the plan wasn't to kill Kevin, but just to poison him enough to scare the shit out of Viv," Shawn says.

"Mike, can you text Luke to find out if he knows where I can find these idiots?" I ask. "Tristin, what did they look like?"

"They all looked like maybe they came from wealthy families. I don't know why I think that, but while they tried to look badass, their clothes looked high-end, like little preppy thugs."

Shawn snickers at the description.

Mike looks up from his phone. "Luke says they live over in Milbridge, on Bar Island. He says they have a little center console they bomb around in. And one of their dads has a forty-footer docked at the marina that they hang out on. They probably never show up on my cameras if they're coming in by boat."

"Let's go check it out. See if we can find them." Shawn says, jumping off his barstool. I chuckle because I can't wait to see these boys shit themselves when Shawn's 6-foot-7-inch frame darkens the dock.

"Tristin, I can't thank you enough for coming forward with this information," I say.

"Anytime, Will, really. I love that dog so much, and Viv, too. The thought of someone trying to hurt him is just so maddening. I generally try to mind my own business while I'm working, but those boys were so obnoxious and bragging about what they had done. I knew I needed to speak up."

Tristin leaves the brewery, and Mike, Shawn, and I make plans to visit the marina. "I know exactly which boat that kid's dad owns. He's the one who told me I was overreacting when I caught them skulking around the docks at night. I'd like to punch his face, too," Mike threatens.

"Do you have any idea when they usually hang around?" I ask.

"I would see them on camera late afternoon. Like they're going to the boat to pre-game before looking for trouble," Mike answers.

"Ok, let's go. If they're not there now, I'll move one of the cameras to capture more of that particular boat so we can see when they return." Mike slaps me on the back as if to say, *We've got this.*

Shawn's waiting at the back door for us, clearly ready to get this show on the road. As generally easy-going as he is, he's the first to stand up for any friend who's been wronged. And he's a strong motherfucker. "Come on, guys. Let's go get those little assholes!"

The marina is quiet when we arrive, at that time of day when everyone is already on the water and won't return until sunset. Mike points out the small yacht secured in its slip, and the three of us head in that direction. As we approach, we can hear some particularly vulgar rap music blasting from the boat's stern. Mike and I move in from the starboard side while Shawn stays just out of sight on the port side. As expected, the underage teens are sprawled on chairs, with a cooler half full of beer and an array of empty bottles littering the boat's deck.

Mike knocks on the side of the boat, catching their attention. Each one sits up straighter, and when they see me, at least two of them go pale. If you spend enough time in Shearwater Cove, you know that I spend a lot of time at Walker's Rock, and these idiots know they're fucked.

"Get the fuck out of here," First Idiot spits. "This is my father's boat. We have a right to be here."

"I know exactly whose boat this is. And honestly, you're welcome to stay right here. It will make it easier for the Staties to find you once we report your asses." Mike isn't the tallest guy, but his broad chest and thick biceps can be a menacing sight, especially when his arms are crossed.

"We didn't do nuthin," Second Idiot whines.

"Oh no?" I question. "Because we heard you were bragging about getting paid to poison someone."

"Must've been that bitch at the ice cream place," Third Idiot mutters under his breath.

"Doesn't matter who it was," Mike starts. "You have two choices here."

"I'm calling my dad. He'll sue your ass." First Idiot's big mouth is going to get him thrown overboard if he doesn't shut it.

"Please go ahead and call him. I'd like him to hear the two options we're offering," I reply. "We'll wait."

The kid calls his father, and I don't hear much of the conversation, but after a few minutes, he hands the phone to me. "It's my dad. He wants to talk to you."

"Hello, Mr—"

"Armstrong."

"Hello, Mr. Armstrong. This is Will Cooper. I have you on speaker. I'm here with your son and his friends and the owner of the marina, Mike Tucker."

"What can I do for you, Mr. Cooper?"

"I have reason to believe that your son was involved in poisoning someone. I also think he and his friends were hired by someone to commit this act. I'm prepared to offer them two options."

"I don't think you're in a position to be offering anything. I'll call my lawyer."

"No, Mr. Armstrong, you don't understand. Between a witness who will testify they heard the boys bragging about getting paid to poison someone and the alcoholic evidence on this boat at the moment, one call to the State Police, and they'll be arrested. As I'm sure you know, you'll also be charged with supplying alcohol to minors." The looks on the three faces staring at me from the back of the boat are priceless—a mix of fear and anger.

"I'm outta here," Second Idiot says, jumping over the port side onto the dock. When he turns to run away, he comes face to face with a very tall, very menacing Shawn. The boy slowly backs up the way he came and steps back onto the boat.

"I think not," Shawn says with a chuckle.

Mr. Armstrong finally speaks. "What's your alternative offer?"

"They tell me who hired them, and we'll forget this ever happened. Additionally, Mike Tucker would like you to find another marina for your boat. You and your family are no longer welcome here."

"That's fair. I'll get my boat tomorrow." The sound of defeat in the father's voice is almost as pleasing as the frightened looks on the boys' faces. He then raises his voice to make sure the teens hear him. "Tyler, get your ass home immediately, and don't plan on leaving the house for the rest of the summer."

"Daaaaad," Tyler whines.

"Tell those gentlemen exactly what they want to know and get the fuck home." The phone call ends. I smile at my friends as we stand on the dock, waiting for them to give up a name.

"I don't know what the guy's name was. He paid us $500 in cash each. Said not to kill the dog, just make him sick. He said if we sent the dog to the vet, he'd give us another $500 each," Tyler said.

"What did the guy look like?"

"City guy. Soft hands. Crazy, weird blue eyes. His skin looked like it was too tight on his face," Idiot Three said.

I look over at Mike and Shawn; both have murder in their eyes. "Tyler, give me your father's number. I'm going to need you three to be available if we need more info." I hold up the picture Viv gave me. "Is this the guy?"

They nod, refusing to make eye contact with us. Idiot Two asks, "Is the dog okay?"

We walk away without answering.

CHAPTER THIRTY-FOUR

Not Everything Has a Price

VIV

When I open my eyes again, it's nearly dinner time. After the stress of the past two days and sleeping on the hard floor of the animal hospital, I needed this nap like nobody's business. Kevin has hardly moved all day. I'm sure the poor guy is feeling the effects of his ordeal much more intensely than I am. I bury my face in the soft fur at the base of his ear and breathe in his comforting doggie scent.

We both crawl out of bed and shuffle to the kitchen in search of snacks. I serve Kevin another portion of his bland food and grab a plate of cheese and crackers while contemplating what to have for dinner. Since Will hasn't texted me, I send him a plea for pizza.

VIV: BRING ME PIZZA

WILL: YOU GOT IT

VIV: AND BEER

WILL: BE THERE SOON

When Will pushes through the front door an hour later, Kevin greets him with a full-body wag. His eyes light up at the sight of the dog's excitement, and I swear I see a glint of tears in them. He leans down to kiss me, and I take the pizza and beer, setting them on the coffee table.

He scooches down to give Kevin well-deserved scratches. "Quite a difference from yesterday," he observes.

"We just got up about an hour ago. I think a nap day was exactly what we needed." I flop down and pat the couch cushion next to me in invitation. Will sits, and Kevin shimmies under our legs—he's been a bit clingy today, and I'm okay with that. After shoveling several pieces of pizza into my mouth, I turn to Will's handsome yet slightly troubled face.

"So, why do you have that look?"

"What look?"

"Like you're dealing with something troubling, and you're working it around in your brain for a way to tell me with the least amount of negative impact. Out with it, Cooper."

Will takes my hand in his calloused palm. "Your ex is here in Shearwater Cove," he says.

My eyes go big, and I can feel the heat of anger slowly creeping up my neck. I take a deep breath to keep myself from losing all of my shit all at once. "Motherfucker."

"He's visited the brewery several times, inquiring about available properties for sale. I pretended to be a realtor the other day, and he was insistent on seeing and possibly making an offer on Walker's Rock, even after I told him it wasn't for sale."

"What the actual fuck?"

"I know. He introduced himself as Mitch," he says. "His face just screams, punch me."

"His last name is Mitchell. What a fucking tool. So what did you tell him about my cabin?"

"I told him I knew the family personally, and they've owned this property for generations and aren't interested in selling. He said everything has a price."

"Typical," I mutter. "Always throwing around money he doesn't have."

"Guy talked like he was a millionaire. Saying he'd pay double what it's worth."

"Quite the contrary. I think he's made some bad deals. Just before I left him, I overheard a phone conversation where he was asking for more time on a loan. I think he just wanted to get out here to the cabin to scare me."

"That just makes me want to beat his ass more," Will says, running a hand aggressively through his hair.

"Generally, the vibe he gives off," I say. "Your face says there's more to the story."

"He hired some local teens to poison Kevin."

"He WHAT?" I spit angrily.

"Tristin overheard those delinquents Luke used to hang out with bragging about it in the ice cream shop, and came to the brewery to inform me. Mike, Shawn, and I visited them down at the marina, and after a few threats, they spilled their guts like snitches in a back alley."

"For fuck's sake. He paid teenagers to poison my dog. That is lower than I thought even he was capable of." My fists are clenched so tight I think I can feel blood from my fingernails piercing my palms. I need to text Hadley, she's going to blow a fucking gasket at this news.

> VIV: YOU ARE NEVER GOING TO BELIEVE THIS!

> HADLEY: YOU KNOW I HATE CLICKBAIT.

> VIV: ERIC HIRED TEENAGE BOYS TO POISON MY DOG.

> HAD: I'M GOING TO KILL THAT MOTHERFUCKER.

> VIV: GET. IN. LINE.

"Hadley is interested in murdering said poisoner," I relay, putting my phone down.

"Of course she is. I'm supposed to meet him at the brewery tomorrow to let him know if I was able to coerce Walker's Rock's owner to let him tour the property."

"Maybe I should say yes, and then I can poison him!"

"Okay, there, Nannie Doss, calm down. I've got some ideas."

"Who the fuck is Nannie Doss?" I ask.

"Some woman who poisoned a bunch of family members in the 1950s. I got sucked down a rabbit hole on the internet one day." He shrugs, and now I'm wondering if my boyfriend has a thing for obscure female serial killers.

"My brain is mush right now," I sigh. "Can we discuss this more in the morning?"

"Absolutely. I feel like I could fall asleep standing up after the last two days, so bed sounds really enticing right about now—and not even in a sexy way."

Kevin's loud bark wakes us from a sound sleep, which is odd because that dog rarely barks. He prefers a menacing growl to express his anger. I rush out of the bedroom to find him looking out the front window with his paws up on the windowsill.

"What the hell are you barking at, puppy?"

Will is close behind me, pulling on a t-shirt. "What the hell is he barking at?"

Peering out the window, I see what looks like a State Trooper's vehicle pulling up in front of the cabin.

"Jesus, what time is it? And why is a Statie here so early?" Will rubs the sleep from his eyes.

"It's 9 a.m. Why the fuck is he here at all? Did you report the poisoning?" I ask, confused as to why a law enforcement officer is climbing my front stairs.

"Nah, we told the boys we wouldn't if they gave up their source—and I wanted to confront the asshole before turning him over to the cops."

I open the door before he knocks. My face obviously reveals my confusion at his presence.

"Hi, I'm Officer Miller with the Maine State Police. I need to speak with you regarding a report we received involving possible animal cruelty at this location. Is this a good time to talk?"

"Yeah, come on in," I say, backing up to let him enter the cabin.

"Thank you," he says.

"What can we do for you?" Will asks as the three of us take seats at the kitchen table.

"We received information that an animal in your care may have been neglected or harmed. I'm here to look into that and hear your side of the story."

"Excuse me? Are you saying someone reported me neglecting my pet?" I touch my chest in shock.

"Yes, ma'am. An anonymous male caller reported it." Pointing to Kevin, he continues, "Is this the only animal on the premises?"

"Yes."

"Has he been admitted to the veterinary hospital recently?"

"Yes. He was poisoned."

"Did you find the source of the poisoning?"

"We assumed it was a bag of fish chunks we found in the yard." I've gone numb. How could someone accuse me of harming the one being in my life I would die for?

"Hold on a sec," Will interrupts, obviously confused by the line of questioning. "Are you accusing Vivian of harming her own dog?"

"Yes, sir. We take these accusations seriously," Officer Miller says.

"I can assure you that's not the case." Will opens his phone and holds up a photo I haven't seen. A photo of me asleep in front of Kevin's kennel at the animal hospital, holding his little paw. A faint gasp escapes my lips, and my heart clenches.

"That doesn't prove anything," the officer says.

"Alright, then. What about three witnesses claiming they were paid to poison this dog?" Will gestures toward Kevin, who lies quietly on the floor, his usual worried expression bouncing between the two men.

"I would need to talk to the witnesses."

"I have the number of one of the boys' fathers. I'm sure you'll need to go through him since the witnesses are minors." Will recites the number, and the officer jots it down in his notebook.

Officer Miller stands up. "I'll go outside to call him."

The State Trooper returns shortly, shaking his head. "I'm heading over to Barr Island to interview the three teens. The father didn't appear to be too impressed with the recent events. He's more than happy for me to come put a good scare into them."

"Do you mind coming back this afternoon?" Will asks.

"For?"

"We'll have some more information for you."

"I'll swing back by after I complete my interviews. And for what it's worth, I'm really sorry to make these accusations, but you understand that we need to follow up on these types of calls," Officer Miller apologizes, his hands squeeze the hat he removed.

"I get it," I finally say. "Kevin is my life. I would do anything for that dog."

"I see that now." The officer bends to give Kev a scratch on the head. "He looks like he's well cared for and happy. I hope we get to the bottom of this and punish the parties responsible."

"I have faith we will," Will says.

Will walks the officer out to his cruiser, and I sink onto the cool wood floor next to Kevin, gently pulling his large, warm head into my lap. "I love you, you big lug," I whisper, ruffling his soft fur. "Let's not eat any weird stuff in the yard anymore, okay?" Kevin lets out a satisfied groan and rolls onto his back, exposing his belly. I oblige with the vigorous belly rubs he adores so much—his tail wags lazily, a silent testament to his pleasure. I'm so relieved to have my boy back to his cheerful, goofy self.

"How are we stocked for breakfast items?" Will asks, coming back inside.

I get up off the floor and check the refrigerator. "Looks like we've got eggs, bacon, English muffins, cheese."

I can feel his warmth behind me. He wraps his arms around my waist and rests his chin on my shoulder. "Sounds like breakfast sammies to me," he murmurs into my neck. I lean into him, incredibly grateful for his love and support. Handling all of this alone would've broken me.

We bring our coffee and delectable sandwiches out to the back deck. I can barely get my mouth around the English muffin stacked with eggs, bacon, melty cheese, avocado, and tomato. Kevin sits nearby, waiting quietly for a crumb of bacon to fall on the deck magically. We're a little apprehensive about giving him any people food just yet, but a little piece of egg shouldn't hurt him. He delightedly licks my fingers until they're spotless, happy to have something other than his bland, post-sickness dog food.

Will's phone pings.

> SHAWN: WEIRD GUY IS BACK.

> WILL: TELL HIM I'M AT A SHOWING AND I'LL BE THERE IN HALF AN HOUR. KEEP HIM TALKING.

"Eric is at the brewery waiting for me. I'm going to bring him back here this afternoon for a showing. Do you want to take Kevin up to my house, or do you want to confront his sorry ass?"

"I want to be here. Both Kevin and I would like to give that motherfucker a piece of our minds."

"That's my girl." He leans down for what I expect will be a small peck but sticks his tongue in my mouth, and I'm now having second thoughts about letting him leave this house.

"I'm going to need more of that later," I murmur against his lips.

"Maybe I could be a little late to my appointment," he smirks, pulling me against him.

"Just go and get this over with. I'll be here when you get back. Oh, and maybe grope me as much as possible in front of that fucking man-baby."

"Don't need to ask me twice. Love you, babe."

"Love you. Be safe. His recent activity is proof that he's completely off the rails at the moment. He doesn't like to lose, and my leaving him and taking the dog with me has caused him to lose his mind."

CHAPTER THIRTY-FIVE

Dog Days Are Over

WILL

Swinging by my house to check on Dad before meeting Mitch/Eric gives me a chance to change into something more professional. I dress in a blue and white checked button-down with the sleeves rolled to my elbows, paired with dark jeans and the new gray and navy Cole Haan sneakers that Viv surprised me with. I've always preferred boots, but these are a great casual alternative and wicked comfortable. Plus, they're something I'd never buy for myself.

"How's it going, Dad?" I ask, finding him watching sports news on TV.

"Good, good, son. How's Kevin doing?"

"He's just about back to normal. Looks like he's going to be okay—thanks to you."

"He gave me quite a scare."

"Us too. I think we've found who was responsible," I say.

"Oh?" His brows shoot up.

"As far as we can tell, Viv's ex hired some teens from over on Barr Island to poison the fish and get it onto her property."

"Jesus Christ. Have you called the Staties?"

"We've been in touch. The whole thing should be taken care of by this afternoon. We'll come up for dinner tonight and bring your pal."

"Be careful out there," Dad calls out as I head out the door.

I know I just brightened his day by promising to see him later for dinner. The limitations on his activity have really gotten him down lately. I make a note to stop by the café later to pick up his favorite dessert.

> WILL: HEY MARY, CAN YOU SET ASIDE A BOSTON CREME PIE FOR ME TO PICK UP LATER?

> MARY: YOU BET, DARLIN'.

Shawn's pained expression when I walk into the taproom clearly indicates that he's not interested in continuing the conversation with Viv's ex for even a second longer. I notice his shoulders sag in relief when he sees me.

"Excuse me, Mitch?" I say as I approach his barstool.

"Yes." He turns in his stool. "About time. I've been waiting for you for an hour." Liar. It's been half an hour, according to Shawn.

"I apologize. I had another appointment, and you never told me what time you would arrive."

"I don't like to be kept waiting," Mitch/Eric mutters.

"You should've made an actual appointment, then."

He scoffs loudly, and it takes every ounce of willpower in my body not to reach forward and slam his smug face into the glossy wooden bar top. I can't fucking wait to never see this guy again.

"I was able to get you a showing at the place on the point this afternoon. If 2 p.m. works for you, I can give you directions to meet me there."

"Well, I guess it will have to be if you can't get me there earlier." The urge to punch hard gets stronger and stronger each time this ballsack speaks.

I hand him a sticky note with Viv's address. "There are a couple of good lunch spots here in town if you want to get something to eat while you wait."

"Yes. Good idea. I'll see you at two." He hops off his barstool, and I chuckle to myself at our height difference. The top of his head barely reaches my shoulder. As badly as I want to blacken his eyes, the fight would be unfair.

Shawn and I watch him leave the brewery, and as soon as the door swings shut, Shawn loses his shit. "That guy is, by far, the biggest douche canoe I've ever spoken to. How did Viv put up with him?"

"She admits it was foolish not to leave him sooner. But it was during the COVID times, with social distancing and all that. I think she felt trapped. And then, with all the health issues concerning her mom, she didn't have time to think about getting out."

"I guess that makes sense," Shawn says. "I'm glad she got out and found her way back here. Don't think I've seen you smile this much since before Silas died."

"I don't think I have. She brought me back to life," I remark. "I'm going to run and get a sandwich from Earl's before I head back over to Viv's. Want me to grab you something?"

"Yeah, that would be great. Just a BLT on toasted white."

Shawn and I eat our sandwiches in silence. The brewery is quiet while people are at places that serve more than just beer at lunchtime. I'm feeling mildly nervous that my plan will fail. It's all about timing, so I hope Officer Miller won't let me down. Driving back to Walker's Rock, I run through my plan one last time.

"Hey, babe," I say as I enter the cabin. She and Kevin are lounging on the couch, watching television. Yes, Kevin watches television. He's very interested in anything with animals or water, so naturally, she's watching some National Geographic show about the ocean—and the dog is riveted.

"Hey, handsome," she calls back. "What time is asshole expected to show up?"

"I told him two. I also got in touch with Officer Miller and asked him to swing by just after two." I lean over her on the couch and softly run my tongue across her bottom lip. Without warning, she grabs the collar of my shirt and thrusts her tongue into my mouth, slowly exploring.

"Now we're even, Cooper." She lets me go, and I stumble back, a little lightheaded by the sudden rush of adrenaline that just shot up my spine.

"Jesus." I shake my head, trying to clear the stimulating haze clouding my vision. "No more of that until we get rid of the visitors who are about to arrive."

One side of Viv's mouth lifts in a mischievous smile. "Okay, Junior. What-ever you say." God, I love this woman. I love how genuine and affectionate she is.

The telltale sign of an approaching vehicle's tires over gravel snaps us back into reality. I take a deep breath—it's showtime. It's time to bid this horrible asshole a fond and final fuck you.

"He's here. Stay inside until Officer Miller arrives. I want him to hear everything Mitch/Eric says."

"Sounds like a plan," she says, pushing me out the doorway. I look back to see her peeking out the side of the curtained window. I know that exact moment she spots her ex because her face turns a sickly shade of gray.

"Hello, Mitch," I call out as I walk toward him, hand outstretched. Once again, he acts as if he doesn't see that I'm trying to shake his hand. I don't hate many people in my life, but this guy... I swear he'd trample an old lady to get the last bottle of water.

"Mr. Harris. So this is it? Looks more rundown up close." Mitch/Eric scoffs.

"Well, the place has only been used during the summers, but has also stood vacant for several years. The owner is just now starting to put some money into updates and renovations."

"Well, my offer will definitely take into account all the repairs that need to be done."

My right fist clenches instinctively. "Why don't we go to the back of the house? That's where the money view is," I suggest.

Mitch/Eric silently follows me to the oceanside of the cabin. "This is Narraguagus Bay, and across the way—"

"I don't give a shit what's across the way," he interrupts. Stay calm, Cooper. "I've seen enough. I'd like to tour the inside now."

"Sure, follow me back to the front door."

"Why can't we enter from the deck?" He says, his voice almost whiny.

"Door's locked." This motherfucker is just asking for a karate chop to the Adam's apple.

As they round the side of the house, I see Officer Miller returning. I glance over at Mitch/Eric and see him flinch slightly. Then the smug look I've become accustomed to spreads over his stupid, weird face. As the State Trooper exits his vehicle, Viv's ex waves and starts jogging toward him as if he's here for him.

"Are you here to collect the abused dog? The one I called about? I haven't seen him, but I'm sure he's in the house!"

"Mr. Mitchell?" The officer asks.

"Yes, yes. That's my dog in there. She stole him from me." He points wildly back in the direction of the cabin.

"Who stole what now?"

"Vivian James. She owns this cabin. She stole my dog from me when she left Boston."

"You're making no sense at all, sir," Officer Miller says. "I'm here for you, to arrest you for animal cruelty."

"Me?" Mitch/Eric's eyes widen. "It's her fault. She neglected the dog."

"I have three witnesses that will testify that you paid them to poison this animal." The Statie's big arms cross his chest, just waiting for this weasel to try something.

"Someone paid them off to pin this on me. It was Vivian. She orchestrated the whole thing."

"Are you willing to risk that in a court of law?"

I honestly never thought this encounter would be so fucking entertaining. Viv's ex is losing his shit. And I especially never thought he'd try to run away—in his fancy, slick-bottomed loafers. He barely gains any traction, and the officer just chuckles as he sprints by, knowing he won't get too far in those shoes.

Just as he starts to run up the driveway, Viv swings the front door wide open, letting Kevin loose. She's been secretly recording the entire scene, so she saw her ex take off. She comes to stand next to me, and we both burst into laughter as we watch the big black lab chase down the soft little man. He tackles Mitch/Eric from behind, burying his face in the loose gravel.

By the time we reach Kevin, all 80 pounds of him is proudly standing on the perpetrator's back, his arms and legs flailing about. Viv calls Kevin back to us, and he promptly obeys {{good boy}} with the biggest lab smile I've ever witnessed. "Who's my good boy?" Viv coos at him. "We don't ever have to see that bad, bad man ever again."

"Looks like you've got yourself in a real shituation here," Viv says to her ex with a chuckle, and holds Kevin's collar so he doesn't tackle him again.

"Shituation?" I ask.

"Just how it sounds, Cooper."

"You fucking bitch," Mitch/Eric mutters under his breath.

Officer Miller cuffs Mitch/Eric and pulls him roughly off the ground by one arm, reading him his Miranda rights on the way back to his vehicle. "Ms. James," he calls out. "Do you want to press charges?"

Viv links her hand in mine as we approach her ex. He sneers at us, his face marred with scrapes and cuts from face-planting in the rough gravel. I know she wants him to get the picture that we're together, a family, a unit, and he'll never hurt us again.

"As much as I'd love to, I'll drop the charges on two conditions and the answer to a question," Viv begins. "First, how the fuck did you find me?"

Mitch/Eric spits gravel onto the ground. "I tracked Hadley's car."

"Interesting. You're lucky she's not here right now because she has murder in her heart for you."

"I'll pretend I didn't hear that," Officer Miller says.

"I would like to file a restraining order against him. Just keep him away from me and Kevin. And lastly, I'd like to be reimbursed for the overnight stay at the animal hospital. Now, can you kindly get him out of my sight?"

The State Trooper pushes Mitch/Eric into the back seat; his head hangs in shame. He's quiet for once. "I'll send a tow truck down for his vehicle. I'm taking him back to the barracks to file the paperwork."

"Thank you, Officer," I say. "We'll all sleep better tonight, knowing Kevin is safe."

"And thank you for your assistance in finding and apprehending him."

"I think Kevin deserves the thanks for the apprehension," Viv says. The hand I'm not holding absentmindedly strokes the top of her pup's head.

"That he does," he says. He walks back over with a small plastic shield meant for kids and pins it to his collar. "There, an official deputy in the Maine State Police."

As soon as they're out of sight, Hadley's red pick-up truck skids to a stop in front of us. She jumps out, her baggy overalls covered in paint splatter. She pulls out a large canvas, her easel, and a toolbox full of paints.

"What's going on?" She asks, noticing Viv and me just standing here grinning at nothing.

"Oh, not much," Viv answers. "We just busted Eric for poisoning Kevin. Just another day."

"Oh my fucking god," she exclaims. "That's the best news I've heard this summer. Is that asshole going to jail? Please tell me he's going to jail! He'll make someone such a nice bottom."

"Nope, I dropped the charges with a guarantee that I'll never hear from him or see him ever again." Viv grins and squeezes my hand. "What are you doing here? Not that I'm not so happy to see you."

"Oh man, I just had a creative jolt. It was weird. I woke up this morning and had a vision of myself painting the view from your deck. So here I am. To paint."

"Can't wait to see the finished product. Why don't you invite Cam to come down a little later, and we can have dinner together?" Viv asks.

"Babe, I told my dad we'd have dinner with him tonight."

"Cam can pick him up on his way," Hadley says excitedly.

"Ask him to pick up my pie at the Cafe, too," I add.

"A perfect end to the day," Viv says. We leave Hadley on the deck and flop onto the couch.

"So you're not going to tell her your ex tracked her car?" I ask.

"Have you just met Hadley?" she asks. "She will hunt him until the end of time and torture him."

"I don't see the problem." I pull her onto my lap and hug her close. I think today is the day we officially start our lives together... with no baggage in the way. "I love you, Vivian James."

"Back atcha, Cooper."

CHAPTER THIRTY-SIX

Homecoming

VIV

The final weeks of summer melted away like salt dissolving in warm water, and Labor Day weekend arrived with its customary fanfare—sizzling backyard barbecues filled the air with the scent of grilled meats. We took impromptu, topless Jeep road trips to explore more of Maine's coastline. Kevin's ears flapped wildly in the cool, salty breeze, a broad smile always lighting up his face.

For Will and me, these last few weeks have been a time of subtle transformation. No longer threatened by my ex, and with Kevin safe, we have settled into our life together. Will appears more relaxed; his eyes often catch mine with a warm smile, as if he can't believe this is our new normal. We're learning how to breathe again without looking over our shoulders.

The cabin's construction is complete, and it is just in time for Mom's memorial service. While the work took some time, the changes inside were subtle. First and foremost, all the plumbing was replaced—I definitely don't want any more flooding. We completely remodeled the kitchen with updated cherry cabinets, marble countertops, new appliances, and an island added to better define the kitchen from the living area, providing us with more seating options for dining. The bathroom was reconfigured to replace the outdated bathtub with a large walk-in shower spacious enough for two. A new roof and improved insulation have us ready for colder weather.

I've gradually begun adding my personal touches to the decor. I would never replace the heirloom pieces that hold so many memories for me, but a couple of oversized chairs and ottomans really enhance the living room's coziness. My favorite update took place in the front corner of the cabin, where my great-grandfather's hunting trophies once resided. The walls now hold two large bookcases that frame a heavily pillowed chaise lounge chair, creating a reading nook. Books, photos, and old hunting treasures now fill the shelves. It's where I feel closest to my mom.

The most significant change has been Hadley moving in with Cam and Lucas. It's strange not to see her all the time, but knowing she's just across town is so comforting. It makes sense since she spends almost every night with him anyway. We found out the other day that Will's uncle plans to move back to Shearwater Cove, so he's happily willing to give up his quarters at the house on the hill and settle into Walker's Rock with me. I believe this change will be good for his dad; I know he hated that his brother was so far away. And it eases Will's mind knowing he won't be alone.

"Good morning, beautiful," Will whispers into my hair as he wraps his arms around me from behind. It's before dawn on the morning of Mom's memorial service. I turn in his arms for a kiss.

"Hmmm, good morning," I say against his lips.

"Are you ready for this morning?"

"I think so. Hadley, Evvie, and Betsy were extremely helpful yesterday in setting everything up. All the food is in the fridge, and we just need to heat the casseroles."

"I meant, are *you* ready? It's not easy to say goodbye, even if it is for the second time."

"I am. Saying goodbye in a place she loved so much will mean so much more to both of us," I say, handing him a cup of coffee. "Also, looks like we're going to get the perfect sunrise."

"I'll be right by your side, always."

"I might need you to hold my hand while I read the eulogy. I'm nervous about that."

"Anything you need."

"I love you so much, Will," I say, holding his face in my hands. I kiss him again, this time lingering. "I need to get dressed. You need to get dressed. People will start arriving in about half an hour.

"I love you, too, Vivian."

As the sun begins its slow rise, our Shearwater Cove family sits in folding chairs scattered around the yard. With coffees in hand at the ridiculously early hour, all eyes are on me as I stand at the edge of the deck. Will stands close by my side, our arms touching and providing me with much comfort.

"Good morning, everyone," I begin—murmurs of good morning ripple through our group of friends. "First of all, I want to thank you all for coming out at this ungodly hour to bid farewell to my dear mother. I have prepared a brief eulogy, and then we'll scatter her ashes into the Bay. At that time, anyone who wishes to speak is more than welcome."

Will gathers my hand in his while I clutch my words with the other. I take a deep breath and exhale slowly to calm my nerves. I feel him squeeze twice, lending me the strength to do this.

"My mom, well, most of you knew her. She was your friend, she was my best friend, and she was the fiercest warrior I've ever known. Many of you might know our story—my great-grandmother, Vivian, died at 39, and my grandmother, Patricia, at 42, both from breast cancer. So, when Mom was diagnosed at 37 shortly after our last visit to Shearwater Cove, it surprised no one. For 16 years, she fought like hell until her body just gave up.

"There was a place my mother held dear in her heart. A place she longed to return to. A place that held her happiest memories, where the air smelled salty, where the light danced differently on the water, where she felt at home in a way no other place could offer. She longed to return to Shearwater Cove, never giving up the hope of making it back here.

"Today, we grieve, but we also celebrate. We celebrate the woman who loved without limits, fought without fear, and lived without regret. While I mourn a life back in this town without her, I celebrate the life I've made here, and I know she would've been so happy that I made it back.

"Rest easy, Mom. Fly on the breeze, float on the ocean, and be free. You're finally home. I love you."

Will gently stuffs a handful of tissues in my hand, and it's only then that I realize silent tears are streaming down my face. His arms wrap around me, pulling me into his chest, where I can feel his chest against my cheek. As I settle into him, I become aware of several of our closest friends gathering around us, their presence a circle of support I've grown to depend on. The overwhelming wave of love from this group crashes over me, filling me with a profound sense of gratitude.

"Vivi, I have a special song I think Maggie would have wanted us to play as we say goodbye," Hadley says, sliding her arms around Will and me.

"Okay, Hads, I'm sure she'll love whatever you pick."

As we walk toward the point of land, each person holding a paper lantern to release in memory of Mom, the sun rests on the horizon, welcoming the new day. My breath catches as I hear the opening notes from the outdoor speakers of the song chosen by Hadley.

Toad the Wet Sprocket's "Walk on the Ocean." My mother's favorite band from when I was little. The *Fear* album played on repeat in our house in the '90s. I feel the tears start again, and I'm quickly gathered into Will's arms. Hadley squeezes my hand.

"You remembered," I whisper to her.

"She still played that one album when we were in college. What, like thirty years after its release?" She chuckles at the memory.

The music fades into the background as, one by one, some of her closest friends from Shearwater Cove come forward to say a few words about her, as her ashes float away with the tide. It was more than I could've hoped for in a send-off for my sweet mother. I whisper to the wind, "I miss you like crazy, Mom."

Finally, turning to face our crowd of friends, I say, "Thank you, everyone, for coming. My mother would come back to haunt me relentlessly if I didn't feed you, so come on up to the house for some of Mary's famous breakfast casserole and Cam's delicious pastries. And of course, plenty more coffee!"

Later that afternoon, after everyone had left and all the clean-up was done, Will and I collapsed onto the bed for a much-needed two-hour nap. Finally, I dug out the envelope my mother had left me. The instructions were clear: I was not to open it until I had returned to Shearwater Cove and we had reached the anniversary of her death.

Will and I sit on the couch, with Kevin squeezed between us, as I slowly open the envelope and pull out a small stack of papers. This feels quite mysterious. The first document is my mother's will, and its contents are familiar to me. We reviewed it before she passed away. She left everything to me—her house, this cabin, and the trust fund my grandmother established for her, similar to the one I received when I turned thirty.

The following document is my grandmother's will, which I had not seen before. Similar to my mother's will, it bequeaths her house, the cabin, and her financial assets to my mom. However, the subsequent items leave me speechless.

"Are you okay, Viv?" Will asks, noticing the look of shock on my face.

I quietly hand him the Apple stock certificate, and his expression mirrors mine. The certificate is dated 1984; the logo features the classic rainbow apple. My grandmother's name is printed on it, indicating that she purchased $13,000 worth of shares. She must have taken the money from the settlement after my grandfather was killed.

"Wait, you didn't know about this?" Will asks. "Where did your trust come from?"

"I had no idea. The trusts she set up for Mom and me came from the settlement she received after my grandfather was killed in a car accident."

"Holy shit," he says, handing the certificate back to me.

"Holy shit is right," I agree.

The final three documents in the stack include a letter to my mother regarding the posthumous sale of stocks for a donation she needed to initiate, a receipt for selling shares valued at approximately $5 million, and a letter to the town of Shearwater Cove identifying my grandmother as the anonymous donor in 2009.

"Oh my god," I exclaim, showing him the letter.

He blows out a long breath. "I don't even know what to say about this. I'm just shocked."

"I know. But hey, the mystery is now solved. What should we do?" I ask

"I honestly have no idea. Let's go see my dad. He must know something."

We grab the stack of paperwork and Kevin, and head for the truck. There would be hell to pay if we showed up at the Cooper compound without the dog. As usual, Bill is watching a Red Sox game when we arrive.

"Hey Dad," Will calls out. "Who's winning?"

"Not these bums," Bill replies sullenly.

"What do we always say? There's always next year?"

"They do have a couple of breakout stars this year, so if they can build on that, maybe they'll be contenders next year." Bill shuts the television off. "What brings you up here?"

Kevin leaps on the couch, and Bill gives him a full-body scratch. He flops onto his back, his tongue lolling out of his mouth. "Who's a good boy?" he asks him while rubbing his belly.

"This," I say, handing him the letter to the town.

He reads it and slowly hands it back, blowing out a breath. "Thank god that's out in the open now."

"Wait, you knew?" Will asks.

"Yeah, I've known this whole time."

"You kept this secret for fifteen years? You're the worst secret keeper I know," Will laughs.

"Maggie needed someone on the inside. I helped her get the funds to the right person."

"Damn," I say. "You and my mom were in cahoots for a while, huh?"

"Oh yeah. With each passing year that the two of you didn't return here, she got madder and madder. She would call to complain to me at least once a year. Your mom was pretty private about her health, so she begged me not to tell anyone we talked. She never had the desire to connect with friends she wasn't sure she'd ever see again."

"Ugh," I lament. "That sounds so much like my mom. She hated for anyone to see her sick or weak."

"So I was the one to make sure your grandmother's wishes were followed exactly as she had laid out. People in this town thought I was crazy when I told them about the paint colors," Bill continued.

"I bet," Will says.

"My grandmother died before I was born, but my mom always said she had a pretty twisted sense of humor."

"So I've heard," Bill says with a quiet laugh.

CHAPTER THIRTY-SEVEN

Plans and Pillow Forts

WILL

Viv and I hunker down on the couch for most of the following day. After the emotionally draining memorial service and the recent revelations from the *envelope*, we truly need a day of nothing. Kevin fully supports our day of rest after his morning swim, which couldn't have been pleasant in the cool, rainy weather that has rolled in. This probably explains why he's buried under a blanket on his dog bed.

We each take an end, using the armrest for support, our legs stretched out in front of us and entwined with each other. Viv's nose is buried in what

I assume is a smutty novel, given how she's chewing on her bottom lip. Meanwhile, I'm catching up on the news on my iPad.

"So what do you think it's worth?" I ask.

"Hmmm?" she looks up at me.

"The Apple stock. I've read stories about what stock bought in the '80s is worth."

"Jeez, I have no idea. I'll see if someone can recommend a financial firm to get in touch with. I'm guessing it's—what's the proper term? A fucking shit ton of money. Maybe 15-20 million?"

I laugh. "Agreed. What will you do with it all?"

"Are you just with me for my wealth now, Cooper?" she asks, pressing her foot closer to my crotch.

I grab her foot and give her a devilish smirk. "Can I help it if I dream of being a kept man?"

"I'll keep you alright," she jokes. "I'll keep you naked and exhausted."

"Promises, promises," I murmur, pulling her legs to me so she's straddling my lap.

"Not in front of the child," she purrs.

"Not even this?" I ask, licking up the side of her neck. She lets out a low moan and arches her back, pressing closer to me.

"Well, that might be okay," she whispers, running her hands through my hair.

"What about this?" I pull the front of her loose t-shirt down and continue to lick downward.

"I think that's nice." She shifts her weight with slow, deliberate movements as she settles deeper into my lap. "Feels like you think it's nice, too."

"Hmmm, it is." I slowly slide my hand down the front of her shorts. "And this?"

She leans forward, pressing herself firmly into my hand. "That's good," she breathes heavily as she rhythmically rides my lap.

"We might be treading in rated-R territory here soon," I breathe, nodding in Kevin's direction.

"He's asleep; just be quiet."

"I think you're the one who needs to be quiet," I tease, circling my finger around her clit.

"Oh, god," she grabs the hair at the back of my head and pulls me to her mouth, her whimpers muffled by my lips.

"Not fair," I murmur teasingly, pulling away just enough to create a torturous distance. Without warning, I slide two fingers inside her, feeling her warmth surround them. Her deep, loud moan echoes through the room with an intensity that jolts Kevin awake. He sits up abruptly and stares directly at us with a bewildered expression.

She lets her forehead fall against mine as we look over at the dog. With our eye contact, his tail starts wagging furiously. Well, shit. That'll teach us. "I think he needs to go out," she says, stepping off my lap and pulling her shirt back into place.

I leave Viv at the cabin, pretending to have work duties, and head to the brewery to meet our friends. She's so engrossed in her book that she hardly notices me when I lean down to kiss her goodbye.

"So, what's the emergency?" Shawn asks, always the impatient one.

"I found out who the town's anonymous donor is." Might as well jump right into it.

"Who?" My friends shout in unison.

"My god." I fall back a step. "Calm down."

"This mystery has been around since we were teenagers, for fuck's sake," Mike leans forward.

"It was Viv's grandmother, Patty."

"Holy shit," Becky exclaims. "And she never knew?"

"Nope."

"No one knew?" Evvie asks.

"Just my dad," I say. "I can't believe the old man kept it a secret all that time."

"No shit," Shawn agrees. "Remember when we tried to throw you a surprise thirtieth birthday party and he asked you what the dress code was?"

"Oh my god," Mike says. "I wanted to murder him—all that planning and sneaking around."

"I remember. I was so grateful to know about the surprise, but I was tragically bad at faking my shock. You guys knew right away."

"The sheepish look on Bill's face kind of gave it away also," Evvie adds.

"So is Viv a gajillionaire?" Becky asks.

"Sort of?" I say. "But you guys know Viv. This won't change her one damn bit. I definitely don't think she'll leave us all behind for the French Riviera."

"Viv isn't equipped for the Riviera," Hadley chuckles. "What are you planning in that beautiful head of yours, Will? And how can we help?"

"Yes, okay, so I have an idea," I say. "I want to arrange for the town to name the waterfront park after Patty officially—the Patricia Walker James Memorial Park, we could call it Patty's Park for short."

"Will—" Evvie gasps. "That's such a fantastic idea. I love Patty's Park."

"Hadley, can you arrange to hang out with Viv next Saturday and get her to the park?" I ask.

"Of course. And she'll never turn down a walk if I ask her," Hadley says.

"Great," I start. "I talked to Earl, and he told me Patty's favorite place to be was next to the water. She loved the salty air, he said, but she never liked to be the center of attention. Let's place the plaque on the boardwalk overlooking the Bay."

"That's a great idea," Becky agrees. "It's right next to the water without being a huge focal point."

"Do you think the benches along the walkway will be enough seating for anyone who can't stand for that long?" Mike asks.

"Maybe grab a handful of folding chairs just in case?" I say, and Mike nods.

"What about the actual plaque?" Shawn asks.

"I've got a guy in Milbridge who does bronze plaques and says he can have it done by next Saturday, no problem. And I'm going to ask my dad to build a nice teak stand to attach it to."

"Ooooh, I love that!" Evvie squeals. "Betsy and I can let everyone know what's happening, so we have a nice crowd for the dedication."

"Perfect," I say, consulting the list on my phone. "I think that's it. I really don't think we need a gathering with food afterward."

"Agree," Shawn says.

"We'll have our group over to the house for a barbecue afterward. Does that work for you, hon?" Mike asks Evvie.

"Absolutely," she says, nodding her head. "We haven't done that in a while. It will be fun. Please make sure Viv brings Kevin because if he doesn't show up, the girls will revolt."

"She wouldn't think of leaving him home. He loves those girls as much as they love him." The image of the girls trying to out-splash Kevin makes me smile. "Wait. Olivia's birthday is next week. Is that going to mess things up?"

"Not at all," Evvie says. "She's having a group of friends sleeping over on Friday night, so they'll all be gone before lunchtime. And then we can have some cake for her during our barbecue."

"Okay, that sounds great," I sigh, relieved. "I'll talk to you all later. I need to go see Dad."

When I arrive at the house, I notice another vehicle with Massachusetts plates. I haven't seen my Uncle Charlie in years, so I eagerly push through the front door.

"Dad," I call out. "Is there a Masshole in the house?"

"You little shit," I hear Uncle Charlie curse as he meets me in the entryway. He grabs me in a borderline violent hug and lifts me off my feet. My uncle is not a small man. We used to call him Uncle Bear when we were little because of his hulking form. He sets me down and gives me a forceful pat on the back.

"How ya been, Unc?" I ask. "Can't wait to have you here permanently."

"I'm good, kid. Just retired from the Post Office, so I'm ready to start my quiet retired life up here with my big brother," he says, jerking a thumb towards my dad sitting on the couch.

Like my dad, Uncle Charlie is a widower. His sweet wife, my Aunt Jenny, died of lung cancer about ten years ago. Never smoked a day in her life. It was such a shock to everyone.

"I'm glad you're moving up here. I know Dad has missed ya," I say.

"Or are you just glad I'm moving here so you can shack up with your girl guilt-free?" He says with a sly smile.

"Okay, that too," I laugh. "I can't wait for you to meet her."

"If you love her, I'm sure I will too."

"When are you planning to move in?" I ask.

"I brought up most of my stuff on this trip. I'm having the movers come with the rest in a couple of days. So I guess I'm here to stay now. I've sold the house after less than 24 hours on the market, and they were looking for a quick closing." He shrugs. "So here I am."

"That's excellent!" I say, clapping him on the back.

"Dad, you got a minute? I want to talk to you about something." I say, flopping on the chair next to his spot on the couch.

"What's up?" He asks.

"I'd like to have an official dedication at the park next weekend to name it The Patricia Walker James Memorial Park formally."

"Kid, that's a wonderful idea," Dad says. "How can I help?"

"I found a guy in Milbridge who will create the bronze plaque, but we need something to mount it to. Thought maybe you could come up with something. Don't you have a bunch of teak in the barn?"

"I do. And I would be honored. What are you thinking?"

"I thought we could place the plaque along the boardwalk, at the spot where the path through the park connects to it. Maybe have a way to attach it to the railing," I suggest.

"I can work with that," Dad says, smiling. I can tell by the gleam in his eyes that he's so thrilled for a project to keep his hands busy. My dad has been working on boats for many years, but his real passion is carpentry. He's happiest working with wood.

"Thanks, Pop. If you guys aren't busy tomorrow night, I'll bring Viv and Kevin up for dinner."

"Your girl has a kid?" Uncle Charlie asks, confused.

"Dad hasn't told you about Kevin?"

"Kevin is Viv's black lab," Dad says. "He's my best buddy. You're going to love that silly dog."

"That dog has a human name," Charlie laughs.

"He sure does. And we're almost positive he understands like a human, too," I say.

"Can't wait to meet him."

"Great, we'll see you tomorrow night." I give both men a wave and head home.

WILL: ON MY WAY HOME. NEED ANYTHING.

VIV: JUST YOU.

WILL: COMING!

VIV: YOU WILL BE.

Jesus fuck, this woman truly has a talent for getting under my skin, in a good way. The need to watch my speed as I drive into Walker's Rock feels like pure torture. The last thing I need is a head-on collision to ruin my night.

I skid to a stop in front of the cabin, the gravel crunching beneath the wheels. I leap out of the truck and burst through the front door into the dimly lit, empty living room. The only sign of life is Kevin, sprawled on his back across the couch, oblivious to the world. Fool.

"Babe?" I call out.

"In here," she yells from the bedroom.

Oh boy.

I push the door open and step into a bedroom bathed in candlelight. Flickering flames cast golden shadows across the walls; the air is thick and sweet with the aroma of vanilla mingling with a hint of lavender from the assortment of candles scattered across every surface. The room feels like a cozy embrace; the bed, which usually resembles a battlefield of tangled sheets and pillows, is now neatly made and topped with a mountain of plush pillows.

Viv sits on her knees amongst the pile, completely naked. Waves of deep red hair cascade over her shoulders, barely concealing her bare breasts. She's peering up at me through long, sweeping bangs, her green eyes bright and teasing. But it's the bottom lip caught between her teeth that has me shedding my clothes in record time.

She makes no secret of her admiration for my body, her eyes raking over me with an intensity that ignites a fire inside. When she crooks an index finger at me, beckoning me with the playful gesture, I find myself powerless to resist. All of my self-control vanishes as I sweep her into my arms with a swift, fluid motion, pulling her beneath me in a way that elicits a delighted squeal from her lips.

So much for the tidy bed.

CHAPTER THIRTY-EIGHT

The Heart of the Cove

VIV

"Hey, babe?" Will says from the kitchen.

"Hmmm?" I look up from my book. "What's up?"

"I made plans to go fishing with Mike and Shawn on Saturday. This summer has been so busy, the three of us haven't had a chance to go out."

"No need to talk me into it, honey. I have plans with Hadley on Saturday," I tell him.

"Cool."

"What would be really cool is if you catch something for dinner," I chuckle.

"I'll do my best, enchantress."

"Oooh, I like that title," I say, winking at him.

"Don't get used to it," he says. "It's going to be really nice today. Want to take a drive with the doggo?"

"Where ya thinking?"

"Have you ever seen Bass Harbor Lighthouse? It's only about an hour and a half away," Will suggests.

"I haven't seen Bass Harbor. Let's go! Maybe we can find a good lobster roll for lunch somewhere nearby."

"I think that's probably an option."

Our drive to Bass Harbor is as uneventful as any trip to that area can be during the shoulder season. The traffic is steady but not as heavy as it is on weekends. The parking lot is half-full when we arrive, and I'm excited to get out and explore with my boys. The house is a private residence, so I leash Kevin, and we head off to check out the grounds. We take the wooden steps that lead down to the boulders at the water's edge, which is the best location for snapping pictures of the adorable lighthouse perched on the granite cliff. The clear blue sky provides a stunning backdrop behind the bright white structure.

"Do you think Kevin will be ok on the boulders?" I ask as we make our way down the steps.

"If not, I can stay back with him while you take some photos. It's such a pretty spot."

Will holds Kevin's leash tightly in the presence of the open ocean. If he ever jumped in here, we would absolutely never get him back on dry land with this rocky terrain. I find a boulder at a safe distance and delight in the view it offers of the lighthouse. I take endless photos of the scenery. I capture more images of Will and Kevin with the glassy, teal ocean behind them, the sun highlighting the rich blue-green hues. We take selfies, and Will and I scooch down to include Kevin in the frame. We find a flat boulder large enough for all three of us and linger in the sunshine until our hunger drives us back to the Jeep.

"Let's see if we can get into Thurston's for lunch," he suggests.

"I have no idea what that means, but if there's a big, fat lobster roll in my future, I'm in," I reply, reaching over to squeeze his hand as we drive the short distance to the restaurant.

Thurston's Lobster Pound sits across Bass Harbor in the town of Bernard, which is part of Acadia National Park—though it is a bit quieter than downtown Bar Harbor. As we approach the restaurant, we are greeted by a building that embodies Down East Maine. The weathered cedar shakes are adorned with lobster buoys of various colors and patterns. The short line to order food moves quickly, and by the time it is our turn, we have both settled on the jumbo lobster roll with chips and iced teas.

The dining area features a spacious deck shaded by a bright yellow awning, where we find an empty table closest to the front edge for the view. It's far enough from the other tables that Kevin won't be a bother, even though he's so exhausted from the lighthouse adventure that he immediately flops down on the deck beneath our table.

As expected, the lobster spills out of its buttery, toasted bun. The tender, bite-sized pieces of claw and tail meat deliver the sweet, salty flavor I adore in the perfect lobster roll. It was lightly tossed in mayo, and of course, Will remembered to ask for butter on the side. The corners of his mouth lifted when I poured the entire side over the sandwich, undoubtedly reminiscing about the last time we enjoyed lobster rolls at the cabin. I try not to moan this time.

On our drive back to Shearwater Cove, we stop at a few antique shops. I discover a vintage trapper basket for the collection of fleece blankets, currently scattered across the back of my couch. Will finds an old brass gimbal compass in mint condition, and the price is so reasonable that we dart out of that shop as if we had stolen something.

Days like today will live in my heart always—and hopefully, these are the kind of memories Will and I will continue to make as we continue our life together.

On Saturday morning, Hadley arrives far too early for normal humans. The upside of this early arrival is the box of warm, freshly baked scones—the blueberry ones, my favorites. It's almost like she's buttering me up for something. I mean, not like Will buttered me up, but shit, now I want butter.

"Why are you here so fucking early?" I ask, watching her pour herself a cup of coffee and taking a sip of my own.

"Cam needed help with some baking this morning, so I got up early to give him a hand," she says, like it's normal for her to get up before 9 a.m.

"A hand? Mm-hmm." I mutter, chuckling. "You must be head over heels in love with this guy. Not much gets you up that early."

"I really am." She dreamily flutters her eyelashes at me.

We snuggle into the soft, cozy blankets on the couch, cradling our steaming mugs of coffee and savoring the buttery blueberry scones. Throughout my life, I've had good friends, but none quite like Hadley. No friend has ever woven themselves into my life with so little effort. We've had our share of arguments, spent years separated by miles, and at times, let boyfriends take priority over each other. Still, I have never feared that these circumstances could jeopardize our friendship.

"Why do you have that weepy look on your face?" she asks, snapping me out of my thoughts.

"I'm just happy you're here. Not just at my house right now, but here in Shearwater Cove. For real. I'm happy you met someone who is obviously so good for you. And I'm happy you're my person. I don't know what I'd do without you," I say, my voice hoarse with emotion.

"Ew, why are you so mushy today?"

"I dunno, just happy, I guess."

"Yeah... you said that already." Hadley rolls her eyes and continues picking chunks off her scone and popping them into her mouth.

I lean over and hug her.

"God, get off me, you weirdo," she scolds, but then puts her arms around me, careful not to spill her coffee since she's still holding on to it. "I love you, Vivi."

"I love you, too, friend."

"Let's get out of here," Hadley says. "It's such a nice day, and who knows how many more of these we're going to get. Winter comes fast this far north."

"Where do you want to go?" I ask.

"Let's go for a walk in the park with the puppers."

"Sounds great. I'll go get dressed."

Today is my favorite kind of weather. It's cool enough for jeans and a sweatshirt, yet warm enough for flip-flops. I definitely prefer cool-weather clothes to shorts and tank tops. The more layers I can wear, the better.

We park the car at the brewery and walk across the street to the park. Cove Street, the town's main drag, is busier than expected, and the park seems to be teeming with people. As we walk down the main pathway toward the boardwalk, I spot many of our friends gathered around. And there's Will—the exact Will who told me he would be fishing with his friends today. What the fuck is going on?

When Will spots us, he jogs over. "Babe, hey!"

"Don't *babe, hey* me, you big fat liar," I say, crossing my arms over my chest.

He can't help but smile at my impudent toddler attitude. "I had to bend the truth a little for the surprise."

"What surprise, Cooper?" I ask.

He places an arm around my shoulders, guiding me toward the rest of the group. Kevin lags behind us, annoyed with me for keeping him on his leash. "Maybe you should just stand here and find out."

Earl steps forward from the crowd and stands at the railing beside something covered with a large sheet. Will and Hadley are on either side of me, each holding one of my hands. Kevin sits politely in front of me. This is weird. Why are they acting so weird?

"Thank you all for coming to the park today," Earl begins. "We'll keep this short and sweet, but I thought it was important to say a few words about a very special person. We recently found out something that has been quite a mystery in Shearwater Cove for fifteen years."

I squeeze Will's hand as hard as I can. "What did you do?" I say through clenched teeth.

"Anyone in this town will say the most asked question is *Why are all the buildings painted in such bright colors?*" Earl continues. "Well, now we know. An exceptional woman made it so. It's no secret that before I married my beautiful wife, Mary, I had a little crush on Patricia James. That woman was a bright light in this town, and she loved it even with its drab, rundown buildings."

I feel tears prick the backs of my eyes, listening to Earl's kind words about the grandmother I never knew.

"Now, when anyone asks about the color scheme, we can say Patty did it. We can also stop calling this beautiful piece of land the waterfront park and call it by the name it deserves. Will, can you do the honors?"

Will walks up to Earl and pulls the sheet from the structure to reveal a beautiful bronze plaque mounted on a lovely teakwood stand.

"Viv, do you want to come read what it says?" Will asks.

Kevin and I walk over to him, and all the breath leaves my body. The tears now blur my vision so I can barely read the words:

The Patricia Walker James Memorial Park | "Patty's Park" | Dedicated September 21, 2024

"You did this?" I ask Will in a gravelly whisper.

"I did. Is that okay?" He looks mildly worried now, considering the river of tears streaming down my cheeks.

"It's more than okay. I can't believe you did all this."

"She was important to this town, Viv. I couldn't not do something," he says, kissing me on the forehead.

"I love you so much."

"Back atcha, James."

"Patty's Park," I murmur. "I love it. My mom would've loved it. And I'm sure my grandmother would've loved it too. Even if she didn't really love being the center of attention—so I've heard."

"So I've heard, too."

I weave through the crowd, shaking hands and hugging those who have known my family forever, while Will stands off to the side, watching over Kevin and allowing me a moment to express my gratitude. I'm filled with such overwhelming affection for this little town and its people—now, my people. As the crowd begins to dwindle, leaving only our closest friends behind, I stand at the beautiful bronze plaque and trace the letters of my grandmother's name. I doubt she had any idea what she was doing when she purchased those shares of Apple stock all those years ago; for all I know, she probably bought it simply because apples were her favorite fruit. She changed the lives of an entire town with her generous donation.

"Viv," Will says from behind me. "We're going to head over to Mike and Evvie's for a barbecue."

"Will, the base this plaque is on?"

"Dad made it," he answers.

"It's exquisite," I breathe. "He should have an Etsy shop."

"A whatsy shop?"

"It's like an online craft fair. God, it's like you've lived under a rock until I moved here." I bump into Will gently, and he exaggerates a stumble.

"Somehow, I don't see Bill Cooper managing an online Yahtzee store."

"Etsy," I correct. I look over and see him grinning, clearly fucking with me.

We're the last to arrive at Mike and Evvie's, and the girls rush my dog like a couple of feral cats. "Kebin's here, Kebin's here!" Amelia squeals excitedly. He loves every minute of attention he gets from the small humans. I release him from his leash, and he runs off after the girls into the yard, most likely heading for a belly flop in the pool.

"Anytime you need someone to dog sit, we'll take him," Evvie says. "Those girls are so in love with him."

"I appreciate the offer. He'd probably never want to come home!" I say.

We eat, we drink, we toast to my grandmother, and we indulge in chocolate cake until we all get bellyaches.

Before Evvie puts the girls to bed, Will pulls out a small package wrapped in Frozen-themed paper. He has already given Olivia the gift from both of us—a Frozen Lego set that she lost her mind over. This small package is likely to get him in trouble with her parents. She tears open the paper to discover a Whoopee Cushion, and a puzzled look crosses her face.

"Blow it up," Will instructs. She does as he says.

"Squeeze it." She squeezes, and the loud fart sound it makes sends her into a fit of giggles.

The look Evvie shoots Will across the table makes me think it might be time for us to go home. He holds his hands up in surrender. "Can't help but feed her prank habit."

Evvie shakes her head and shoos the girls upstairs, and Mike gives Will two thumbs up when his wife can no longer see him.

CHAPTER THIRTY-NINE

One Last Song for the Summer

WILL

"Do you guys know if anyone has a portable karaoke machine around here?" I ask Shawn and Mike as we sit at the brewery's bar.

"I think Tiny has one," Shawn says.

"Yeah, he's the only one I know that has a good one," Mike says.

"Why the fuck does Tiny have a karaoke machine?" I ask, thoroughly confused by this new development.

"Why the fuck do you need one?" Shawn asks.

"I think he used to use it on his old boat when he had larger groups on his charters. Now, he just uses it at parties." Mike says, giving me a strange look.

"Interesting. Okay."

"So you're not going to tell us why you need one?" Mike asks.

"Absolutely not. I just have an idea."

"You know what scares me about this conversation?" Shawn asks.

"The fact that Will can't sing for shit?" Mike replies.

"Exactly." Shawn picks up his beer in a mock toast and takes a long swig.

"What do you think about having a goodbye summer party next weekend? It's the end of September, and the weather is starting to shift. This will probably be one of the last outdoor barbecues until spring," I say, trying to change the subject from my singing abilities. Or lack thereof.

"Great idea," Mike agrees. "Please don't say we're having it at my house."

"Nah, we'll have it at Walker's Rock," I say, and I see Mike's shoulders visibly relax.

"Oh, thank god," he says. "Evvie has basically threatened to chop my balls off if I plan one more gathering on our back deck. With the girls back in school and her back at the salon full-time, our house is crazy enough."

"Has Olivia gotten a chance to use her new Whoopee Cushion?" I ask.

"Oh my god, she got my mother so good yesterday. I thought my head might explode from holding in my hysterical laughter. My mom's reaction was priceless," Mike laughs. "She simply said, Excuse me, and acted completely normal."

"So great. Perfect Betsy response," I say. "So, bring the kids, invite your parents. All are welcome to the party."

"Babe?" I call out as I open the front door to the cabin. There's no answer. "Vivian?" I say a little louder. This house isn't so big that she can't hear me. I can see Kevin lying on the back deck in the last sliver of sunshine before it disappears behind the house. I peer through the French doors leading to the deck, but I can't see her anywhere.

As I open the door to step outside, she suddenly bursts around the corner with a very loud, "BOO!"

"JESUS CHRIST ON A CRACKER!" I yell, jumping approximately one mile into the air and clutching my chest.

When I can finally breathe again, I catch sight of Viv literally rolling on the floor with laughter. Kevin leaps to his feet, his confused gaze shifting from his mother, who is lying on the deck, laughing like a hyena, to me, desperately checking to make sure I didn't shit myself.

"Vivian Patricia James, you are in BIG trouble," I warn as I stalk towards her. She skitters backward on her hands like a crab desperate to escape my wrath. I grab her by an ankle to keep her from getting away, and once I subdue her flailing arms and legs, I toss her over my shoulder.

"William Cooper, put me down this instant!" She orders, pounding her small fists on my back.

"Nope, you wanna play, we're gonna play," I say, a hint of roguery in my voice.

"If you ever want me to touch your cock again, you will not throw me in the water," she yells, seeing me heading for the dock. Kevin is hot on my heels, no doubt wondering if this is a new game we're playing.

"Woman! Stop hitting me. You got your kicks; now I get mine." I shout, reaching the end of the weathered dock. With a swift motion, I toss her high into the air, watching as her arms and legs thrash wildly against the sky and she hits the water with a spectacular splash.

She emerges from the frigid water, her breath escaping in a sharp, angry gasp. "Help me out, you cretin!"

I extend my hand to help her onto the dock, but she's quicker than I expect. With a surprising twist, she braces her feet against the dock's support beam and, using every ounce of strength, she takes advantage of my forward lean, causing me to plummet headfirst into the water. Kevin remains seated at the end of the dock, looking at us as if we might be the biggest fools he knows. He is aware that the water is damn cold.

We're still laughing as we sprint to the warmth of the cabin to shed our soaking wet clothes. Viv pulls me into the bathroom and the steaming hot shower, where we stand curled into each other, letting the water warm our skin. We remain in that position for what feels like an hour because I can't bear the thought of any space coming between our wet bodies. But if we linger any longer, we'll find ourselves back in the cold water again.

"Dinner?" I ask as we both dress in warm sweats.

"Nachos!"

"Sounds good to me," I agree.

We enjoy our monstrous plate of nachos, then crawl under the warm duvet, still chilled from our evening swim. "Babe, I'd love to host an end-of-summer party next weekend out here. It will be a great way to welcome the fall weather, and before we know it, we'll hardly see our friends anymore because nobody wants to venture out in the winter."

"Great idea," she says, burrowing into my side. "While part of me looks forward to cozy nights in front of the wood stove with you, I will miss the carefree summer days spent on the deck."

"Yeah, it always kinda bums me out, but that's just the nature of living in Maine. You have to take the snow if you want to get to the sun." Exhausted, I pull her close and feel the dip in the mattress as Kevin climbs onto the bed and curls up at our feet.

With our *So Long, Summer* soiree in full swing, I navigate through the crowd in the backyard, searching for Tiny. My dad and Uncle Charlie stop me to ask where Kevin is, and I direct them to the living room couch. I nearly run into a camp chair that is already testing its limits by holding both Hadley and Cam, who are making googly eyes at each other, utterly oblivious to the activity around them. I finally find Tiny, who is talking to Jack and Earl about his upcoming fishing charter.

"Tiny," I tug his shirt sleeve, pulling him away from this conversation. "Sorry, guys, I need him real quick. Dude, do you have the goods?"

"In my car. Do you need it now?"

"Yeah, I'd like to get it set up while Viv is playing corn hole with Becky and Tristin."

"Okay, come on," he leads me around the cabin to his car.

After setting up the karaoke machine, I turn off the Bob Marley playlist that has kept heads gently bobbing all night, receiving a few grumbles in response. I tap on the microphone and say, "Is this thing on? Hey, everyone. Hi. This isn't usually something we do at our parties, but I thought a little karaoke might be fun."

Someone yells from the back, "Yeah, as long as you're not singing, Cooper!"

"Heyyyyyy," I reply in my best offended whine. "Tiny's got a huge catalog of your favorite hits, so come on up if you want to sing."

Amelia tugs at my pant leg. "Uncie Will, can I sing Frozen?" I glance over at Tiny, and he shrugs, clearly unsure of what she means. Olivia approaches us to say that she wants to sing the "Build a Snowman" song, and surprisingly, it's available. The two sisters' duet is so fucking cute, there's not a guest who's not riveted to their performance. Surprisingly, even Hadley and Cam come out of their bubble to watch.

I'm surprised by how many of our friends want to sing. Tristin, who is usually so quiet around crowds, delivers a stunning performance of Sabrina Carpenter's "Espresso." Dr. Jane's daughter, Nora, performs an incredible rendition of Janis Joplin's "Piece of My Heart"—her voice carries that same raspiness as Joplin's. And in what may be the best performance of the night, Tiny sings Teddy Swims' "Lose Control."

With everyone gathered around the deck, I give Tiny a slight nod. "Hey again. I know there have been many requests for me not to sing, but I have a dedication." Groans erupt from the group. "Viv? Can you come up here?"

"Oh god," I hear her say. "What are you doing, Cooper?" She nervously wrings her hands, waiting to see how I might embarrass her.

The music begins, and a few people give me a strange look. Train's lead singer, Pat Monahan, has a distinctive voice that is not easily imitated. Here goes nothing.

"Vivian James, this song is for you."

My voice wobbles as I start singing. Viv covers her mouth with her hand and looks up at me with a questioning expression. It's clear it takes her a moment to recognize the song.

I take a deep breath; this gesture can be as grand as I hope, or it can fall flat and fail miserably. I close my eyes and continue to sing.

Gasps come from the crowd when I reach the chorus. I hear a choked sob from right in front of me, and when I open my eyes again, Viv's face gleams with tears. I keep going.

"Vivian?" I swallow hard, and her glistening green eyes lock on mine.

She doesn't let me finish. She climbs onto the deck and leaps into my arms, burying her face in the crook of my neck. I hear her whisper, "Yes, always and forever, yes."

I set her back on her feet and step back to give myself enough room to get down on one knee. From my back pocket, I pull out the one-carat, bezel-set diamond and platinum ring I bought in Portland last month. This was the only ring that even remotely spoke to me when thinking about what would be perfect for Viv.

"Vivian James," I begin. "I have loved you since we were fourteen. Without even realizing it, I've loved you every day since that first day we met at the ice cream shop. The years we were apart were just a placeholder for this moment, and now, I'm never letting you go. Marry me?"

"Today and every day, yes." She holds out her left hand, and I carefully slide the ring onto her finger. The diamond sparkles in the lights strung around the deck. Her eyes are still wide with surprise as I bury my fingers in her hair, drawing her closer until our lips meet in a kiss. As we slowly pull apart, a grin spreads across our faces, reflecting the love that fills the space between us. "I love you so fucking much, Will Cooper."

I wrap an arm around Viv's shoulders, and we turn to face the crowd of friends who have just been shocked into silence by the engagement. "She said yes!" I exclaim, and the entire yard erupts into cheers. Our friends surround us on the deck with hugs and congratulations—each one of them has been a part of my life for as long as I can remember.

When the crowd clears, Hadley stands waiting for her turn. She's the only person who knew what I had planned. We talked at length about what this commitment would mean to Viv, especially considering what she'd been through: losing her mother and being tormented by her ex. She's Viv's family, and her blessing was the one I needed.

"Hadley," she whispers. "Did you know?"

"I did. Who else was going to bless this engagement?" Hadley chuckles. "Vivi, you deserve all the happiness in the world, and Will's going to be the one to give it to you. I love you, my little friend, and I can't wait to grow old in this town with you and our guys."

Someone turns the music back on loudly, and Bob Marley sings of "One Love."

Epilogue: A Season for New Beginnings

VIV

The long, cold winter has finally, at last, given way to brighter skies and warmer days. After months of limited sunlight and record snowfall, the first whispers of spring seep into Shearwater Cove, transforming both the air and the mood. Our neighbors happily emerge from their homes, like bears emerging from hibernation.

Will and I were married on New Year's Day, keeping it simple with a small ceremony right in the brewery's tap room. We were surrounded by our closest friends, family, and, of course, Kevin. The space felt extra special, still twinkling with holiday lights that warmed up the whole room. Even though the Christmas tree in the corner had been up for ages, its piney scent still drifted through the air. Nearly every surface was brightened by baskets overflowing with greenery and poinsettias, making everything feel especially cozy and festive.

I wore a long, cream-colored sweater dress paired with a cropped, faux-fur jacket in the same hue. My hair cascaded in long, loose waves down my back. Will looked incredibly handsome in a charcoal gray suit and a red tie. His hair was, of course, tousled, and his beard remained longer than usual, just how I like it. The gray suit emphasized the color of his eyes, resembling an incoming storm—dark, mysterious, and full of mischief.

Mike's mom, Betsy, who serves as the town's Justice of the Peace, officiated the ceremony with tears glistening on her cheeks as we exchanged vows. Betsy cried throughout the event, clutching a tissue and declaring how beautiful we looked beneath the holiday lights. When she pronounced us husband and wife, she whispered, "This is perfect," barely able to speak through her tears. She couldn't help but believe that my mom would have given Will a very high approval rating. "Five stars, at least," she said, wiping her eyes, as everyone around us cheered and popped champagne bottles.

Neither of us brought up the dumpster fire of a year that had led us here, anxious to start the new year and our married life together on a positive note, leaving the past behind.

April Fool's Day marks four months of marriage, and we tread lightly around each other all day, both waiting for the other's inevitable prank. We haven't spent this holiday together before, so we're unsure of what the other might do, and neither of us brings it up in conversation.

Every glance is cautious yet expectant. I open drawers slowly, half-expecting a rubber snake to leap out at me. Our interactions are teeming with suspicion; everything feels like a potential trick. Each time I use the toilet, I make sure there's no plastic wrap over the bowl. By the day's end, I find myself flinching whenever Will moves. Yet still, there's nothing.

I finally relax as we crawl into bed to watch television before falling asleep—both of us exhausted from being on high alert all day. When I hear Will's soft snores, I pad softly to the bathroom to pee one last time, navigating through the dark as I usually do. While relieving myself, I feel warm wetness on the back of my legs and immediately regret not checking for the plastic wrap.

"Will Cooper! You're dead meat, buddy!" I yell from the bathroom while I clean myself up.

As I whip open the door to stomp back to the bedroom to wake him up and give him a piece of my mind, I walk straight into a wall of packing tape stretched across the doorway. It's a large area of tape and I unceremoniously bounce off it, landing on my ass on the bathroom floor. There's no denying the silent laughter coming from the hallway as Will surveys the success of his prank.

"Payback's a bitch, Cooper," I say, walking past him as he remains bent over in the hallway, laughing his ass off.

On April 4th, we celebrate Kevin's second birthday. The weather is unseasonably warm, so we take him on our first road trip of spring, where he, as usual, thoroughly enjoys the wind blowing through his ears. Our destination is West Quoddy Head State Park, which I've been eager to visit since last summer. The red and white candy-striped lighthouse is the easternmost point of the United States, so far east that our cell phones think we're in a different time zone.

We spent most of the late morning exploring the five miles of trails that wind through the state park, stopping frequently to take pictures at the lookout over Quoddy Channel, which separates the U.S. and Canada, as well as the cliffs of Grand Manan Island. We chose the scenic route through Cutler Harbor and found a small sandwich shop to grab lunch while enjoying the view.

On the way home, we stop by Tucker's Tasty Treats for Kevin's favorite pup cup treat. Will and I order our usual hot fudge sundaes, and the three of us sit at a small table in front of the shop. We wave to friends enjoying the lovely day, some of whom pause to chat about, what else, but the weather.

In the car, heading back to Walker's Rock, I take Will's hand in mine. "This day couldn't have been more perfect," I say.

He glances in the back seat quickly to find Kevin sound asleep. "For him, too," he adds.

"For sure. I mean, he's two now. Nearly an old man." I laugh, and Will squeezes my hand.

Will gets a phone call from Shawn asking for his help at the brewery, so he drops the birthday boy and me off at home before heading back out. A short while later, I hear his truck tires crunch on the gravel—he'd been gone barely enough time to get to the brewery and back, so he must've forgotten something. Instead of coming inside, he texts me.

> WILL: BABE, CAN YOU COME OUTSIDE? BRING KEVIN.

> VIV: WHAT'S GOING ON? HE'S SOUND ASLEEP ON THE COUCH ALREADY.

> WILL: HE MIGHT WANT TO SEE THIS.

> VIV: OKAY, I'LL WAKE THE ANGEL.

Kevin wakes up slowly, stretching and yawning before getting off the couch. He shakes off the sleepiness with a full-body tremor and follows me to the front door. Neither of us is prepared for what Will called us outside for. In his arms, Will holds a tiny black lab puppy. A rush of déjà vu washes over me in waves, reminiscent of when Kevin was a puppy—the same fur so black it appears blue, the charcoal nose, and the bubblegum pink tongue hanging loosely from the side of its mouth. This little one is a carbon copy of him.

As Will walks toward us, carrying the puppy that lies limp in his arms, I cover my mouth to stifle a sob I choke back. Kevin lets out a low whine, and I can feel the beat of his tail against my leg as it wags excitedly.

"Will," I breathe out.

"I thought Kevin might like a buddy for his birthday," Will says, with a shrug.

I reach out to relieve him of the puppy and can't help but squeeze it just a little too tightly. It buries its face in the crook of my neck, and I feel gentle licks from the small, rough tongue.

"Meet Daisy," Will finally says.

"Daisy! My favorite flower," I exclaim.

"I know," he says, wrapping his arms around us.

I lean down and set the little girl on the ground, and she immediately flops over on her side, revealing her belly to Kevin. He looks at me, obviously not sure what he should do. I scooch down and scratch the scruff at his neck and whisper in his ear, "This is your new little sister, buddy. Your job is to teach her all that you know and keep her safe."

He slowly lowers his head and licks her soft, pink belly, eliciting happy growls from her, and then turns to smile at us. I think he likes his birthday surprise. Welcome to the family, little Daisy.

The end.

Interested in listening to the Spotify playlist for *That Little Town Street?*

Acknowledgements

To-Do List Item: Write a Book

To my husband, Scott, thank you for not looking at me like a crazy person when I told you I was writing a book. Thank you for your patience, especially during the hours I sat on the couch, bent over my laptop.

I would like to express my deepest gratitude to my beta readers for taking the time to read something that I wasn't sure I would actually finish. The notes and comments were thoughtful and so appreciated. A special thank you to Debbie for reading this thing in its earliest days, giving me valuable insights and suggestions while it was still just a wee work in progress. Thank you also to Bailey, Michelle, Tristin, Martha, Ashley, Jess, Jamie, and Jan. It is because of all of you that I kept going...

A special thanks to Bailey for designing a cover for this book that completely embodies the essence of how I hope this book makes you feel. And for the cute little wave doodles. Bailey works primarily in single color—black and white, blue and white—so a full color cover was something new for her. Visit her on Instagram @baileydebiase.ink or www.baileydebiase.com.

Thank you, Bonnie, my friend of 35 years, for being my veterinary liaison. And my friend for 35 years.

Thank you, Dr. Chiara Battelli, MD, for providing the information I needed on breast cancer, as well as being my own oncologist-extraordinaire... 4.5 years cancer-free.

My entire adult life, I've wanted to write a book. I've started many and finished none... until now. Maybe it took middle age and a twisted imagination to get me here at last. Or maybe it was the 100+ books I read in 2024 that led me to believe I could do this. Whatever the reason, I'm glad I made it.

When I began writing this book, I wasn't sure I'd finish it (sort of like all its predecessors.) I didn't want to tell anyone I was writing because then failure would be public. But then I figured if I started telling friends, and letting them read it as I wrote it, I would be held accountable to finish.

Not only did I finish, but keep an eye out for more adventures from our friends in Shearwater Cove.

About the Author

Stacy Elizabeth is a native Mainer (pronounced Maine-ah). She grew up in Portland and now resides in Gray with her husband, juggling their many house projects. She's a child of the '70s, a teenager of the '80s, and a proud Gen Xer who drank from a hose, lost skin on scorching hot metal slides, rode bikes without a helmet until the streetlights came on, and lived to tell about it. She loves books, lobster rolls, tacos, really sour beer, and her big, giant, crazy family. Follow her on Instagram: @stacyelizabethwrites

Spotify Playlist for *That Little Town Street*:

www.ingramcontent.com/pod-product-compliance
Lightning Source LLC
Chambersburg PA
CBHW020015120726
47903CB00004B/1294